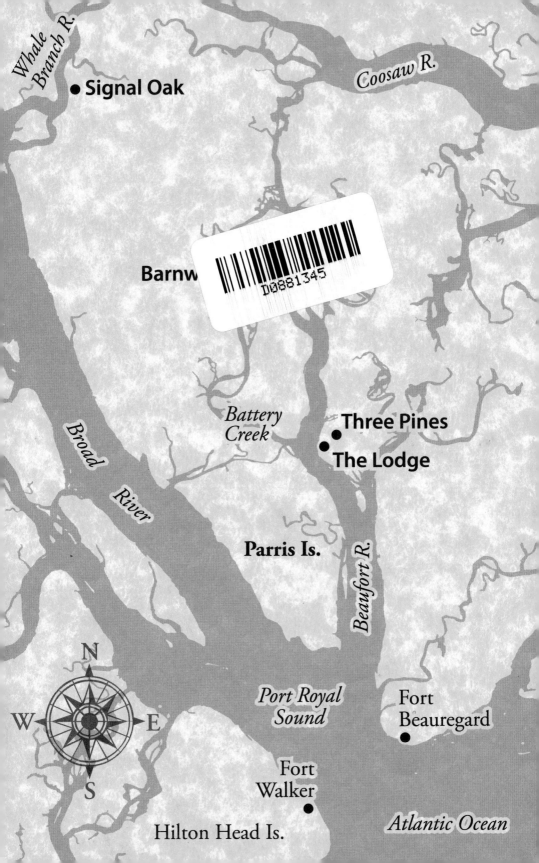

THE
HOME
GUARD

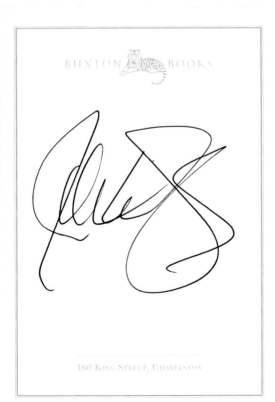

BUXTON 🐅 BOOKS

160 KING STREET, CHARLESTON

Other works by John Warley

Fiction

Bethesda's Child

The Moralist

The Moralist II

A Southern Girl (Story River Books, Pat Conroy, editor,
a University of South Carolina Press Imprint 2014)

Non-Fiction

Stand Forever, Yielding Never:
The Citadel in the 21st Century (Evening Post Books 2018)

Published Essays

"Lingering at the Doors" (*This I Believe on Fatherhood,*
Jossey-Bass, A Wiley Imprint 2011)

"One Cadet's Lamentations" (*Our Prince of Scribes,*
University of Georgia Press, 2018)

THE
HOME
GUARD

A Novel of the Civil War

JOHN WARLEY

EVENING POST
BOOKS

Published by
Evening Post Books
Charleston, South Carolina

Editor: John M. Burbage
Designer: Gill Guerry
Cover Illustration: Gill Guerry

First printing 2019
Printed in the United States of America

A CIP catalog record for this book has been applied
for from the Library of Congress.

ISBN: 978-1-929647-42-2

For Marilyn

LIST OF CHARACTERS

Carter Barnwell, a Beaufort boy of 12 when the book opens.

Anna Barnwell, Carter's mother.

Preston Barnwell, Carter's old brother, a Confederate soldier.

Martha "Missma" Gibbes Barnwell, Anna's mother-in-law and Carter's grandmother.

Gabriel Heyward, Carter's cousin serving with the Charleston Light Dragoons.

Newton Spruill, a U.S. Navy officer stationed in Beaufort.

Sonja Sunblad, a 14-year-old girl, daughter of Christina Sunblad.

Christina Sunblad, Sonja's mother, a missionary from Pennsylvania.

Grace, a slave, mother of Sparrow and Lark, young twin girls.

Polk, common law husband of Grace and father of Sparrow and Lark.

Abigail Gregorie, Anna's aunt and Charleston resident married to Daniel.

Daniel Gregorie, Abigail's blind husband.

Luke Gregorie, Daniel's brother, who lives in Columbia.

Reggie, Carter's African American friend who lives on the Barnwell property.

Jacob Roan, supervisor of Three Pines plantation on Cane Island.

A NOTE ON LANGUAGE

The story of the Civil War in Beaufort cannot and should not be told without African-American characters. Their spoken dialect before and during that era was Gullah. As Rowland, Moore and Rodgers noted in their excellent *The History of Beaufort County, South Carolina, Volume I, 1514-1861*, "The linguistic and cultural uniqueness which survived among the sea islands has long been referred to as 'Gullah,' and the origin of the term has been vigorously pursued and debated by historians, anthropologists and linguists." [p. 349] A majority of African Americans brought to South Carolina in the early nineteenth century were from Angola and Congo, and one theory is that the word Gullah derives from a spoken contraction of Angola, "N'gulla."

Whatever its origin, it proved difficult for non-Gullah speakers to understand. A small sample may prove instructive. A Gullah proverb currently on display in the South Carolina Historical Society headquarters in Charleston reads as follows: "Ef oona ent kno eh oona da gwuine, oona should kno eh oona kum frum," which means, "If you don't know where you are going, you should know where you come from." Capturing a spoken language on the printed page has vexed modern writers, including me, and there is likely no perfect solution. The dialogue included in *The Home Guard* is an attempt to convey the essence of the language of the times, and to do otherwise risks conversations that could not possibly have taken place between 1861 and 1865 in the South Carolina Lowcountry.

PROLOGUE

I n November 1861, the Civil War came to the scenic, antebellum town of Beaufort, South Carolina. A Union soldier wrote to the folks back home:

"The city of Beaufort is, I suppose, one of the handsomest places in the United States. It was inhabited only by the rich, retired planters of the South and they spared no pains nor expense in making it beautiful with art, and nature could not develop itself more handsomely than it does here. The weather is pleasant the year round. The large shade trees cannot be surpassed for their beauty. Their flower gardens are superb and there is not a single house but what is clustered around with orange, lemon and fig trees; grapes they have in abundance, and in fact everything that the most fastidious could desire to make them happy and contented."

Seven months after the war began with the firing on Fort Sumter in Charleston Harbor, the Lincoln administration, anxious to blockade the Confederate coast, sent an armada of Union ships down the eastern seaboard. Those ships bypassed Charleston and anchored just off Hilton Head Island, near the entrance to Port Royal Sound, through which any invading force would have to pass to reach Beaufort, some twelve miles inland.

On the morning of November 7, Union warships attacked, and in three hours they reduced the two Confederate forts guarding the entrance to the Sound. Beaufort lay defenseless. When word reached town that the forts had fallen, Beaufort's white population, some fifteen-hundred fled in what became known as the "Great Skedaddle." Left behind that day were a host of fine mansions and an estimated ten-thousand suddenly free African Americans. Union forces occupied the homes and the town for the duration of the war.

Carter Barnwell, a dreamy-eyed boy of twelve, knew little of war on the day his world collapsed around him. Born and raised in Beaufort, as Barnwells had been for generations, he knew best the streams and marshes of the Lowcountry. Winds and tides were as much a part of him as his fingerprints. His only battles had come against feisty redfish or when he hooked a small shark in the surf. All that changed when, while fishing on the beach, he looked toward Charleston and saw the Union ships, dozens of them, coming over the horizon. Before he and his dog, Soot, could launch the skiff, a gunshot from a warship hit Soot in the left hindquarter. As he tended to the dog's wound, he stared at the ships and wondered what his world had become. He was about to find out.

NOVEMBER 7, 1861

CHAPTER 1

Carter watched his mother, Anna Barnwell, cinch the last strap on her leather valise.

"There," she sighed. "If I cram another thing in it, you won't be able to lift it."

As she brushed back a fallen wisp of hair, the boy thought of how seldom he had ever seen her when she wasn't perfectly composed, with her hair neatly held in place by a tortoiseshell comb.

"Is the silver well buried in the back?" she asked. "You were gone for quite a while."

"I hit some roots that slowed me down, but the hole is deep, filled with dirt and covered with pine straw."

She looked at him, her shoulders slumping as she exhaled. "I never thought it would come to this; packing to leave the only house this family has ever known. I am glad your father isn't here to witness it. I doubt those Yankees will take care of it. Are your things packed?"

"Yes, ma'am."

"Time is short. If I dwell on what is happening, I'll turn into a sniveling ninny. Let's go upstairs to help Missma with her things. I need to remind her to bring her wolfskin robe."

Together, they ascended the stairs, Anna wondering if perhaps for the last time. At Missma's closed door, she knocked. No answer. She entered the room, Carter trailing. Missma was not there. She called.

"In here," came Missma's voice from an alcove off the bedroom used for storage. The door was shut.

Anna said, "Missma, what are you doing in there?"

"What I said I would. Staying in Beaufort."

Anna and Carter looked at each other, then at the door. "I know how hard this is," Anna said. "Hard on all of us. But we will be back before you know it.

9

Staying just . . . isn't possible."

"Silence."

Anna turned the knob and shouldered the door. "Missma, have you locked the door?"

"I have no lock, but it is secure."

She turned to Carter. "Go find Daddy August. And tell Rosa to come up right away."

When Anna heard Carter's quickened footsteps on the floors below, she again addressed the door. "Are you standing in the dark?"

"Sitting," Missma said.

Anna saw that Missma's rocker was gone from its usual place by the window. Carter returned, panting. "Rosa said Daddy August left. She's on her way."

Fear edged into his mother's voice. "Missma, we have to leave. Everyone in town is leaving, and I mean everyone. The *Cecile* is pulling out at five and after that we cannot leave. Pleeeease!"

Silence.

Anna looked at her son, shaking her head and muttering, "What now?" She took a deep breath. "Missma, think about this. It breaks my heart to say it, but in twenty-four hours the Yankees will be in this house. They may burn it or they may loot it or they may stay here—I do not know what will happen. They could shoot anyone they find here. We are traitors as far as they are concerned. All I know for certain is that whatever happens will not accommodate you and your needs. You simply cannot stay here. Do you not see that?"

From the other side of the door came Missma's voice, steady and almost breezy. "I never said I would not leave this house. I swore I would not leave Beaufort."

"But . . . but where else could you go? All the neighbors—everyone—is leaving."

"We have the Lodge."

Anna's eyes widened. "The Lodge! Can you be serious?"

"Never more so."

"With all due respect, that is utterly impossible. It may be the most impractical idea I've ever heard. We are all heartsick that the forts fell—"

"As I predicted."

"Yes, you predicted it but none of us could imagine leaving Beaufort, and now we must. We must all leave!"

Anna left the door long enough to glance out the window. On the street, buggies, horses and carts moved toward the wharf from which the steamer *Cecile* would depart.

"Missma, Rosa is nearly as old as you are and can barely walk. The thought that she can take care of you—"

"Who mentioned Rosa?"

Frustration turned to anger as she turned back to the door and screamed, "Have you taken leave of your senses? For the love of God you cannot stay alone."

"Carter can stay with me. It will be a great adventure."

Anna pirouetted at the door, her body rigid, her face thrust upward and her hands clenched in bloodless fists at her side. The pendant on the simple necklace she wore now rested near her shoulder. Carter had never seen her so frustrated.

"Let me understand. You and Carter will live in the Lodge on Cane Island while the entire town of Beaufort evacuates for what could be the duration of this war?"

"Precisely."

Carter returned his mother's look with a shrug, answering the question she no longer needed to ask. She pounded her fists on the door. "It is not enough on me that Preston is off fighting and could be killed any day, and now you want Carter to stay in the middle of thousands of Yankees! It is . . . selfish. Purely selfish, and frankly it is insane."

Missma's voice shifted, now heavy with the weight of fatigued resignation. "Sadly, I agree. It is selfish. I am very sorry to make this demand on you and Carter. At age eighty, I have earned some rights. I cannot leave. I will not last in Charleston."

"What makes you think you will last any longer here, cared for by a boy and put up in some drafty hunting lodge that is at least sixty years old? What will you eat? What if you get sick? Can you at least open this door so we can discuss this as rational human beings?" Anna was still screaming.

From the other side of the door came a creaking of wood on wood. Anna looked toward the ceiling and silently mouthed "Thank you," expecting the door to swing open.

Instead, Missma said in a hardened voice, "It is a terrible burden on us all that I did not pass on last night or last year. But my mind is made up. I knew those forts wouldn't keep the Yankees out and I've had days to think this through."

"And what will happen to Carter when you . . . pass on?"

"They will not harm a twelve-year-old. Not even awful Abe Lincoln is that cruel."

"I need Carter with me," Anna said, now close to tears.

"I need him more," Missma replied, her voice barely audible.

Anna turned to her son. "Can you do something about the door? We must get her out of there."

He shouldered it to gauge its resistance. "I can get the axe."

"Oh, dear God," his mother said. "Did you hear that, Missma? The axe!"

With Carter in search of the axe, Anna paced before the door. She pressed the knuckles of her knotted right fist against her teeth, willing herself to remain calm. Then she heard Rosa's ancient shuffle on the stairs.

11

Rosa finally arrived at the top of the stairway. Unsure of her year of birth, she claimed sixty, but had repeated this for several years. Cataracts clouded her eyes, shaded a milky blue by the rheum of age. Weight loss had left her with the weakness of a child. She stood beside Anna to catch her breath.

Anna motioned to the door. "Rosa, do you know anything about this? She's locked herself in there and has some idea she and Carter . . . well, it is too ridiculous for words."

"No ma'am, Miz Anna." She held Anna's stare longer than usual before her cloudy eyes misted. "I come to say bye."

For a moment Anna forgot the Missma crisis. "If we could take you, would you come, Rosa?"

Rosa's gaze fell to the floor. "My people here. I 'spect I gwyne stay. Barnwells been good to old Rosa. I thank you fuh that."

Anna reached to embrace her, an embrace Rosa accepted but did not return. With eyes still cast downward, Rosa said to the door, "Bye, Miz Martha."

"Goodbye, Rosa," Missma said. "God bless you for all your service to this family."

Anna reached to her neck and unclasped the pendant necklace. "Please take this, Rosa."

Rosa nodded. Anna put it around her neck. Rosa left, fingering the necklace, as Anna turned back to the door.

"Missma," Anna said with feigned nonchalance, "you realize that I will have to stay. Because of your decision, I must remain here, come what may. A woman your age has certain needs that a boy of twelve cannot provide."

From beyond the door, "Nonsense. A woman *your* age cannot stay among Yankees and darkies. You would not last a day without regret. I am at an age beyond risk."

Sorrow broke over Anna like thunderous surf. Preston off to war, the loss of her home, her way of life, Beaufort, Rosa, her friends scattered to points north and west, and now Carter and Missma. She collapsed, her back to the door. When Carter arrived with the axe she was sobbing as if visited by some biblical sadness. He reached down to pat her shoulder. He had seen her cry only twice; at his father's funeral, and the day Preston left for Virginia. His touch provided some comfort, for she stood, smoothed her dress, dried her eyes on a handkerchief tucked in her sleeve, and instructed Carter to follow. In the hallway, she placed a hand on each of his shoulders.

"Son, I have never been so confused. I don't know what to do, and I have no time to decide. Can you get her to the Lodge?"

"Yes, Mother."

"As soon as I get to Charleston I will think of something. I will be only sixty miles away. We will not abandon you."

"Preston is fighting Yankees. I can take care of Missma."

She managed a smile. "I will just have to leave it in your hands."

"Will you tell Missma goodbye?"

"I am too angry. You tell her for me. Now hurry. You want to leave in day-light. I must get to the wharf or I will miss the steamer." She turned and walked toward her room. The echo of her retreating footsteps was as lonesome a sound as he could remember. He followed. At her vanity table, she made a half-hearted attempt at straightening her hair and drying her tears. Together they descended the stairs. Carter picked up the valise and they began the walk to the dock.

The street was a one-way thoroughfare toward the river, with a few of their panicked neighbors rushing to get aboard the waiting *Cecile*. From a piazza, they heard "Anna! Anna!" Mrs. Hortensia Hull waved a handkerchief to beckon them closer. They had both known the seventy-four-year-old all their lives. As they stood in the yard looking up, the nearly hysterical woman explained that the portrait of her mother could not be left to be sullied by the Yankees and she pleaded with Carter to help her move it from the wall over the mantel where it had hung for twenty-nine years.

"But to where, Mrs. Hull?"

"Well . . . with me. It must come with me. Those ungrateful Negroes to whom I have been ever so kind for all these years have left and I have no one to help."

Anna spoke. "I'm afraid there isn't time, Mrs. Hull, and nowhere on the boat for such a large portrait, even if Carter could somehow get it there. Please bring your things and come. The boat is leaving soon."

The *Cecile* rocked gently at the dock, her decks crowded with townspeople. Carter carried the valise up the gangplank as his mother followed. At the rail, they embraced. She promised to write upon arrival in Charleston though later, on her journey north, she realized that no mail service would get it to him. As he disembarked, he passed winded and still frantic Hortensia Hull, who appeared to be leaving without a single personal article save the clothes she wore.

Carter sprinted back to the house.

• • •

"She's gone, Missma. What now?"

A muffled thud sounded and the door swung open. Missma stood by her rocker. "I will need my chair," she said. "Will it fit on your boat?"

"Yes, ma'am."

She handed him a cloth carpetbag, bulging at its seams. She reached into her walnut bureau and extracted her buggy robe, wolfskin with fox trim, lined with red flannel, that would provide ample protection against chill on the water. "One more thing," she said, reaching back into the bureau. From behind a blanket

13

she lifted down a gallon jug of clear liquid.

"Water?" asked Carter.

"Not exactly," she said.

He carried her chair to his skiff before returning for her and her carpetbag. As they walked, she listed for him the items from the house they would need on Cane Island. He made several trips to find and load them, sweating through his shirt in his hurry to leave before sundown.

Lastly, he returned for Soot, his black St. John's water dog, which lay on a blanket near the wood stove still recovering from a gunshot wound to its hind leg. For the second time in a week, he carried the dog to his boat and set him down gently at Missma's feet.

• • •

Anna stood at the rail of the *Cecile* as her son shoved off from the dock and set sail for Cane Island. Missma sat in the bow, the wolfskin cinched close and her head shawled and held high. Soot panted beside her. Between Carter and the tiller, her rocker had settled into an awkward niche. As they disappeared around the bend, the last rays of sunlight reflected off the Beaufort River.

CHAPTER 2

arter's skiff, a gaff-rigged, fifteen-foot sailboat, made good time on a fair breeze. Missma hummed, her voice amplified in the hush of evening. The only other sound was a faint lapping of the tide against the boat. Because the breeze and the boat were headed in the same direction, he was not forced to tack, which was fortunate given the bulk of the rocking chair over which his boom would have to be lifted. In addition to Missma's personal articles, they carried bedrolls, blankets, mosquito nets, a cast iron pot, three jugs of water, some bread, two jars of fig preserves, slices of ham and bacon, a few eggs, two chamber pots, a lantern, a rifle, a shotgun and ammunition, some matches, Carter's fishing pole. And Missma's jug of liquid, which was not exactly water.

He pushed the tiller to bring the boat gliding into a low bank on the shore of Cane Island. As the boat stopped, she said, "Well done, young man."

"Thank you, ma'am." After a pause, he asked, "When was the last time you were here—in the Lodge?"

She looked up, where a few stars winked in the twilight. "Oh my, I was here in . . . 1799. It was new then. I was newer, too."

"It is not nice like home."

"Well, no," she said. "A hunting lodge is not supposed to be like home. Help me out of the boat."

With the lantern in one hand and his grandmother's hand in the other, he led her up the path through a stand of tall pines and water oaks that separated the Lodge from the boat landing. When they cleared the trees, the Lodge loomed ahead. It was one-story, wooden frame, built on a tabby foundation four feet above ground. Two wide porches spanned its length, one facing the river and, on the back side, the other facing the break of trees they had just come through. His father brought him here often to hunt and fish. His father also maintained it, putting on a new roof shortly before he died.

"There could be snakes," he said.

"I'm sure there are. We will just have to make some noise to let them know they need to leave."

They arrived at the steps leading up to the porch as Missma's eyes adjusted sufficiently to make it out. They mounted the steps. Missma kept a hand on the railing as she climbed. He lifted the metal latch and the door creaked open. They entered and stopped in the middle of the room. A stone fireplace dominated the south wall.

"A little heat and light and we will be fine," she said.

"I will bring your chair, then get Soot and some wood."

"Yes, please do."

"The lantern can stay here. I know the way."

Twenty minutes later, a fire illuminated the hearth and began to warm the air. After repeated trips to the boat, he had unloaded all they brought and secured it against tidal drift. Missma slid her rocker to a spot at the edge of the hearth, then motioned for him to join her. From the table he took one of four caned chairs and placed it at the opposite edge. He sat tentatively, almost apologetically. Soot curled at his feet, his muzzle resting on one paw. In the fireplace, seasoned oak logs he found behind the Lodge crackled, shooting embers in all directions. Missma cinched her shawl around her shoulders and arms. Staring into the fire, she said, "So much change in such a short time." Carter, also eyeing the flames, nodded but said nothing.

"I am sorry I upset your mother," she said. "I hoped against hope the forts would hold. When they did not, I had to act on my decision. Boys your age should not have to care for old ladies."

"Will Mother be safe?"

"Yes, child. She will be fine unless she worries herself sick over you and your brother."

"Preston has seen fighting. I pray for him." He swung his head toward her. "Will we still get his letters?"

"No. Everything changed today. No mail, no school, no friends, no . . . comforts. But you and I will find a way. We will stay in touch with Preston and your mother and Uncle Daniel and the rest of our people."

"How?" he wanted to know.

"By deciding what works. We must spend all our days here deciding what works." He stared at her. Shadows cast by the flames deepened the lines in her face. She looked ancient, more specter than woman. Sensing this very appearance, she said, "I am old and weaker than I was, but do not forget that I grew up on these islands. There is nothing here I have not seen."

"You have not seen Yankees," he offered respectfully.

"I have seen worse. The British—do not get me started at this late hour. We must be practical. Our situation is severe but not impossible. Tomorrow morning, as early as you can manage, you need to return to the house for supplies we left in all this chaos. If you delay, there will not be anything left. I will make a list."

"What if they stop me?"

"I doubt there is anyone to do that. Had the Yankees arrived in town, we would have met them on the river tonight. But this trip may be your last. You must bring everything you can."

The fire burned brightly. Both stared into it to manage the silence. After a time, Missma said, rather formally, "I must speak with you about our . . . living conditions. I will ask you to nail to the rafter a quilt I brought. I will need some privacy, as will you. I will sleep there," she said, indicating the wooden bunk along the north wall. "I will manage my chamber pot for as long as I am able. I can cook, but we will require food that only you can bring us. Do you think you can manage that?"

"Yes, ma'am."

"Good. I know you can. We both love fish, and unlike our neighbors the fish did not leave when the Yankees arrived. We must have water. Have you tried the pump?"

"No, ma'am."

"First order of business tomorrow morning. Let it run a spell, until it pumps clear."

He spread the bedrolls on their bunks. Using an iron wedge from the wood-box and standing on the table where they would take their meals, he nailed her quilt to the rafter.

What a day it had been he thought as he slipped under the mosquito netting. His eyes were nearly shut when he heard her stir. She walked to a spot by the door where he had left her liquid. She lifted the jug by the glass loop near its throat and brought it to the table. From her robe she took a small, silver jigger. She filled it, replaced the stopper, and carried both behind her partition. Then, all was quiet as they passed their first night in this new life.

CHAPTER 3

For the rest of her life, Grace remembered the moment she heard the first distant echo of Union guns in Port Royal Sound. To her and the other Negroes, that would always be the day of "When Big Gun Shoot." But in her slave cabin on Cane Island, she could not tell who was firing at whom, only that nothing like what she was hearing had ever been heard in her years at Three Pines Plantation. Her twin daughters, Sparrow and Lark, ran to her, hugging her waist and looking upward for reassurance. She patted their braided hair, hoping Polk would come. He had left for the fields at sunup.

She stepped outside, the girls still clinging, as her neighbors along their shanty row emerged, all looking in the direction of the ever-increasing explosions, their expressions a mixture of curiosity and fear. Since word came of ships anchored off Hilton Head, speculation had bloomed like the cotton all around them. Polk thought the ships would move on down the coast, while others, who helped build the Confederate batteries on Hilton Head and Bay Point, insisted that those forts made Beaufort immune from capture. A few, Grace among them, wondered aloud if deliverance was at hand; if the arrival of the fleet was Massa Abraham coming to free his children.

Grace turned from the sound to see Polk walking briskly toward her. He motioned her inside with the nod of his head, scowling as if to indicate brief, unpleasant business. He told her they needed to be ready to leave on short notice. Perhaps this morning. She saw him straining to be calm in deference to the girls.

"The man say we go if dem forts fall."

"Where we go?"

"Dunno."

Grace eyed him skeptically. "Dem forts fall, we stay."

News of the battle's outcome reached Three Pines in early afternoon. A shirtless Negro on horseback rode across the sea islands spreading word of Union victory to those whose masters were in the process of abandoning them, leaving them free. He rode a well-bred mare from the stable of the rider's owner who, cursing the rebel defeat, could no longer feed or shelter his horses, or take them with him.

Smits, the mulatto overseer at Three Pines, stationed the plantation's two buckboards in front of the main house. From the bed of one he bellowed that they had one hour to pack a day's rations and prepare to leave. The buckboards could carry sixteen; the rest would have to walk. Smits disappeared inside.

An hour later, he emerged. The teams waited patiently in their traces, but no occupants of slave row had come. With his bull whip in his right hand, Smits started down among the shacks, now deserted and still. He peered inside the first three before yelling out that they had until sundown to appear or he would hunt down every man, woman and child and see to it that they were sold to Cuba. From their hiding place in the woods, Grace squeezed Polk's hand and cautioned the girls to remain still.

Grace heard a twig snap behind her and turned to see Mingo, who whispered, "He come in here, we kill 'um." Polk shook his head. Grace knew that if any man then hiding in the woods had cause to kill Smits, it was Polk. "Let him be," she said.

Long past sunset, voices rose up in the darkness. The twins shivered, and Grace pulled them closer as Polk passed word he would venture out, but she too began to shiver at the thought of Polk confronting the detested Smits. To reach the main house Polk would have to walk through the field of cotton he had planted, tended and would be forced to harvest with Smits in charge. He disappeared into the darkness. When he returned, he told them one buckboard was gone and there was no sign of the overseer.

Within minutes, the entire slave population of Three Pines surrounded him. He told them Smits is gone, taking his clothes with him, but reminded them he could return. He recommended everyone go home until he could learn more about what happened and what it meant. Someone asked what he planned to do in the morning. He told them he would work in his vegetable garden, then added, "I ain' pickin' no cotton," which elicited amens and hallelujahs.

In the cabin, Lark asked about Cuba. Grace patted her hand and told her not to worry, though for most of her life Grace herself had harbored an intense fear of Cuba from early childhood images conjured by her grandmother, who never set foot on that island. She pictured it as a place where slaves were roasted on spits before being eaten by dogs. But Smits "just mouthin'" when he threatened to send them to Cuba, Grace assured Lark.

"How you know?" Lark asked.

Grace eyed Polk, who said, "You know some nights I leave when it gets dark? Real quiet like I crawl under de main house. Dem floors got holes and cracks. Listen to Smits tell his woman 'bout Cuba. He say all niggas 'fraid of Cuba. Den he laugh."

Polk said the girls needed to know Cuba was a long way from Beaufort by ship and that it was no place a slave would ever want to be. Grace wondered if they might no longer be slaves.

"Too good fuh true," Polk said.

"Maybe," said Grace. "But I hearin' talk."

"Heard talk all my life," countered Polk.

"You ain' never hear talk while all dem ship out dere."

Polk shook his head. "Too good fuh true."

The following morning, Grace and Polk rose early. If Smits returned during the night, smoke would be rising from the chimney of the main house. They saw none. At the house, there was no sign of Smits. After looking in every room, they emerged onto the porch, where she noticed something she couldn't remember having seen since before Lark and Sparrow were born: smoke rising from the chimney of the old hunting lodge by the river.

CHAPTER 4

The *USS Wabash* arrived off Hilton Head a few days before the battle. United States Navy Lieutenant Newton Spruill surveyed the shoreline. Sand and dunes stretched into the distance, dotted by scruffy trees that reminded him of broccoli florets on thin stems. The sole signs of life, a boy and a black dog on the beach, watched the ship. From the forecastle came the call that the ship was approaching Port Royal Sound, its destination. Spruill spit over the side, pondering again the miserable combination of circumstances that brought him to God-forsaken South Carolina.

Spruill loathed this land despite never having set foot upon it, for the South had brought him only misery and promised even more. His wife back in Boston was the buxom, leggy, honey-dipped daughter of a former Mississippi governor whose charms when they met included the delightful expression, "Oh darlin', that's just sooooo true," uttered with a sultry wink. Enchanted, he had married her over the wishes of both families. They honeymooned in Europe, where Ashley Ann had taken a riveted interest in the current fashions and little else, including him. Upon their return to Boston she complained incessantly about the cold, a particularly ominous habit given the fact that it was then only October, and by New England standards a mild one. Her complaints escalated to include his choice of friends, the drafty house, his preference for cigars, his hours at the printing business and her clothes allowance. When she lobbied for relocation to Mississippi he firmly refused, after which her absences from the house grew more frequent. At the end of three warring, fang-bared years he confronted her with his suspicions of infidelity, to which she had replied, "Oh, darlin', that's just soooooooo true." When she winked he swung his fist. The blow glanced off her chin but served her nicely when she demanded some expensive jewelry as her price for not having him arrested. He had scoffed at the idea of arrest, but as she seemed quite chummy with several high-ranking members of the police force, he couldn't be certain she was bluffing. Shortly after the shots on Fort Sumter, he joined the Navy as a way distancing himself. On his first voyage, he dropped his wedding ring into Boston Harbor. Another distancing. Just thinking about Ashley Ann raised his blood pressure.

The *Wabash* slowed as the Sound loomed in the distance. An armada would eventually anchor off these shores. Spruill was confident Union firepower would teach the traitors a lesson that would be heard all the way to Richmond. The boy on the beach ran toward a skiff pulled up near the dunes, the dog trailing a few yards behind. That's one of them, Spruill thought, probably on his way to warn the enemy. A young one, but a rebel for sure. Who else could it be this far south? He unholstered his pistol, a .44 caliber Colt, pointed it toward the beach, and pulled the trigger. The dog went down onto the sand momentarily. When it stood, its left hind leg dragged behind. On three legs it followed the boy for a few yards, then collapsed. The boy turned, running back to where the dog lay. Spruill watched as the boy, on his knees, turned his gaze from the animal's haunch to the deck where Spruill stood.

Spruill sensed a presence at his elbow. "What happened?" asked Lieutenant Luther Locklear.

Spruill pointed in the direction of the beach. "Some rebel kid and his dog. Just letting them know the U.S. Navy is here to settle the fight they started."

Locklear raised a telescope. "That's a pretty young boy. Were you aiming at him?"

"Not particularly, but I figure it's open season on anything that moves in this swamp."

Locklear avoided eye contact. "You might want to run that by the captain. Maybe you should aim at gulls like the rest of the men do. I'm not sure our orders include shooting children, rebels or not." As Locklear walked away, Spruill saw the boy lift the dog and carry it to the skiff.

The *Wabash* served as the flagship for Commodore Samuel F. DuPont, commander of what the Federals were calling the Port Royal Expedition. It anchored off the Sound as, over the next three days, straggling ships delayed by a storm off Cape Hatteras continued to arrive. When he wasn't on watch, Spruill remained in his quarters, made increasingly nervous by the ship's chatter about the upcoming battle. From the deck he could see the two Confederate forts guarding the Sound. The one on Hilton Head, Fort Walker, appeared particularly menacing, and the large guns bristling from its parapets added to his anxiety. On Bay Point, Fort Beauregard stood perfectly positioned to catch Union ships in a murderous crossfire when they advanced toward Beaufort. He had never experienced combat, a fact known to the other officers on board.

Thursday, November 7th, dawned so clear and cloudless it would have passed for suspension of weather itself, as if Nature had decided that the battle's outcome should be determined by stratagem, grit, heroism, preparation, and blood thirst and not by favoritism of winds or tides. On board the *Wabash*, Spruill left the war room, where Commodore DuPont had dictated the order of battle, set to begin at 8 a.m. A thin line of perspiration formed in Spruill's mustache and along his hairline. He sensed a tempest in his stomach and loosening in his bowels. As he returned to his quarters, barefoot tars hauled ammunition to the enormous guns that would open the assault. More ominously, surgeons spread crude instruments of amputation on tables equipped with shackles.

The *Wabash* was a three-mast, steam driven forty-eight-hundred-ton frigate that, twenty years earlier, would have been on a windless day such as this one as mobile as Fort Walker. Today, she crowded her sails and pulled in her spars to reduce to absolute minimum the target she would present to the forts' gunners. On ships around the *Wabash*, sailors scampered into the rigging for a better view of the fight. Spruill stopped to gaze at Fort Walker's low profile, her ramparts clearly visible from that distance. To calm his nerves, he thought of the letter he would pen to his sister Hazel that evening, touting a great victory, revenge for Sumter and Bull Run, and his role in the drama about to unfold. He avoided speculating on alternatives, like lying on the deck looking skyward as a surgeon hovered over him, or burial at sea. For an instant Ashley Ann flashed to mind. He vowed he wouldn't give her the satisfaction of dying in the South. He went below, vomited in muffled bursts he hoped went unheard by the crew, and returned to the deck to assume his battle station, trying to pitch his facial anxiety at a level expected from a veteran. He set his jaw and muttered, "Let's kill some Rebs."

On DuPont's signal, the assault began. Led by the *Wabash*, the warships crossed the bar and entered the Sound, headed on a course equal distance from the forts to either side, threading a watery needle with little margin for error. A puff of smoke burst from the side of the *Wabash*, then another, then another, followed by booms that echoed south to Savannah. Behind the *Wabash* in a line came *Susquehanna*, *Mohican*, *Seminole*, *Pawnee*, *Unadilla*, *Ottawa*, *Pembina* and *Vandalia*. The forts answered, smoke rising from the ramparts as the gunners gauged the fleet's range and motion. The Sound soon boiled into a stew of whistling projectiles.

When the trailing *Vandalia* delivered its ordinance, the *Wabash* turned toward Hilton Head, joined by *Susquehanna* and the gunship *Bienville*. In a line led by *Wabash*, they rained shell after shell upon the fort from a distance of less than 600 yards. To their front, the *USS Pocahontas* left the safety of the sea and moved into a position from which she could bring flanking fire upon the occupants of Fort Walker, absorbed in the *Wabash's* relentless broadsides.

In an irony of war destined to be repeated over the next four years, kin fought kin. The captain of *Pocahontas*, Union Commander Percival Drayton, knew full well that his guns were trained on his brother, General Thomas Drayton, who commanded the Confederate forces in the forts. The older brother, Thomas, risked all. Not only was his life in jeopardy, but his plantation home, Fish Haul, on Hilton Head was but a stone's toss from Fort Walker, where his men scurried in preparation for the attack. If Fort Walker fell, total personal ruin would follow ignominious military defeat. (After Fort Sumter, the brothers had met in St. Michael's Church in downtown Charleston. They shook hands, wished each other well and followed their consciences. They did not speak again for years.)

On deck of the *Wabash*, Lt. Spruill was reasonably certain he would be dead by noon. Ten feet from his battle station, he watched an entire gun crew cut down by shots screaming across the deck. Two of the crew lay motionless, one moaning and contorting in a fetal contraction, and the other propping himself on his left arm while his right dangled by some tendons from his shoulder. Spruill called for medics, then reported the casualties to the executive officer and lingered on the quarterdeck to avoid returning to the carnage. He also avoided Fort Walker, his executioner, hoping grimly that death would come swiftly, sudden and unseen, and he was dwelling on this, seeing in his mind's eye a formal interment in dress whites when he realized that the ship had passed out of range of the fort's diminishing fire. This epiphany of survival left him euphoric until orders were issued for the *Wabash* to come around for another pass at the fort. His tremors proved groundless. By the time *Wabash* was again abeam of Fort Walker, the Confederates had bowed to overwhelming force by evacuating, as did those manning Fort Beauregard. By 2:30 p.m., the Stars and Stripes fluttered lazily over Fort Walker.

CHAPTER 5

From the rail of the *Cecile*, Anna Barnwell watched Carter and Missma disappear around the bend of the Beaufort River with the sense of finality she might have experienced watching her own funeral. The small skiff, growing smaller, seemed to contain not only her loved ones but her world, or what was left of it.

When the boat was no longer visible, she lingered at the rail. The glorious sunset struck her as bitter irony, with the wide savannas of Lowcountry marsh, as common to her life as air and speech, never looking so hauntingly magnificent, as if donning their most radiant blends of blue, gold, ocher and brown to take a final bow before the curtain fell. Around her, sober, grave and maudlin faces were faintly illuminated by torches, lamps, running lights, charcoal braziers and fiery cigar ends. Some women and a few men wept silently as the town receded. Many would never see it again.

As night descended, their prospects were as uncertain as the unseen bend in the river ahead. There was not one among them who anticipated that the life to which they were headed in any way resembled the life they just abandoned. In days and weeks to come, a few might see the irony, also bitter, of earlier wrenching exoduses from the shores of West Africa, but on this, the first day of a war some prayed would come, they were shocked, beaten and silent; so many sad stars moving in a dispirited constellation toward a new world. Anna instinctively held her head high and her shoulders straight, but inside she fought the urge to jump overboard and swim back, toward home, Missma and Carter. It all happened too fast. She couldn't believe she allowed Missma to checkmate her in such a fashion, but what choice did she have?

Suddenly fatigued, she sought a seat and found one next to Hortensia Hull, who with her head in her hands wept in gasping sobs. Anna put her arm around her shoulder, leaning close to say that if the elderly woman was cold, she could borrow Anna's wrap. Mrs. Hull shook her head but did not look up. Anna patted the woman's knee in consolation. "We will get through this," she whispered, but not at all certain they would.

And there was that pain again, the same one she had been suffering for months, the one Dr. Gaffney had said could be a tumor or cyst. He had recommended she see a specialist in Charleston and she had every intention of doing so, but then the war started and other priorities intruded. If there was any silver lining to this dislocation, it would be the medical attention she had put off. At times the pain grew so intense she struggled to breathe.

She tried to focus on contact with Carter. She would need to get word to him of her safe arrival at Uncle Daniel's in Charleston. She would reassure him that she was just up river, and that they would be reunited soon. But who will carry such word, and how can they be reunited? It wasn't as if the *Cecile* would be making a return run into a war zone. Now that the Union would occupy Beaufort, would she need Yankee permission to join Carter and Missma at the Lodge? Was Preston safe, and how would his letters reach her in Charleston?

And how was it possible that weeks of speculation that the Union fleet might target Beaufort failed to inspire a contingency plan addressing the kinds of challenges that threatened to overwhelm them now? If she, at home in the "Cradle of Secession," found herself at such perils, was it possible the South was equally unprepared for what it had brought upon itself? The future darkened before her, testing the congenital optimism she always assumed she possessed.

A rhythmic creaking of the paddle wheel and constant churning of water made conversation with those around her nearly impossible, which was just as well she thought, as every passenger likely had a tale of woe to share. Most seemed content to sit quietly, contemplating as she did what this sudden uprooting portended. Her gaze upon the receding water rose and fell with the boat, lulling her into a trance, or perhaps it was mere fatigue. What had happened today? It came to her that despite telling herself the forts could fall, despite packing in advance of that fall, despite *knowing* she might be forced to leave Beaufort, she had not prepared herself for the past four hours. Not really. Clearly, she should have taken Missma's statement, "I will die in Beaufort," more literally.

Her mother-in-law had an iron core, but to have brought Carter in as a co-conspirator? He was still such a . . . child, a fawn-eyed innocent whose skills at hunting and fishing and boating put him well beyond his years, but war? Abandonment? What skills did he bring to the very adult crises that today's events had wrought?

So unlike Preston, who had volunteered to fight at the first chance because something within him had been preparing for war since he was a small boy, and if not war then an equally mature challenge. Preston possessed his father's manliness, an edge that rendered him short on words and long on action. Preston hunted to kill deer and wild boar. He fished to fill his bucket.

Carter hunted deer and turkey to walk in the woods. With rifle or shotgun casually slung over one shoulder, he ambled along in something close to a dream state, watching squirrels chase each other up and down pines, spotting a cardinal fly from the low branch of a water oak to a higher perch, sensing the eyes of a raccoon or possum on him as he walked. When he encountered deer, it was usually by accident—misfortune for the deer because the boy was an excellent shot. But even his skill as a marksman was inadequate to bag a turkey, a breed that never strayed into hunters by accident. Turkeys took concentration, and they had more than he did. He told her how he loved rising early to position himself in a duck blind, but she knew it was mostly to watch the first rays of daylight break over the marsh, illuminating the mist that had infused the spartina grass during the night. He might study a marsh hen at ebb tide, lightly traipsing over pluff mud, only to be startled by the squawk of ducks overhead. Preston fished with practiced efficiency, hauling in his line mechanically and netting the fish with a fluid, swift down-and-up motion. Carter netted a trout cautiously, from behind, leaving net and fish in the water to see the flash of colors as the trout shimmied in the net. Anna knew that her younger son, on the cusp of manhood, would soon lose the downy innocence that endeared him to her so. His shoulders would broaden, his voice would deepen, and his evanescent attention span would likely become more focused. She suspected his youth had ended today, and she wondered when he would learn it.

Carter dreamy and inattentive? What about *her*? Hadn't she just left her last and youngest child in the care of a feeble octogenarian? In a *war*! What kind of mother did that? The kind confronted with a horrible dilemma and no time to sort it out, she consoled herself. The kind blindsided by a manipulating old woman reaching the end of her string. She would tell Missma a thing or two when she saw her next . . . if she saw her next. It was all too sudden, too horrible, too impossible.

Lights of Charleston loomed ahead. The boat docked at midnight. On the wharf, a frenetic mix of friends and relatives waited, having heard telegraphed news of the exodus and hoping their loved ones were aboard. She turned back to Mrs. Hull, now stoically silent. "Do you have someone meeting you?" Anna asked. Mrs. Hull managed, "I hope so."

Anna rose to find a place at the rail, scanning the crowd for Aunt Abigail and Uncle Daniel. She saw both standing at the far corner of the pier. In his right hand Uncle Daniel, blind from birth, held his cane and appeared to be listening to Abigail as he stared blankly ahead. Abigail's arm shot up when she spotted Anna among the passengers. Anna returned to Mrs. Hull, helping the older woman to her feet and assuring her that she wouldn't be abandoned. Anna picked up her valise, the only item she brought, and together with Mrs. Hull they patiently made their way to the gangplank. Mrs. Hull leaned on her for support until she saw a young man on the pier, her grandson she said.

As Anna walked toward Abigail and Daniel, she heard snatches of exclamations: ". . . burn Charleston," ". . . headed this way." Ahead, an argument ensued in a cluster of men who had just learned from an evacuee that they did not burn Beaufort before they left. "You surrendered the town intact?" the incredulous Charlestonian demanded. "And all that cotton?"

Abigail, a short, buxom woman, embraced Anna as she would a daughter.

Anna retained her composure until she turned to Uncle Daniel, with his vacant stare but kindly face that seemed to mirror the abject sorrow that had descended upon her during the journey. He pulled her to him. His neatly trimmed beard rested on the top of her head, and pipe smoke permeating his suit filled her with a nostalgia that dissolved her. As her eyes welled and her sobs began in short bursts, Abigail patted her back. Anna fought for control, regained it, and calmly explained that Carter and Missma were safe in Beaufort, that it was a long story, and that she would relate it fully when the tumult of the pier was behind them. Together, they walked to the carriage, Anna carrying the valise in one hand while her other arm rested in Abigail's, who guided Uncle Daniel, tapping his cane as they walked. At the carriage, Anna greeted Leo, the house servant and driver employed by the couple for twenty years. Leo was a free black who had taken the last name of his employers: Gregorie.

Leo guided the horse and carriage through the city. A steady clop-clop echoed from stately structures along Meeting Street—structures that seven months earlier held onlookers cheering the bombardment of Fort Sumter. Visually, the houses were unchanged from that time, or from years when Anna attended teas or soirees in them, but tonight they were all spent energy, like a party after the last guest departs. Perhaps, she thought, somberness was only her imagination, or the lateness of the hour, or the semi-desertion of the streets, but whatever the source Charleston, the gayest of cities, seemed sad to her.

By the time the carriage arrived at the modest Gregorie home on New Street, Anna had related Missma's tactic of the barred door, her refusal to leave, her demand that Carter remain and their evacuation by boat to the Lodge.

"They were both welcome here, of course," Abigail assured her.

"Both welcome," echoed Uncle Daniel.

"It would have been a bit crowded, but we would make do," Abigail continued.

Anna sighed. "It was no reflection on you. Of course they would feel welcome here. But you know Missma and how . . . unbending she can be."

Uncle Daniel nodded his head firmly at this. "Stubborn as a mule, that woman."

It was past 2 a.m. when Anna fell into bed in the guest room. She was asleep before she completed her nightly prayers.

CHAPTER 6

S onja Sunblad gathered the stallion under her for the final fence leading back to the barn. The fact that she and the horse, recently renamed d'Artagnan, had never failed to clear the split rail did not lessen the pounding in her heart, her scissor-like clamp on the animal's flanks nor her manic grip on the mane. A fall from this height could be disaster, and for that very reason the jump was her favorite. For a few seconds over the rails she experienced matchless exhilaration, the sensation of flying.

But not today. Something was wrong, and she knew it the instant the horse sprang from its hind legs, which slipped as it vaulted forward. Those same hind legs caught the fence on the descent. Horse and rider were no longer parallel to the ground but nearly perpendicular. As the turf on the far side rose, d'Artagnan's forelegs buckled and Sonja flew over its head, rolling as she landed and with uncommon nimbleness avoiding injury beyond pride and a hip that would bruise by morning. The horse, too, seemed unhurt, stumbling to its feet and eyeing her as if to confirm it was as surprised as she was. She stood, walked to the animal, patted its withers and said, "A fine birthday present that was."

Horse and rider walked toward the barn. Sonja blended the Nordic features of her Swedish parents, with blonde hair, bright blue eyes like her father's, and her mother's lithesome curves, just then beginning to emerge. She was in mid-passage from girl to woman, a daylily near dawn, and today she turned fourteen.

When she entered the farmhouse, her mother, Christina, looked up from her reading, the most recent issue of *Harper's Weekly*. So engrossed was she in news of the war that she appeared not to notice Sonja's disheveled clothing, her hair awry, the dark stain on her pants where her hip met dirt. Sonja pouted, feeling the need for sympathy but not surprised by Christina's focus. It was as though the firing on Fort Sumter severed not only the Union but her maternal bond as well. Since April, Christina's interest in the war had passed into obsession.

"Did you have a nice ride, dear?" her mother asked.

"I took a fall at the end. D'Artagnan missed the jump."

Christina smiled mechanically, seemingly on the verge of saying something like, "That's nice," when what Sonja told her registered. She put aside the paper, asking as she rose, "Are you hurt?"

"My hip is a little sore. I will be fine."

Christina embraced her, resting her chin on Sonja's shoulder now that they were of equal height. "You always say that—'I will be fine.' Sometimes I wonder.

You said it when you knocked your tooth out and when you broke your foot."

"And when father left."

Christina drew back and held Sonja's shoulders at arm's length, sighing. "Yes, then too," she said. "I know how difficult it must be, especially on days like today. Perhaps by your next birthday—"

"Mother, he's not coming back. It's time you knew that."

"In his last letter—"

"In all his letters, but nothing changes. He will not leave Sweden, and we are on our own, but I will be fine."

Christina renewed her embrace. "You have been a brave, strong girl. He should be very proud. I know I am."

In her room, Sonja lifted her copy of *The Three Musketeers*. How lucky to be a man, she thought. Men could seek adventure while women, she was learning, had to wait for it. And what if it never came? She sat on the bed, favoring the unhurt hip and envisioning her next birthday on their same Chadds Ford, Pennsylvania, farm with her same friends and routine chores. Unless her father returned, which she was sure would not happen, her life at fifteen promised to look very much like today.

She tried to picture her father, gone four years. The image was a blurred mosaic of features surrounding his glacier blue eyes. When her younger brother Peter died of typhoid fever at age three, her father told them he needed to visit the homeland where his parents and sisters lived. He would be gone a few months. The hired man could keep up the farm in his absence. His letters since, written in a hurried scrawl that sloped downward at the end of each line, always professed his love for them and always promised a return "soon." When the hired man left and not even that brought him back, Sonja knew he had no intention of returning, yet Christina clung to the hope. In the months following his departure, she had maintained an artificial cheerfulness, smiling too broadly for Sonja's benefit and putting the best face on dispiriting news, such as the cow being struck by lightning ("She didn't suffer.") and Sonja's broken foot ("It will heal stronger than before.").

When his letters arrived, Christina opened them in Sonja's presence. With the letter resting in her lap, she smiled as if to say they were about to get the long-awaited news of his return, and she broke the seal as if opening a gift. With a dramatic flair, she re-read with underscored relevance any allusion to ship schedules or his longing to see them or the harshness of the Swedish winter. When finished, she returned the letter to her lap with a deep sigh, her optimism rewarded. But as time passed, the sigh at the end confirmed Sonja's intuition, and in the days following those letters her mother grew morose and depressed. She cried often and slept later. Sonja worried that she would cease to be able to teach the Swedish immigrants she tutored in English. That income had been their salvation when the hired man left without notice.

But today, her mother looked and felt better. Sonja attributed the upswing in her moods in recent months to a most unlikely source: the war.

"Listen to this," Christina said, folding the November 2, 1861, issue of *Harper's Weekly* in half and adjusting the distance as she read. "'The Great Naval Expedition. By the time these lines are read by the public the Great Naval Expedition will have reached its destination, and we therefore violate no duty to the Government in illustrating its departure on pages 696 and 697. What precise point it is intended to attack no one knows but its leaders and members of the Administration; but we may rest assured it will deal a blow where it may be felt, and that the rebel army on the Potomac will not hear of its landing without emotions of very lively concern.'"

"I wonder where it landed," said Christina.

"May I see the illustrations?" Sonja asked. "Those poor horses." In one illustration a horse was lifted by sling onto the deck of a vessel; in another the crowded stalls below deck were shown. "How can they do such a thing? It is cruelty."

"It is war," Christina said looking over her shoulder. "A cavalry is not much use without horses. Look at the ships. I cannot imagine standing up to all those ships, and from all I read the rebels have no navy to speak of. Wherever this expedition landed will feel the full weight of this war, and it serves the rebels right."

NOVEMBER 8, 1861

CHAPTER 7

On the morning after the battle that forever changed his life, Carter sailed home. Was it still his home? Union troops would surely occupy it in a day or two. So much for the Confederate forts on Hilton Head and Bay Point that folks insisted would protect Beaufort. Both had fallen in three hours. How could adults, his people, have so underestimated the enemy? If they were wrong about the forts, maybe the whole war was a mistake. Too late now. His only choice was to make the best of it and survive.

From a mile away he saw and heard commotion along the waterfront. An old steamer offloaded gray-clad soldiers, whose slow, uninspired gait implied a long night and recent defeat. They made their way through dozens of Negroes milling along the docks, speaking Gullah and looking like they had just come in from the cotton fields. He couldn't recall ever seeing so much activity so soon after sunrise. A phalanx of black faces lined the wharf as he lowered the sail and tillered his skiff alongside the dock, as second nature to him as tying his shoe. He secured the boat and made his way to the street. He had taken only a few steps toward the Barnwell home when a soldier, seated on a step, called out to him.

"Hey, son, what brings you into town? We heard everybody high tailed it."

"Need a few things we left behind, sir."

The soldier looked up and down the street. "'Cept for all these niggers it looks like pretty much everything got left behind."

"Yes, sir. When the forts fell folks took what they could carry."

The soldier nodded, dropping his head as he did so. "I know all about that. We marched all night from Fort Beauregard. Captain Davis says we got a long walk ahead."

"If you're heading for the ferry it will take all day. May I ask who you're with?"

"Company C of the 12th. We're the last. Everybody behind us is wearing blue."

Carter said, "I watched the battle from Land's End. Those ships—"

"Fort Walker took a pounding. We got in a few licks but those Yankee guns were too much. I felt for those boys in Walker. Yep, they got tore up." He stood. "Better see where the captain went. He's trying to get us some vittles afore we head off."

"Good luck, sir."

Carter turned and walked west, the chatter of the docks receding and a ghostly quiet replacing it as he approached the Barnwell home. Here the street was utterly deserted. He crossed Bay Street and Dr. Gaffney's yard to the Barnwell home, a three-story landmark of Georgian design, with wide piazzas and columns twelve feet high. At the steps he paused, looking toward Lady's Island, where bolls of white sea island cotton stretched to the horizon. This was all about cotton, he thought. His mother off in Charleston, his brother Preston fighting at Manassas, his grandmother waiting for him back on Cane Island, his home lost. For cotton.

The cry of a crow flying low overhead brought him back to the purpose for this trip. He needed to do his work quickly. Union soldiers were bound to begin exploring. If Yankees found him here, his war could end today. Entering the house, standing in the foyer, he paused to listen, conscious that he was nervous about being in a place where he had every right to be. He dug his grandmother's list from his pocket and began to search.

The largest item was the butter churn. He took that to the boat first, planning to fit smaller objects around it. Working steadily, he located a small footstool, a hammer and nails, some spices from the kitchen, laudanum from the medicine chest, and several books, along with another lamp. He picked up an artillery shell canister used as a doorstop. It was not on the list, but his father said it was a relic of the war with Mexico.

In his room on the second floor he grabbed a small daguerreotype of his father and the cigar box in which he kept his arrowhead collection and the letter from Preston. He looked around to see if there was anything else he considered essential. Would he ever spend another night in this room?

Back on the first floor, he had just retrieved candles from the dining room sideboard when he heard laughter from the street: Daddy August. There were others, some Negro women and girls. Daddy August yelled for them to catch up, and from the slur in his voice he sounded drunk. The women yelled back at him, giggling and telling him to shush his mouth. The voices became louder, nearer. Instinct told him he should hide. He climbed the stairs, pausing at the second-floor landing before continuing to the third. At the top of the stairs he lingered at the banister as the party of Negroes entered the foyer.

"Well, Lawd de king, lookee dat," he heard Daddy August say. Moments later, the thunderous crashing of breaking glass mingled with gales of laughter. Daddy August yelled to Chloe that it was time for some dancing. Someone pounded the keyboard to the piano as shouts of glee rose up the stairwell. He heard what sounded like a window break. He stood listening as wood split, glass shattered, doors slammed. When he heard them coming up the stairs, he took a step back. He could no longer see them, but the trail of their laughter led to his mother's bedroom. A bureau drawer opened. Moments later Chloe yelled that she would be "queen 'o we" as she walked onto the landing in a dress his mother sometimes wore. In a maniacal voice, Daddy August called for help. A piece of furniture scraped across the hardwood floor, and from the clinking together of crystal bottles Carter knew it was his mother's cherry vanity. That vanity had given him his first glimpses of his own image. As his mother sat on the polished bench to arrange her hair, he would crawl up beside her, his legs too short to reach the floor. She smiled into the tri-paneled mirrors as he wondered at his own reflection. Her hair in place, she sometimes applied rouge lightly to her cheeks before playfully dabbing a spot of it on the end of his nose.

Carter edged back to the railing. Daddy August grunted as he lifted the vanity over the second-floor balustrade and dropped it to a thunderous crash landing on the floor below. When he threw his head back to laugh, his eyes met Carter's, who stood frozen at the banister. The Negro pointed a thick finger, his eyes bloodshot and marauding. "Hey, boy," he yelled. "I done polished dem mirrors for de last time. We is free! You hear me, boy? Free!" He descended the stairs. Minutes later the voices retreated, and all grew quiet.

Carter started down the stairs but had taken only two when he heard footsteps coming up. Heavy footsteps—boots. A Yankee? He regained the third floor and slipped into a shadow at the rear of the gabled room. Moments later the boots' owner emerged onto the landing. Carter's heart felt barely contained within his chest and he was certain it must be audible to the man whose back was now to him ten feet away. The newcomer wore a uniform and was holding a revolver in his right hand. He walked to the gable and looked out. From profile, Carter recognized Gabriel Heyward, his cousin. As he stepped from the shadow, a board creaked beneath him, and before he could call out Heyward wheeled and fired. Carter saw the muzzle flash and felt a sting in his right earlobe.

"Cousin Gabe," he stammered.

Heyward's eyes widened as he lowered the gun. "Damn, boy" he said. "You hit?"

"Maybe."

Heyward approached, reaching with his left hand to Carter's ear, where blood dripped. "I almost sent you to Jesus." He holstered the weapon and extended his hand, tousling Carter's hair. Heyward was medium height, handsome, with piercing green eyes and perfect teeth. "Your momma's gonna have my hide. You got to let a man know you are there."

Carter fingered his ear, then looked at the blood on his hand. "I didn't know it was you at first."

Heyward nodded. "Truth told, I'm just getting used to this revolver they issued me. Trigger seems a mite touchy. Here, put this handkerchief on it. Not a real good beginning for my career as a soldier—shooting my own cousin."

"It doesn't hurt much."

Gabriel smiled, his perfect teeth exposed. "One day you will thank me because the little scar it will leave is going to drive the ladies wild." On the subject of driving the ladies wild, Cousin Gabe was an expert. "I guess you saw what they did downstairs."

"I heard it."

"I've been waiting for them to leave. Lord, they tore up the place. Where is your ma?"

"Gone to Charleston."

"Uncle Daniel's?"

Carter nodded as he looked his cousin over. "Where did you get that uniform?" Heyward wore a single-breasted tunic buttoned from waist to neck and matching pants. No insignia adorned it, and but for the brass buttons and holster it could have passed for an oddly tailored suit.

"Joined the Charleston Light Dragoons two weeks ago. Pretty nice, eh? And let me tell you, son—the ladies? They love old Gabe even more in this outfit. I have had to warn a couple of them about smudging my buttons."

"The Charleston . . . ?"

"Light Dragoons."

"Never heard of them."

"You will. The hardest riding, hardest drinking crowd that ever strapped on a saber. We bivouacked up at Huguenin's place. Captain sent me down because those Charleston boys do not know the town."

"What about your folks?"

Gabriel's grin vanished as he inhaled. "Lost it all. Everything. They went to Summerville. That's the other reason I came—to check on our place. After seeing what went on here, I may pass it by. Say, where's Granny? Charleston?" Gabriel was the only person in Beaufort who called Missma "Granny," and for some reason she did not mind. His charms ran to women of all ages, as he was aware.

"She's with me," Carter said. "At the Lodge."

Gabriel's eyebrows arched, his green eyes flashed and the grin returned. "That old place?"

"Not so bad."

"How did that happen?"

"Missma locked herself in her room. Told mother she was born in Beaufort and would die in Beaufort and she wasn't leaving. Mother banged on the door, she yelled and she screamed—I've never seen her that way—but nothing she said could persuade Missma to leave. When she told Mother I would be staying with her at the Lodge, I thought Mother would faint."

"You knew about this?"

Carter shook his head. "Had no idea. Up to that minute I thought all three of us would head to Charleston like everyone else in town."

Gabriel's lips turned up in a wry grin. "Granny can be one tough bird. So you two are together at the Lodge?"

"Yep."

"For how long?"

"I guess as long as this thing lasts."

"That could be a whole year."

"That's what they say. Or as long as Missma lasts. Mother says she has a weak heart."

Gabriel shook his head, smiling. "That woman's not got a weak anything. Any news of Preston? Those boys made us right proud at Manassas."

"Last letter said he was okay. Still in Virginia. You know Preston. Not too many details."

"He'll be a general before you know it. Those Yankees have their hands full with him."

Carter looked at the floor, and for a moment the silence in the house was complete.

Gabriel tousled his hair again. "Do not worry about Preston. He'll be fine. Let me tie that handkerchief around your ear. It will look strange but it beats bleeding to death."

As Gabriel secured the bandage, Carter looked up. "Are we going to win?"

"Does a hound dog lick his balls? Of course we are going to win. And when we do, your brother and I will be war heroes and the ladies will line up for the thrill of touching us, which I just may let them do."

"What's it like in the . . . Dragoons?"

Gabriel turned and walked to the window looking out on the Beaufort River. The view stretched for a couple of miles, to the bend at Port Royal and to Parris Island beyond it. Carter followed, and for a moment they stared out at the placid river. "Well, I've only been in a couple of weeks, but so far I cannot complain. Before we left Charleston it was champagne for dinner and a party in town every night. Lord, those boys love a party almost as much as I do. Since we got to Huguenin's, things are a bit different. We drill some, but mostly we play cards and wait around for the action to start."

"When will that be?"

"Smart money says real soon. We got this new general, Lee is his name. R.E. Lee. West Pointer, I hear. They sent him down to protect the railroad, which we figure the Yankees will try to take out. 'Course, to do that they will have to get around the Dragoons, and that will not happen."

"When can I join the Dragoons?"

"How old are you now?"

"Twelve. Almost thirteen."

"A while yet," he said with a kindly smile.

"They shot my dog."

"Soot? Who shot Soot?"

"I don't know. Some Yankee. I was fishing on the beach when the ships showed up a few days ago. We were running for the boat when I heard him yelp. I picked him up and carried him. He's limping pretty bad but he'll be okay. What kind of person shoots a dog?"

"Maybe they were aiming at you. You're sure it came from a ship?"

"Only place it could have come from."

"Damn, boy, this war just started and you and Soot have both taken bullets."

As Gabriel stared out the window, his perfect teeth disappeared and a frown replaced the grin. "Is that what I think it is?"

Carter followed his gaze down-river. "Ships."

Visible now in the distance were tendrils of smoke streaming in the breeze, and below them three ships rounding the bend at Parris Island.

"Gunboats," Gabriel said. "Here they come. You better get back to Granny before the Yankees land."

"I have to pass them on the way to the Lodge."

"Keep your head down and hug the shore. Try to look seven instead of almost thirteen."

"What will you do?"

"Ride back to Huguenin's. I've seen what I came to see."

Carter grabbed his blanket full of supplies, straining at its weight and bulk, and joined Gabriel on the stairs. At the second-floor landing, Gabriel turned and gripped his shoulder. "The Dragoons may need some help defending the railroad. Maybe you keep your eyes and ears open for what goes on down here."

"Like a spy or something?"

"Yeah. Can you do that?"

"Sure. I want to help. I owe them one for Soot."

"Good. Meet you at the Lodge one of these days. I am real sorry I shot you. Forgive me?"

Carter grinned and nodded.

At the back door, Gabriel untethered his horse from a post, mounted and took off at a canter, waving as he rode.

Carter picked up his sack and walked toward the front door. He stepped around the wreckage of his mother's treasured vanity, now a pile a wood and glass. As he passed the dining room, he saw the Canton Blue china strewn across the floor, the cabinet overturned, and its doors ripped from their hinges. In the foyer, he recognized a dress of his mother's crumpled against the base of the grandfather clock. He picked it up and put it in his sack. Remnants of china littered the floor. The hands on the face of the grandfather clock had been knocked off, and without them its rounded wooden eyes seemed to be surveying rooms that had known only perfect order, as amazed as Carter that the Barnwell foyer, hallway and parlor now lay in ruin.

At the doorway he looked up and down the street, deserted. He lugged his supplies to the skiff, his eyes on the river, his bandaged ear beginning to throb, and his mind focused. With the wind at his back, he figured he had a chance of beating the gunboats to Cane Island and thereby avoiding any risk of confrontation. But the wind was not to his back, and the time spent tacking brought the gunboats closer with every change of direction. Then the gunboats stopped, idling just off the tip of Port Royal. He assumed one of them had run aground. Their delay gave him needed time. When he had Cane Island in sight, they resumed their trip up-river, coming toward him in single file. He tacked toward shore, crouching beneath his sail, as if by lowering his profile he could lower the boat's. He could see sailors on deck, and several on board the lead gunship came to the rail. One pointed to him. He held his breath in anticipation that it would change course to head him off, but it maintained a line straight toward the town. He reached shore just as the last ship cruised by in the wake of the one ahead.

Soot barked from inside as he neared the Lodge. Missma opened the door.

"What happened to you?" she asked, her eyes focused on his bandage.

"Cousin Gabe shot me. Not too bad."

She shook her head and scoffed. "That boy is all devil. Come inside and tell me what happened."

He entered the Lodge and walked to the hearth, where Soot lay curled by the fire. He petted the dog's head, eyeing the hind leg where traces of blood had coagulated around the wound.

"He hasn't moved from that spot all morning," Missa said, motioning Carter toward the table. "Sit," she instructed. She removed the handkerchief. "Lost a bit of your lobe. You'll live but let me clean that blood off."

She walked to the hearth, where a cast iron pot hung suspended from a trammel. Holding one corner of a rag, she dipped it into the pot. "This may sting for a moment." She gently brushed away the dried blood from his ear and neck. "Tell me what happened."

He related his arrival at the house, his retreat to the third floor at the approach of Daddy August and his band of celebrants, the loud music and violent destructions, and the sudden appearance of Gabriel Heyward.

"He didn't mean to," Carter said. "I guess I surprised him."

Missma's face aged visibly, its wrinkles deepening. "A couple of more inches and you wouldn't be here."

"Gabe says I'll thank him later because the ladies will love it."

Missma's face brightened. "If that does not say it all about that boy. I have never met anyone so head-over-heels where young ladies are concerned. I wonder if he would feel the same if it was his ear, knowing how much he likes what he sees every time he passes a mirror."

"What did he mean?" The sting had receded, replaced by a dull throbbing.

"He means that some girls like men of danger, and a scar from a bullet gives them a certain aura."

"What's an aura?"

"An atmosphere, a . . . feeling."

"He joined the Light Dragoons."

Missma nodded. "A perfect fit."

"You know of them?"

"I should say I do. They've been around for years—since I was a young lady at least."

"What are they like?"

"Like your cousin Gabriel. Wild, good-looking, rich boys that chase foxes and dresses. If I had a daughter I would keep her under lock and key when the Dragoons were around. How is that ear feeling?"

"Better. How does it look?"

"Swollen, but Cousin Gabriel just might be right this time."

"He told me they have to protect the railroad."

"And let us all hope they do a better job than those who were to protect Beaufort. I warned your mother those two forts wouldn't be enough to hold off the Union Navy."

"He says he will come to see us; that I might be able to help."

"What kind of help?" There was tension in her question.

"He didn't say exactly. Maybe spy on the Yankees."

She placed a bony hand on his shoulder and looked down. "You must think that over very carefully. The Yankees are not the British. They will not shoot or imprison an old lady and her grandson who are simply trying to stay alive. But spying? That's a horse of a different color. Do you understand?"

He broke eye contact and nodded.

She squeezed his shoulder hard. "They shoot spies, and not in the earlobe."

"They shoot dogs, too."

"He'll be alright. He's strong, and dogs heal themselves mostly."

That night, he stretched out on his pallet, tired but unable to sleep. From the other side of the counterpane separating him from his grandmother's corner of the Lodge came her rhythmic snoring. He lit a candle and from the cigar box extracted Preston's last letter.

39

At Camp
Lewinsville, Virginia

Dearest Mother:

After the waiting I complained about in my last letter, we finally saw some action. Minor's Hill is about three miles from here. The yanks took off running as soon as we fired a volley their way. Our boys think they have no stomach for this war. Colonel Kershaw told us we proved ourselves and that he was proud of us.

We have been told the yankees are moving into the area and there could be a battle. Just yesterday we captured some poor devils from the 9th Pennsylvania who wandered too far from their camp. The yanks took the farmers Hugh Adams and George Gunnel to prison for feeding us and giving us fresh fruit from their orchard along the Lewinsville Road. I pray for their release as their kindness has kept us well provided and reduces homesickness with their pretty daughters.

No matter what you may have read in the papers about the Virginia boys coming down with the grip and measles, our camp is clean and we have not had any cases of disease. We are on a small stream called Pimmitt Run and the water is fresh and clear. Two of our camps are upstream and we all benefit from an abundance of timber for our shelter and fires. If you can, please send me a new shirt and drawers as the weather here is much cooler than home.

I must leave you now as we are preparing to move toward Munson's Hill about 6 miles east with the rest of the men from South Carolina. Do not worry.

I close with my love to you and Carter and Missma.

Your Son
Preston

Carter's trip that morning had opened his eyes to the magnitude of change wrought by the war. A mere forty-eight hours ago, he slept in the room he had known since infancy, in the home that had been his and his family's for generations. He had risen before dawn to get to Land's End in time to watch the battle that by then everyone in Beaufort knew was coming. From the veranda at Dr. Jenkins's he marveled at the size of the Union armada anchored off the bar in Port Royal Sound, ship after ship stretching to the horizon, or so it seemed. Then came the line of warships, headed straight for where he and Reggie and dozens of anxious islanders stood waiting to see if the forts on Hilton Head and Bay

Point would hold. They saw puffs of smoke from the warships before the roar of cannon reached them. The forts answered, and soon the entire Sound was filled with an acrid smoke that made his eyes water. Around him, men he had known all his life talked of what was at stake, of how a Union victory meant total ruin.

As the ships steamed in an elliptical pattern half way between the forts bombarding them, the outcome seemed in doubt for a time. But eventually the response from the forts slowed, then stopped. All lost, the men on the veranda had agreed. He remembered how Miles Wilson, who brought him and Reggie in his buckboard to Dr. Jenkins's, had cursed the Yankees, saying that he had arrived on the piazza as a well-to-do gentleman and was leaving as nothing much more than a beggar. He told Carter and Reggie to unhitch his horses from the rig and ride them back to town. "I got no more use for them," he had said.

• • •

Carter stared up into the darkness of the Lodge's ceiling. His ear throbbed, pulsing with his heartbeat. He remembered Dr. Gaffney telling him they were "goners." He'd asked his mother if that meant they would die. "No sugar," she said. "It means we will have to leave. The whole town will be overrun with Yankees."

He thought about his mother, standing at the stern of the *Cecile*, waving to him as the paddle wheeler headed north toward Charleston and he and Missma sailed south to Cane Island. Was that just yesterday?

The war had now come to them and he and Soot had scars to prove it. He blew out the candle and drifted off to sleep on his second night in the Lodge.

CHAPTER 8

Pre-dawn chill in the cabin woke Grace. She gently untangled the twins' arms, draped over her beneath a blanket too thin. Polk snored steadily on his mat nearby. Her bare feet, toughened by years without shoes, did not register the cold dirt beneath them. With an old strip of metal that once served as a handrail on a carriage, she stirred the embers in the stove to life, then added two logs. In the glow cast by the renewed fire, she watched the twins huddle together, tempted to add her body heat until the cabin warmed, but she was too excited to return to the mat. Since yesterday, she had felt the presence of some new fullness. She could not locate it nor could she describe it beyond what she whispered to herself a dozen times: full, on the verge of overflowing. Was this what it felt like to be free? She had to find out. Today.

Polk opened an eye at the sound of her stirring. She leaned over him to say she must go into town to get the news. She would walk all the way to the landing on Lady's Island if she must. Polk responded with a grunt. She slipped into the only dress she owned, a brown muslin castoff, and pocketed a chunk of cornbread for the trip. It was still dark when she passed the three pine trees at the entrance to the plantation. There was enough waning moonlight to see how tall they had grown since she and Polk first arrived ten years before.

By the time she had walked for an hour, the sun was up. A buckboard full of her people passed. The driver, a toothless old Negro man in a slouch hat, halted the team as she climbed aboard. They were going where she was going. Morning mist covered the road, and the wagon seemed to be riding on a cloud. No one uttered the word "freedom." The talk was of food. Word of the soldiers' regular and plentiful meals had already reached the islands. To be near the soldiers was to be near the food and away from hardscrabble plantation life. More wagonloads of folks will follow, they told her. She thought of all the hours Polk spent in their vegetable garden, every day when he worked one task and on many days when he worked two. A man who could work two tasks and still garden had done a full day's labor, but that extra effort kept her from worrying about dependence on soldiers to eat. What she wanted was not food but freedom. The sway of the rig induced sleep in a few of the passengers, but Grace had never felt more alert and alive. And full. There was that feeling again.

Soldiers crowded the landing at the ferry, so it was noon before Grace and her traveling companions were allowed to cross. Her last trip into town was three years before, when she visited her half-sister Portia. The buildings were as she remembered, but nothing else looked remotely familiar. Bay Street appeared to her as a giant carnival. White soldiers and black men, their intoxication evident, paraded up and down the street, yelling and singing songs foreign to her. The formidable front doors of the old mansions stood open as revelers went into and out of them at will. From upper windows, clothing and furniture cascaded into yards. She spotted Daddy August, whom she knew from time spent at Portia's. He and five or six others were trying to remove a piano from its home. They tilted it sideways, but the legs would not fit through the door. She heard wood snap as one by one the legs broke to gleeful laughter. They slid the piano onto the piazza, where it remained upside down as the men moved toward the next house. A drunk soldier veered toward her, but she recognized lust and sped up to a near run. By the time she arrived at Portia's door, she was breathless. At her first knock the door opened.

"Get in here, girl," Portia told her. "The devil on the loose in Buford."

As Grace caught her breath, Portia told her of the soldiers that had come to occupy the Barnwell home. They had been friendly and sober, she reported, and had told her she would be paid for any services she chose to perform in the kitchen or laundry. "You believe that? Paid sho' 'nuff money!"

But what, Grace wanted to know, had the soldiers said about freedom? That was what she came to learn.

"Freedom?" Portia asked. "Dey say everybody free. No more master. De white folk done skedaddle and dey ain' comin' back."

Grace felt the fullness rise within her. It flooded her eyes in tears she could not stop.

CHAPTER 9

Anna slept late. When she arose, aromas of breakfast filled the first floor and wafted upstairs. In the dining room, Daniel sat at his customary seat at the head of the table. Morning sunlight filtered onto his shoulders. His hands were folded in his lap, on top of a linen napkin. On hearing her enter the room, he smiled. "I was about to send Abigail up to check for a pulse," he said. "Good morning."

"Good morning," Anna said, and touched his shoulder on her way to the kitchen, where she and Abigail embraced. "Let me help."

Abigail brought Daniel his plate. "Biscuit at noon," she said. "Eggs at three o'clock, grits at six, bacon at nine." They used this system at each meal to prevent Daniel from having to feel for his food. Once oriented, he ate with rare complication. His coffee was always to his right, and above that the fig preserves he was so fond of. Butter was to his left, flanked by salt and pepper. He ate with utmost patience, savoring his food with small bites thoroughly chewed. Abigail ate rapidly, setting her plate aside and replacing it with the Charleston *Courier*. She read, "The election of Electors of president and vice-president of the Confederate States will take place today."

"No drama there," Daniel observed. "Just as before under the old Constitution."

Abigail said, "Mr. Rhett is at it again in the *Mercury*, I hear. Criticizing President Davis before he has even been formally elected." She ended with a small huff of impatience.

Daniel said, "At the risk of speaking ill of our cousin, Barnwell Rhett has a case of aggravated envy. His choice for president has looked back at him in the shaving mirror for thirty years."

"He has the disunion he worked so hard to bring about," Abigail agreed. "It will be the ruin of us all." She returned her gaze to the newspaper. "It seems pointless to read the report from Beaufort while we have a more current one sitting at the table with us."

Anna, who had eaten little, sipped coffee. "I cannot believe the forts fell so quickly. Carter witnessed it from Dr. Jenkins's piazza at Land's End. He told us the Yankee ships fired constantly. I fear for the casualties we must have suffered." She lowered her eyes. "And Carter is out there somewhere in the middle of it. With his grandmother. It's like waking in the middle of a horrible dream."

Abigail reached over to pat her hand. "We must do some shopping today.

You'll need some clothes."

"I must get word to Preston. He won't know I am here."

Daniel dabbed his mouth with his napkin. "We took care of that first thing this morning," he said. "I telegraphed the Army. They will make sure he gets the word, although they said it would take some time—a few days, they said."

"Oh, thank you, Uncle Daniel," Anna said. She had long admired the old gentleman, a cotton broker with far more success than the tangible evidence suggested. He and Abigail lived modestly in a quiet section of the city, just off Broad Street. He had a brother, Luke, also a cotton broker, who lived in Columbia. Both brothers were products of a marriage between second cousins, Edgar and Helen, who were warned that their union posed a risk. Edgar and Helen eventually had six children, all sighted except Daniel, who had been, with one exception, more successful than his siblings. Abigail read for him and to him, and together they were formidable. Uncle Daniel possessed a highly developed feel for long-staple cotton. When bales arrived on the docks for transport north or overseas, he rubbed a sample from each between his thumb and forefinger to verify the quality he had represented to the buyer. Early in his career, he was known to order entire substandard shipments returned to the plantation on which they were grown. The growers knew better now. He brokered for six plantations, all in the Lowcountry, to buyers in London and Boston, and he anticipated the business he had spent his adult life building would be devastated by the war.

He said, "I realize you just arrived, but have you given any thought to what you would like to do? Use our home as your own, of course, but beyond that?"

Anna straightened. "On the boat last evening I saw so many friends and neighbors that will be staying in Charleston, but I don't know where. One thing I would like to do is make a list of who is here and their temporary addresses. We'll need to stick together to get through this."

"A worthwhile project," Abigail said. "I would love to help."

"And I will need to see a doctor, as I was advised to do by Dr. Gaffney in Beaufort. Even if I can find a way to join Carter and Missma at the Lodge, I dare not put off that consultation any longer than I have."

CHAPTER 10

November 8, 1861
Beaufort, S.C.

My dear Hazel:

At long last I have the opportunity to compose a letter worthy of the events I am living through in this war. Your brother has been in the thick of the action, as I shall relate.

I address you from the porch of a house I suppose the rebels would call a mansion. I am seated in a hammock, of all things, but they are ubiquitous here and somewhat comfortable if one can find precisely the proper position for sitting or reclining. Today is quite temperate, so different from our Boston Novembers, not that I would not give all I own to be back there instead of here, in this pitiful backwater. The porch overlooks the river, scene of the fierce battle I will describe herein and from which I was most fortunate to escape unharmed. Please save for me the account in the *Globe* of the battle of Port Royal Sound, which I know you read with interest and no small amount of dread for your dear brother's safety.

I last wrote on the eve of the great battle, so I will begin where I left off. On the morning of the 7th, I was summoned by Commodore DuPont to his stateroom to consult on the plan of attack. I was most encouraged by his display of such an open mind regarding my suggestions. Modesty prevents me from claiming too great a share in the successful outcome but suffice it to say the Union's first major victory could have ended differently had my role been other than it was.

There could have been no grander spot to watch history made than the quarterdeck of the *Wabash*, where I was assigned. I marvel even now at the calm confidence I felt as I assumed my battle station in full view of the crew and senior officers. All around me men displayed visible evidence of the fear some felt going into battle. Their anxieties were palpable, and it must have reassured no few of them when they looked up toward me and the ship's officers. Leaders must lead, and I did.

When the battle commenced, the *Wabash*, as the flagship, drew the heaviest attention. The benighted enemy may be mired in the eighteenth century, but to give the devil his due they can shoot artillery with murderous aim. We took a number of hits amid-ship, keeping our surgeons fully engaged. Our brave sailors fought through the agonies of burns and amputations, determined to live long enough to see the southern rabble get its grim reward. Through the smoke of battle and the whistling of shells overhead I shouted encouragement, issued orders, and performed in a manner that will undoubtedly yield promotion, as my efforts could hardly have gone unnoticed by the powers that be. As I watched our glorious flag raised over the traitors' fort, I felt the satisfaction that can come only from battlefield glory and devotion to cause.

When the battle ended we were ferried to the beach of the island they call Hilton Head, where the rebels' Fort Walker lay in ruins. I counted 14 enemy dead. Those who turned tail to run will no doubt be hunted down and shot like the dogs they are. That said, candor compels me to report that the conduct of our infantry, newly landed, was less than professional. I saw inebriated Marines shooting into the air and yelling like it was the Fourth of July. Those who were less drunk went through the abandoned rebel tents, plundering pistols, swords, watches, tobacco and money left behind by their fleeing owners. As much as such hooliganism repels those of us who seek to set an example, it is gratifying to know that these spoils of war will grace sideboards and libraries in New England for generations to follow.

Adding to the confusion on the beaches were the contrabands, the official term used to describe the Negroes. They came out of nowhere, some falling at our feet in gratitude and others clasping their hands skyward in prayer. They sing as often as speak, and speak a dialect that is almost impossible to understand—indeed, one enlightened southerner who was raised in these parts interpreted for us, and only through him were we able to learn that the contrabands had been told that we planned to sell them into slavery in Cuba. We surmise this Cuba threat was a method by which some plantation owners hoped to discourage their slaves from deserting on our arrival, but it is clear the rumor has little credence among a majority of the poor contrabands, whose patched and depleted clothing, if it can fairly be called clothing, defies description.

Near sundown on this triumphant day we were exposed to yet another barbarism in this desolate land—an invisible gnat of some kind that inflicts utter torment upon its victims. I was told, again by

47

the gentleman raised locally, that the mildness of the day accounted for their presence, and the onset of winter will banish them until spring. If true, winter must set in at once, as I find these horrid pests intolerable. The contraband seem immune, but perhaps that is to be expected after so long an acclimation.

I found myself detailed to one of a number of gunboats assigned the task of reconnoitering the town of Beaufort. I take this privilege to have been accorded in part for my performance in the battle and in part for need of reliable and accurate reporting on conditions. We are an advance party of sorts, sent to scout buildings and facilities to be utilized by the senior command that will relocate here in the coming weeks. We had a pleasant enough trip up the Beaufort River, which was devoid of boats or commerce with the sole exception of one skiff I pointed out from the deck, a small sailboat piloted by a young white boy going who knows where.

The town we entered must have been nice enough in its day, for the homes here are opulent by Southern standards, according to those claiming to know. The styles are Greek Revival and Federal (ironically) with white columns, large sweeping porches like the one on which my hammock is suspended, and shuttered floor-to-ceiling windows that catch what breeze there is. As I say, nice enough in its day, but its day has passed, as shown by the broken furniture strewn about the yards and streets. Every house we entered had been vandalized and plundered. Lest we judge harshly, we must remember that these contrabands have lived with the yoke of subjugation around their necks for generations, and who can fault them for taking or destroying the property their sweat and tears made possible. More power to them is my motto. Yet it is a mess, but the structures are sound and will do nicely for the purposes needed.

I confess to one profound shock on my inspection tour. The public library here is extraordinary. Who would have guessed these back-country ingrates would be sufficiently literate to support a fine library? It is on par with many in New England, although one wonders if it is perhaps maintained just for show. The building is round and columned, suggestive of Jefferson's Monticello, but hardly on as grand a scale from sketches I have seen of the Virginia estate. I perused the stacks for half an hour, noting collections of Shakespeare, Wordsworth, Ben Franklin, Darwin, Gibbon, and what must surely be every word ever written by Sir Walter Scott. There is even a ten-volume set of our own Massachusetts Historical Society. When I expressed my grudging admiration within earshot of a captain, he promptly assigned me the responsibility for it. Its fate will be discussed in the coming days, he told me. As for now, the building is open and a search for keys to the door locks proved fruitless, so open it will remain. However, there is little reason to believe it is at any risk, for the contrabands cannot read and thus feel no need to take retribution on a collection of helpless books.

I trust, my dear sister, that you are content and comfortable. I am neither, but that is war. I assume you have had no communications from the unspeakable woman I married. Being here in the deep South, where the serpent was birthed, gives me insight into the forces that shaped her, and she is indeed a product of those forces. Now that I have trod South Carolina soil, I can only imagine what Mississippi is like. Heaven help us, and heaven give strength to our president and our great cause.

With greatest affection,
Newton

NOVEMBER – DECEMBER 1861

CHAPTER 11

"How's your ear?" Missma asked Carter on the morning after his wounding.

"Sore." He added wood to the fire as she warmed herself near it.

"I wonder if your mother will ever forgive me."

"Did you know she would get so upset?"

"I don't fault her. To have one son fighting in Virginia and leave the other in the middle of a war was asking too much of her. And of you."

"Why does she need to see a doctor in Charleston?"

With the room warming, Missma loosened her robe. "It's a female problem. Dr. Gaffney recommended a specialist in Charleston."

"Is it serious?"

"It can be if not treated, so it was important for her to go. If that sounds like I'm justifying myself, it's because I am. She has every right to be furious. I would be."

"Is the Lodge like you remember it?"

"Very much so. I doubt you were born when we owned this entire island. We sold it, or most of it, to Thomas Boykin. Your father couldn't bring himself to part with the Lodge, so he kept that and some acreage. Ten, if memory serves."

"Does Mr. Boykin live in the house over there?"

"Oh, no. He lives in Pendleton. His overseer looks after the place here. If you'll come with me, I'd like to walk around a bit."

They walked outside, beyond the outhouse, where two paths diverged. The path to the left led to the shore and the boat; the one to their right through the break of trees to the cultivated fields of Three Pines, bountiful this time of year in a profusion of white cotton ready for harvesting. Along the winding path approaching the cotton fields stood live oak, cedar, crepe myrtle, pines and palmettos, all competing for sunlight. As they walked, she asked if he came here often.

"Yes, ma'am. Father told me it was my job to keep the paths clear, so I try to do that."

At the edge of the field they stopped. "I have a project for you," she said. "The floors are quite dirty. I suspect you and others who hunt here haven't been very careful about taking your boots off." As they returned to the Lodge, she suggested he haul sand with the promise they would see a dramatic improvement in the floors, muddied and scuffed.

She told him to find the whitest sand available on the island. He filled a woven basket used to harvest fruit, as she had said the task would demand a substantial quantity. He carried the basket to the Lodge, where she instructed that sand be spread across the floor. That done, she sent him in search of corn shucks, telling him to look near the slave cabins at Three Pines. He walked through the tree break and around the plantation's billowing cotton, guided by smoke rising in the distance from chimneys of the cabins. Near one he found a plot of fallow land with desiccated corn stalks, which he stripped while glancing at the cabins, conscious that he was in someone's vegetable garden. But for the smoke, there was no sign of life among the cabins.

Back at the Lodge, Missma stuffed the shucks into the holes of an odd-shaped wooden board Carter brought from his last trip into town. Attached to the board was a long handle. Together the shucks, board and handle created a crude mop. In the fireplace, boiling water bubbled in the cast iron pot. Into the pot she dumped a healthy ration of lye soap, stirring the potion with a long wooden paddle, which was also on her list. The brew gave off an acrid smell that filled the Lodge. She dipped the mop into the boiling concoction, letting it rest in the cauldron long enough for the shucks to become saturated. She removed the mop, then applied it to the sand on the floor at her feet, scrubbing hard. When she had cleared an area two feet square, she doused it with cold water from a pail resting on the hearth. Then, to Carter's amazement, she kicked off her shoes, placed each leg into a crocus sack, and shuffled back and forth across the small area subjected to the scalding. The effect was, as promised, dramatic, bringing to him the realization that he had never seen the actual floor but only the layer of grime to which he and the other hunters had contributed. It took him an entire day, following her example, but eventually the floor matched Missma's two-foot square. By the time he changed the shucks for the final time and shuffled the sacks to dry the floor, he was exhausted.

On their fifth morning at the Lodge, Missma said she thought she heard rats. "Near daybreak. Very clearly," she said as she stirred the fire to heat water in the small kettle. The mild temperatures of early November had been ushered offshore by a cold front. She cinched her wolfskin robe as she stabbed the poker into awakening embers. "If we must learn to live on little food, so must they. Not so much as a crumb. If you catch us a fish, I'll fix the grits."

Carter nodded and walked toward the door, looking over his shoulder at Soot, but the dog stayed by the fire, its muzzle resting on its front paws. Thirty minutes later, he returned. He handed Missma a large redfish, scaled and gutted. "I caught it from the bank," he said. From his pockets he extracted three oranges. "There is a tree full of them near where I tied the boat."

"Beautiful," she said. "Now peel that potato for me and we will eat well this morning."

After breakfast, he grabbed axe and wedge and spent the morning splitting wood. Downed oaks and cedars would provide seasoned hardwood for the winter, so felling trees was not necessary. He hovered over an upturned log. Sweat stung his eyes as he brought the blunt edge of the axe down on the wedge, its tip angled into the log's grain. The wedge disappeared, the log divided, and the process continued. They may starve, but they will not freeze, he told himself.

Back inside, he found Missma seated in her rocker, knitting. He shed his hat and wiped his forehead with a rag he carried in his back pocket.

"You're working hard," she said.

"We will need lots of wood this winter. And it beats cleaning the floors. Missma," he said from a chair by the table, "why don't the Yankees just leave us alone?"

"Because this would not be much of a country without the South, and the South has said in no uncertain terms it wants to go its own way."

"Because of the Negroes?"

"Yes."

He nodded. "I guess if I were a Negro I would want my own land and not have to work so hard on other land I could not keep."

"I believe I would feel the same," she said.

"Is it wrong what we do?"

She lowered her knitting needles to her lap, holding her breath a beat longer than usual, weighing her words. "If by 'we' you mean the Barnwells, then no, I do not think we do wrong. Your mother sold off all the field hands when she sold Longleaf after your father died. She freed the house servants, Rosa and Portia, although she did it quietly because it is not legal to free slaves. Your mother made certain they were clothed and fed, she sent for Dr. Gaffney when they got sick, and she never separated a family. They loved her for that."

"Then why did they not go with her? And why did Daddy August tear up the house?"

Missma sighed. "Because if by 'we' you mean the South, then yes, I think we did wrong. One human being should not own another. Simple as that. I wish we had freed them all years ago. Then we could have avoided this awful mess we have on our hands now."

"Why did we not free them?"

"As I said, it's not legal. Your father once told me he planned to free them in his will, but he died long before any of us expected. Your mother raised no small number of eyebrows in doing what she did, but she escaped punishment because she was a widow and because Portia and Rosa were house servants. Daddy August was a field hand needed at the house after your father died, and no planter in Beaufort could have freed a field hand without being prosecuted."

She swept her needles toward the window. "Acres and acres out there. Picking cotton is hot, hard work. The plain truth is that we do not have enough whites to do it. We got ourselves in a fix by having to depend on them so much—the Negroes, I mean. And I blame that on John C. Calhoun, not that it is a popular view around these parts, Mr. Calhoun by all local opinion being a god among men."

"What did he do wrong?"

"He fought industrialization. He never believed we should build factories here like they were building up north. Said he would ruin any man who tried to manufacture anything, and he could do it, too. Can you imagine? If you cannot make anything, you have to buy it from folks that do, and to do that takes money. Yes, I blame Mr. Calhoun for much of this war."

"Why did he think it was wrong to make things?"

"I would ask him that very question if he had not taken the coward's way out of an argument by dying."

"And Daddy August?"

"Let me just say that I thank the Lord your mother was not here to see what that man did to her house. It would kill her to think he had so little respect for one who treated him so kindly. I prefer to think it was the whisky in him."

"Do you think I can visit her in Charleston some day?"

"Of course, child. You have my word."

"But who would take care of you?"

"Do I look helpless?"

"No, ma'am."

"Nor am I. Not yet, anyway. We will see what tomorrow brings, which is all we can do. I worry you will get lonely here with just an old lady for a companion. I can't replace Thomas or Ben or Sims or any of your friends that left. Did you see Reggie in town?"

He shook his head. "I looked for him, thought sure he would be tending his plants like he does."

She tilted her head to one side. "We haven't talked about school."

"That's the only good thing I see about these Yankee ships coming. No school."

"You think that is good, do you? Well, think again. You are a bit young to worry about money the way your mother does, but you do understand that the family is now without means."

"Without means?"

"Ruined, financially speaking. Your mother and I have a little gold put away, and some savings, but when that runs out, we will have nothing. Our home? Gone. Longleaf? Long gone. Negroes? Sold or freed. That means little of value to pass along to you when your time comes."

"Can we get the house back?"

"I doubt that very much," she said. "Your future will depend on education. I was willing to force you to stay with me, but I'm not willing to cost you a proper education. Because school as you have known it is not possible, we will turn to books, the only real source of learning."

He groaned.

"I heard that. You will thank me later. We will need a source of books. I wonder if the Yankees know what a fine library Beaufort possesses. I will give the matter some thought."

The next day, he shot a duck. Missma slow cooked it in wild rosemary she picked that afternoon from a berm where the rosemary was surrounded by poison ivy. That evening, roasting yams added to the aromas filling the Lodge. Just after sunset, they ate. Carter banked the fire for the night as Missma dozed in her rocker when a sharp knock on the door brought her out of her slumber. Carter instinctively reached for his shotgun. Soot growled. Before either could speak, the voice at the door said, "Your favorite rebel. Open up."

Carter caught her wink and smiled as she called loudly, "Are you armed? I do not want my ear shot off."

Gabriel Heyward came through the door with the casual confidence of a seasoned cowboy approaching a wild-eyed stallion. "Hmmmm," he hummed, "someone had duck for dinner." He approached Missma's rocker, took her proffered hand, and kissed it with a cavalier flourish. Her eyes followed each bend and nod as she accepted his greeting with a debutante's coyness. His beard tickled her hand at the knuckles.

"We have extra," she said. "Carter, get your cousin a plate."

Gabriel surveyed the room. "Not bad, all things considered."

"Then I doubt you have considered all things," she said. "But it feels more like home each day. Poor Carter has the worst of it. His grandmother takes him hostage and his cousin tries to kill him."

He grinned his wide smile. "Fortunes of war, Granny. The boy startled me. How is that ear, cousin?"

"Missma cleaned it up. It feels better."

She said to Gabriel, "Would you like some tonic? You had a long ride to get here."

He whipped a leather-covered flask from his hip pocket. "I never travel without my tonic, and if there are no objections I will take some with my meal."

They were seated at the table. "The Yankee brass has moved into town," he said between bites. "General Stevens has taken over the Smith house. Appears he will run things from there. We don't know what they are planning, of course. The best guess is they will make a run at the railroad and the depots. They might not get around to that for a while, because they have a couple of immediate problems that ain't going to be easy to solve."

"Such as?" she asked.

He took a pull on his flask. "Such as harvesting a cotton crop without any help from the people who have been doing it for a hundred years. And then there are all the slaves—nine or ten thousand of them, free and confused, stumbling around mumbling about Moses and Jesus and all sorts of stuff. Those holier-than-thou abolitionists will finally get their prayers answered, and I wonder how many Boston hypocrites will invite a few dozen of them to come live in the guest quarters."

Carter asked, "How did you come?"

"Same as when I saw you at the house, only then I had no time to go by our place, and this time I did. Staying here tonight and leaving at first light if that suits."

"Surely," said Missma. "Carter said you might need him."

"That's why I came." He ceased eating, placing his knife beside the plate as if to call this very intimate meeting to order. He looked at Carter. "We need help. All our information comes from a few loyal old black souls who may or may not be trustworthy down the road. If the Yankees are planning to attack the railroad, or make a run up to Charleston, lots of folks in Beaufort will know before it happens. We cannot allow them to take that railroad. All the plans being made to defend South Carolina assume we can transport our boys from Charleston to Savannah and anywhere in between in one day, and that can be done only by rail. It also carries food and ammunition to the troops. We have to hold it."

"You want him to spy. That will be dangerous."

"It's war, Granny. Everything is dangerous." He turned his gaze back on Carter. "You asked me when you can join the Dragoons. Can't help you there, but every town needs a home guard, those left behind who will protect it when things get rough. And things are already rough here."

Missma spoke. "But spying is particularly dangerous. You understand my meaning."

"They won't hang a kid that has not yet seen a whisker in the mirror."

"No, they may shoot him." Carter's eyes widened. "The boy and I will discuss this. I feel responsible for him. I want to make certain he appreciates the risks. I will discourage him, but he will have to decide."

"Fair enough," said Gabriel. "In a day or two I will come back for his answer."

"Bring a cow," Missma said.

Gabriel laughed. "I guess ya'll could use a few things."

"Some chickens and a rooster," Missma said. "And Carter will need a horse."

"Done thought of that," Gabriel said. "Got one tied up outside for him." He turned to Carter. "Go take a look if you like. We call her Sunset because that's when she foaled, but you can name her anything you want. She's yours now."

"Thanks, Cousin Gabe."

Missma said, "More bird?" Without waiting for a reply, she placed a slice on his plate.

As he picked up his knife, Gabriel said, "We don't have much time for him to decide. In a few days the Yankees will get organized and begin exploring these islands. I can't risk getting caught. That's some mighty good duck, Granny."

She nodded in acknowledgment. "He will risk getting caught, too."

"Can't be helped."

"Of course it can. He can refuse."

"But he won't. He will do what he can for the cause."

She sighed and looked away. "This is something I did not consider when I made my decision to stay. If he is hurt or captured, I will not be able to face his mother."

"Day after tomorrow, about this same time, I will come back. If I fail to show, it's because the Yankees are on Lady's Island sooner than expected."

"Do not forget the cow," she said.

CHAPTER 12

I n Pennsylvania, Sonja Sunblad clutched a pillow pressed to her abdomen as relief against the monthly cramps she had begun to experience. The last thing she wanted to do today was ride into Philadelphia to church over marginal roads in the teeth of winter.

Just after first light her mother entered her room. She put the lantern on the bed stand and leaned over. "How are you feeling?"

"Miserable." Sonja winced. "Sharp pains."

"A woman's burden," said Christina. "The trip into Philadelphia will take your mind off it."

"The trip into Philadelphia will kill me. Do we have to go?"

"Sit up. I brought something I want you to see." The *Philadelphia Inquirer* article reported wandering masses of hungry, nearly naked Negroes in and around Beaufort, South Carolina, trailing the Army because they did not know what else to do. The former slaves, liberated by the Union victory in the Battle of Port Royal Sound—what the Negroes call the Big Gun Shoot—have descended upon their camps, obstructed their drills and drained their food supplies. In turn, the soldiers have foraged the plantations, raiding the fields and stores of corn and potatoes the Negroes grew and rely upon to see them through the winter.

"Very sad," said Sonja. "I want to sleep."

"Who will help these poor souls?" Christina asked.

"Someone whose insides are not on fire. Do we have to talk about this now?"

"Get up and get dressed. Your oatmeal is on the table. We leave in half an hour. You may bring your pillow."

"Mother, I know what this is all about. Ever since you suggested we move you have spoken of nothing but the war. We are going all the way to Philadelphia to hear more of the same, are we not?"

"To hear a wonderful speaker, and please do not roll your eyes because this is important. Dr. William Henry Furness is to preach a major sermon on what is being called the 'Port Royal Experiment.'"

Sonja did not read the papers and journals her mother read. She was vaguely and distantly aware there was a war on, but as of yet it had not touched her personally. When she thought about it, she shared her mother's view of slavery as abhorrent, both because it was her mother's view and because the Lutheran church they would otherwise be attending today condemned it. Her absorption for the past three months had been her school work, her chores, her horse, her friends, the changes in her body. She hoped her mother's fascination with the rebellion would subside; that she would come to her senses about selling the farm.

To her surprise, the long buckboard ride into the city did relieve her cramps. By the time the service began, she felt human once more.

At the First Unitarian Church of Philadelphia, from a pulpit high above the congregation in a building that on that day held more communicants than had ever been envisioned by the architects who designed it, Dr. Furness delivered a sermon that spoke directly to mother and daughter.

"In every life," intoned Dr. Furness, "there comes a day of judgment far earlier than the one you have heard so much about. Oh, I know!" and here both hands shot skyward as he warmed to his theme, "I know you feel the need to prepare yourself for that day the Bible tells us is coming, the day when we lay our earthly cares aside and come face to face with our Lord and Savior. Brethren, I tell you that for each of you within the sound of my voice, there comes a day unlike other days, and it is here. It is now. God's children in Southern bondage cry out for mercy and for justice. For generations they have endured the wet, the cold, the hunger, the lash and the noose. Our brave soldiers are fighting and dying to free them from the shackles of slavery, and we pray for every success the Almighty deems fit to bestow. But armies cannot comfort the afflicted, and soldiers cannot bind up the hurt felt by these oppressed souls. It falls to us, God's more fortunate children, to answer the cry from the South, to set aside our petty struggles and to fly where we are needed most. What is that need? Food and clothes, to be sure, but much more than that: education. Teachers are desperately needed in South Carolina. If God has granted you the ability to teach, now is the time to bring our black brethren out of ignorance by your good works. This much I know; on the final day of judgment those answering this call will reside in God's heavenly kingdom, for this is truly the Lord's work."

As they mounted the buckboard for the return home, Christina's eyes blazed with an excitement Sonja had never seen.

"What did you think of the sermon?" Christina asked.

"I would hate to be a slave," Sonja said.

"It must be terrible," her mother agreed. "And when we see something that is terrible and could be corrected, we must act. The scripture instructs us so."

"We cannot fight."

"No," said Christina, her eyes straight ahead but still fired, "but we can teach, as Dr. Furness said." Then, feeling Sonja's stare, she added, "It would not mean leaving Pennsylvania forever. And surely you see how difficult the farm is becoming for us."

Back in Chadds Ford, Christina read aloud from a recent issue of *Harper's*. "On the arrival of the United States steamship *McClellan*, Captain Gray, she was surrounded by boats loaded with fruits, sweet potatoes, chickens etc., gathered by the slaves, who importuned the Captain to purchase their small but many cargoes." She looked up to gauge Sonja's reaction, turning toward her the illustrations of the fruit sellers and the town itself. "So different from Pennsylvania. So . . . exotic. I realize there will be perils, but we are resourceful women and we can handle whatever comes our way." She bobbed her head decisively, as if to put an exclamation point to her confidence.

"But I love Pennsylvania."

"And I loved Sweden. Your father and I left all our family and friends to sail across the ocean for a better life, more opportunity."

"Did you regret it? Father must have, because he went back."

"He missed his brothers and sisters more than I realized, and after Peter died . . ."

"I barely remember him."

"Your father or Peter?"

Sonja sighed. "Both, I suppose. It seems like it has been you and me forever."

"I still have hopes your father will return. South Carolina could be a great adventure for us while we wait."

"Mother, I'm not waiting. I don't believe he's coming back. Besides, I would miss Heidi and Ingrid and my friends."

"And make new ones there, I feel sure."

"Suppose I don't like teaching? And who will teach me? If I hate it, can I leave?"

"If you give it a fair chance and you hate it, we will leave."

"Do you promise?"

"If you promise to give it a fair chance."

CHAPTER 13

Carter accompanied Missma to lay out the land behind the Lodge. They passed the outhouse and walked the path leading away from the river. Her gait was steady, but she placed her hand on his shoulder as a precaution against tripping over the vines and brambles that were beginning to infest the path. When they emerged from the break formed by the woods, waist-high cotton, in alabaster profusion, stretched for acres.

"Worthless," Missma said. "We cannot eat cotton. I would bet my eye teeth that no one will come here to harvest this. Chances are good with all the chaos it will rot where it stands. Whoever owns this field is gone like the rest of them. Old man Boykin owned it once. Perhaps he still does. Gabriel may know, but it hardly matters."

An autumn wind blew off the river, rippling the cotton so that the entire field appeared to be a sea of lapping whitecaps. Set against darkening clouds on the horizon, the cotton appeared faintly luminescent. She plucked a boll from a nearby stalk. "When I was a girl, indigo grew here. We used big vats to soak the leaves and extract the residue. I remember the osnaburg sacks hanging from trees."

"What is an osnaburg sack?"

"A special sack that allowed the indigo to dry. They were everywhere. I must have been nine or ten when the crop and the vats and the sacks disappeared. Cotton took over."

"Is the cotton business dead like indigo?"

"It is if we lose the war, and I am afraid that is just what will happen."

She dropped her head reflectively. "To think that one week ago this crop meant income, prosperity, wealth . . . and now? My, my." Then, lifting her head, she looked at him directly. "Have you given any more thought to your cousin's plan?"

"I want to do it."

"He thought you would. What do you think your mother would say?"

"She will worry. I remember how she cried when Preston left. But everything has changed and I need to do my part."

"You have considered the risks?"

"There are risks in what I do now. Hunting, even fishing. Storms come up quickly here."

"Still, the Yankees are a risk unlike any you have taken. We really do not know what they would do if they arrested you as a spy. I don't believe they would execute a boy, but some kind of jail or confinement seems highly likely. Are you prepared for that?"

"I'm not worried about me. I'm worried about you. How could you manage here without me?"

"I couldn't. That is clear. I suppose they would allow me to join your mother in Charleston, but I can't be sure of that. It seems these days we can't be sure of anything."

"Was staying here a mistake?"

"Very likely, but it was something I had to do. When you get my age you may understand. Growing old is a predictable decline, and not a pleasant one." She gazed out at the cotton. "I dread it. This grand adventure of ours, such as it is, will keep me from that rut. At least for a time."

"Cousin Gabe's idea may be a mistake, but like you say, it is something I must do."

She turned her head and smiled at him. "Your father would be proud. Like the time you shot the turkey."

They returned through the break toward the Lodge.

"We need to plant," said Missma.

"What will we grow?"

"Corn and potatoes mostly, but it's too early to plant them now. We can make it through the winter on what we have but come spring we will be busy—both of us."

"Thanksgiving is coming," he said. "Will we have Thanksgiving?"

"Can you shoot us a goose or duck?"

"I think I can."

"Then we will have a Thanksgiving feast. We must work to keep our spirits up. And while we are on the subject of spirits, come back inside so we can discuss your schooling."

When he had added some logs to the fire, he sat across from her.

"Don't look so pained," she ordered gently. "I know there are a hundred things you like better than your studies, but none of those is more important."

He lowered his eyes, resigned.

"Do you know," she asked, "that your mother was teaching Reggie to read?"

He shook his head and returned eye contact.

"Your mother insisted that Reggie tell no one. I suppose if he had it would have been you. Teaching slaves to read is illegal, so your mother was quite insistent that it remain their secret. But she also thought the law absurd. Reggie was a quick learner, she told me. He was just about to start a new reader when the Yankees arrived."

"What will happen to him now?"

"That might depend on us. I could teach him myself if he still wants to learn.

You need to find him and ask. If he wants to continue, bring him here so we can make some plans. I have an idea that could make everyone happy."

Carter nodded. "What will they do when they find out we live here?"

"The Yankees? I doubt they will care if we stay out of their way and keep our noses in the business of trying to stay alive. They have all the troubles they need with cotton ready for harvest, thousands of slaves who do not know where to go or what to do, and our boys waiting for them at Pocotaligo and Coosawhatchie. One old lady and a boy will be very far down on their list of worries."

"I can find Reggie in Beaufort. He's been here before, so he knows the way. What should I tell them if they stop me?"

"The truth—that you and your old broken-down grandma are living in a shack on Cane Island and you don't know a thing."

"If they ask me about Preston?"

Missma's eyes narrowed. "That's a bit more difficult, because Daddy August and the others may have told them your brother is off fighting. You don't want to get caught in a lie. Just say he went to Virginia, you haven't heard from him in weeks, and leave it at that." She paused. "Tell them you don't know if he's alive or dead. That's the sad truth."

Carter's face contorted, his lower lip trembling. She reached across the table and took his hand.

"He's fine, child. I know he is. I feel it. Don't worry about things you can't do anything about. Your mother is fine as well. Between you and me and Gabriel we will find a way to communicate with them, and soon."

He steadied, then managed a small nod, as if to have reached some resolution. "I will find Reggie tomorrow."

"Good. And while you are there, dig up a few of those strawberry plants from along the back fence. We can set those out here."

But the next day dawned cold and harsh, with a strong prevailing wind from the north that made travel to Beaufort impossible. Carter resigned himself to a day inside, pacing. Missma pulled her rocker close to the fire and stayed immersed in *A Tale of Two Cities*. "You need a book," she told him, "and I know the perfect one if you brought it from home. *Robinson Crusoe*. I can't believe I didn't think of it before now." She stood, disappeared behind her partition, and emerged with a thick volume. "Excellent," she said. "Your life is not exactly like Robinson Crusoe's, but it's closer than you ever imagined it would be."

He took the proffered book and said he would begin it tomorrow.

"You will begin it this very moment."

The howl of the wind could be heard from the chimney and gusts of cold air rattled the windows. He stoked the fire and opened the book. "He's from England. I thought you hated the English."

She removed her oval pince nez, marked her place and closed her book. "Sadly,

62

my dislike of the British must be tempered by several facts."

"What does 'tempered' mean?"

"Moderate, lessen, or ameliorate."

"Amel . . .?"

"Ameliorate. It means to make better, in this case less harsh."

He looked doubtful.

"We are, of course, descended from the British, and try as we may nothing can change that. Your grandfather was born in London, though he was brought here as an infant. It's difficult to hate an entire ancestry, especially your own. But their writers are wonderful; Mr. Dickens and Mr. Shakespeare in particular."

"What about Mr. . . . Defoe?"

"Very good also."

"Why are the British so bad?"

"That's a long discussion, one we will have on a day when it does not distract you from your reading." She smiled at him.

The following day the weather improved. The wind shifted, permitting tacking that brought him into town. As he tied up to the dock, he gazed toward Bay Street and felt at once an estrangement from the place where he had spent his life. The street was deserted, the shops closed. At the intersection of Bay and Carteret streets, a wagon with a uniformed driver faced away from him. He began walking toward his former home, his heart pounding and his hands trembling. As he passed the Sea Island Hotel, he heard a shout.

"Hey, boy." A soldier stared down at him from the second-floor balcony.

He stopped. "Yes, sir?"

"Where are you going?" The man was small and bearded, and wore no cap.

"To find my friend, sir."

"I thought all you people left. Where do you live?"

Carter pointed vaguely downriver. "On one of the islands."

The soldier called inside, and moments later another soldier appeared. This man was taller and plump. The shorter soldier pointed at Carter and they held conversation he could not hear. The taller man laughed audibly. Together, they went inside. Carter, aware that he had been holding his breath, resumed walking. He encountered no one else before arriving at his house, which he did not enter. It may be occupied, it certainly had been looted and damaged, and he had no real business inside. He circled around to the back, where Portia and Reggie lived in a small, neatly maintained outbuilding. He knocked. Reggie opened the door. They exchanged grins and Carter entered. He had been there many times, and it was almost as familiar to him as his own home.

"Is yo' momma here?" Carter asked in Gullah.

"No. She be stayin' out. Be back before dark. You on Cane?"

"Yep. Missma and me at the Lodge. Are the Yankees in our house?"

"Bout ten of 'em moved in a few days ago."

"What do you do with them here?"

Reggie described his routine, which consisted mostly of tending the flowers, shrubs and trees around the house. Some soldiers approached him several days before, telling him that a full occupation of Beaufort was a couple of weeks away and that they may require his help in locating fruits and vegetables for the officers and their staffs. He told Carter the soldiers were nice.

"How yo' momma be?" Reggie asked.

"I don't know," Carter said. "We haven't heard from her since she got to Charleston. Missma wants to know if you want to keep reading. She says she can teach you until Mother comes back. If you come to Cane we can hunt and fish again."

Reggie nodded.

"Missma asked me to bring back some strawberry plants. Can you help me dig up a few?"

The boys walked to the back fence, where Reggie indicated the ones that should be transplanted. Carter asked for a shovel and approached the first one, driving the blade downward at an angle. Reggie, grinning, stopped his arm before he could dig again, explaining that the blade should be horizontal to the bush, with more circumference than Carter had allowed. When the plant had been freed from the soil holding it, Reggie wrapped the roots in burlap. They took turns digging and wrapping until four plants were prepared for transport. With a plant in each hand, the boys walked to the skiff, encountering no one on the street.

"Want to come with me now?" Carter asked.

Reggie didn't answer, but jumped aboard.

Back at the Lodge, Missma greeted Reggie and suggested the boys get some oysters. The tide was low, the day milder than when it began, and within the hour they had gathered a bushel. Seated on the porch, Missma insisted on doing the shucking, "Since you boys brought them and we must all do our part." She was precise in her movements, inserting her shucking knife at the hinge points and applying what appeared to be effortless pressure. As the oysters were set before them, Carter and Reggie slurped them down, tossing the shells into the yard.

When they had finished, and the porch was cleaned, Carter suggested they go deer hunting. Missma said that first there was business to be discussed. She told Reggie that she was willing to tutor him and recommended he come once a week. "Carter can come get you and take you back. You boys can hunt and fish once your lesson is over. Would you like to do that?'"

Reggie glanced at Carter and said he would.

"Reggie, do you know where the library is?"

"Yes'um."

"Good. Can you go there to see if it is open? We have a few books here, but we will need some others for your reading lessons. This one in particular." She wrote out the words '*Carolina Sports* by Elliot.' "Copy this in your own hand and take it with you to the library. This is the book you are looking for, but it would be best if the Yankees don't know we are involved. That could cause trouble for you. Do you understand?"

"Yessum."

On the skiff during the return trip, the boys made a plan. In one week, Carter would sail to a point below the town and out of sight. They had fished from this particular bank many times. Reggie agreed to meet him there an hour after sunrise. Carter guided the skiff to this bank, where Reggie jumped out and disappeared through the foliage lining the shore.

Carter sailed back to the Lodge. As he secured the boat at the landing, he heard a cow bellow. Cousin Gabe had come through. The animal was tethered to the porch. It had soft eyes and large udders. Missma and Gabriel were inside. As he entered, he heard Gabe saying, "not so dangerous." They were seated at the table, and the corners of Missma's mouth turned down in a pronounced scowl. They both looked up as he closed the door behind him.

"Welcome, cousin," Gabe said. "How is that ear?"

Carter fingered it. "Almost healed," he said.

"Let me look," Gabe said, rising. After a brief inspection, he tugged it gently. "Nice scar. The ladies will fall all over you, thanks to me. Have a seat. Granny and I were just discussing your role in our war for independence."

Carter asked, "Milking the cow?"

Gabe and Missma laughed.

Missma turned serious. "Tell him exactly what is involved."

"Fair enough," Gabe said. "I told you how valuable the railroad is and we know the Yankees are going to try to capture it. Our ranking officers, the big boys, seem surprised they haven't tried before now. This new commander, General Lee, is real busy making life more difficult for them if and when they decide to attack. Hell, they even ordered me to dig out part of a new defensive perimeter. That dog won't hunt, because I didn't join the Dragoons to move earth. Anyway, we'll be ready when they come. What we need is a warning, and that's where you come in. They will use gunships to get their troops up the rivers to within firing distance of the defenses. Those gunships will be coming up the river you just got off, and they will pass right by this Lodge. You could not be in a better spot to watch them unless you were living on the second floor of the Verdier House, and that happens to be occupied by the folks planning the attack. So, what we need you to do is keep your eyes open for gunboats and get word to me as soon as possible."

"How can I do that?"

65

"Tricky, but I think I know a way. Take Broad River to the Whale Branch so you avoid the town. A mile before the ferry, on the south side, there's a small island. Huge live oak and nothing else. You can't miss it. We know where the Yankee pickets are and they can't see what goes on in that tree or below it. The lowest limb is covered partly by water at high tide, but the next lowest is an easy climb. We have a spotter across the creek who can monitor that tree with a telescope. We cleaned that second limb of everything except a large piece of Spanish moss hanging in the middle of the limb. We need you to find that tree in the next day or two. When you find it, remove the moss. That way we will know you've been there. When you learn something we should know, hang a big piece of moss from that limb, then leave a note in the small hollow of the tree where that limb meets the trunk. When we have something for you, it will be in that same hollow. Go at night when you can, and carry a castnet in the boat so you'll always have a logical excuse to be there."

Missma said, "If you call sailing five miles to crab at night logical."

"I will do it under one condition."

"I reckon I know what that is," Gabe said. "You want word from your mama and Preston."

Carter nodded.

"Deal. Think of it as the new Confederate post. No stamps required. Oh, and you will need this." He reached into his rucksack and pulled out field glasses. "Brand new, and strong."

"This is dangerous," Missma said, looking at Carter.

"True enough," Gabe replied evenly, at that moment looking older and more mature. He reached for his hat. "My captain says this visit must be the last. Too many Federals in the area. When I got the cow, I said my goodbyes to the Negroes at the plantation."

"Thank you for that cow," Missma said.

"She's a good one." He stood, grinning. "Time to move. The next time you see me I'll be a general in charge of our entire Army."

Missma said, "That possibility makes me wonder if it is too late to change sides."

CHAPTER 14

Lt. Newton Spruill surveyed a table piled high with books. He thought back to the letter he had written his sister telling her the newly freed slaves posed no threat to the library. In fact, before the locks could be changed the contraband vented frustrations there, too, knocking books off shelves and scattering them across floors. Some of the heavier volumes, tossed through windows, had been ruined by morning dew before their ejection from the building had been discovered. Those left inside showed bruises on their covers but were otherwise in need only of reorganization. That was now Spruill's job, thanks to his assignment as interim librarian. Armed conflict at sea did not suit him, he had decided. Memories of the Battle of Port Royal Sound still loosened his bowels. When his captain suggested that, with Spruill's printing background, he would be a perfect fit for the work needed at the library, Spruill fought the urge to hug the man.

The soldier assigned to assist Spruill was Hiram Kemp, a twenty-two-year-old scallop harvester from Maine who had spent his life on the water and who, despite a mere three years of classroom instruction, read voraciously and loved books. "Pearls," he called them. He and Spruill spent long hours at the library on days when their training duties allowed. Spruill's dislike of such consistent and close contact with an enlisted soldier gave way to grudging admiration for Kemp's devotion to literature. In Spruill's view, Kemp's comprehensive knowledge of the published word almost compensated for his lack of gold braid.

When Spruill wasn't ordering his underling to tote, dust or shelve books, he passed the time telling Kemp about Ashley Ann, or Satan's Mistress as Spruill had taken to calling her. Early in these diatribes, Spruill realized that Kemp's experience with women had been virtually zero. His long stretches on scallop boats, his devotion to his invalid mother, plus a preternaturally shy disposition contributed to Kemp's sexual naivete. Spruill lorded his worldliness over the younger man, spicing up his tales with prurient details, most of which came from Spruill's imagination. In one such verbal exposé, he described in sorted detail Ashley Ann's obsession with three Italian longshoremen with whom she slipped away to meet under cover of darkness. "I followed her a couple of times," Spruill said. "Her cries of passion coming from the boathouse spoke of unquenchable lust. That night I retrieved her undergarments from a hamper. Let's just say that I doubt a stallion in heat could have produced more seed." Kemp's eyes bulged. In truth, Spruill's hyperbolic slander had been inspired by a dinner at which Ashley Ann had suggested that their waiter, a handsome man of Mediterranean complexion who might have been Italian, be left a generous tip. At other times, Spruill worked himself into maniacal anger, his jaw tensing and his eyes dilating as though Satan's Mistress was in the library with them, taunting Spruill with, "Oh, darlin', that's just sooooooo true," a phrase Spruill mimicked with withering virtuosity.

Spruill worked alone on the afternoon two uniformed officers entered the library. He knew by sight Brigadier General Isaac Ingalls Stevens, commander of Army forces in Beaufort.

"Good afternoon, Lieutenant," Stevens said.

Spruill tensed and saluted. "Sir."

"Lieutenant, this is Colonel Reynolds. He's a Treasury agent who has been sent by Secretary Chase to turn all the rebel cotton into cash. I'm sure you two will be seeing each other from time to time."

Stevens turned to Reynolds. "Spruill here thought he was volunteering for war and finds himself a librarian." Stevens grinned good-naturedly.

"I enjoy my work here, General," Spruill replied. "Pleased to meet you, Colonel."

"Where are you from, Spruill?" Reynolds asked.

"Boston, sir."

"I'm a Rhode Island man. May we look around?"

"By all means, sir."

Stevens and Reynolds toured the stacks. Except for Spruill, the library was deserted. Gas lamps augmented dimming natural light. Ten minutes later the two officers returned to the desk where Spruill stood.

"Impressive," Reynolds said, glancing toward Spruill.

"You should have seen it a month ago," Stevens said. "When the rebels left, the Negroes went wild for a few days. You can hardly blame them. But since so few of them can read, we thought the library would be the last place they would take revenge, but we were wrong. They did not take much out but they certainly made a wreck of what was here. Spruill has spent a lot of time reorganizing it."

Spruill beamed. "Thank you, sir. I do my best."

Reynolds turned to Stevens. "Pardon the question, General, but does anyone use this library?"

"We're a month from a formal opening and regular hours. Spruill and his assistant have been doing inventory and cross-indexing so we can find things. I want it for my troops and the sailors. I wish I had more time to read, but between official dispatches and meetings my days and evenings are full. The men have time on their hands, so I welcome this."

"Perhaps I should recruit the men to harvest cotton," Reynolds said.

Stevens laughed. "How does that sound, Lieutenant?"

Spruill said, "I prefer it here, sir."

"I feel certain the Colonel was joking, Spruill," Stevens said. Then, turning serious, he said, "Morale is a problem. The troops want to fight. That's why they came. They want to take it to the rebels so they can get back home. I want the same thing. Being idle is very frustrating."

Reynolds said, "Maybe this question is better put to General Sherman, but why no attacks? The Confederate railroad must be a good prize."

"I can answer that as well as he. The logistics of dealing with the contrabands have overwhelmed us. We are spending all our time and much of our energy feeding and housing them. The troops see this and it gives them little patience with the Negroes."

"I see," said Reynolds.

"But thank God that is about to end," Stevens said. He pointed north. "Several miles up that river the rebels are building batteries at Port Royal Ferry and Seabrook's Ferry. Big guns. Those ferries provide access to the mainland, so it's a logical place for them to defend. They know that to get to the railroad we must get to the mainland. We're taking some gunboats and troops up there to let them have it."

"A Christmas present for President Lincoln?"

Stevens shook his head. "I wish, but too much planning ahead to make Christmas. We will marshal the troops New Year's Eve and launch on New Year's Day. It will start 1862 with a bang. And a victory. That should improve everyone's morale."

Stevens and Reynolds shook hands. "Thanks for the tour," Reynolds said.

"My pleasure. Glass of port before you go? I have some back at the office."

"Sounds perfect," said Reynolds. "Good day, Spruill."

• • •

Two days after Christmas, Spruill and Kemp worked in the library. Kemp, who wrote a neat and fluid script, sat at the main table indexing. Spruill labored back in the stacks. Kemp looked up to find wide-eyed Reggie staring at him.

"Can I help you?" Kemp asked.

Reggie lowered his eyes. "Come fuh borrow de book."

"Ahh, what book do you want?" Kemp asked.

Reggie handed him a small slip of paper on which was printed, "Carolina Sports by Elliot." Missma had insisted Reggie print this himself. Kemp looked at the note, then back to Reggie, hesitating before saying, "Wait here." He left to find Spruill.

Reggie gazed around the building he had seen all his life but never entered. His eyes redirected toward the floor as Kemp and Spruill returned. Spruill held the note, and his approach and tone signaled exasperation.

"The library is not open," he snapped. "Who sent you here?"

Reggie, eyes down, shook his head but said nothing.

"Did you write this note?" Spruill demanded.

Reggie nodded.

"You can read?"

Another nod.

Kemp said, "Go easy on the boy, Lieutenant. He looks harmless enough. You can't fault him for wanting a pearl."

"I fault his people for what they did to this library. Senseless destruction."

Kemp, by now practiced at humoring Spruill, said "I doubt this here pickaninny had anything to do with that." He looked at Reggie. "Am I right, boy?"

Reggie nodded.

"Well, I'll wager he knows who did it."

"No, suh, I ain' know 'um."

Spruill appeared to soften. "I have seen this book. It's here somewhere. I suppose there is no harm in letting him have it for a time."

Kemp smiled at Reggie as Spruill disappeared into the stacks. "Take a chair," Kemp said.

Ten minutes passed. From the stacks came, "Aha!" Spruill returned holding a small volume. "I knew I had seen it," he said with obvious satisfaction. He walked to where Reggie was seated. "Are you sure you can read?" he asked.

"Yessuh."

"Prove it," said Spruill. He opened the book randomly and handed it to Reggie upside down.

Reggie oriented the book as Spruill looked over his shoulder. The book was open to page 161. Reggie read in a nervous, halting voice, "to have been . . . struck . . . by four out of the six shots . . . fired . . . at him—and the . . ."

"Doctor's," Spruill snapped. "That word is 'doctor's.'"

"Doctor's," repeated Reggie. "Doctor's shot, of . . ."

"Enough," Spruill said, turning to Kemp as if Reggie was no longer there. "Get his name and address and give him two weeks."

"Fair enough," Kemp said as Spruill returned to the stacks.

"You did real good," Kemp said. "What is your name?"

"Reggie."

"Just Reggie?"

"Yessuh." He described where he lived but Kemp could not comprehend it. Kemp lowered his voice and said, "Never mind about the address. Just bring it back soon. You can stay here to read."

Reggie remained seated. He opened the book and began reading, mouthing the words silently and sounding them phonetically as Anna had taught him to do.

Spruill returned. He and Kemp chit-chatted about camp life, the food ("getting worse by the day if you ask me," Spruill said) and news from home. They seemed to have forgotten Reggie's presence. Then, apropos of nothing they had been discussing, Spruill asked, "Has your leave for New Year's Day been canceled? Mine was."

"No," said Kemp. "Why would it be?"

"Big operation," Spruill said with obvious self-importance. "Gen. Stevens and Col. Reynolds briefed me on it last week. I told them it was about time we hit those ferries up the Coosaw. They agreed. I expect they'll put me in command of a gunboat or two. Unless I miss my guess, 1862 is going to start on a very sour note for Johnny Reb. If your leave is canceled, you may be on one of the gunboats they send up river."

Reggie had stopped reading, but he had not stopped listening.

CHAPTER 15

With Abigail's help, Anna sought out other Beaufortonians banished to Charleston. Each one they found seemed to have information on at least one or two others. What would become known as the Barnwell List grew daily. Anna pledged to reproduce and distribute the list as soon as it was complete. Mrs. Adeline Porcher heard of the list from her brother and paid a visit to New Street to make certain her name and address were added. She had just departed when there was a knock at the door.

"My, my, Gabriel, you look handsome in that uniform," Abigail said, holding him at arm's length for a full view.

"Aunt Abigail, a modest man would deny it, but we both know I am not that man."

After hugging him, Anna asked if he had come from Beaufort.

"I saw them both at the Lodge."

"Come sit and tell us everything," Abigail insisted, grabbing his hand and ushering him to the sitting room, where Uncle Daniel smoked his pipe. They exchanged greetings.

"How about a dust cutter, Gabriel?"

"Uncle Daniel, I am a member of the Charleston Light Dragoons. We are forbidden by our charter to refuse alcoholic refreshment. A morale issue, I am told."

Over glasses of plum wine, Gabriel related his visits to Cane Island.

"But how did you know they were there?" Anna asked.

"The Dragoons are stationed at Huguenin's Plantation. Granny sent Carter back to the house for some things before the Yankees took over the town. I happened to come along on a scouting mission and ran into him."

"I know he was glad to see you," Abigail said.

Gabriel hesitated, looking toward the ceiling. "Well, yes and no."

"And no?" Anna asked.

"There was a small incident," he said. "Nothing really. The scar is healing nicely."

"Scar?" Anna said. "What scar? Where?"

"Earlobe. I shot him. It was an accident. He startled me. That boy should know better."

Anna brought her hand to her mouth. She shook her head, unable to speak.

"Relax, cousin," Gabriel said to her. "He will be fine. Something to tell his grandchildren. Anyway, here is what I came to tell you. I can get mail to him and Granny from time to time. We worked out a system, so if you want to write him send letters in care of Quartermaster Holmes, C.L. Dragoons. I will make sure they get through."

Anna clasped her hands together. "That's the first good news I have heard in days!"

"I thought that might cheer you up," Gabriel said. He related living conditions at the Lodge but omitted Daddy August's ransacking of the house.

"And what about your parents' place?" Abigail asked.

Gabriel shrugged. "They asked me to burn the cotton so the Yankees can't sell it, but I couldn't bring myself to do it. Some of the field hands stayed, and others have gone to Hilton Head because they think the soldiers will feed them."

He stood, downed the remainder of his wine, and put on his hat. With his congenial grin he said, "I am called away, either by duty or a young lady on Tradd Street, and I leave it to you to decide which."

A few days after Gabriel's visit, a letter arrived for Anna. She recognized Preston's pinched script on the envelope. His letter was dated October 27, 1861:

> Dear Mama:
> I know you are worried but do not. I am doing my part up here. The weather is cooler now. We have not seen action since Lewinsville. That was nothing compared to Manassas. We are camped near Washington. I volunteered to visit Abe Lincoln but they would not let me go. A boy named Lewis is my age and from Sumter. He has twelve brothers and sisters. We share a tent. We talk about hunting together after this war is over. I want you to tell Carter we are holding a place for him in our regiment. Your loving son, Preston

Anna reread the letter until she had virtually memorized it, after which she folded it for safekeeping in the small jewelry chest she brought from Beaufort.

She felt driven to help, and compilation of the Barnwell List consumed neither her full day nor her energies. On the evening of November 22, she attended a lecture delivered to the Ladies Clothing Association. The speaker was the Reverend Robert W. Barnwell, a Beaufortonian by birth and another of Anna's many cousins. But few of those cousins were as impressive as this one. Barnwell was thirty years old and until the outbreak of the war a full professor at South Carolina College, having been elected chairman of sacred literature and moral philosophy at the age of twenty-six, and having declined the presidency of the College of William & Mary at age twenty-seven because he did not wish to leave his native state. His religious commitment prevented him from joining the Army, but many of his former students had gone to Virginia to fight and Barnwell wanted to contribute to the Southern cause. He did so by establishing field hospitals in Virginia where wounded Confederates were being treated. On this night, he pleaded for a dozen women to go to Virginia for a month to six weeks to attend to the soldiers and to relieve the exhausted Virginia women who had borne the burden thus far. After his talk, Anna sought him out, embracing him and beaming with pride at the compliments showered by the ladies encircling him. When the crowd had dispersed, she told him all she knew about what had transpired since she left Beaufort. In turn, he informed her that his mother stayed in Columbia and his father was still in Germantown, Pennsylvania, where he was being treated by a noted specialist for an illness Barnwell did not name.

"I am thinking of volunteering," she told him. "It would put me closer to Preston."

"If you could give us a few weeks, it would be wonderful. Several ladies signed up tonight." Barnwell was intense, with dark, piercing eyes but a ready smile.

Anna hesitated. "I suppose I should resolve this mess with Carter and Missma first. I have to find a way to get them here, to Charleston."

"I long for Beaufort," Barnwell said. "Virginia is becoming humanity at its worst."

In the days that followed, Anna tried to focus on making herself useful, both to her hosts and their city. The trauma of sudden exodus had begun to subside. Anxiety over her loved ones never disappeared, but it had been mitigated by Gabriel's visit, Preston's letter, and her brief reunion with Robert Barnwell. Abigail took her shopping, supplementing the few things she brought from Beaufort with new clothes favoring her understated style. Some shops they visited displayed Christmas merchandise, so the holiday spirit Thanksgiving lacked for her was building gradually. The Barnwell List now held just over two-hundred names and addresses. Last week, Abigail read an article in the *Courier* soliciting nurses for the Charleston Wayside and Soldiers Depot, a train station being converted into a haven for sick and injured troops. Anna volunteered, needing more to do to help the cause and to take her mind off the perils confronting her family.

She kept an appointment with the surgeon recommended by Dr. Gaffney, and the results of his examination were also on her mind. When he palpated her stomach, her abdomen, her back and her lower spine, she winced often and cried out once. He told her to return in a month, that she probably suffered from an ovarian cyst, and that surgery might be required.

On New Street, her bedroom felt more like home. After Abigail and Daniel went to bed, on most nights she read until the combination of fatigue and worry brought heavy eyelids.

On the afternoon of December 11, Leo drove Anna downtown for a social engagement growing out of her attendance at the Ladies Clothing Association lecture. At a tea hosted by Mrs. Edna McCall, the talk was not so much about clothing as about news that General Lee and his staff would be arriving at the nearby Mills House that evening for several days of meetings regarding area defenses. When Anna accepted Mrs. McCall's kind invitation to stay for supper, she sent word to Leo that her return to New Street would be delayed. They were joined for the meal by three of the LCA's managers, and it did not take Anna long to perceive tension running the length and breadth of Mrs. McCall's well-set Thomas Elfe dining table. As was her habit at such affairs, Anna listened as closely to what went unsaid as to the articulated, tactful and restrained criticism of the absent Miss Hester Drayton who, it became plain, was liked by not a single woman at the table. Mrs. Eldridge Lesesne, her hand pressed to her clavicle as if to cushion herself from the shock of what she was about to say, went so far as to suggest that Miss Drayton could be "somewhat independent," which Anna took to mean pushy and arrogant. In point of fact, Anna was being wooed as a potential manager, the ranks of which had been depleted in direct response to certain actions by the somewhat independent, thoroughly disliked Miss Drayton.

Dinner ended at eight. Anna sent for her carriage, and she was standing in the doorway, thanking Mrs. McCall and bidding her good night, when Mrs. McCall stopped in mid-sentence to say, "Oh, dear."

"What is it?" Anna asked.

Mrs. McCall pointed. "The steeple, there, at St. Michael's. That red lantern means there is a fire."

The two women descended the steps to the pavement. Alarm bells began to ring as cries of "Fire!" echoed from neighboring streets and alleys. As Leo halted the carriage nearby, he stood pointing northeast, where an ominous glow illuminated the night sky.

Mrs. McCall said, "For a moment I was afraid it might block your way home, but I see now that it will not. But you had better get started."

Anna climbed into the carriage, facing back to track the progress of the fire. The sky was brighter now, with sparks breaking free of the red areola on the horizon. And the wind, dead calm when she first arrived at Mrs. McCall's for tea, now blew with some force directly into her face. Not a good sign, she thought.

As the carriage progressed south on Meeting Street, the street filled with shouting people, causing the carriage to first yield, then stop. Fire engines hastened in the direction of the blaze, now with large tongues of flame set against a backdrop of radiant heat, and even though Anna could not feel that heat, she sensed its threat. Leo got down from his seat to hold the horse's bridle, patting its withers and speaking soft reassurances. They proceeded slowly, Leo leading the horse, and had almost reached Broad Street, where they would turn west, when Anna saw a building at the far end of Meeting Street burst into flames. "My Lord," she exclaimed aloud, "it is coming for Mrs. McCall!"

75

Back on New Street, Uncle Daniel and Aunt Abigail were preparing for bed when they heard the alarm bells. Daniel stepped to the window, opened it, and sniffed air that puffed the curtain inward.

"Daniel, what is it?"

"Smoke. I smell smoke."

Together they walked out onto the piazza. Abigail pulled her shawl close against the chill.

Daniel said, "I want us to walk to the corner. Perhaps we can see something from there."

"At this hour?" Abigail asked.

"Yes."

They re-entered the house long enough to change clothes. Minutes later they walked up New Street, Uncle Daniel tap-tap-tapping his cane as Abigail guided him. At Broad Street they paused. "Scan the horizon," he said.

The wind was steady and when they turned into it Abigail saw the glow. "There," she said. "Coming from the wharfs on the Cooper River." She turned to Daniel. "Far away. Several miles."

"I do not like it," he said. "This wind . . ."

"A cotton warehouse, most likely," Abigail said. "Those are common."

"Yes," he acknowledged, "but I never smell them from here. What do you see now?"

"The glow . . . is larger." Cinching her beaver overcoat, she said, "I hope Anna is safe. So chilly. Shall we go home?"

"No," said Daniel. "You have a better view here."

They stood in silence, facing the distant glow that seemed to gain arc by the minute. Abigail leaned into him for warmth, her face pressed against his coat and her teeth chattering in the chilly night air. The wind picked up. Uncle Daniel stood ramrod straight, sniffing. "That is quite a fire."

Others now appeared on front steps and piazzas. Like Abigail, they could now smell the smoke. The night sky of Charleston was transformed from a faraway burnish to a living thing, with flames erupting higher with each passing minute. And closer. They heard more alarm bells, their clanging carried on the wind. Then, an explosion. The Gas Works?

"Oh, dear," Abigail said. "I believe it must be spreading downtown." She turned to Daniel. "Surely we are in no danger here."

"It all depends on the wind," he said. "And the wind is getting stronger."

Around them, people were beginning to shout and point. Lights came on in houses that had been dark. Some arriving on the street were in nightshirts and housecoats. A few were barefooted. A general panic set in, but the fear was for the beautiful city that was clearly now at risk. No one yet imagined the fire could threaten them or their homes at this distance.

Except Daniel. "Abigail, we must go to the house. Hopefully, Anna and Leo will return soon. Pack some clothes and our silver in a suitcase. Pack one for Anna and Leo, too." So strong was the wind that he raised his voice to be heard.

Abigail recoiled. "You do not suppose Anna and Leo are in the middle of that?"

"Leo knows the dangers. He will be making every effort to get them safely home. I pray they come soon."

Not long afterword, each packed a suitcase, clothes in Abigail's and valuables in Daniel's. When she had packed bags for Anna and Leo, she asked, "What now?"

"We go back to the corner and wait."

As they returned to Broad Street, she said, "Daniel, Ellen Robertson's house is dark and she is nearly deaf. I should make certain she is up if you think there is any danger to this street."

"Of course it is not certain," he said. "But this wind . . ." He turned his face into it. "It is a gale. You had better make sure she's awake."

Two hours passed. Others, including Ellen Robertson, who was asleep and unaware of the fire, gathered at the corners, their attention focused east down Broad Street. The smell of smoke turned to smoke itself, warmer than the night air and burning the eyes of those looking windward. The flames were higher because they were closer. They heard a series of explosions, but Daniel could not pinpoint the location.

Daniel waited in silence for Abigail to sight Anna and Leo, who were indeed in the middle of it. People moved furniture and clothes into the street, either in hopes of preserving it if the fire took the home or in preparation for moving it to a safe place. But no one could predict what would be safe from this fire, which had unworldly reach and power. Already it had leapt entire blocks to ignite homes Anna and Leo passed minutes before. Leo abandoned the thought that his horse would respond to the whip. The animal was thoroughly spooked, and it was all Leo could manage, with a steel grip on the bridle, to keep horse and carriage moving forward. In the carriage, Anna's eyes burned with smoke, then cleared when the incessant wind shifted. She saw a mattress in the middle of the street with a mother and three children huddled together. Moments later sparks landed on the sheet, sending the woman and children shrieking down the street. Anna heard the same series of explosions that Uncle Daniel heard, but they seemed to her fatally close. She ducked her head with each one. Twenty yards in front of the carriage, a fire company attempted to hose down a home sufficiently to act as a firebreak. Six black men manned the hand-pump engine. As the carriage approached, Anna watched them rise and fall in a rhythm and heard them singing:

Go Down Deep, Go Down Strong,
Bend de back and sing de song.

An acrid phosphorus smell, close to gunpowder, assaulted her nostrils, and she wondered if the entire city was about to explode. Behind her, far down Broad Street but not far enough, she saw fire leaping the street, and within seconds houses on both sides blazed. For the first time, she considered the possibility she may not be able to outrun this fire and that she and others would die on this street. She could not take her eyes from the inferno behind her. A mere six hours ago, she rode down this same street, admiring the fine homes, and despite the war most decorated brightly for Christmas.

When the wind slacked momentarily, Leo was able to break the carriage free of the pandemonium around them. He mounted the driver's seat, cracked the whip over his horse's head, and steered for the least congested path ahead. He did not slow until they arrived at the corner of Broad and New Streets, where he saw Abigail waving furiously.

Daniel called up to him, "Go to the house. Get the bags we packed. They are just inside the front door. Do not linger. Come back here at once." In front of the house, Anna leaped down, tripping over the hem of her dress but managing to avoid a fall. She rushed to the door. Moments later she and Leo were back in the carriage with the bags, headed for the corner. From the carriage, the four saw and heard the fire approaching.

Abigail let out a painful moan. "Dear, God. The Cathedral. I thought it was fireproof."

"What?" Daniel demanded.

"Flames are all around the spire. The cross on top—glowing."

"The heat," said Daniel. The Cathedral's cross reached 285 feet into the air and was visible from anywhere in the city. When it crashed to earth in a crescendo of sparks, flame and ash, it was as if a fiery coffin has been slammed shut, snuffing out Broad Street's antebellum luster.

Mansions on the north side of Broad were the last barrier. If the fire leapt Broad Street, New Street would be defenseless. Daniel insisted on a running account of what was happening, with Abigail's tone telling him more than her words. "It cannot cross Broad," she said, but there was no conviction now and as often as she repeated it she knew it could. When the homes on the north side virtually exploded in flames, Leo climbed down to repeat his pattern of holding the horse at its bridle and whispering reassuring words to the animal, which wanted to rear. The wind was again howling. Cinders from the north side infernos blew horizontally across Broad Street. With the collapse of each roof, profusions of sparks flew south, straight into the waiting homes on the south side. As the first home on the south side incinerated in what seemed like seconds, Abigail buried her head in Daniel's coat and sobbed.

"We need to go," Daniel insisted.

"Do we have room for Mrs. Robertson? She will be lost."

"We make room," Leo said. "Run get her, Miz Anna."

In a field safely removed from their neighborhood, they watched what they could not bear to see. Anna knew the worst had come. She tried to think of anything of value she would lose tonight, and wondered if by chance, when Abigail packed her things, she remembered the Barnwell List or Preston's recent letter.

By dawn, the flames had died, the neighborhood a smoking ruin. The newly homeless staggered back to confirm what they instinctively knew. The house on New Street was a total loss. The chimney alone remained standing. The next day, when the embers had cooled, Abigail walked the spaces where she had spent so much of her life. She found only the brass knocker from the front door which, though disfigured by heat, was still serviceable. She wrapped it in a cloth.

Charlestonians spared the fire's devastation opened their homes to those whose loss was complete. Daniel, Abigail, Anna and Leo spent nights after the fire at the home of friends on Church Street. The transition was hardest on Uncle Daniel, who navigated the New Street house as though sighted, and who now collided with his surroundings.

On Sunday morning, Anna sorted through her radically reduced wardrobe for something suitable for church. Abigail pleaded exhaustion, so Anna alone attended services at St. Philip's, a venerable Episcopal parish church destroyed by fire in 1835, but this time only singed. She had never felt greater need for spiritual infusion. From a pew in the middle of the church, she listened to the Reverend William Bell Howe deliver his sermon entitled "Cast Down, but not Forsaken." The lesson was drawn from—it can only be from, Anna thought—the story of Job.

Howe had acquired that certain look of divinity when he ascended the pulpit. In starched white robes, he impressed the weary congregation as God's messenger on earth; in this case, scorched earth. He recounted the familiar tragedies inflicted upon Job before asking the essential question: do temporal calamities like the fire infallibly point to great crimes; crimes which have "invited the severe vengeance of an offended God?" Anna stared at him, transfixed. She pulled her elbows into her sides, as if to hold herself together, for she felt she was coming apart in front of the congregation and God Himself, who had taken Howe's place in the pulpit. Yes, she thought, yes. That was her question. What were her sins that had brought about this war, that had her older son in combat at age seventeen; that stranded her younger son in enemy territory; that rendered her dear uncle and aunt homeless in the declining years of their exemplary lives. Yes, God, she wanted to know, and she demanded an answer then and there as to why this torment had been visited upon her.

Howe thanked God for "sparing you from beholding, a second time, your 'holy and beautiful house, where your fathers praised God, burned up with fire, and all your pleasant things laid waste.'" He stated the obvious: that such a fire as the city had just experienced, and that left so many of the church's communicates homeless, would have been terrible at any time, but to have come while "we are threatened by an invasion from ruthless foes, all necessities and comforts of life difficult to procure, engaged in ministering to the sick and wounded," added insult to injury and exacerbated the tragedy. As with Job, so cumulative did the disasters appear as to have taken on the blush of vengeance. But, no, Howe assured. The parish was being tried, not punished. Job was a good man whom God tested, and the ancient and noble parishioners of St. Philip's were good people whom God was likewise testing.

Yes, that must be so, Anna thought. Their cause was just, and therefore God must be trusted to restore that which He had taken from her and hers. Their faith would be rewarded as Job's was rewarded. She left the service with a renewed sense of peace and optimism.

CHAPTER 16

Carter surveyed the shoreline, spotting Reggie at the agreed upon place from half a mile out. He felt again the alienation from his home and town. He was a stranger here, in the place he had lived all his life. Beaufort belonged to Reggie now, and to Portia, and to Daddy August and all the uniformed Federals walking Bay Street and plying the river. It felt permanent, this strangeness.

From this point on the river he could see his home, where so many of his memories prior to November 7 nourished the security he felt there, and now those same memories nagged him as reminders of loss. He thought back to the Christmas his father presented him with his first hunting rifle, a Happoldt 50 caliber with its polished walnut stock and engraved trigger guard. The parlor fire warmed the room on that unseasonably cold morning, and the heated cloves and cinnamon his mother traditionally prepared gave off an aroma that came to define Christmas morning as surely as her special ambrosia of oranges and coconut recalled the dinner served later. Preston and Anna and Missma watched as his father handed him the rifle. His father didn't say much—he never did—but the act of placing the rifle in his hands told all Carter needed to hear. Indelible was the pride-filled smile on his father's face, the heft of the weapon, the collective gaze of his family.

As his boat neared the shore where Reggie waited, memories of that Christmas gave way to the vision of his last visit, of Daddy August's rampage, the sounds of breaking glass, of smashed furniture, of his mother's vanity hitting the first floor with fatal force, shattering the little bottles she used to give herself the same scent as the garden after a summer rain. He missed her, and that too felt permanent, notwithstanding Missma's persistent assurance that it was not.

With Reggie aboard, they sailed back to Cane Island. Reggie knocked for admission to the Lodge as Carter walked to the field that would feed them next spring and summer. Mid-morning sun warmed his back as he hoed the earth for planting. The soil was rich, sandy and pliant. As he dug, the cow, staked nearby, watched him with bovine indifference. Missma named the cow Lundy after a cousin on her father's side who Missma insisted the cow resembled. Carter believed all cows look alike, but Missma, when he shared this view, said that all people look alike to cows, which, she said, are valuable but essentially stupid. "Like Daddy August," she could not resist adding.

Inside, Missma expounded on *Carolina Sports*. "I chose this," she told Reggie, "because I thought a book on hunting and fishing would interest you more than other books." She asked him to read, gauging his level of proficiency. "We have work to do," she said, "but you are further along than I realized. You read quite well, all things considered. We will begin at the beginning, with the chapter on devil fishing. Don't worry about understanding it all. You will not. We will work on the more difficult words, and when you have mastered those, you will understand. Agreed?" After two hours, she called Carter in to eat. "One more hour of lessons," she said, "and then you boys can catch some fish."

Over the simple meal she had prepared, Missma asked Reggie if he had any difficulty getting the book. He related his trip to the library. He told them two Federals were inside when he arrived. One, in what Reggie had come to recognize as a Navy uniform, was very nasty. He accused Reggie's people of ransacking the library for no reason and causing the people who rescued them no end of problems. The other man, in an Army uniform, was nice. The Navy man didn't want to lend the book, didn't think Reggie could read, and made him read from it to prove he could. The Army man argued with him, saying that lending books is what the library was there for.

Then he paused, looking down.

"What is it?" Missma asked.

Reggie told them the mean one, the Navy man, complained because his leave was canceled. When the nice one asked why, the mean one said he had to go on a raid on New Year's Day. He said they were going to hit the ferries up the Coosaw.

"You are sure the man said New Year's Day?"

Reggie nodded.

"At the ferries?"

He nodded again.

Carter and Missma exchanged glances. She stood. "Well, I just hope and pray no one is killed. On either side. I suppose that is fantasy in a war, but I will hope and pray for it nonetheless."

That evening, Missma and Carter discussed next steps.

Missma said, "New Year's is three days away. Any warning to our boys will need to come tomorrow."

"Is it a land attack, or a water attack, or both?" Carter wondered.

"We can't be sure, but they will need boats for certain." She disappeared behind her partition and emerged with pen and a sheet of paper. On it she wrote: "Information received today is that Yankees will launch attack on Coosaw ferries on New Year's Day. No details known." She folded the note and handed it to him. "This is not much, but better than nothing. You should leave early tomorrow morning."

"You are helping me to spy, Missma."

"For the moment. If that note fell into Union hands, better my handwriting than yours. You can always say you were asked to deliver it but had no idea what it said."

"I hope there is a letter from Mother."

He awoke early the next morning and knew immediately from the stillness of the air, the complete inertia of the leaves and Spanish moss, that sailing was impossible. The Beaufort River mirrored the few clouds above with unruffled fidelity, its waters lake-like calm in the dead air. He scanned the morning horizon for signs of a front moving in, but even the few clouds seemed painted in place on the canopy of blue above them. He chopped wood to take his mind off Cousin Gabe being hit by a surprise attack. Missma reminded him that they could not control the weather any more than the Federals, but they both knew steam rendered that truth only half-true.

But the weather was fortuitous. Later that morning, he watched from the porch as twenty barges designed to ferry cotton in shallow water were towed up the river to Beaufort. He did not know the significance of this, but it was unlike anything that had come up the river thus far, and the timing of Reggie's report made it potentially quite significant. Missma revised her note to include this information. That evening, a faint but felt breeze promised he could sail at first light.

It held. His sail filled as soon as he shoved off, the warning note pinned inside his pocket. He cleared the tip of Parris Island and was soon skimming along the eastern bank of the Broad River. At Barnwell Island, he veered into the Whale Branch, eyeing what he had come to think of as Signal Oak. As he neared it, he saw clearly that the moss he draped on the second limb last week was gone. The tide was at flood, so he tied to the second limb and pulled himself up, tightrope walking along it until it met the trunk. He reached into the hollow and felt a rush of excitement when his hand encountered two envelopes. On one appeared his name, on the other Missma's, both written in his mother's hand. He placed the warning note in the hollow, thrust his letters into his pocket, and reached upward for a large clump of Spanish moss. He retreated to the center of the limb, draped the moss over it, and dropped into the boat. Two minutes after landing, he was sailing.

As he rounded the point to re-enter the Broad River, he felt the tide begin to ebb. That would hasten his return and reduce the work. He relaxed, suddenly conscious of how tense he had been for the past few hours. As he glided past Lemon Island, he was congratulating himself on a successful mission when he saw in the distance a hull. Then another one. Yankee gunships, headed upriver. His pulse quickened and his heart pounded against his chest.

A small creek lay just ahead and he made an instant decision to enter it. He tacked, sailed a hundred yards, and stopped. He lowered his sail, and waited. Spartina grass obscured his view downriver, and he did not want to raise his head above it. Instead, he turned to face the entrance to the creek, where the boats should pass. Minutes crawled at an agonizing pace. Then he heard the thump, thump of steam engines, very distant at first but then closer. The ships were approaching his creek. They steamed by, fully visible, with four sailors on the deck of the first, five on the second. Guns stood unwrapped—he saw their outlines plainly. The sailors appeared not to have noticed him, and their collective attention was to their immediate front. He breathed easier as the thump, thump receded upriver. Then it stopped. In the new stillness, he heard voices from the decks but could not make out what was being said. He stood cautiously in the boat to peer over the marsh. The gunboats had stopped a quarter mile past the entrance to the creek. He heard the splash of one anchor, then the other.

He weighed his options. It was early afternoon, with dusk still hours away. He assumed these ships were positioned for the attack planned for the morning. If that was true, they would not move again until dawn. He could not exit the creek without being seen unless he waited for darkness. He considered sailing anyway. If they called to him, he could ignore them and sail on, confident that they would not shoot a boy who they would assume had been fishing. On the other hand, they had hours to kill this afternoon and could give chase to ask him questions. He did not want to answer questions about who he was, where he lived, or why he was there on this day. If, by waiting for dark, he could avoid such inquiries, he would do it. He reclined in the boat and took his mother's letter from his pocket.

December 16, 1861 Charleston

Dearest Carter:
Your cousin Gabriel has promised me you will receive this letter. I pray it is true, and that you and Missma are well. Given your isolation on Cane Island, it is doubtful you have heard about the Charleston fire. Know that Uncle Daniel, Aunt Abigail and I are all safe, although we are now homeless because every house on New Street was destroyed. A neighbor now as homeless as we said the fire was set by some slaves down at the waterfront, but no one knows for certain.

Regardless how it started, I owe my life to Leo, Uncle Daniel's driver. We were returning from supper downtown as the fire spread to Broad Street, our way home. Houses burst into flames before my very eyes. I heard ear-piercing explosions, expecting to see things all around me disappear, only to realize that they came from several blocks away, deliberately discharged to protect the hospital, the medical college, the jail and the workhouse. Our poor horse, so traumatized. Leo calmed the animal enough to get us safely away before the world collapsed behind us. Everyone assumed there would be significant loss of life, but as of today no deaths have been reported, which is a miracle given that over five hundred homes were lost. Lovely downtown buildings are in ruins. The Circular Congregational Church burned, and Institute Hall, where they signed the Ordinance of Secession, is completely destroyed. St. Andrew's Hall is gone. The Cathedral of St. John and St. Finbar, surely the most majestic building in the entire city, burned as we watched. Flames shot all the way up to the steeple's gold cross, and by the time it fell it had been heated to an unearthly glow. We heard a rumor that the Cathedral's fire insurance lapsed the week before. Some of these treasured buildings might have been saved had the fire department been at full strength, but so many of the men have left to fight the Yankees that only skeleton crews were left to respond. Such a tragedy.

When the fire had nothing left to consume and the wind finally died down, Leo drove us in the carriage to view the damage. You cannot believe what we found, or did not find, as seems more fitting. The chimney is all that remains of the home. Aunt Abigail found a door knocker in the rubble. Otherwise, all is lost. It breaks my heart as they have lived there for their entire married life of thirty years. During my month with them I learned how terribly this war is affecting Uncle Daniel's business, and now this.

As bad as this was, it could have been worse. General Lee, who is in charge of all our Lowcountry defenses, arrived in the city hours before the fire broke out. He and his senior staff were evacuated from the Mills House, which was spared despite being in the fire's path, saved by boarders who took wet blankets to the roof to smother the embers blown from other buildings.

We are staying for the moment with dear friends, but it is only temporary and we do not know where or when we will find more permanent quarters. I will write to you as soon as I know. Uncle Daniel has mentioned Columbia, where his brother lives. Uncle Luke is a widower, his sons live out west, and there is room for us there. Uncle Daniel loves his brother, but they do not see eye to eye on this war as Uncle Luke wanted South Carolina out of the Union a decade ago and both Daniel and Abigail fear we have made a horrible mistake by seceding. I have the impression it is a subject best avoided, but that will be impossible under the same roof. Nothing is decided.

Gabriel told me about your ear. I cannot believe it! Your own cousin, although nothing he does on the wild side should surprise any of us. I worried that you would receive a wound before this war was over, and now you have one. I thank God it is not serious. Days ago I received a letter from Preston. It was lost in the fire but I read it so many times I have it memorized. He is camped at a place in Virginia outside of Washington, D.C. He mentioned a friend named Lewis. They share a tent and love of hunting. Now that I am once again homeless, I do not know when or how his next letter will reach me. Of this I am sure—Gabriel will always find me so please, please, please write when you can. You may tell Missma that I miss her. I have not forgiven her, but you need not mention that. I suppose I should feel grateful that at least you and she were spared the awful experience of the fire. I have never seen anything in life to compare to it. The sheer power of those flames fanned by the wind is a vision I will carry with me always. My dear son, take care of yourself and Missma. We must all be strong, and with God's help we will survive this terrible time.

Your affectionate and loving Mother.

At last the sun set. Darkness settled onto the creek and marshes. Carter poled the skiff from the bank, pointed it toward the river, and thrust downward until the tide took over. The sail was still down. Over his shoulder, he saw gas lights on the decks of the gunboats and in the stillness the voices of the crew carried. He floated for a mile, then set his sail into the few remaining hours of the year 1861.

Despite the late hour, Missma met him at the door. He explained the long delay in returning before handing her both letters. The one addressed to her she clutched to her breast before slipping it into a pocket. She moved her chair closer to the hearth, spreading Carter's letter in her lap.

When at last she looked up, she said, "What an ordeal. And now homeless, but at least they are alive."

"Maybe that is all the bad luck for this year."

"That depends upon what the other letter holds."

He watched her expectantly. She withdrew her pince nez from her pocket and brought it to her eyes slowly, so slowly that she seemed to be predicting the news contained on the two sheets of paper she withdrew from the envelope.

"Just as I feared," she said, looking up. "The surgeon agrees with Dr. Gaffney. Your mother has a growth on one of the female organs. A tumor. It must come out. She will decide in January whether to undergo an operation to remove it."

"Is that dangerous?"

"Quite dangerous. Your mother is in the care of a Dr. James Carter. She says he may be a cousin, but related or not he is acknowledged as the best at the Medical College. He will take on cases others won't, and the operation she needs is quite rare."

"Won't she be in great pain?"

"In my day it would have been unthinkable, but today they have something called ether. They put you to sleep so you feel no pain as they do what must be done."

"Is there a chance she might not wake up?"

"As you are learning much too early, there is risk everywhere. All we can do is face it as best we can and hope that 1862 brings us all safely back together.

1862

CHAPTER 17

His leave canceled, Lt. Spruill spent New Year's day aboard the gunship
Seneca, one of the two Union vessels that had caused Carter to seek
the shelter of the marsh the day before. *Seneca* and *Ellen* sailed up the Whale
Branch, passing within shouting distance of Signal Oak as they steamed to
Seabrook's Ferry. There, they supported an infantry unit that demolished a
Confederate battery under construction. The commander of the *Seneca* shared
his disappointment that his boat had failed to inflict casualties and his surprise
at finding the battery undefended. "It's as though," he said, "they knew we
were coming."

• • •

February 15, 1862
Beaufort, S.C.

My dear Hazel:
   I am utterly distraught! You cannot believe what has happened.
The time and energy I have given to the library you know full well
from my letters. I dare say that the system I put in place would serve
as a model for libraries everywhere to emulate. The care with which
I inventoried the books, the Spruill Cross-Indexing system that I
so meticulously thought through and implemented, and in which I
took so much pride as a path to promotion—all is for naught!! And
to think this treachery, this betrayal, comes not from the perfidious
rebels but from one of our own!
   You will recall my account of General Stevens bringing to the
library a Col. Reynolds. That gentleman (although I now affirm the

88

difficulty of linking that description with his name) was introduced to me as the man designated by Secretary Chase to organize the harvesting of cotton for sale and thereby assure revenue for our noble cause. Can it be that he does not know books from cotton? Yesterday, a gang of his henchmen consisting of the universally loathed cotton agents appeared at the library, brandishing an order signed by Col. Reynolds that my entire book collection be boxed up and transported to the wharf for shipment north. Evidently, it is Col. Reynolds's intent to sell it. Can you believe anyone would do such a thing? Can our cause be so desperate for funds that we must resort to this . . . treason?

I am aghast, as I intend to let be known. I am not without friends in high places, as you know from prior correspondence, and they shall hear of this. Is my labor to be cast aside as if these past months of night and day effort were mere child's play? Shall the troops here, who Lord knows have an abundance of time on their hands, have no facility with which to edify themselves? And what of the Spruill Cross-Indexing System? If the books are sold piecemeal, it will be utterly useless. And if they are sold as a lot, there is no assurance the buyer will preserve it intact. And what of my promotion? This could delay it by weeks, possibly months, although its inevitability cannot be doubted notwithstanding this setback. I have half a mind to march down to headquarters to seek, no demand, an explanation from General Stevens, who cannot be happy at this development, and indeed may not even be aware of it.

Dear Hazel, there is other news to report, but I cannot bear the further stress and anxiety that comes from detailing this disaster. I am taking a powder and retiring for the evening, all the while remaining your affectionate brother.

Newt.

CHAPTER 18

The Sunblad farm sold almost immediately. In April, Christina and Sonja boarded the steamer *Oriental* for the trip south. As Christina introduced herself to fellow passengers, Sonja kept to herself, fearful of the ship as she had never before traveled on water, resentful of having to leave her home and friends, and convinced her mother made an impetuous decision they will both soon regret. Added to this list of laments was an overriding one that Christina did not observe until Sonja brought it to her attention: there was not a single person on board near her age. So much for meeting new friends, Sonja thought.

Her sense of isolation was eclipsed by a new sensation shortly after the *Oriental* entered open water. It began with what felt vaguely like a headache. Her throat went dry. She sought out her mother below deck.

"I don't feel well," she said.

"Oh, dear," said Christina. "I should have warned you about seasickness. You are a bit green."

"What can I do to make it go away?"

"Go up on deck and try to keep your eyes on the horizon. The fresh air should help."

"Did you have this when you and Father came over?"

"I'm afraid so. Mine lasted for a week."

"A week! You should have warned me. You kept it from me."

"Go up on deck."

Sonja stood at the bow, trying her best to focus on the horizon, but the growing miasma in her stomach made it difficult. She clung to the rail, tightening her grip as a sour taste invaded her mouth. She knew she would be sick, and soon. She walked along the rail toward the stern, out of sight of most passengers on deck. The deck dipped, and when it rose her stomach rose with it. When she opened her mouth its contents spewed forth. Her head throbbed. She grabbed the rail for support as the next wave of nausea overtook her. She wretched, bending nearly double.

From behind, she felt Christina's hand on her shoulder. "I had forgotten how awful it was," she said. "Would you like to lie down?"

Sonja shook her head.

Christina offered her a biscuit. "Perhaps something to settle your stomach."

At the sight of it, Sonja turned back toward the rail, vomiting violently.

Passengers on the *Oriental* included teachers and superintendents from Boston and New York in addition to those from Philadelphia. One woman who did not wait for Christina to approach her was Laura Towne, who exuded quiet confidence as she introduced herself as the representative of the Philadelphia Port Royal Relief Committee. That committee had gathered impressive stocks of clothes and other essentials now on board the *Oriental,* and it would be Towne's job to organize their distribution among the plantations in Beaufort. Towne's training in homeopathic medicine would be a valuable skill in view of the paucity of medical professionals available to treat the Negroes.

By the third day of the voyage, Sonja felt sure she would die. She went below for only the briefest periods. For the past two nights, mercifully mild, she had slept on a deck chair facing into the wind, a blanket pulled around her like a shroud and the fresh air on her face furnishing the only relief she could find. The fact that she had nothing left in her stomach to void did not spare her periodic trips to the rail to wretch. She had eaten nothing since boarding the ship. In sympathy, Christina slept beside her, offering encouragement but little else.

By day four she began to feel better. When Norfolk appeared distantly off the starboard bow, she sipped some broth and kept it down. They were within sight of the enemy, though all the ships in view flew the Stars and Stripes. Christina, Laura Towne and others gathered at the rail to point and chatter. The girl watched as her mother gesticulated, grew animated in conversation, laughed and nodded, and it occurred to her that this community, a shared purpose among other adults, was what her mother had craved all along. Perhaps it explained this entire venture. At least one of them was happy, thought the girl, who could not remember a more miserable week in her life, with the prospect of more over the horizon the ship was lunging toward.

One morning she felt the air turn discernibly warmer, and with it a smell foreign to her. She walked to the rail as several passengers extended their arms, pointing to Charleston in the distance, where it all began. She breathed deeply, and the smell swelled her lungs. She reasoned that its source must be some combination of warmth, humidity and exhalation from the land mass the ship now skirted. To her surprise, she found it pleasant.

Five hours later, a pilot boat met the *Oriental* in the Sound and guided it across the bar. The dock on Hilton Head loomed. Uniformed sailors secured the lines as the ship came to full stop at the pier.

In a reception building still under construction, they were greeted by some of the original so-called Gideonites, the first group of fifty-three missionaries and teachers who had arrived a month earlier. On March 3, 1862, forty-one men and twelve women left New York aboard the steamship *Atlantic.* The New Yorkers among them were evangelicals, mostly Unitarians and Methodists, while the Boston contingent was characterized less by religious fervor and more by education, graduates of Harvard, Yale and Brown from families with deep roots in New England and solid abolitionist bent.

The new arrivals heard welcoming remarks from Mansfield French, a minister and former college president in whose care the twelve female Gideonites had been placed. He assured Christina, Sonja, Laura Towne and the others that they had arrived in a land of upheaval in a moment of destiny, but all in accordance with God's will and His plan to raise the Negro from centuries of subjugation. Some of the Bostonians looked young enough to be Christina's sons, but to Sonja they were another reminder of the absence of anyone her age.

When the reception ended, a naval officer approached Sonja and Christina. He introduced himself as Lieutenant Newton Spruill. In his hands he held an envelope with their names written on it. He smiled at them both, but his stare lingered on Sonja. He handed the envelope to Christina as his gaze remained fixed.

"Your destination," he said.

Christina opened the envelope. "It says we've been assigned to a plantation called Three Pines. On Cane Island. Do you know it, Lieutenant?"

"I do indeed. One of the smaller islands not too far from the town. I would be happy to take you there."

"That's very kind. We are at the mercy of others here."

"I'll speak to those in charge. It should not be a problem and it would be my pleasure to show you a bit of the countryside. For all its shortcomings, this area has its charms. I understand you will be taken into Beaufort to spend tonight. I'll call on you in the morning."

On the boat ride into town, Christina said, "Lt. Spruill seems nice. Handsome, too."

"I suppose," Sonja said, yawning. "How long did they say this trip would take?"

"They didn't, but those must be the lights of the town ahead. Sonja, did you notice anything about the lieutenant?"

"He's not very tall and his eyes are dark."

"He also didn't take those eyes off you. When you are a little older you will be aware of such things, but it would not hurt to begin now. A reality of this adventure of ours is that we will be surrounded by men. Most will be well intended but some may not. You're reaching an age when you will need to know which is which."

"What I know is that I am very tired and want to get off this boat."

Christina extended her arm around Sonja's shoulders. "On that, dear girl, we are agreed."

CHAPTER 19

S onja awoke from her first night at Three Pines with the denial that came from complete dislocation. Nothing around her seemed remotely familiar. Exhaustion had allowed her to sleep. The last thing she remembered was a bent, ebony woman entering her room, mumbling words that, while soothing in some odd way, were completely incomprehensible to the girl. The old woman might just as well have been speaking Swedish as she spread a thinly meshed net over the bed. The bed was not soft, but neither was it rolling with the motion of waves or currents.

Sonja placed her bare feet onto an uneven plank floor. The whole room tilted slightly in the direction from which the sun was rising. She wrapped herself in a blanket, opened the door and proceeded down the hall. The door to her mother's room was open. Through a window she saw Christina sitting on the porch. She exited the back door to join her.

"There is coffee," Christina said brightly, as if that fact justified all they had been through and could anticipate. "It was made when I got up. I never heard anyone come in, or start the fire, or make a sound. In fact, it was the aroma that woke me. Have some?"

Sonja nodded. Her mother entered the house and returned with a mug, steam rising. Sonja cupped it for warmth and yawned. "What now?"

"We should walk about to get to know the place. Look at it. It is strange but magnificent, don't you think?" A thin mist rose from the ground, so that trees in the distance appeared to be growing out of clouds.

"It looks haunted," Sonja said.

"The sun will burn this off, I feel sure. There is a woman here, called Auntie Peak, who speaks English. The others speak Gullah, as we were told on the ship. But Auntie Peak speaks both, so we can ask questions and get answers."

Sonja yawned again. "What am I going to do all day in this place?"

"Help me to help them. That's why we came, and once we settle in a bit you will feel differently."

"I doubt it."

A door closed in the distance. Moments later Auntie Peak rounded the corner and mounted steps to the porch. "Mornin', missus," she said. Her dress was plain and rough broadcloth, her hair piled under a kerchief knotted at the front. Thin and hunched, she managed her osteoporosis like a weight on her back, her head tilted toward the floor. She may have been forty or sixty. "I see you found da' coffee."

"And it is so good," Christina said. "Thank you for making it."

"My job," Auntie Peak said plainly. "I git up breakfast fuh you now."

"Can we help?" asked Christina.

Auntie Peak looked up long enough to grin a toothless smile. "Dat ain' the way we do it here." She disappeared inside. Thirty minutes later, aromas emerged from the house. When the women on the porch were summoned, they sat down to fresh eggs, bacon, grits, baked biscuits with molasses and milk.

"The best breakfast I've had in years," declared Christina.

"Very good," echoed Sonja.

Christina and Sonja donned plain dresses for this, their first full day on Three Pines. Auntie Peak took them first to her cabin, from which three children ranging in age from four to eight emerged. The children were sullen, bashful and did not hold eye contact as Christina assured them it was nice to meet them. The youngest, a boy, hid behind Auntie Peak's dress. Sonja gazed down the row at other slave cabins, shocked that these housed living souls. Most appeared doomed by a strong gust of wind.

Next, Auntie Peak conducted them on a tour of the plantation's perimeter, pointing to landmarks by which they could discern neighboring properties. Men, already in the fields, waved to Auntie Peak as she passed. The white women felt the stares as they walked.

By noon the women returned to the house, where they unpacked and organized their clothing and the few personal articles that accompanied them. Both rooms contained basic necessities: simple pine dressers, a mirror atop the dresser, a cane chair, a vanity holding a porcelain washbasin, a chamber pot. In Christina's room, there was a cedar chest at the foot of her single bed. The women's rooms adjoined. Across the hall, a third bedroom was reserved for Jacob Roan, the plantation superintendent. Three Pines was too small to justify a full-time superintendent, so Roan traveled among three plantations assigned to him.

After a simple lunch of cold ham and field peas, Sonja decided to explore. She hoped this was safe. Her fear stemmed not from any overt threat she had experienced, but from the strangeness of it all. Fields under cultivation were bordered not by orchards or meadows but by marshes and water. She saw no fences. The land was flat, without the slightest undulation or grade. She had spent her life on a farm, but not like this one, where dark field workers bent to their tasks, sometimes humming. She circled a cotton field and entered a break of palmetto and scrub pine. There was the tracing of a path, and she pushed ahead with her eyes down for snakes, as they warned on the ship. When she looked up, a boy stood ten feet away.

He had been working in the garden when he heard someone or something coming through the break. He went to investigate, standing at the edge of the break as the sound of cracking twigs and repelled branches neared. When Sonja came into view, he dropped the spade he had been holding in his right hand. "Hello," he managed.

"Hello," she said.

He had never seen eyes so blue, nor hair so blonde, nor a face so arresting. She was taller than he by several inches. "Who are you?" he stammered.

"Sonja," she said. "My mother and I arrived last night."

"Where from?"

"Chadds Ford. Near Philadelphia."

He nodded absently, suddenly out of his trance and nervous. He couldn't think of anything to say, so he simply stared. She approached him.

"Do you live here?"

He pointed toward the Lodge. "There." Her eyes were impossibly blue. The top of his head reached her chin. "With Missma, my grandmother," he added.

"I live back there," she said, pointing in the direction from which she came.

"Three Pines?"

"Yes."

"Why do you live there?"

"Because we came to teach the Negroes."

"Teach them what?"

"To read and write mostly."

"You could get into trouble. There is a law."

"My mother says it's our Christian duty. I don't know about the law. It must be something the rebels made up. We heard terrible things about them."

"What things?"

"They beat the poor Negroes and starve them and sell them like cows and lots of things like that."

"We are rebels, Missma and me. We don't do those things."

Sonja's eyes widened. "You are a rebel?"

"That's what they call us now. Because of the war."

Her tone hardened. "Then you must do those things."

He shook his head. "No. We are nice to our Negroes. You can ask Missma."

"I never met a rebel. Where are your mother and father?"

"I don't have a father. He died when I was eight. Mother went to Charleston when the Yankees came. Everyone left."

"You didn't leave."

"Missma wouldn't go. She said she would rather die in Beaufort."

"How old is she?"

"Over eighty."

Sonja looked back over her shoulder. "I better go back. Mother will worry. I guess we are neighbors. What is your name?"

"Carter."

He watched as she retreated.

Back inside the Lodge, Missma asked if he was feeling well. "I met a Yankee today. Out back. She lives at Three Pines."

Missma studied him more intently. "A Yankee woman? Next door?"

"She said she and her mother came to teach the Negroes."

"How old is this Yankee?"

"Older than me. I . . . don't know. She said we do bad things to the Negroes. I told her we don't."

"I see," said Missma. "It's not surprising that a Yankee girl would say that. What is her name?"

"She has blue eyes. That's all I remember."

Four days later, Missma suggested they invite "the Yankee girl" to tea. "Just to show her we don't have horns," Missma said. "But then I don't suppose we can send her a letter. How can we issue an invitation?"

"She walks the property," Carter said. "I see her out there. Every day she walks." He pointed to Three Pines.

"Oh?"

"I have chores and the garden, so I see her."

"Well, then perhaps you can ask her for tomorrow. Mid-afternoon?"

"For what when?"

"Tea. I said tea, at mid-afternoon."

"Oh, yes."

"Tell her to dress casually. We don't stand on ceremony here. And her mother is welcome also."

That evening, he reported that she said she would ask her mother, that if her mother approved she would come, and that she did not believe her mother's duties would allow her mother to attend. "Her name is Sonja."

The next afternoon, Missma stood in the doorway of the porch looking toward Three Pines. Carter sat in the Lodge, staring blankly at the Beaufort River. The day was unseasonably warm, with heat and humidity common to mid-summer.

"She's coming," Missma announced over her shoulder. She studied Sonja as she neared the Lodge. "Oh, my," she said, just loud enough for him to hear. The girl wore a plain cotton skirt, navy in color, and a loose white cotton blouse.

"Welcome," she called when the girl neared the porch. Sonja mounted the steps and Missma proffered her hand. Sonja nodded uncertainly, looked away as she saw Carter, and took a seat at Missma's invitation.

"It's so nice of you to visit us," Missma said as she seated herself. "I understand from my grandson that you and your mother have come to teach the Negroes. That's noble work. But we have had so much war in recent months, I suggest we avoid the subject entirely. Would that suit you?"

"Yes," said Sonja, her relief obvious in the breath she expelled, as though she had been holding it since she entered.

"You and your mother came to us from . . .?"

"Chadds Ford, Pennsylvania," said Sonja. "We sailed from Philadelphia. We live on a farm near the city, or we did."

"Horses?" asked Missma.

"Several," said the girl, smiling for the first time.

"I grew up riding," Missma said. "Tell us about your favorite. There is always a favorite."

Sonja described d'Artagnan, a chestnut her father bought for her before he left. She maintained eye contact with Missma, who prodded with questions, while Carter stared at the girl.

Missma served tea before turning the conversation to Sonja's school. "You must miss your friends desperately," she said.

"I do, I do," Sonja said. She described her friends in some detail. "You must never tell a secret to Heidi," she said with authority. "Everyone knows Heidi cannot be trusted to keep secrets. Ingrid can be trusted, but not Heidi. But she's fun because we learn from her about the others," Sonja said with a demure giggle. When Missma asked about her voyage from Pennsylvania, Sonja related her extreme seasickness. After what seemed to Carter only minutes but was in fact a half hour later, Sonja announced, "I must go. Mother will expect me. Thank you very much for the tea. I have enjoyed myself."

"Please come again," Missma said, walking her to the door. "And please give your mother my regards."

Sonja turned suddenly. "I almost forgot. Mother wanted me to ask if there are any pecan trees nearby."

Missma turned. "Carter would know better than I."

Carter, who had not spoken a word during the tea, said, "I can show you," and walked down the steps as Missma closed the door behind him.

"Is it far?" she wanted to know. "I can't go just now. Can you draw me a map?"

He dropped to his knees and cleared a space on the ground, grabbing a nearby stick. "Here's Three Pines," he said, drawing a rough rectangle, "and here is the Lodge," which he marked as an X. "And over here are the pecan trees." He placed a small circle some distance from the plantation boundary. He scratched a zigzag line. "There's the creek. You have to go here to cross."

"So to get there," she said, kneeling to the ground, "I would go here." She trailed her finger along the border of Three Pines. As she bent to point, her blouse separated from her chest, exposing the upper portion of a very white breast. He felt he should look away but he could not. The breast was firm, as though there was too much flesh to be contained within it, bounded by it, and near the surface thin blue veins, lightly filigreed, converged, disappearing as they neared the nipple, half concealed, but those veins held his stare as they would hold his dreams that night and for nights to come. Something in their branching, their flow in and through her, had awakened something in him. As she took in the crude map, a strange arousal stirred within him. His breath grew shallow. He couldn't understand why he was unable to look away, just as he had been unable to truly understand why he no longer saw his mother, why his grandmother had become his surrogate parent. He needed his old life, but it was gone and he was powerless to bring it back, to hunt and fish with Preston and wake up in his bed in town and hear his mother calling him to come down for breakfast. And now, with no control over his life, he found he couldn't even perform the simple act of looking away from a sight that he instinctively felt to be forbidden. When she suddenly stood to go, he felt sure she must have sensed his stare, but she merely thanked him and said she would see him again sometime since they were neighbors.

In the days that followed, he grew moody and restless, two things he had not been up to then. He asked Missma a question he asked only an hour before. He had to be reminded to do things he routinely did without prompting. He smiled or frowned for no apparent reason. He read his book without turning a page for half an hour. He walked the path behind the Lodge and disappeared beyond the break, hoping for a glimpse of her.

A week after tea, he returned from the break with pace. "She has never gigged for flounder," he said, although Missma had not asked. "No moon tonight. We should get some."

"Boat or on foot?" she wanted to know.

"Boat. I know a place close by."

Sonja appeared at the Lodge just before sunset. From somewhere she had obtained dark pants, which she wore belted high on her waist, well above her emerging hips. Her dark cotton shirt looked like a man's; possibly a mate to the pants. It hung loosely about her shoulders and arms. Her hair was pulled back into a simple ponytail. Her greeting to Missma was reserved but respectful. "Mother says I have two hours. Will that be enough?"

"Plenty," said Missma, while he wished for longer.

"You need a gig," said Carter. "Like this." He handed her the gig he made last month, a narrow pole with a sharpened end. She ran her hand over the smooth surface and her finger across the point. "Follow me," he said. They entered the woods near the Lodge. Carter selected a sapling and with two hacks from his hunting knife felled it. He trimmed it, sharpened the point, and handed it to her. "There. Your first gig," he said. "I made yours lighter than mine."

"Is that because I'm a girl?"

He stammered. "I . . . I guess so. You can have mine if you like."

"I was teasing," she said. "Is this all we need?"

98

"We need light." For this he returned to the woodpile near the Lodge. He picked up several pieces of pine from the ground, chopping all but one with a hatchet where the wood met the knot. He put several of the knots in his pocket. Sonja said nothing, but he was aware of her eyes on every move he made. "Wait here," he said.

"Where are you going? I want to see everything."

"Then come into the Lodge." He grabbed the piece of wood he had not trimmed and went inside. He thrust the knotted end into the fire, where it flared up enough to brighten the cabin. "We're ready," he said.

It was now dusk. An ambient flame from the improvised torch lit the way to the boat. "You get in and hold the light," he instructed.

She hopped the gunwale and turned to take the light. She doesn't move like a girl, he thought. Her movements were strong and assured, tomboy-like. He passed her the torch and the gigs, untied the skiff, and shoved off.

"Are we going to sail?" she asked.

"No wind," he noted. She blushed, but in that light he could not see her pale. "And the shallows are close."

Standing in the stern, he poled the skiff thirty yards to a series of hummocks just offshore.

"That wasn't much of a boat ride," she said, and he could not tell if she was again teasing.

"We didn't go far," he said, "but the water we crossed is deep in spots. Don't ever try to walk it. Can you swim?"

She shook her head no, looking away.

He took the torch from her and forced it into a notch in the gunwale. The air was still. Light from the torch illuminated the two of them, but blinded them to the mainland, the marsh and the sea. It was as if they were enclosed in a giant bubble of phosphorus. Carter wanted to stay here all night, forever, with her. In their bubble, there was no war, no Yankees, no soldiers. She turned her head to look out, and the light glistened off her ponytail. Maybe, he thought, a strand of that hair would remain in his boat. He would find it and keep it and smell it and taste it and put it under his sleeping mat.

"So, do we fish?" she asked.

"Yes."

"Show me how."

He took his gig from the bottom of the boat and moved to the bow. He stood. "You need to see this," he said. She joined him in the bow, leaning on the gunwale for support. Their arms touched, but she seemed not to notice. "Your eyes have to get used to seeing what is down there," he said.

"What am I looking for?"

"Fish eyes. They reflect the light." He studied the water, which was quite clear to the depth of the bottom, two feet down. He moved along the gunwale. "There," he said. "See it?"

"No."

"Look at the bottom. The flounder is almost the exact color of the mud, but not quite."

"I still don't see it."

Carter raised his gig and hurled it downward. The water roiled as mud ascended, and for an instant all was obscure. He raised the gig, using both arms. At the end of it flapped a large flounder. Sonja's eyes widened and for a moment she recoiled. He carried the gig to the stern, stepped on the fish to extract the gig, then attached the fish to a stringer. "Supper," he said. "Your turn."

She picked up her gig and placed herself where he stood.

"Try over here," he said, motioning. She moved to a spot where the water below was calm and the bottom had not been disturbed.

"Won't the others leave because you caught one?".

"Flounder don't think that way. They bury themselves in the mud and hope we go away."

"I can't see anything."

He came to her side. They were again touching. He could smell her, although he could not say what the smell was. He leaned closer, to get his eyes near hers. "There," he said, pointing. "A tiny reflection. See it?"

"Yes! I see it."

"Look around that. You are looking for a shape like the one I just brought up."

"Yes, I think I see that, too."

"Then gig him."

He backed away to give her room. She imitated the motion she had watched him perform. With impressive force she thrust her gig downward, but its entry into the water was at an angle and the gig deflected enough to miss the fish. Her shoulders slumped.

"Don't worry," he said. "That was a good first try. Now you know what you are looking for."

He poled the boat to another shallow a few yards away. She tried twice more before bringing up a small flounder, but her face lit up as if it were trophy size. Carter took another turn and again speared a large fish. She clapped her hands in approval. He beamed.

The torch burned low and time with it. She said she needed to go home. Back on shore, he lifted the stringer of fish and carried it to the break. He volunteered to walk her home, but she said she could manage. "I had fun," she said as he gave her the fish. Then, without warning, she reached with her free hand to his head and tousled his hair. "You know a lot for a kid," she said. She turned and walked toward Three Pines. He watched until the night swallowed her, touching his hair where her hand had been.

CHAPTER 20

B ecause Sonja and Christina had come to teach, they made it their first priority after settling in at Three Pines. Sonja selected an abandoned 15' x 15' slave cabin as the only practical place to hold classes. Far from ideal, its floor was dirt. Two windows, neither glassed or screened, helped air circulation only marginally while admitting flies, mosquitoes and gnats. A fireplace furnished heat. There were no chairs for students, and no desk for her.

She instructed the younger children, ages five to eight. A quick census showed fifteen in her group. Her first class was memorable for all that went wrong. She rang a cowbell to summon them. In fifteen minutes, only three students arrived. As they all lived on the same street leading from the main house, she walked hut to hut to track down the truants. From the mothers of the younger, she got explanations in Gullah she found impossible to understand. The urge to seek out Auntie Peak to interpret was strong, but this barrier to communication had to be overcome. By liberal use of hand gestures, she got assurance they would send the children "directly." The older ones, whose parents were already in the fields, were simply not there. She returned to the schooling cabin, now empty, the three prompt students having ignored instructions to remain. She rang the bell again. This time eight students drifted in, including the three who reported initially. She decided to begin. The children would sit on the floor until some furniture could be secured. She told them her name and asked them to repeat it back to her. They sat mum. She asked their names: "Hood," "Rina," "Oakie," "Rebecca," "James," "Flood."

The last two were identical twin girls: Sparrow and Lark. Sonja learned Sparrow's name from Lark, the more outgoing. Their hair was braided, their faces scrubbed. Like the others they were barefoot, but their identical dresses, made from flour sacks, were clean, with a scarlet sash tied at the waist. She learned from Lark that they were six years old.

Sonja had brought with her some illustrated children's books with big letters and florid pictures. Her first lesson would be to read *Benjamin the Bee* to the class. She showed them the first page, a brightly colored black and yellow Benjamin smiling as it hovered over a sunflower. She began to read. Flood stood and walked out. Rebecca, about eight, turned to Rina and began to chat in Gullah. Sonja could not understand a single word the girls uttered. James slapped Oakie on the back of the head, which produced from Rina a braying laugh. Only Sparrow and Lark sat silently, listening. Sonja called for quiet. She began page two. A new student walked in. He said his name was Morse and he was twelve. Rina and Rebecca giggled at his responses. Sonja suggested he was too old for her class, but he sat anyway. At her explanation of what they were doing, he listened to her read page two before standing up and walking out. At page three, Rina began to sing, which made Rebecca laugh and try to cover Rina's mouth.

Sonja learned from Christina later the same day that Christina's experience with the teens and adults in her class mirrored Sonja's. None had ever taken a class or sat for instruction. They did not know they lived in a state called South Carolina, or in a country called the United States, or on an ocean called the Atlantic. The only city or town any could name was their own, which they called "Bufed." Some believed babies were found in the hollows of trees or nestled into marsh grass. None of their parents were or ever had been married. The new teachers had work to do.

With Auntie Peak to translate, they visited the cabins to begin what would obviously be an ongoing process in educating both parent and child as to what was expected when school was in session.

The last stop on Sonja's round was the cabin where Sparrow and Lark lived. Her knock at the loosely hinged door was answered by Grace. An aroma that Sonja would come to identify as frying fatback filled the room, which was the cleanest and tidiest she had visited. Grace had smooth, dark features and bright white teeth. Sonja estimated her age at thirty-five. Seated at the plain wooden table was Polk, a muscled middle-aged man who stood when Sonja entered. Grace and Polk had lived together at Three Pines for ten years. Sparrow and Lark, now huddled together in a corner of the cabin, watching intently, were their only children.

Sonja thanked Grace for getting the girls to school and for their attentive behavior once there. "Dey wants to learn," said Grace. "Thank you for teaching we."

When Sonja left, Grace turned to the girls, praising them for earning their teacher's praise.

"She nice," Lark said as Sparrow nodded.

Polk, seated again, said, "She white fuh true."

In the days that followed, Sonja wondered if she would quit were it not for Sparrow and Lark. Sparrow seldom uttered a word, but her eyes were always bright with eager anticipation. When Lark answered, Sparrow nodded or, less often, shook her head imperceptibly in disagreement. When the lesson ended, they left holding hands.

A presence since Sonja and Christina arrived had been Gordon Fry, a stout little Irishman with a bulbous red nose.

"And what do you do here, Mr. Fry?" Christina had asked on the second day. She and Sonja were taking their morning coffee together when Fry stepped onto the porch to introduce himself.

"I work for Colonel Reynolds. I'm a cotton agent, and it's my job to see this year's crop gets in the ground so's come November we will have something to harvest."

"So you work with the Negroes?" Sonja asked.

Fry gave a short, punctuated laugh. "The Negroes work for me, doing the same work they've always done, only we pay 'em instead of whipping 'em. The whipping days are over at Three Pines. And I get paid a commission based on what they produce. Did pretty well last year, but this here's a new year and we got to make sure it gets done right."

"How long do the Negroes work?" Christina asked.

"Depends on the man," Fry said. "One task a day minimum."

"Task?"

"That's how work is measured here. When a man has done everything needs doing on a quarter acre, he has finished a task. Some finish by noon, others longer. Depends on the man."

Sonja asked, "What do they do then?"

"After they finish? Whatever they want. Some sleep, some tend their plots."

Two weeks after she arrived, Sonja saw Fry in the field with Polk, whose head hung while Fry gesticulated as if angry. She reported this to her mother, who mentioned it to Jacob Roan. Sonja, Christina and Roan were seated on the porch when Polk was sent for.

It was nearly dusk. An early spring hush had settled over Three Pines. In the distance, candles in the Negroes' cabins gave off barely perceptible light and the aroma of frying fatback reached the porch, where the lamps had not yet been lit. Polk emerged from the semi-darkness.

"You send fuh me?"

Roan said, "I saw you and Fry having some words. Wondered what that was about."

"He be wantin' two tasks a day."

"And you want to quit after one so you can work your garden."

"Yessuh."

"You get more pay when you work two, do you not?"

Polk said, "When we get pay. Seem lately we be gettin' 'cuses, not pay. When I work de land, I know zackly what I gwyne get and when I gwyne get it."

"I'll speak to Colonel Reynolds about that. I know they are having some problems getting money to the plantations to pay folks. Thank you, Polk."

When he left, Roan said, "Polk's worked that plot for ten years, I'm told. I don't blame him for wanting to spend more time there than in the fields. Fry can be a real driver. When it comes to his commissions or Polk's garden, Polk might just as well resign himself to two tasks a day."

Sonja sat in silence, despairing at what her world had become. In the span of a month she had left behind all she had known for this forsaken plantation, surrounded by strangers and bereft of anything she recognized as her former life with the sole exception of her mother, who seemed transformed in ways Sonja had yet to discern. In place of Ingrid and Heidi and her other friends were now Negroes who spoke a foreign tongue and the rebel boy at the Lodge. As to teaching, she was wasting her time and her life. She did not care what a task was, or how many of them Polk worked, or whether cotton got planted, or whether the Union Army under General McClellan would take Richmond. She may one day forgive her mother for this, but it would not be soon. She left the porch for the seclusion of her room.

CHAPTER 21

In early May, Carter watched Missma stand in the door of the Lodge to catch the smallest puffs of breeze off the river. Over her shoulder she told him the weather was occupying her thoughts as it had not done for many years. Thus far, the spring had been a fruitful one. The seven rows of corn they planted in March showed signs of bounty. The sweet potatoes, also sown in March, were always harder to assess, but because spring rains had not saturated the soil she said she remained cautiously optimistic. And how she looked forward to fresh peas in the fall. His labor in the garden had given him new respect for farming's challenges. He felt it was his responsibility to produce enough food for their survival, mindful that no matter how hard he worked, nature would have the final word.

Back in late February, she had taken him to an area behind the Lodge large enough to support a crop and exposed to sufficient sunshine. Together they walked until she planted her toe in a spot, instructing him to drive a stake. Three stakes later, a plot more or less rectangular outlined what would be their garden, and their salvation. "When you have cleared that plot of every living weed, vine, stalk, stump and root," she said, "we will proceed to the next step. I thank God for Reggie. If he hadn't brought seeds we would be in a fine fix." Three days later, using the hoe brought from the house, she demonstrated how to break up and hoe under the remaining vegetation. "This is called listing," she told him. "This time next year, most of what you will be hoeing under will be a few corn stalks from this year's crop."

Carter asked, "Will we be here next year?"

"I see no quick end to this war. We must plan for the worst and hope for the better. Now we build the rows. We will need the manure the cow has produced, but it will not be enough. You will need to bring up some pluff mud to supplement what we have available. That's hard work, and I wish I could help, but I can't."

"That's alright, Missma, I can do it."

She smiled at him. "Of course you can."

In late March, she showed him how to plant the grains of corn, three or four grains to each hole and spaced two feet apart. When he asked if the plants needed more room to grow, she told him that the early shoots would be thinned to allow just that. Next they planted the seed potatoes. Since those early spring lessons, he had spent part of each day purging the rows of weeds and grasses growing around the fledgling sprouts.

His work in the garden comprised only part of his daily routine. On most days, he and Soot left at sunrise to fish or hunt. He returned for breakfast, then milked the cow. He did his garden work in the morning, before the afternoon sun began to bake the plot, and it was on those afternoons, when there is no respite from the heat, that he was thankful he and Missma did not raise cotton. From an orange tree in the break separating the Lodge from Three Pines, he saw the contrabands laboring in the fields, straw hats or head-handkerchiefs covering their heads, bending to plant cotton and moving as if suspended in an invisible molasses. His reason for climbing the tree was not, however, to commiserate with workers but to catch a glimpse, however brief, of Sonja. At Missma's insistence, he read for an hour or two after the light lunch Missma prepared. In late afternoon, he had conditioned himself to chop wood, and while it could be taxing physically, he could do it in the shade. When the breeze was fair, he and Soot sailed past Signal Oak, where he hoped a letter or message awaited. Missma accompanied them on several such sails, reveling in being outside and feeling the wind on her face. On days Reggie came for his reading lesson, they sometimes hunted or fished even if the tides or conditions were not the best. Reggie always walked the garden, but his interest remained stronger in plants, flowers and trees. Twice he had helped Carter haul in mud for fertilizer, and on both occasions expressed relief that no mud was used at the house in Beaufort.

Carter came through the break, his excitement evident in his pace. As he neared the Lodge, he saw Missma walking in the garden. "I went to Three Pines. Sonja invited me."

"Oh? Did you meet her mother?"

"Yes, ma'am."

"Was she nice?"

"Yes, ma'am. She asked me to teach Sonja to swim. She is worried about that with so much water here."

"I should think she would worry. How old is that girl?"

"Fourteen."

"High time she learned. I wonder if the mother knows how."

"No, ma'am, she doesn't. She said Sonja will teach her if I teach Sonja."

"And when do the lessons start?"

"Sonja is changing her clothes now."

"Where will you take her?"

"To the bend in the creek. There's not much current."

Thirty minutes later, Sonja appeared, clad from neck to foot, with a long sleeve shirt buttoned over an undershirt and bloomers that reached to her ankles. "You must be hot," said Carter, who wore only a shirt and shorts.

"I am. Let's find the water."

He led her through the woods bordering the Lodge to a spot on the bank where the creek went off at an angle. The bank was firm, and behind it spartina grass shielded the bend. He took off his shirt and slipped into water above his knees. She watched him from the bank. "Are you afraid of the water?" he asked. "It's okay to be afraid."

"A little," she said. "Are there things in there?"

"What kinds of things?"

"Alligators? Sharks?"

"No sharks come in this far, and alligators don't want anything to do with us. There's nothing in here that will hurt you."

"Promise?"

"I promise. Come down here where I am."

She sat on the bank, sliding in cautiously until she was standing beside him. "Mud is oozing between my toes."

"Don't worry about the mud here, but there are places where you can sink up to your knees."

"What's the first thing to do?"

"Just what we are doing."

"But we're just standing here."

"You will learn faster if you are comfortable in the water." He grinned and chopped his hand down, sending a splash. She turned her head and put her hands out to deflect it.

"Hey, none of that," she said.

"You have to get wet sometime. Okay, let's get wetter." He dropped to his knees, resting them on the bottom, the water just below his chin. She followed. Her shirt, with air pockets in the sleeves, bloated around her.

"So cooling," she said.

"Now taste it," he told her, scooping some into his hand. "Don't swallow, just taste. Do you taste the salt? Salt helps you float. The water here is not nearly as salty as the ocean."

"I want to swim in the ocean one day," she said.

"You will. We will," he said, stressing "we" in a way that seemed to go unnoticed by Sonja, who remained focused on the lesson.

She began to move her arms as if treading water. "I like it so far. What's next?"

"Do this," he said, ducking below the surface and holding his breath for ten seconds.

She ducked, but resurfaced immediately, pushing her hair from her face.

"Try this," he said, taking a big breath, holding it, and then submerging.

She managed to stay under for four or five seconds before she exhaled and surfaced.

"You did better," he said as she wiped water from her eyes. "Want to try more?"

"Yes. I want to learn this."

"Next you should try to float, on your back. That will show how the water can help keep you up. But I should hold you at first. Is that okay?"

"You're the teacher."

"Stretch out like this," he said, in a float position facing up.

"I will sink," she said.

"No, because I am going to hold you up until you feel comfortable."

"You will not let me sink?"

"I will not let you sink."

He placed one hand between her shoulder blades and the other in the small of her back. He was touching her, holding her, as he had dreamed so often of doing. She looked up at him with her blue eyes, her face tense with nervous uncertainty and her body rigid in his hands.

"Try to relax," he said, but he was anything but relaxed, and he could have spent the entire day doing just this.

Gradually, as her face remained skyward, he felt her muscles loosen. She managed a smile. "I'm floating," she said.

"Now I'm going to lower my hands just a little, but they will still be under you. You will not sink. I promise."

He lowered his hands until they briefly disengaged, her body descending to them as her torso slipped momentarily below the surface. "Relax," he instructed. After several more repetitions, she floated free of his support for several seconds. "See? You have it. Maybe that's enough for your first day."

They left the water for the bank. The sun warmed them as Sonja wrung out her clothes. When he had put on his shirt, they sat on the bank, their feet dangling in the water.

"Mother is arranging some tutors for me," she told him. "If she has her way I will be a teacher by morning, a student by afternoon. I can't tell if she is really that concerned about my education or if she just wants to keep me busy so I won't be so miserable."

"Are you miserable?"

"Wouldn't you be?" she said, her voice rising. "If you had to leave your home and your friends and live in some strange place?"

"But I did have to leave my home and my friends to live at the Lodge. At least you have your mother here. Where is your father?"

"He went back to Sweden. He's been gone a long time. Mother still hopes he will come back, but I believe he will stay." Her voice softened. "So we are the same. Are you miserable?"

He picked up a clod of mud and tossed it into the creek. "I'm not happy, but I'm trying to make the best of it. Mother says always try to make the best of a bad situation so that's what I want to do."

"Well, I don't. I want to go home."

"Before you learn to swim?"

She hesitated. "After. After I learn to swim." She sighed heavily. "But I promised Mother I would give it some time, and it's only been a few weeks, so I guess I'm stuck here. Maybe the Union will take Richmond and the war will end and we can both go home."

"Is the Union attacking Richmond?"

"With thousands of men and guns. Maybe I shouldn't tell you since you're a rebel."

He shrugged. "I would tell you things, but I don't know anything. Missma and I don't get much news."

"Did you hear about that black man who stole the ship in Charleston?"

He looked at her, doubting. "What man? What ship?"

"His name is Little or Small, I forget which. When the rebels weren't looking, he took over their ship and sailed away in it. He just did it. Mr. Roan—he's our superintendent—said the black man worked on this rebel ship and waited for a night when the crew went to town, probably to get drunk. He dressed up like the captain and he and his friends sailed the ship past all the rebel forts. Mr. Roan said he, the Negro, is a hero and he is from Beaufort."

Carter, who had heard nothing of Robert Smalls' brazen coup to commandeer *The Planter*, stared at the water.

"What is the matter?"

"Nothing."

"I think I know," she said. "Your side lost a ship."

"Would you be happy if a rebel stole a Union ship?"

"Of course not, but the Union is doing the right thing in rescuing Negroes to give them freedom and a better life."

"I'm glad their life is better, because mine sure is not."

"You don't have to teach me to swim."

"I was not talking about that. Teaching you is fun. I meant all the rest of it. One day I will sail you into Beaufort. You can see our home, or what used to be our home. Missma says we have lost everything."

"You have the Lodge," she said.

"As of today. Who knows what will happen tomorrow."

"I'm certain your house in town was very nice. We saw some grand homes when we arrived. But have you seen what the Negroes at Three Pines live in? The Lodge looks like a mansion compared to them."

"Those are for field hands. We didn't have field hands."

"I will take you to them one day. You can see for yourself."

"It's not my fault we had a nice house, and it's not my fault the field hands don't have nice houses."

"I didn't say it was your fault. Just like it was not my fault my father left and not my fault I had to leave my friends because Mother came here. So I suppose you and I are stuck and we just have to make the best of it."

He smiled. "I thought I said that. We have to make the best of it."

She paused reflectively. "You said you don't get much news here. How do you get any?"

He hesitated. He could not tell her about Signal Oak. "The Negroes, mostly. We know a few of them in town."

"Oh. So can you teach me again tomorrow?"

"Yes. Yes I can."

"What will we do tomorrow?"

"Same as today. When you can float on your back, it will be time to face the water."

"Will I be swimming?"

"Soon."

"See you tomorrow." She stood. By then her clothes were almost dry. She brushed off her bloomers and disappeared into the brush leading to Three Pines.

On the day following, he arrived at the bank early, watching the break from which she would emerge. Dressed as she was the day before, she smiled and waved as she approached, proceeding past him and into the water. A good sign, he thought. She dropped to her knees, submerged her head, and stayed under longer than the day before. Raising her head, she sputtered and wiped water from her eyes. "I'm ready to float," she said. "You won't let me sink?"

"I promise."

He supported her as he had done the day before. She was much less tense today, and the touches became less frequent as she gave herself over to the buoyancy of the water.

"Very good," he told her. "Ready for the next lesson?"

"I think so."

"This is called the dead man's float. Watch me." He lay face down in the water, arms and legs spread wide, and stayed there a long time. He wondered if she was beginning to worry. He stayed down until his lungs screamed for air. He felt her hand on his hair, pulling up. He surfaced, breathing heavily and grinning.

"That was cruel," she said. "I wasn't sure . . ."

"Now you. I need to hold your waist."

"Hold tight."

"Take a deep breath, relax, close your eyes and spread your arms and legs as far as they will go. I will not let you sink."

She did as instructed. He encircled her waist with his hands, looking down as her blonde hair spread against the pale green surface. He felt he was holding something fragile and at the same time dangerous, like a lethal poison carried in an eggshell. He loosened his grip as he sensed her floating. She began to sink, and he reasserted his grip. After half a minute, she stood.

"You have it," he said, and she smiled. "Ready to swim?"

"Yes."

He demonstrated a dog paddle, then held her waist as she imitated. She was keeping her head too far out of the water, but he remembered doing the same when he learned. When she tired, they again sat on the bank, catching their breath in the sunshine of a bright mid-morning.

She picked up the conversation where they left off the day before. "So that means you never hear from your mother?"

"What?"

"Your mother. If you get your news from the Negroes, you never hear from her."

"We . . . hear things about her. Mother liked the Negroes and they liked her. I guess she knows people in Charleston that know people here."

"I'm an only child," she said. "Are you?"

"I have an older brother. He's in Virginia fighting the Yankees."

"What is he like?"

"Preston? He's the best brother ever. After my father died, Preston taught me to hunt and fish like my father taught him. He taught me to swim, like I'm teaching you."

She turned her face to him, smiling faintly. "Did you learn as fast as me?"

"Faster," he said, returning her grin. "In one day."

"You are lying," she said.

"Yes, I am."

"I had a brother once, but I never knew him. He was born before me and only lived a short time. My father went back to the old country after that. He never got over it."

"That's very sad. I know he would have been a great brother."

She made no response to this. After a silence broken only by a mockingbird in a nearby tree, she said, "We should go fishing again."

"Or swim in the ocean."

"I don't feel ready for those waves."

"You will be. Soon."

"You are a good teacher."

"Thanks. You learn fast."

"Thank you."

"How is your teaching going?"

"I have fifteen children between five and eight years old. Some days I have three or four, and some days they all show up. They have never had a set sched-ule and sitting still to learn is new to them. Sometimes I'm in the middle of a lesson and one will just get up and walk out. They have to learn how to learn and teaching them takes all the patience I have. But I see progress, and they are sweet children. Especially two. Twins named Sparrow and Lark. My favorites."

The sun had dried their skin and nearly their clothes. She shifted forward, dangling more of her legs in the water, while he made random marks with his fingernail in the bank between them. She paddled her feet, roiling the otherwise smooth surface.

"Would you like to ride my horse sometime?"

"Do you mean it? I would love that. I miss my horse so much."

"Whenever you want," he said. "I don't ride often, and Sunset needs the exercise."

"That's so generous. I'm glad we are neighbors, even if you are a rebel." She stood. "I have to go."

He was rising from the bank when she shoved him, sending him backward into the creek. Sputtering, he surfaced to see her running away, laughing over her shoulder. He climbed onto the bank and started after her, but soon realized she was quite fast and he had no chance of catching her.

Carter rose early the following morning. The sun was just coming up when he saw Sonja walk through the break toward the creek. She was carrying a large cloth and a slab of soap. He almost called out to her when he realized she did not intend to swim, but to bathe. The cloth was a towel. What to do? She didn't swim well enough to be on her own in the water, yet the bend in the creek was gentle, particularly at this early hour. She shouldn't be alone, yet if she intended to bathe, clearly she needed to be. He felt butterflies flutter in his stomach as he followed her at a safe distance.

In the woods overlooking the bend, he stealthily climbed a tree with a clear view of the bend. He saw her drop the towel on the bank, then look around. She faced the water, with her back to him. She began to undress. As before when he glimpsed more of her than he should have, he had an instinctive feeling he should look away, but he could not. As he stared, his mouth going dry, she took off the long-sleeved shirt and the undershirt. She unfastened the drawstring that held the bloomers to her hips. The bloomers slid down, and she stepped out of their crumpled mold. She was naked. He held his breath. He stared at the crescent cleft between her legs and felt the need to tighten his grip on the limb supporting him. She reached down, picked up the soap, and eased into the water, submerging to her neck. She wet her hair and lathered her head, running her splayed fingers repeatedly through the mass of blonde. She stood, her back still to him, and bent down to rinse her hair, massaging her head and wringing water from her hair. She turned toward the bank, reaching for the towel. He saw her breasts, and below, a triangular mass of light brown pubic hair. He had never seen a woman naked.

He watched her dress. She left the bank, walking into the woods and passing within a few feet of his tree. He inhaled, praying she did not look up and certain the thumping of his heart must have been audible on the ground. He remained utterly motionless, refusing even to disturb the mosquito that was feasting on his forearm.

Once, when he was seven, he broke a dining room window pane playing with Reggie outside. When his mother asked who was responsible, he blamed Reggie. He remembered the shame he felt, lying to his mother and fingering his friend. That was his baptism into shame, and he felt it now. Days after the broken window, nagged by guilt, he had confessed to his mother. But he could never bring himself to tell Sonja he spied on her. Never.

For the rest of the week they met at the bank for her lessons. She was learning too quickly. Soon she would no longer need him to hold her, encourage her. On the day she dove from the bank and swam out twenty yards with a competent crawl stroke, he knew this special time was nearly over. She mentioned needing to teach her mother.

Although he was awake at sunrise, he had not seen her return to the bank with her towel. He told himself that he would not follow her again; that now that she could swim he could not justify pursuit in the name of her safety; that to return to his perch in the tree would be an admission that his only interest would be seeing her undress. He told himself that spying on her was wrong and that he would not do it. She was his friend. It was wrong and dishonest to spy on a friend. He spied on the Yankees, but they were his enemies, the ones trying to kill Preston in Virginia and the people who caused his mother to flee. Sonja was a Yankee, but she was his friend. No, he would not spy on her again.

And yet . . . at night he could think of nothing else. He wondered what it would be like to join her; for both of them to undress and swim naked. No woman had seen him naked since he was a young boy, and certainly not since downy hair had appeared under his arms, above his penis, and even a few on his chest. And how would he feel if, being naked with her, his penis did what it always seemed to do when he thought about her naked. If she saw him that way, would she understand what it meant? How much did he understand? But no, he will not spy on her again. He will not.

He did his chores with his mind elsewhere. Was it his mind? His stomach got queasy when he saw her. His pulse began to race. His palms moistened. It was his heart, not his mind. Was this love? Was this what love felt like? Was this what his mother had felt for his father? All he knew for certain was that it was unlike any feeling he had ever had, the closest he had ever come to magic.

CHAPTER 22

Through Jacob Roan, a rumor reached Three Pines that the Union man in charge of the Department of the South, Major General David Hunter, intended to form a combat unit of black soldiers. Roan told Christina and Sonja that he very much doubted it. "We need men like Polk to get the cotton crop. We're struggling to find enough men as it is. To take the ones we have makes no sense."

After dismissing the rumor as "so much idle speculation," Roan handed Christina a note from Laura Towne. Despite the warm relationship kindled between Towne and Christina during their time on the *Oriental*, they had not seen each other since disembarking in Beaufort. The note invited Christina and Sonja to come to church with Roan on Sunday, May 11, and to spend the night. Towne wrote that she had recently received a shipment of clothes from the Philadelphia Port Royal Relief Committee, and she wished to enlist Christina's help in distributing it to the contrabands at Three Pines. Christina handed the note to Sonja. "I want to go," she told her daughter. "You come, too."

Roan drove the buckboard's reluctant horse with gentle, patient ease. It was a fine Sunday morning, the air clear and without humidity. A faint breeze, augmented by the motion of the buggy, kept the travelers cool. When Christina, seated between him and Sonja, asked who they could expect to see aside from Laura Towne, Roan answered, "Edward Pierce will be there. He's based at Pope's Plantation as well."

"Who is Edward Pierce?" Sonja asked.

"An impressive young man who everyone knows to be the eyes and ears of Secretary of the Treasury Chase. In fact, it's possible none of us would be here if it was not for Pierce."

"How so?" Christina asked.

"You have heard the Negroes referred to as contraband? That term was coined by Major General Benjamin Butler, the commander of Fortress Monroe in Virginia. About a year ago Butler had a difficult problem when three slaves crossed our picket lines at the fort. They told him their owner, a Virginia lawyer named Mallory, planned to send them to North Carolina to dig rebel fortifications. Mallory heard they were there and demanded that Butler return them because of the fugitive slave law. Butler was not about to turn them over. He told Mallory the law didn't apply because Virginia had left the Union and the slaves were contraband of war, so that is where the term originated."

"When other slaves heard that Butler was protecting runaways, the fort was flooded with them. I heard something like nine hundred appeared in just a few days. Butler needed someone to be in charge of all those people and he found Edward Pierce, who happened to be assigned there as a private in the Third Massachusetts Regiment. But Pierce was no ordinary private. Not only was he a Brown and Harvard law graduate, but he had been the personal secretary to Secretary Chase. By all accounts Pierce did a splendid job managing the contraband, then wrote about it in an article published in *Atlantic Monthly*. He claimed the contraband would make good soldiers if properly trained and equipped, and many in our government agree with him. So Edward Pierce is a man to be reckoned with."

As they arrived at the church, hundreds of Negroes greeted each other outside. A goodly number wore bright clothes reserved for such occasions. Many of the women sported vivid turbans, a few adorned with a jaunty feather from a duck or eagle. The breeze that followed the buggy caressed the live oaks and enlivened the Spanish moss. Christina spotted Laura Towne standing on the church steps and waved. Standing beside Towne was a handsome young man she introduced as Edward Pierce.

Inside, the congregation heard Mr. Horton preach rock-ribbed scripture, reminding those gathered of how much greater they are than the beasts of the field. Hymns, sung full-throated by beautiful black voices with lilting sopranos and resonant bass, floated through open windows into the woods beyond. Neither Christina nor Sonja had ever heard such music, and Laura Towne smiled at their delight. A downy-headed, wizened old man asked the Lord to bless the "good folk what comes to help we."

After the service, Christina and Sonja accompanied Towne to Sunday school, where she told her class of twenty-five of Christ's love for children, and how kindness to each other would earn them a place in Heaven.

Laura joined Roan, Christina and Sonja in the carriage for the trip to Pope's Plantation, where Towne lived. Many of the Negroes remained in the churchyard to talk and laugh, while others started for home. When the carriage passed a group of a dozen, Sonja said she noticed several who carried their shoes into church and were now carrying them home. "Why would they do that?" she asked.

Laura Towne laughed. "Most likely to show they have shoes. That was not always the case before we arrived."

At Pope's, the trio from Three Pines watched Edward Pierce distribute the weekly wages to the contraband. This was of particular interest to the women because it was a ritual they had been unable to see or perform. The laborers at Three Pines had been belatedly paid the week before the women arrived, but since that payday certain "administrative problems" had been cited as the explanation for a shortage of specie among the cotton agents. Roan admitted he found the situation "intolerable" and acknowledged that the morale among the field workers at Three Pines suffered as a result. Edward Pierce was evidently better connected, for regular pay appeared to be a fact of life at Pope's. Pierce stepped to the front porch and called for everyone to assemble. Within minutes the area was packed with eager black faces, raised expectantly. Pierce called each name from a list. The men and women who stepped forward received between seventy-five cents and three dollars each, depending on the number of tasks performed. Upon receipt, each man made a backward scraping motion with one foot. The women curtseyed.

Later, at tea, the talk was of the rumor, received from a Union Army lieutenant the week before, that a rebel force of twenty thousand was massing to retake Beaufort and the islands. It produced nervousness among all, but particularly the Negroes, who had feared just such an attack since When Gun Shoot at Bay Point. Edward Pierce had just expressed his profound skepticism that such an attack was or ever would be forthcoming when two riders approached the house. They were Captain Hazard Stevens, son of the local commander General Isaac Stevens, and an orderly. Their expressions upon entering the house told of grim business. Capt. Stevens handed Edward Pierce an order issued by Gen. Hunter to send every able-bodied Negro of fighting age to Hilton Head, "today."

Pierce looked from the order to Stevens's unsmiling face in disbelief. "He cannot mean this. It is . . . insane. How are we supposed to work these plantations with these men gone? Does Gen. Hunter have any idea of the fear these men hold of Hilton Head? The very mention of the place will send them into the woods. Is your father in Beaufort? I will see him today."

"Yes, sir, it was he who instructed me to deliver the order, but between you and me he was none too happy about it."

Pierce handed the order to Roan and faced his guests. "Ladies, you will excuse me. This strikes me as something of an emergency. I will appeal to Gen. Stevens." He turned to leave. "One more thing. The order strictly forbids any discussion with the contrabands about this. I suppose we must honor that command until I can get to the bottom of the business."

Roan turned to Sonja and Christina. "So much for my theory of idle speculation. Hunter actually expects to impress all these contrabands into the military. I agree with Pierce; many will take to the marsh."

Christina said, "But wouldn't the contraband want to fight for their freedom?"

"Some will, to be sure, but many more are afraid of Hilton Head, as Pierce said. They've been told for years by owners and overseers that Hilton Head is the starting point for places they don't want to go, like Cuba."

Laura Towne joined them, lowering her voice as she told them the house servants, who saw and heard all, were alarmed. Their worst fear was that the white people who came to help them would abandon them to the retribution of their old masters, and the rumor of a massing Confederate force had them in a panic. "So now they have two reasons to fear Hilton Head. They don't want to go for fear of being sent to who knows where, and they don't want to see us go for fear that we will abandon them." She nodded subtly toward a servant across the room collecting cups. "Josiah asked me if I planned to go to Hilton Head, and I knew what he was thinking. The others put him up to it, I feel sure."

"What did you tell him?" Roan asked.

"I told him no, but you heard Mr. Pierce say we were not to discuss this with them, so I left it at that. Josiah seemed relieved."

But after dark, when a company of Union soldiers entered the yard, panic set in. Towne implored the servants to remain calm. Josiah said, "Massa comin' back," and sent several women to the marsh to keep lookout for the rumored Confederate force.

Towne pleaded. "I'm sure there is no danger, Josiah. Those poor ladies will be eaten alive by the mosquitos." Better the mosquitos than their old masters, he replied. Besides, he said, if the rebels weren't coming back, why were all these Union soldiers there.

Towne spoke to the company's commander, who told her they had been ordered to divide into squads, that each squad had been assigned a plantation, and that they were to round up all black recruits for transport to Hilton Head.

"These men will be marching all night," Towne said.

"Yes, ma'am. They'll be tired and hungry, but those are our orders."

Christina asked, "Is one of your squads going to a plantation named Three Pines?"

The commander checked his list. "They left a little while ago."

Christina turned to Sonja. "They'll take Polk and the others."

Early the following morning, Capt. Stevens mounted the porch at Pope's as Towne, Christina and Sonja looked on. Flanked by two armed soldiers, he called for all able-bodied contrabands to come forth. Slowly, the men arrived from the fields and stables, apprehension on every face. Stevens instructed them to come closer. When they were assembled in the yard below him, he told them that Gen. Hunter had sent for them and they must go to Hilton Head. He paused as the two soldiers flanking him pointedly loaded their pistols.

When the message had been delivered, Stevens sought to soften its impact. He told them they would not be made to fight against their will, and that they would be allowed to return to Pope's if they wished, but today they had no choice but to go.

Laura Towne then spoke. "I hope you will all be back again in a few days with your free papers, but if you are needed, I hope you will stay and help to keep off the rebels." The men seemed resigned, some even enthused. They were to leave without further delay. Two broke out to say goodbyes, followed to their cabins by a soldier. Most were wearing neither caps nor shoes, which the women brought to them from the cabins, then huddled together with children in protective clusters. The men marched off, first to be transported to Beaufort, and then to Hilton Head, where five hundred likewise conscripted Negroes arrived the following day.

Sonja tugged at Christina's sleeve. "Grace and the girls will die if they take Polk."

With their weekly supply of bread and a large assortment of clothing to be distributed, Roan, Christina and Sonja left for the return trip to Three Pines. On the main road leading back, they met a large body of contrabands flanked on each side by Union soldiers. Roan stopped the carriage to let the procession pass. From the back, they saw a hand rise and wave. Polk's hand.

Grace, Sparrow and Lark waited for them in the lane. Grace had been crying, the girls holding her hands. Christina repeated the assurances she heard given at Pope's, predicting his return soon. Grace dried her eyes on her apron, comforted if not convinced.

A week later, Polk was back. Happy, he told them, that he wasn't taken to Cuba, as so many feared, and relieved that the Army had kept its promise that no man would be required to serve against his will. He did not mind fighting, he told Christina and Sonja, but without him Grace and the girls would suffer and his garden would fallow.

Christina teased, "And you would not be able to see this cotton crop through."

Polk flashed a toothy grin. "I thought 'bout dat, too."

CHAPTER 23

On a balmy afternoon in mid-June, Carter told Missma he was going to Signal Oak to place a letter he had written to his mother.

> Dearest Mother:
> I hope you get this letter and that you are well. Missma and I are making the best of things at the Lodge. Now that summer is here we eat shrimp at least once a day and Missma fixes it in different ways. I try to cut wood every day because we burned so much last winter.
> We don't get much news of the war, but we get some when Reggie comes for his reading lesson and from the missionaries that have come to Three Pines to teach the Negroes. One of them is a girl named Sonja. She is a little older than I am. She is very nice for a yankee.
> Missma is making me read Robinson Crusoe by a man named Defoe. I did not want to read it at first but she gave me no choice and now I am glad she made me do it. Robinson Crusoe and I have a lot in common, which you already know if you have read the book. Missma was not sure you have. After a shipwreck, he is stranded on an island and must figure out how to stay alive. He does not have anyone to cook for him and no missionary near his age, so I feel sorry for him and better for myself. I am near the end and feel sure he will be rescued. Missma and I hope we will be rescued, too, but do not worry about us because we are fine.
> Love, your son Carter

Missma had also written letters and wished to go. Soon they were navigating the Broad River, Soot perched in the bow like a lookout. His hind leg was now fully mended, though he limped at times. To their right, a dolphin broke the surface to eye them. Soot stood, alert, on point, ears raised. Carter commanded him to stay. At Signal Oak, he secured his line and took the letters to be left. Waiting in the tree hollow was not a letter but a note:

"Cousin, We need to talk. Wait half an hour for me to arrive. If I do not, there is a Yankee nearby."

He climbed down from the tree and showed Missma the note. They sat in silence, surveying the waterways and marshes. He began to fish in the event they were being watched. From the mouth of the creek on the far shore they spotted Gabriel Heyward paddling a canoe toward them. He was dressed not as a soldier but as a fisherman, a canvas-colored slouch hat covering most of his face. In minutes he pulled beside them.

"Howdy, cousin. Good afternoon, Granny. I need to make this as quick as possible. Cousin, how is the surveillance going down there?"

"Pretty quiet."

"How about the 50th Pennsylvania? Heard anything about those boys lately?"

"No, why?"

"Because the 50th Pennsylvania hit us two weeks ago at Pocotaligo. They brought their friends, 8th Michigan and 79th New York. We lost a couple of pretty good men. My pal Allen was one."

"I . . . didn't know."

"We beat them back. We know you can't be everywhere. And don't take this hard. We have missed bigger things than this with twenty sets of eyes on the job instead of one."

"Two sets," injected Missma.

"Sorry, Granny, I meant two. Anyway, lives depend on this information, including the life of yours truly." He paused to grin. "And the ladies of Charleston and Savannah will never forgive you if you let something happen to me."

Missma said, "I keep him busy at the Lodge. And then there are those swimming lessons."

"Swimming lessons?"

"A daughter of the missionary at Three Pines," Missma said.

"Oh?" Gabriel looked at Carter. "Cousin? Is this something you need to talk to Cousin Gabe about? Is she pretty?"

Carter dropped his head, staring at the bottom of the boat. "I guess." But Missma, out of his vision, nodded her head once, emphatically.

"I see," said Gabriel. "You be careful with those Yankee women. Why, out of concern for you, I may just have to sneak through the lines and investigate this fraternizing with the enemy." He winked at Missma.

"Sorry about 50th Pennsylvania, Cousin Gabe. And about your friend Allen."

"Just keep your eyes and ears open, and don't do what I do, which is think about women all day." He reached into his shirt and withdrew two letters, handing one to each. "I know you will be glad to get these. Hope the news is good. I need to skedaddle."

"Wait," Carter said, jumping from the boat back to the low branch of Signal Oak. He retrieved the letters from the hollow, returned to the boat, and handed them to Gabriel. "If you see Mother . . ."

Gabriel nodded, placed the letters inside his shirt, pushed his paddle against the skiff, and was soon lost among the waning shadows of the day.

June 5, 1862
Charleston, SC

Dearest Carter:

My dear son I hope this letter finds you, and finds you well. Your last gave me such comfort that you and Missma are making the best of the horrible circumstances brought on by this war. Who would have guessed you for a farmer? My pride in you and what you are doing for Missma is complete.

Enclosed is a letter from Preston addressed to you. I also received one. I hope yours is as reassuring as mine. He sounds so much like himself, yet I sense his military service is aging him beyond his eighteen years. Surely they will give him leave to come home soon.

We are still in Charleston, but our days here are numbered. Because of the fire, the shortage of houses is acute. Uncle Daniel, Aunt Abigail and I have managed to stay together thanks to the kindness of the Singletons, but we cannot impose on them forever. Last month we learned what we had feared about Uncle Daniel's home. It was insured for fire, but claims overwhelmed the insurance company and it is bankrupt. Thank God we were able to get valuables from the house before fire consumed everything.

In all likelihood, our next move will be to Columbia. Uncle Luke has offered, which was kind. Now that the question of fire insurance has been answered, I am urging Uncle Daniel and Aunt Abigail to visit before accepting Uncle Luke's offer. They know the house, of course, but the war has changed things everywhere.

Spirits here ebb and flow with news of the war. Weeks ago we rejoiced at what was being called here a victory at Shiloh, in Tennessee, but the loss of General Johnston is a blow. Casualties were horrible on both sides, and all I could think of when I heard them was to give thanks that Preston was nowhere near Tennessee or Mississippi. The loss of Fort Pulaski leaves Savannah vulnerable, but what is one more vulnerability with all that is happening? No one I have spoken with believes that General McClellan will capture Richmond.

The Union blockade has resulted in shortages of nearly everything. I was so relieved when spring arrived because we shivered for much of the winter. Even oak for the fireplaces was in short supply, and the prices for what was available outrageous. If I had not been so chilled I would have laughed, knowing how much oak surrounded us in Beaufort. At least that is one discomfort that you and Missma should not be suffering at the Lodge.

What a joyous day it will be when this war ends and we are all reunited, as God intends us to be. It is the thought that keeps me going.

All my love, Mother

• • •

May 31, 1862
Somewhere near Richmond

Dear Brother:

I hope you get my letter. This war sure has turned everything upside down. You at the Lodge with Missma, Mother in Charleston, and me here in the boondocks of Virginia. I wrote you a long letter back in January when we were in winter quarters at Centreville. The boys and I built some huts there because tents are no match for winter up here. But I thought of more things to tell you, so I put the letter in my haversack when we moved to Blackburn's Ford and on the way I slipped on a log crossing a creek and the letter was ruined. My friends in the fighting 2nd will not turn loose of that one. My friend Lewis says they will put on my gravestone "He fell in the creek."

We are on the march again now that spring is here. I am glad because the sooner we march the sooner this war will end. Thanks to General McClellan, the one they call Little Mac, we are getting a fine tour of the swamps around Richmond. Little Mac aims to take our capital, but General Lee has other ideas and he is ten times the general that Little Mac will ever be.

Our Captain Cuthbert is a fine man and sees to it we have fair shelter and enough food to fill our bellies. Thanks to him, we get some Charleston papers a week or two after they are published. The Captain picks out things he thinks will interest us and reads to us around the fire at night. Some of the boys get sleepy, and a time or two I've had trouble keeping my eyes open, but usually I stay awake. A few days ago he read a poem from Henry Timrod published in The Charleston Mercury. I liked it so much I asked if I could have it and he tore it from the paper then and there. I keep it in my kepi, and I hope it puts as much steel in your spine as it did mine. He wrote:

> At last, we are a nation among nations; and the world
> Shall soon behold in many a distant port

Another flag unfurled!
All the boys cheered as the Captain read that line from the paper.

Brother, I have killed a man. It happened on Nine Mile Road
near a place called Fair Oaks. I was not expecting him as his unit
was in retreat and we had taken no enemy fire that morning. I have
wondered since if he was lost. He stepped from behind a tree to
draw a clear bead on me. He fired and I heard that bullet come right
past my ear. It is strange what you think about at a time like that
because I remember thinking that if he had hit me we both would
have scars on our ears, yours courtesy of Cousin Gabe and mine
thanks to a Yankee that is now dead. We stood there looking at each
other. When I shot I knew he was going to die and he knew it too.
He did not suffer. At Manassas I fired at lots of Yankees, and I may
have killed a few, but I never knew for sure. Knowing for sure makes
it different. I have had a few nightmares. I see him standing there
waiting for my bullet. We are back in tents now, so only Lewis hears
me. The boys told me to take something for a souvenir, but I did
not want one. I only wanted to know his name. Edward Lacey from
Lebanon, Pa.

We are moving out again so I will close. I hope to avoid creeks
from now on so you will get this letter. Tell Missma I will write to
her soon.

Your Brother, Preston

p.s. Do not tell Mother about Edward Lacey. It will upset her and
I will tell her myself.

• • •

May 24, 1862
The Lodge

Dear Anna:

I write to once again reassure you that Carter and I are well and in
good spirits. You and I can both be proud of what a fine, responsible
man he is becoming. We lack here only things that absolutely must
be purchased. My stock of tea is low, and if I cannot find a source of
it I will miss it. We are never hungry, thanks to Carter's skill at hunting and fishing. When the corn, potatoes, peas and tomatoes come
in, we shall eat as well as ever.

I must tell you about the missionaries who arrived at the Boykin place, which is now called Three Pines. They are from Philadelphia, a woman who may be about your age and her daughter, two years older than Carter. I have yet to meet the mother, but the daughter has been here several times. She is a stunning creature and becoming a woman in every sense. To report that our boy is smitten would not do justice to the puppy love I see in his eyes every time they are together, which has been frequently of late because he has taught her to swim. Who can doubt the need for it here, but I am somewhat surprised her mother consented to her consorting with the "rebels," as they call us here. I surmise both mother and daughter are abolitionist to the core, but perhaps I am prejudging, as I have not met the mother, who is teaching the Negro children on Three Pines. I wonder if either of them had ever spoken to a black person before they arrived. I am confident the swimming lessons were all quite chaste and innocent, and the girl, Sonja, gives no sign of returning his ardor. Hopefully, the poor boy will not get his heart broken, as did you and I and everyone else who has lived and loved.

The surgery described in your last letter must have been a major ordeal. How fortunate you were to find a skilled doctor like James Carter to perform it, and how brave you were to risk it. At least it is now behind you. I quite agree with Dr. Carter that you should not travel. Even if the Union would assure safe passage to Beaufort, you cannot risk the trip. Your health is too important, and the potential complications he outlined dire should any come to pass. Stay where you are until the medical situation is resolved and you have completely recovered your strength. We miss you, of course, but Daniel and Abigail would as well.

I pray you have forgiven me for all of this, and that I can one day again occupy a warm place in your heart.

Fondly, Missma

CHAPTER 24

By late June, a summer swelter settled over the Lowcountry, pressing down on fields and marshes like a suffocating gravity. Palmetto fronds drooped, oleanders sagged. Spanish moss dripped like candle wax from lethargic oaks. Buds of crepe myrtles could not muster energy to bloom. The air hung heavy with humidity, opaque, as if some unseen fire was smoldering, emitting haze to replace oxygen. Carter seized the morning hours for his work in the garden. He picked early corn and planted peas. The peas would vine along the corn stalks for harvest in the fall.

Missma confronted, for the first time since leaving Beaufort, a dwindling supply of her nightly tonic. After giving Reggie his reading lesson, she asked if he had seen Daddy August.

"Yes'um."

She rose from the table, walked behind her partition, and emerged with the gallon jug, eyeing him playfully. "Reggie, do you know what this is?"

"Licker?"

"Yes, licker. It helps me sleep, and Daddy August makes it. If I give you something to pay him with, could you get this bottle refilled?"

"Yes'um. I try."

"Good. I have enough to last another week." She handed him a small gold coin. "This should be sufficient. Please put it in a safe place."

Days after the visit to Signal Oak, Sonja appeared at the Lodge to invite Carter and Missma to Three Pines. "Mother wishes to thank you for the fish and for teaching me to swim. She asks that you come tomorrow, in the morning when it is cool. Around ten?"

Missma said, "We have no clock here, but mid-morning should suit us all. Tell her we accept her kind invitation."

The walk to Three Pines taxed Missma's strength. Although Carter kept the pace leisurely, she arrived out of breath and looking her eighty-one years. Christina greeted them on the porch, where the table had been set with tea cups, slices of pound cake and a bowl of fresh strawberries. Christina's smile was tight, her manner formal. When they were seated, Missma recovering her breath and Carter fixing his eyes on the door in expectation of Sonja emerging, Christina said, "Safe to say this time last year none of us could have anticipated being where we find ourselves." Her hands were folded primly in her lap. It was unclear if she expected a reply.

"That is true for my grandson," Missma said. "I, on the other hand, saw this war coming and always assumed I would one day be 'in residence' at the Lodge."

Christina was about to respond when Sonja walked out of the house to join them. She spoke to Missma but her greeting to Carter was merely a glance.

"Hello, dear," Christina said. Then, turning back to Missma, she said, "And how could you be certain war would come? The Union did everything in its power to avoid it."

Missma gave out with a breathy 'hmmm.' "And imbeciles like Barnwell Rhett did everything they could to provoke it."

"I am not familiar with Mr. Rhett," Christina said.

"Be glad," said Missma.

"Is he not our cousin?" asked Carter.

"Everyone in Beaufort is our cousin, or was," she said. "How is the teaching? Do you find the Negroes eager learners?"

"Some, certainly," said Christina. "But whenever I am inclined toward frustration, I remind myself that they have never in their lives sat for classroom instruction."

"Did you teach them in Philadelphia?" Missma asked.

"We farmed there. There were no contrabands."

"I see. We farm here, as you know, but without contrabands, as you call them, not an acre of cotton would be planted."

Christina's shoulders squared. "But surely slavery is too high a price to pay for cotton."

"I do not defend slavery," said Missma. "It is abhorrent, and if any good comes from this war the practice will end forever."

"So you are an abolitionist?"

Missma paused before answering. Carter recognized that certain look she got when she strained to be diplomatic. "Am I an abolitionist?" she repeated. "I am an old woman about to be abolished myself. I live in fear that my grandson will be abolished on some battlefield in Virginia. It is certain that life here in Beaufort and my home as I knew them have been abolished. A life I loved is no more, and it will be generations before the South recovers from this war. If by abolitionist, you mean freeing the slaves, we did that years ago and I would do so now. If you mean losing everything dear to me in life, then no, I am not an abolitionist."

Christina cleared her throat while reaching for strawberries. "Yes, well, we want to thank you for the fish Carter has brought. And for teaching Sonja to swim, which gives us both peace of mind as far as the water is concerned. She gave me my first lesson yesterday. I will have to get used to mud between my toes."

"There are other dangers," said Missma. "Other than the water. Women your age and her age must be careful."

"Mr. Pierce has been explicit on that point."

Missma asked, "Do you intend to stay?"

Christina and Sonja exchanged a glance. "It depends," said Christina. "On whether I continue to feel I am contributing to the betterment of these poor people. And on whether Sonja's education is suffering. We brought books and can get more . . . still."

Missma said, "A distinct advantage of being a blockader instead of the blockaded."

"Perhaps we can share some of my books," Sonja said.

"Yes," said Carter, a bit too quickly.

"That is very kind," Missma said.

On their return to the Lodge, Missma asked him if he had mentioned Signal Oak to Sonja.

"No, ma'am."

"Good. And you must not."

• • •

Carter decided to go with Reggie in search of Daddy August. He hadn't walked in town in months, and he wondered if any changes he noted should be reported to Gabriel. As the boys sailed together, Carter contemplated a confrontation with Daddy August about the destruction in his home, of his mother's things. He would not have considered such a thing six months ago, but life at the Lodge, the daily exertions required there, and his emanation into puberty had combined to set an edge.

They had no trouble finding Daddy August. The location of his still was known to all in the community, black and white. Reggie told Carter that Daddy August drank much of what he made; that from mid-to-late afternoon, he sat in a cane chair under a tree at the edge of woods just outside town and that from the chair he took orders, collected money and delivered what he made. After sunset, he disappeared into the woods to supervise production of his white lightning, which he called "Daddy's debil brew."

The boys approached the cane chair.

Daddy August called to them in a loud voice, slightly slurred. "What chu comin' here fuh? You boys ain' old 'nuff fuh Daddy's debil brew."

When they arrived at the cane chair, where Daddy August sat like an African potentate, Carter stared at him evenly as if to say, 'I know what you did and you know what you did, and how could you have done that to us?' But he realized any confrontation with Daddy August in his condition was likely to cost Missma.

Reggie held out the jug. "Miz Martha needs some mo'."

He ignored Carter, whom he saw almost every day of the boy's life and had not seen since the moment on the stairs after he destroyed Anna's vanity. He said to Reggie, "You mean dat old goat still kickin'? I sure she be dead now. You bring Daddy some money?"

"They say pay when delivered."

"Dey do?" Daddy August roared. "Well, we gots some special rules where de enemy goes. See, the niggas what buy from me is my friends, and the soldiers what buy from me dey workin' for Massa Abraham, so dey pay on delivery. But you buyin' for the enemy. Yep, special rules. Pay in advance. Can't trust no enemy. You bring de old goat's money, boy?"

Reggie reached into his pocket and extracted Missma's small gold coin. He handed it over, where it disappeared into Daddy August's large, extended palm.

"So," said Daddy August, "we got ourselves a bidness deal, sho 'nuff. I got to make me a batch or two for my regulars, but you come back in three days and we see what we kin do. Yep. Three days. Den we see."

Reggie was alone when he returned. Later, he reported to Carter and Missma that Daddy August said he had thought it over and concluded that it would be unpatriotic for him to supply Missma with his brew. "Comfort to de enemy," he called it. When Reggie asked about the gold coin, Daddy August laughed, saying he could not remember getting any coin from Reggie.

• • •

"It is time," said Missma, "for you to begin reading *A Tale of Two Cities*." It was evening. Carter had brought chairs onto the porch, where they sat in darkness. Around them throbbed the night sounds of the marsh and woods; bullfrogs and cicadas and owls and crickets. The humid night air was at last breaking the day's heat.

"I thought you said I was too young."

"You were. Months like these age all of us quickly. It is very much a book about what you are going through now."

"A war?"

"Do you know anything about the French Revolution?"

"When they cut off heads?"

She nodded, but he could not see her in the darkness. "A civil war, but mostly in Paris. The rich aristocracy starved the peasants past a breaking point. The people rose up and executed royalty and all those who were perceived to have sided with the king."

"What are the two cities? Paris must be one."

"London. As you read it, think of London as the North. New York, Philadelphia, Boston."

"And Beaufort is Paris?"

"Beaufort is Paris. There are differences, of course, and when you find those we can discuss them. It's not all conflict. There is also romance, but I don't suppose that interests you." She grinned into the darkness.

"Romance is . . . alright."

"One day you will understand it better than you do now."

"Maybe it will be like *A Tale of Two Cities*. Maybe I will understand it sooner."

"Perhaps. You are getting to that certain age where things begin to happen."

"I wish I knew more about girls."

"That is not a conversation a boy your age usually has with his grandmother. We will look for another time when you and Gabriel can talk. He knows everything you will need to know, and I fear much more."

Neither spoke for several minutes. The bullfrogs and cicadas reached their evening crescendo.

Missma said, "Sonja is a very pretty girl. And pretty girls can have a powerful effect on boys your age. Is she nice to you?"

"She treats me like Preston did. Like a little brother."

"That may change, or it may not. When I was her age, about fourteen, a boy who lived nearby was sweet on me. He must have been about your age. I paid no attention to him. He didn't exist as far as I was concerned. Then one day, it seemed like overnight, he was a head taller than me, and our ages were not important. That can happen."

"Did you kiss him?"

"As a matter of fact, he kissed me."

"Oh. Did you like it?"

"Very much. I wondered why he waited so long."

• • •

Just after sunrise the next morning, he saw Sonja come through the break, headed for the creek. She was alone, carrying her bottle and her towel. He ran into the Lodge as a first response to temptation. He told himself he would not follow. Sonja was a friend and he would not spy on a friend. He would not.

Then, he grabbed the field glasses and followed.

CHAPTER 25

In October, Carter stooped to pick up oysters. He stood knee-deep in cool water and selected large singles from the waterline of his favorite oyster bed, his first harvest of the season. Missma said that morning she believed she could make it through the winter and the war, however long it lasted, if she could get fresh oysters. He took a knife from his pocket, shook the shell vigorously to remove some clinging mud, then pried open an oyster. He brought it to his nose. If there was disease or infection, he would smell it. But the smell was perfect, a briny blend of all he loved about the great salt marsh. Missma would be pleased.

That evening, after eating oysters both roasted and raw, they were asleep when Soot began to bark and a familiar voice accompanied loud pounding. "Do not panic," the voice said. "It's your favorite rebel."

Gabriel Heyward, dressed in dark clothing with a hat slouched over his eyes, entered carrying a saddlebag.

Carter rubbed his eyes. "Cousin Gabe. What time is it?"

"After midnight."

They heard Missma rising. Carter kindled the banked fire. As the flames rose, Gabriel's shadow played eerily upon the wall, like the apparition he seemed at this sudden intrusion. Missma emerged from behind her partition, cinching her robe as she stepped cautiously toward them.

"Sorry to bust in on you, Granny," Gabe said. "Urgent business and I don't have much time. I brought some things." He set the saddlebag on the table, extracting from it a pouch of tea, a bag of sugar, a jar of molasses, a metal tin and a package wrapped in heavy brown paper. "Dried beef," he said, "and some lamp oil."

The sight of the tea brought Missma fully awake. "I may have to revise my opinion of you," she said, picking up the pouch, opening it, and inhaling. "I have never smelled anything so wonderful. I'll heat some water."

Gabriel said, "Here's the situation. We have some Negroes that pass us information from time to time. They slip through the lines to visit their people that came with us when the Yankees arrived. Conjugal visits."

"What's that?" Carter asked.

"Granny can explain it when I leave."

Missma said over her shoulder, "Explain it now. He's at an age when he needs to know that and more."

Gabriel said, "They sleep together. Got it?"

"Yes," Carter said after a moment's hesitation.

"The information we get from them has been hit and miss. Usually what they tell us is useless and often just plain wrong. We have to weigh everything against the possibility they have turned on us, or the Yankees have planted a story to throw us off. Those boys are not stupid. Yesterday, two Negroes showed up to pay their monthly respects, if I may put it that way. One claims that several weeks ago he was recruited to work on toting materials for a big barge being built at Hilton Head, and that another barge was already completed beside it. That means most likely that they are getting ready to bring some artillery our way and these barges will haul it. He said all the talk among the soldiers is about a 'thing' that gets under way on the night of the 21st. The other Negro confirmed that something is getting ready to happen. The troops have been told to prepare three days cooked rations and to bring ten days raw rations with them. He claims no one knows the destination, but they assume it is the railroad."

Missma brought cups to the table. "Tea?"

Gabriel nodded.

Missma said, "We have no calendar. What is the date?"

"October 15, so time is short. Here is what we need from you. If this is really in the works, they will be moving troops, either up-river to leave from Beaufort or down-river to mass at Hilton Head. If it's Beaufort, we know they are headed our way. If it's Hilton Head, they may have a target in or around Savannah, but they could also be looking to bring the big guns up the Broad River. You have the catbird view from here. We need to know who is going where, and time may be short to get word to us. Try to get to Signal Oak as soon as you see a trend. A transport or two one way or the other is not a trend. If this thing is what the Negroes described, the Yankees will be doing some major moving."

Missma asked, "Why not just assume they are after the railroad?"

"Good question, and the answer is that most of our boys are stationed at Savannah and Charleston and transporting enough of them here to defend against a major attack is a pretty big operation. Besides, it ties up the railroad when it could be hauling supplies."

The Lodge fell silent as Gabriel and Missma sipped tea.

"Have you seen Mother?" Carter asked.

"Not in several weeks. They are still considering a move to Columbia."

"Can you spend the night?"

"I wish. I have to get back across the Coosaw before sunrise or risk spending the rest of this war as a guest of Lincoln, and that would occasion mass hysteria among the lovelies of Charleston."

Missma said, "If only you could develop some confidence."

"I'm working hard at it, Granny."

"Before you go, I need a favor you are uniquely qualified to perform. Carter, would you leave us for a moment?"

Gabriel said, "My horse needs something to eat. He has a long night ahead."

Carter left them seated at the table, wondering why he was asked to leave. Minutes later Gabriel emerged, the empty saddlebag slung over his shoulder.

Near the lean-to that housed Sunset, Gabriel's horse grazed.

"Is there bad news?" Carter asked. "Has something happened to Mother or Preston?"

"Nothing like that," Gabriel said. "Tell me about this girl."

"Sonja?"

"Nice name. What is that?"

"Swedish. She's nice."

"Granny says she's a looker. She wants me to have a talk with you about your pecker."

"My . . . pecker?"

"That's what we mostly call it in the Dragoons. You know what I mean?"

"Yeah, I know."

The night was dark, each able to the see the other's silhouette.

"Does this Sonja make your pecker stand at attention when you think about her?"

"I guess."

"Good. That means you're on the right track. It's none of my business what you two do, but it might help to know if you have had . . . contact with her."

"I taught her to swim."

Gabriel smiled, a gesture barely visible to Carter. "Now here is what you need to know that you may not know. Women bleed between their legs, from an opening your pecker is going to want to enter and spend time in. It's called a vagina. Between you and me, it's a heavenly place that can't be described or appreciated until you get there. Can I assume you have never seen such an opening?"

Carter glanced down.

"Thought not. The bleeding comes monthly, and the women call it their troubles. It lasts for about five days, and you have no way of knowing when it will start or end. You must rely on her for that, and she better be right because if she's not, or if she's lying, as some do, your time in the heavenly place is going to result in a Carter Junior before you want one. Are we clear?"

"How do you avoid Carter Junior?"

Gabriel dug into his pocket and pulled out a flat, squared piece of paper. He reached for Carter's hand and pressed it into his palm. "I never go anywhere without this, but I sure as hell won't need it tonight." he said. "Slip it over your pecker when the time comes. It may be too big, but maybe not. It's called a condom. Sometimes the ladies will suggest a French Shield. I would stay away from those unless you lose this."

133

Gabriel pulled his horse's head up and swung into the saddle. "Long ride ahead. If you have to go to Signal Oak at night, take something on fire you can wave at us, a pine knot or a cloth. Wait for someone to come. We can't risk a note for something this important. And be careful."

"I will. Thanks, Cousin Gabe," Carter said, still holding the condom tightly in his sweaty palm.

Missma walked out of the Lodge onto the porch. "Thank you for these beautiful supplies," she said. "I really cannot pay for them."

"Compliments of Jefferson Davis, Granny. Take care of yourself."

Sitting on his mat by a lone candle, Carter unwrapped the condom and stared at it. He re-wrapped it, undressed and slipped beneath his mosquito netting, wedging the folded paper under his mat. He fell asleep absorbed in images of a mysterious blood.

For the next several days, he spent time on the porch, scanning up-river and down with his field glasses. Traffic on the water seemed as usual. He reasoned that a major military operation would require several days and concluded the information obtained from the Negroes must be wrong. But in early afternoon on the 21st, he trained his field glasses on a ship steaming down-river. It was a transport. He read the name emblazoned on the paddle wheel: *Boston*. Soldiers crowded the deck, standing at the railing or smoking in clusters. Another transport followed: *Ben Deford*. Next came *Patroon*, followed by *Uncas*. Next in line was *Marblehead*, a gunboat rather than a transport, but likewise teeming with soldiers.

He had seen enough. This was a trend if ever one sailed that river. He ran inside, told Missma what he had seen and that he must leave for Signal Oak. She insisted he take two legs of roast duck she had planned to serve for supper. He wrapped the duck legs in a cloth, stuffed them into a rucksack with the field glasses, and headed for the skiff, Soot at his heels. He remembered the instruction about fire, and he knew now that he could not reach Signal Oak in daylight. He returned to the Lodge. They had only a few matches left, so he deposited embers from the fireplace into the artillery shell cartridge used as a doorstop in Beaufort. He grabbed a handful of wood chips for kindling.

The wind blew out of the southeast, perfect for his sail up the Broad River, but first he must cross the Beaufort River to Archer's Creek, the narrow ribbon of water bisecting Parris Island. He tacked toward the mouth of that creek when, to his right, he saw another transport coming at him. He had not considered the possibility that the *Marblehead* was not the last transport to leave the wharf in Beaufort. He sailed just ahead of the ship, bobbing in its wake as he entered Archer's Creek. The crew had to have seen him, but it did not acknowledge his presence.

He believed the tide was high enough to avoid grounding in the creek but coming back it would be impossible. Even now he was forced to get out to push the craft at severe dogleg turns. He sank into mud to his knees. He fed chips into the artillery casing, as he could not afford for his fire source to die out. Mosquitoes fed this time of day, and he was besieged by hundreds whenever the wind slacked. By the time he entered the wider segment of the creek, he was winded.

Light on the Broad River was fading when he tacked to starboard and the sail filled. By the time he turned into Whale Branch, it was dark. The boat hugged the shoreline, perched on a delicate aquatic tightrope; too close meant grounding and further delay, while too far risked missing the island. He was relieved to make out the vague contours of Signal Oak ahead.

With the boat secured, he took out the cloth from his rucksack. He unwrapped the duck legs, broke some meat off for Soot, and devoured the rest. He tied the cloth to the end of a paddle and dipped a loose end into the shell casing. The oil from the roasted duck would aid ignition. When it flared, he waved the paddle overhead slowly from side to side three times, then doused it in the water.

He waited. The Whale Branch was utterly still. Minutes later he heard the splash of oars and wondered how anyone could have reached him so quickly, but the sound carried in the stillness and the canoe did not arrive for what felt to him a long time.

He heard Gabriel's voice. "How's your pecker, boy?" The canoe appeared out of the darkness and pulled alongside. Both lowered their voices to whispers as Carter briefed Gabriel on what he had seen. Gabriel listened intently, then emitted a low whistle.

"This is major. They are massing several thousand troops, not counting whatever they have mustered in Hilton Head or brought in by the ocean. Ten to one they are headed here tonight, meaning you best get the hell out of here."

"I know it won't make up for your friend Allen but maybe it will help."

"It's good work, cousin. I'm proud of you and I'm going to see you get a medal for this. Until then you can be sure you have the thanks of a whole lot of men behind me in those woods. Now get going."

His return was slowed by the same wind that made the trip to Signal Oak faster. He tacked repeatedly, taking advantage of every puff of breeze. When he entered the Broad River again, his progress was even slower. He looked for some object or landmark by which to measure his forward progress, but the shore was an amorphous mass of darkness and the sky was not much more.

Suddenly, from out of the gloom, he heard, "Who goes there?"

His cheeks flushed and he felt his pulse begin to race. He must think fast. He scanned the dark in the direction of the voice but saw nothing but night.

"Who goes there?" the voice demanded, louder and more insistent.

"A . . . fisherman," he managed to say, and in the same instant realized he had no fish on board. He felt for his cast net below him and eased it over the side, then pulled it back. At least he could show wet gear. He was sure these were Union soldiers.

"Drop anchor," the voice instructed. "We are coming to you."

As he stared, a skiff four times larger than his own emerged from the darkness. He saw Union markings, then made out several faces peering at him from over the gunwales. One held up a lantern, illuminating Carter, Soot and the boat's interior but blinding him to his view of them.

"Coming alongside," the voice said. "Secure a line."

Moments later, Lt. Newton Spruill lowered one leg into the skiff. Soot growled a low distrust until Carter ordered him to be quiet.

"Fishing, eh? Here? At this time of night?"

"Yes, sir."

"Catch anything?"

"Not yet, sir."

"You must be a rebel?"

"I am thirteen, sir."

"Where do you live? I thought all the rebels skedaddled."

"Cane Island, sir. I'm taking care of my grandmother. She was too sick to leave. I have to fish so we can eat, sir."

"I know that island. There is a woman and her daughter living there."

"Yes, sir."

"What is your name, boy?"

"Carter Barnwell, sir."

Spruill gazed around the boat, then called up. "Hand me that lantern."

He again inventoried the skiff, shining the lantern as if he expected stowaways. He spotted the shell casing. "What's that for?"

"I keep it for warmth. It can get cold out here at night. I put these chips in it to keep it going."

Spruill nodded reluctantly. Seemingly satisfied, he placed the lantern to his side, on the thwart opposite Carter.

"Let me see that haversack."

Carter handed it over.

Spruill extracted the field glasses. "Where did you get these?"

"A gift, sir, from my father, sir, before he died."

"When was that?"

"Just before the Yankees . . . the Union, arrived."

Spruill turned it over in his hands, holding it close to the lantern. He took particular interest in a flat spot between the lenses, rubbing his finger over it several times. "This is a good piece," he said. "A man could see a long way with these. Or a boy."

Carter did not respond.

136

"What do you use these for?"

"I have to hunt and fish, sir, like I said. These help me spot things in the marsh. I can look at patterns on the water and tell if there are fish below. Things like that."

"I have seen a pair like it recently. Would you like to know where?"

"Yes, sir."

"On a Confederate we captured." Spruill leaned forward, his knees touching Carter's. He held out the field glasses. "See that flat spot where the end of my finger is?"

"Yes, sir."

"The only difference between your glass and his is lettering in that spot. Want to guess what the letters are on his glass?"

"No, sir."

"C.S.A. Confederate States of America. What do you have to say about that?"

"Nothing, sir. Mine do not have C.S.A. on them."

"I can see that. Don't talk back to me, reb."

"Sorry, sir. I meant no disrespect."

Spruill reached for the cast net at Carter's feet, rubbing netting between his thumb and forefinger to confirm moisture. He examined the interior of the rucksack in the light of the lantern. At length he replaced the field glasses in the rucksack and handed it to Carter with a flick of his wrist. Then he said, "I'll make a full report of this, and I plan to check your story. I have my eye on you, boy. Is that clear?"

"Yes, sir. Clear, sir."

From the Union boat, a voice came down. "Lieutenant, we have more soundings to make. Best get moving."

Spruill picked up the lantern, gave Carter a long final look, and lifted himself back into the Union craft. When the line was untied, the larger skiff glided into the night.

CHAPTER 26

"We need pecans," Missma said. "Let's find those trees you told Sonja about."

They struck out for the woods. It was mid-November, a fine fall day at the peak of autumn splendor. Missma employed the walking stick Carter had cut and planed. Dry twigs snapped beneath their feet as they made their way from the creek's shallow crossing. When they stopped beneath the pecan tree, he became conscious of the total stillness in the air and a complete absence of sound. He set down the basket he brought to hold the harvest.

Missma stooped, picked up two pecans, removed a trace of clinging husk from one, then squeezed them together, cracking one. With her fingernail she extracted half the nut, popping it into her mouth. "Excellent," she declared. "This tree alone will take us through the winter."

As he began to gather the fallen pecans, she asked, "How are you finding *A Tale of Two Cities?*"

"They are in Paris now. It is more interesting. You never told me why you hate the British so much."

"I suppose this is as good a time as any. It is because of what they did to my dear father."

"He fought in the War for Independence, didn't he?"

"That he did. Did you know I was born on the very day we won our independence at Yorktown? October 19, 1781. I have always taken great pride in that fact. I tell folks the United States and I were born on the same day."

"Was your father like Cousin Gabe?"

Missma chuckled. "Lord, no. For one thing, he was married, something I'm not sure your cousin will ever be. For another, he suffered from wounds he received in the war."

"He was shot?"

"Much worse. He was nearly hacked to death by British sabers. That is why I loathe the British. To make you understand, I will need to give you some history. At the beginning of our revolution, Beaufort was divided between Tories, those loyal to England, and Patriots, who sought independence. Most towns in the South were that way. But in Beaufort, Tory sentiment was fueled by what its farmers and merchants felt to have been a raw deal cut in the First Continental Congress that met in Philadelphia during September and October 1774. To bring pressure on the British to consent to the colonies' independence, delegates to that first Congress agreed to a trade embargo. No products raised or manufactured in the colonies would be sold to the British. With our state's dependence on rice and the economic hardships that would flow from the inability to export it, the South Carolinians secured an exemption for rice from the embargo. Are you following so far?"

"Yes. But if South Carolina got an exemption, why would people in Beaufort be Tories?"

"An astute question, young man, and the answer is that in Beaufort we grew indigo, not rice, so our crops were embargoed. The delegates who negotiated the deal were rice people. So anyone in Beaufort who called himself or herself a Patriot had to back that patriotism with acceptance of economic calamity. Some were simply unwilling to pay that price, and those made up the significant Tory population in Beaufort.

"So we suffered as early as 1775, but the serious fighting did not begin until years later. Late in '78, I believe it was, a British general named Prevost captured Savannah and made plans to invade South Carolina. General Washington, bless his soul, realized we needed help and sent a good size force here under the command of a man named Lincoln, Benjamin Lincoln. But they didn't stop Prevost and Prevost didn't stop with Beaufort. When spring came, he moved his men toward Charleston, the real prize. They camped outside Charleston on Johns Island. But the Patriots were not about to surrender Charleston, which at that time was the state capital. General Lincoln moved his forces into and around the city, and Prevost, who had advanced to Charleston by land, now found himself outnumbered by a superior force. Worse for him, his retreat by land was blocked, meaning he would have to retreat by the inland water passages, a difficult if not impossible task.

"My father, Captain Robert Gibbes, was in the Patriot forces defending Charleston. He commanded the Beaufort Militia, attached to a larger company under the command of Captain John Matthews. Matthews owned a plantation on Johns Island not far from where Prevost's troops were dug in. To keep an eye on British movements, Father and Matthews encamped on plantations adjoining one owned by a man named Fentress, a distant cousin of ours. When Fentress learned that Patriot forces were stationed nearby, he invited the officers to dinner.

"Father told me Fentress's plantation was built in the grand Southern style, with majestic live oaks flanking a long road leading to the mansion. He and Matthews must have looked like father and son cantering down the lane, because Father was a mere eighteen years old and Matthews was thirty-five. Matthews was later elected governor. I notice you have stopped gathering pecans."

"I am listening with a feeling that something bad is going to happen at this dinner."

She stooped to pick up a cluster of nuts. "If I can work while I tell it, you can work while you listen. The dinner turned out fine as meals go. There was a war on, but this was a cousin who invited them. From the moment they arrived, their expectations were met. Fentress led them into the house with its grand dining room. That night, only three places were set, one at each end of a long mahogany table and one halfway between, taken by Father. Fentress toasted their health and Matthews, according to Father, said that he looked remarkably chipper for a man living hard by a host of British regulars. 'They won't bother me,' said Fentress. 'Now that General Lincoln is in town, I expect to wake up one fine morning to find the whole lot of those Redcoats gone south, and devil take them, too.' Oh, Fentress played his hand like a master.

"When Fentress asked Father how things were in Beaufort, Father related the hardship that the embargo was imposing on indigo growers like him. When Fentress mentioned rumors of smugglers protected by the British Navy once they reached Savannah, Father admitted that some of that went on and that it was almost impossible to stop. Fentress's idea of how to stop it was for the Patriots to win the war, and I have no doubt they all raised a glass of Madeira to that idea.

"After supper, over cigars and brandy, was when Fentress did his real work. The entire evening had been to set the stage for when Father and Captain Matthews were most relaxed. Fentress asked questions which must have sounded logical enough coming from a Patriot. As far as they were concerned, Fentress was a Patriot landowner with a large British force nearby, so it made sense for him to ask about what defenses were in place to protect his plantation. Matthews said he had about a hundred men at his own plantation, and that Father was in command of a unit of twenty-five at Campbell's Plantation, which was next door to Fentress's. Can you guess what happened next?"

"Fentress told the British."

"Father and Matthews had no sooner left by the front door than Fentress must have left by the back, mounted a saddled horse and rode toward Prevost's encampment.

"At dawn the next day, a low-lying mist covered the fields, and out of that mist came a company of British regulars. Matthews and his unit awoke to find themselves surrounded, their surrender demanded. Matthews complied.

"A mile away, a smaller British force appeared at Campbell's, where the Beaufort Militia was awakened by a banging on the front door and an urgent British voice. 'Captain Gibbes, I am Lieutenant William Rogers in His Majesty's service. You and your men come out without your weapons. We have you surrounded.' From inside, Father demanded to know what quarter would be extended if the Patriots laid down their arms. Rogers replied that no quarter would be given for rebels. 'Then we shall fight,' said Father. 'Men, defend yourself to the last.'"

Carter asked, "So he was wounded in the fight that followed?"

"Had that been the case, my view of the British would be quite different.

It was, after all, a war, and in war soldiers are wounded or killed. No, what happened on Johns Island that day was not war but deceit and treachery of the worst kind. Throughout the house, our boys cocked their muskets and took up positions at the windows. Rogers retreated to the edge of the mist. Moments later, a dozen Redcoats emerged from the haze, their rifles at the ready. From behind this front line, Rogers called out, 'I have reconsidered. Surrender and you shall have honorable quarter.'

"Father was suspicious of this sudden change of heart. He opened the door and stepped onto the wide piazza. 'How can I trust your offer of honorable quarter?' he demanded. 'By my word as an officer and a gentleman in the service of His Majesty' was Rogers' reply, at which point Father instructed his men to stand down. Rogers called out that they should come out and lay down their arms. On Rogers' word, Father ordered his men into the yard to stack arms. Naturally, the men did as they were told. Father drew his pistol and tossed it to the ground.

"Then Rogers yelled out, 'Ready, fire!' A dozen Patriots fell where they stood. Father's men scrambled for their weapons, but a new line of Redcoats replaced the first and cut them down. Rogers gave the order to charge, and from the mist forty British came with bayonets raised. Even now, so many decades later, I get furious at the treachery. So much for the word of an officer and a gentleman in His Majesty's service.

"Father was wounded like most of the rest. He said he felt his left shoulder explode. He fell back, stunned, but then dove to retrieve his pistol several feet away. At the second volley, bullets zipped overhead, and for a moment all he could think of was Fentress raising his glass to toast victory the night before. He reached the pistol, and his hand closed around the grip just as a bayonet pierced his side. He tried to raise the pistol, but a British boot kept his wrist pinned to the ground. The boot's owner thrust downward, bayoneting Father's back. The last thing he remembered was the heat of the fire in his left shoulder where the bullet entered, and a glimmer of relief as he saw several of his men disappear into the mist at full stride. At least, he thought as he lost consciousness, the massacre will not be total and some will live to tell what happened." She paused to pick up more pecans. "I do believe we are going to fill this basket." She cinched her shawl against the afternoon chill beginning to set in.

"Now for the romance part of the story. I know you will be interested in the romance."

He heard her but was busy gathering and did not answer.

"My mother, Eliza Elliot, lived with her father and sisters on Peaceful Retreat, a plantation several miles from Campbell's. She was the oldest of the seven Elliot daughters, with strict orders from their father to stay inside until Johns Island ceased to be a war zone. Word of the British treachery, spread by the few soldiers who escaped, shocked the Elliot family as it still shocks me today. Father was

141

a third cousin and had spent time at Peaceful Retreat in years before the war. Mother sent Isaac, a house servant, to Campbell's. The gruesome scene that greeted him there made him want to turn the buckboard around. Bodies lay everywhere. Even the horse pulling the buckboard shied at getting close. Isaac confessed to Mother that his one thought was to leave as soon as he could. He sensed the place was haunted, with ghosts hovering above the dead. Just when he thought they were all dead, he heard a low moan. He saw Father's lips move. Mud and blood caked his uniform. 'Lordy mercy,' said Isaac. 'Marse Robert, yuz alive.'

"Isaac put Father in the buckboard and carried him back to Peaceful Retreat. When they took him into the parlor and laid him on a sofa, Mother said she nearly fainted at the sight. But her shock was temporary, and within minutes she was preparing a bedroom upstairs. When he had been brought to it, she stripped his shirt and pants to assess the wounds. She gasped, counting seventeen, mostly in his chest and arms. With hot water she cleaned them, grateful for his sake that he had again lost consciousness. As she lingered over him, she thought of the times they had played hide and seek as children, of hayrides taken when her mother was still alive.

"The doctor arrived. He pronounced Father unlikely to survive due to the great risk of infection, internal bleeding, and probable unseen damage to vital organs. Mother held her opinion, convinced that Father's will to live could overcome his injuries. During the following week, she stayed at his bedside. She forced water into his mouth drop by drop. She wet his forehead when fever spiked his temperature. She changed his bandages and his sheets. On the day he opened his eyes and recognized her, she told me she wept. 'Eliza,' he whispered, but could say no more, falling back asleep.

"In a month, he took his first steps, leaning on her and grimacing in pain. As he grew stronger, he continued to lean on her, leading her to suspect he simply liked the intimacy of it, as did she. Without words, they were leaning on each other, as they would do for the forty-one years of their marriage."

In an oak tree near the pecan, two squirrels chased each other. "They are amusing themselves, waiting for us to leave so they can get back to business," Missma said. "Our basket is nearly full. Are you sure you will be able to carry it?"

"Yes, ma'am."

"I was perhaps six years old when I asked Father, for the first time, why he limped. He answered me somewhat vaguely. 'I was wounded in the war,' he said, wheezing from a lung not fully healed. I asked Mother, who provided a more detailed response. 'The most dishonorable conduct,' she said. 'As bad as his wounds were, he has never forgiven himself for the deaths of his men. He has felt guilt ever since.'

"I was too young to know what guilt was. Mother said it was the feeling that comes with doing something you should not. Shame. I asked if the British soldiers would feel shame for what they did to Father, and she said she would like to think some do, but that we will never know.

"As I grew older, I took over more of Father's care, partly because my two brothers and three sisters occupied more of Mother's time and energy. He was not an invalid, unable to move without assistance, but he had trouble dressing himself, with increasingly limited range of motion in his arms and shoulders. When I helped him with his shirt, I stared at the scars left by the bayonets, cursing the British. 'You must not be bitter,' Father counseled, but I asked how he could not be bitter. 'It was war. Those things happen in war,' he said, but I thought it was murder and said so.

"Father took my hand and pulled me to a chair beside him. His smile was so warm I remember it still. He told me that as he lay on the ground at Campbell's that day, he thought he was dying. He was sure of it. From what little he could see, he knew to a certainty some of his men had been killed. Each time he closed his eyes, he thought it was for the last time. When he opened them to see Isaac, he thought he was in heaven, and that Isaac had died and had come to greet him. He said that nothing that had happened since that awful day was anything he ever envisioned for his life. He called Mother an angel for caring for him day and night and an angel for marrying him, broken body and all. Then he told me I had been a joy beyond description and that he made it a habit to focus on what he had instead of what he lost. I will never forget that conversation. He was the sweetest of men, with every reason to be otherwise."

Missma looked skyward. "I believe it is about to turn colder. We have our quota. Let's leave some for the squirrels."

Carter picked up the basket with both hands.

"You are getting so strong," she said. "I don't think I could budge it."

"It is not too heavy, Missma."

"We can stop to rest on the way home." She smiled, but it was a rueful smile. "I guess the Lodge truly is home now."

They started back. He daydreamed as they walked, imagining himself wounded on a battlefield in Virginia and Sonja coming to rescue him. He said, "That was a great romance your father and mother had."

"One of the greatest." Then wistfully she added, "I had one, too. His name was Marc, but we will save that for another time."

CHAPTER 27

Christmas Day of 1862 dawned clear and bright at the Lodge, the air crisp enough to impart a holiday spirit despite its pale reflection of holidays past. Carter had invited Sonja for dinner, and she had promised to come after church. He built the fire higher than usual, both for its warmth and spiritual buoyancy. Missma spent the week leading up to it by making a wreath for the door out of holly trimmings, pine boughs and some ribbon she salvaged from an old dress. Pine boughs and cones also served as table decorations, and when warmed by the fire brought the aroma of the woods inside, where it mixed with the succulent vapors of a duck and a rabbit Missma was roasting.

In mid-afternoon they took their seats at the table. Spread before them were corn, peas, sweet potatoes, a bowl of shelled pecans, oysters on the half shell, candied apples, cornbread, and a smoked trout. The duck and rabbit were being kept warm, awaiting only Sonja's arrival. "I regret we have no wine," Missma said. "Otherwise I defy anyone to deny this is a holiday feast." Then, more reflectively, she said, "Our second Christmas here."

Three taps in quick succession signaled Sonja's arrival. They both recognized her knock. Carter opened the door. Her cheeks were roseate, a pretty natural blush from her hike to the Lodge in crisp air. Under her arm she held a bulky sack. When she had taken her seat at the table, setting the package at her feet, Missma asked that heads be bowed.

"Dear Lord, we ask your blessings on the food we are about to receive. We ask that You protect all our loved ones, wherever they are on this Christmas Day, and we pray for the day when we will all be united again. In the name of Your precious Son, our Savior, Amen."

"I am one lucky girl," Sonja said. "I get to eat two dinners today."

Missma gave her a wry smile. "Well, strictly speaking, what you are eating now is dinner, and what you will eat this evening at Three Pines is supper. Strictly speaking."

Sonja described the church service between ravenous bites of everything on the table. "Are those oysters?" she asked, pointing.

Carter said, "Try one. Like this." He squeezed a little fresh lemon juice on one, then tipped the shell to allow it to slide into his mouth.

"And since I mentioned Southern ways a moment ago," Missma said, "you should know that if things were . . . other than they are, he would be using a petite fork instead of the method you just observed."

"They look . . . slimy."

"They are an acquired taste," said Missma. "I could not stand them until I was a grown woman."

Sonja followed Carter's lead with the lemon wedge. She raised the half shell to her lips, eyed it skeptically, then tilted it as he had. When the oyster entered her mouth, she closed it. Her eyes widened. She bolted from the table, ran to the door, onto the porch and reached its edge just before heaving the concoction into the yard. When she returned sheepishly to the table, Missma and Carter were convulsed in laughter. "As I say," said Missma, struggling for breath, "it is an acquired taste."

When dinner ended, Missma told Sonja she had a little gift. "I am sorry that among the shortages here at the Lodge is a suitable wrapping." She handed her a set of knitted gloves, beige in color but with a dark pattern stitched into the points. Sonja slid them on. "They are beautiful," the girl said, and it was clear she meant it. "And I had none, so this is a wonderful surprise."

She picked up the package she had brought. Looking at Carter, she said, "These are hardly new, but hopefully they will fit." She brought out a cotton shirt and pants. "You have outgrown your clothes I noticed. Mother got these to distribute to the contrabands, but I figure they won't miss two pieces."

Carter held them up. "This is great. I brought one of Preston's shirts and pants with me and these will be fine until I'm big enough for those. Thank you. I have something, too. He left the table, reached under his sleeping mat, and withdrew a long stick. She rose to meet him as he was coming back.

"A gig!" she exclaimed. He handed it to her. She rubbed her hand over the surface, pausing near the larger end. She looked at him, then back to the gig. "Sonja," she said. He had carved her name in script into the wood.

"So we can keep ours straight," he mumbled, looking away.

"I love it," she said, hugging him before he could react. He blushed. "We must go again. I can't wait to try it out."

"It's hickory," he said. "I will last forever, but don't use it like a walking stick because it will dull the tip."

"I promise," she said, thanking them for the meal.

"Even the oysters?" Missma said with a wink.

When she had gone, Missma gave Carter his gift, hardly a surprise since he had seen her knitting a sweater for weeks. And it was much needed. He had grown in the past few months; his clothes no longer fit. Shoes would be high on his list of needs in the coming year.

"And now I have something for you," he said.

"What can it be? Will I like it?"

"I think you will." He left her, returning moments later with a jug of clear liquid.

She beamed when she saw it. "Halleluya!" she said. "How did you get it?"

"Reggie told Portia what Daddy August did. She has been buying a little at a time from him so he wouldn't get suspicious, then adding it back to your bottle." She removed the cork and dipped a little finger in, touched it to her lips and smiled.

"It's the best gift I could receive. I just may survive this war yet."

1863

CHAPTER 28

On January 1, 1863, Sonja and Christina arose early. In front of Three Pines, a hay wagon awaited. Jacob Roan had tied blue and red ribbons to the harnesses of the horses. Roan took the reins as the women seated themselves on hay bales in the wagon bed. Polk, Grace, Sparrow, Lark and a dozen others piled in, bringing with them bags of food and fruit. A holiday mood enveloped the wagon. With songs and hymns to accompany them, the trip to the ferry passed quickly. They reached it in time to board General Rufus Saxton's steamer, the *Flora*, carrying guests to his camp on the Beaufort River three miles below the town.

On board were other missionaries and hundreds of contrabands from plantations on the various islands. These were the true guests of honor, because today their legal status would change to "freedmen." By the time *Flora* and the other boats completed their shuttles to Camp Saxton, five thousand guests would be present to see and hear history made.

An impressive scene greeted them. A giant American flag served as a backdrop to the raised platform from which speeches would be made. Christina and Sonja, among the first to arrive, secured a front row view, from which they would miss nothing. Thousands of Negroes, dressed in their finest clothes, pressed inward to hear. The women wore an infinite variety of colorful headdresses, from understated shawls to opulent profusions fit for African queens. The men, adorned mostly in browns and blacks, displayed a splash of color in a neck scarf, a pocket rag or a jaunty headband on second hand hats.

Gen. Saxton welcomed all. Prayers and hymns followed. Speaker after speaker proclaimed the arrival of a new day. The man selected to read the Emancipation Proclamation was Dr. William H. Brisbane, a former plantation and slave owner who freed his slaves years before the war and took up the abolitionist cause. In the shadow of a mammoth tree that would from that day forward be known as Emancipation Oak, Dr. Brisbane intoned the words they had come to hear. These people were now free. What never could have been envisioned by their ancestors, torn from the shores of Angola and Ivory Coast, had come to pass.

Sonja, seated next to Laura Towne, whispered, "So all the slaves are now free?"

Towne shook her head discreetly. "The Proclamation applies only to slaves in rebel states within areas controlled by the Union. I've heard the actual number put at twenty thousand, with half of those right here in Beaufort."

Gen. Saxton introduced Colonel Thomas Higginson, who Saxton had recruited to command the first mustered company of black soldiers, designated as the 1st South Carolina Infantry. Higginson was white, and his pride in his new command was obvious. He and his men wore the unit's uniform—bright scarlet trousers with blue tunics. As he accepted the unit's colors, a gift from a Puritan church in New York, Christina and Sonja became conscious of a chorus building behind them. Rich voices blended as the words and tune spontaneously spread. The crowd of freedmen had begun to sing "My Country, 'tis of Thee." Song ended and composure restored, Col. Higginson introduced several black soldiers for short speeches to mark the occasion. They urged those in the crowd to join their ranks, as some would do. A poem and songs followed before Saxton invited all the missionaries up on stage to take generous applause for their efforts in Port Royal. Laura Towne was there, linking arms with Sonja and Christina on stage.

The formal program concluded, Towne, Christina and Sonja walked to Camp Saxton, where white tents were neatly arrayed. The pungent aroma of barbecue reached them. Pits had been dug for a dozen oxen, roasting on spits since early morning. Served with the beef were generous portions of molasses, hard bread and tobacco. Some freedmen had stayed away, unable to overcome long-standing fears of a trap that would see them transported to Cuba or some remoter destiny, but those who had made the journey were well rewarded.

The women did not eat because they had been invited to dinner and a dance with Gen. Saxton and his staff at Heyward House, his town headquarters, following the celebration.

At dinner, they were served by the same servants who would have attended them the day before, but there was a palpable change in the demeanor of those bustling food and beverages from the kitchen. It was as if the strains of "My Country, 'tis of Thee" had floated into town and lingered over the table.

After dinner, in the parlor, the missionaries exchanged accounts of life on their respective plantations. They shared teaching experiences. Sonja, again conscious that no one in the room was her age, nevertheless warmed to conversation with Hanna Morgan, age twenty-two and from Philadelphia. Their similar classroom challenges gave them a bond that bridged age. Hanna had just related a poem one of her students wrote when she stopped in mid-sentence to say, "Oh. There is Lt. Spruill." Sonja saw Hannah blush as Spruill approached. Sonja vaguely remembered him from the night the *Oriental* docked at Hilton Head, and the trip to Three Pines the following day.

"Good evening, ladies," he said, his eyes lingering on Sonja. "Just the person I wanted to see."

"Me?" Sonja asked.

"If memory serves, you and your mother are at Three Pines on Cane Island. I recently encountered a rebel boy fishing in the Broad River. He said he and his grandmother were living there. Do you know them?"

"Carter. Yes, I know him. They live near us."

Spruill nodded as though her confirmation carried significance. "I found it quite odd that he would be there at night."

"He sometimes brings us fresh fish."

"The contraband . . . eh, freedmen . . . can bring you fish, can they not?"

"But he fishes from a boat. The fish are different. Better."

"Well, I've been intending to pay you a visit to talk about it, but with the holidays I've been busy. I will ride out before too long. Your mother is well I take it?"

"Quite well, thank you. She's here if you would like to speak to her."

Spruill nodded to Hanna, excused himself and left the room. Sonja and Hanna joined a group gathered around Gen. Saxton, who was talking about a tax sale planned for the spring.

"In my judgment it is bad business," said Saxton to a group that included Towne and Christina. "I fear speculators."

Towne said, "As you know, General, I live at the Oaks. Is it possible it will be sold?"

"It's up to the Tax Commissioners. There are three of them. I intend to let my concerns be known in hopes changes can be made prior to the auction."

Christina asked, "And what precisely do they intend to auction?"

"As it stands now, all rebel property on which taxes have not been paid, which is all of it because the rebels aren't here to pay."

"Is that fair?"

Saxton smiled mischievously. "Fair? Probably not, but this is yet another price the rebellion must pay for Fort Sumter. But I worry that unless some restrictions are put in place, we will wake up to find all the land owned by people who live thousands of miles away, when it should be made available to those who live on it and work it."

"Exactly," Towne said. "Some of it should be sold to the freedmen."

Saxton agreed. "These large plantations should be broken up into smaller parcels that could be set aside for freedmen with a modest amount to invest. To be truly free they need to own the land they work."

Christina asked, "Could we submit a bid?" Her question surprised Sonja, who was thinking of Grace and Polk.

"I don't see why not," Saxton replied.

Towne said, "Speculators worry me greatly. We've come too far to let the poor freedmen be victimized by profiteers."

"We have come a long way," Saxton acknowledged. "Today's ceremony, for example. Unthinkable a few short years ago. But we would all make a mistake to believe the major questions about our black brethren have been answered, at least to the satisfaction of people who don't live and work with them daily, as we do."

"And what are those, General?" Christina asked.

"Let's be honest. Even among our abolitionist friends, there are reservations. Will the freedmen work productively in the economy that replaces slavery? Will they do for a wage what they were forced to do by threat of the lash? Many believe they are too docile for combat, so will they fight for their own freedom? Can they learn on the level of whites? These are the questions being asked. And I can tell you that many of my soldiers doubt these things. They are here to save the Union, and were that not their cause, they would be back at home in New England."

"We know they can learn," said Towne. "We see the evidence every day. And I believe they will fight if properly trained and paid as are white troops."

"Col. Higginson here shares your optimism, don't you Colonel?"

"I do indeed," said Higginson. "Did you see the pride in my regiment when the colors were presented today? Of course the test will come in combat. We are all aware of that. I relish the chance, and I think my men do as well."

Saxton said, "But you will admit there are those who predict they will cut and run."

Higginson, respectful of the senior officer who was responsible for placing him in this command, made a faint nod but said nothing.

Into this awkward pause, Towne injected, "There will always be the naysayers."

"And some of those naysayers make policy in Washington," replied Saxton. "Many are in Congress and the War Department. I have heard what we are doing here described as the Port Royal Experiment, and while I think the phrase a bit condescending, it does reflect popular skepticism. If it is an experiment, we must make certain the right results are reached. The future of the freedmen depends on it. And now, I believe I hear the strains of a cotillion. Shall we find our way to the dance floor?"

CHAPTER 29

"When is your birthday?" Sonja asked.

"Next month," Carter replied. They sat on the porch at Three Pines.

"I should get you a gift."

"You shouldn't bother with that."

"Isn't there anything you want?"

"I'd like the war to end. I need to see my mother, and for my brother to come home."

"I'm just a girl, not a magician."

He stretched his arms upward and placed his hands behind his head. "What I really want is for you to take a boat ride so you can use the gig I made for you."

"Wouldn't that be fun? I'll ask mother if I can go." Her eyes drifted toward the lane. "There's a rider coming."

Carter studied the uniformed rider and as he drew closer recognized Spruill, who dismounted, tying his mount to a hitching post by the porch. He tipped his hat to Sonja before looking directly at Carter. "I didn't expect to find you here."

Carter stood. "I was just leaving." As he started toward the Lodge, Spruill took his chair.

"A nice affair, Saxton's party."

"Yes, it was," Sonja agreed. "Let me see if Mother is inside."

"No rush," he said, watching Carter retreat.

At that instant Christina emerged onto the porch. "Hello, again," she said.

Spruill stood. "And a pleasure to see you."

As Sonja got up to leave, he said, "I was hoping you would be part of this discussion. Based on our conversation at General Saxton's I think you may be able to help."

When they were again seated, Spruill stated his business, speaking to Christina but with frequent sideways glances at Sonja. "As I mentioned to your daughter on New Year's Day, I was on patrol in the Broad River before Christmas when I came across that rebel boy fishing, the boy that just left your porch. He seemed to me to be quite nervous."

"I suppose," said Christina, "that being confronted by a Union officer would make one nervous. For a rebel, Carter seems nice enough and he certainly has been thoughtful in bringing us fish and game."

"But it wasn't just his demeanor that concerned me," Spruill said. "Fishing at night so far from this island seems odd, and then there was the matter of the field glasses." He related the capture of the Confederate field glasses the day before and the similarity of the one Carter owned. "True, the boy's glasses lacked the C.S.A. identifier, but for that they were identical. He said they were a gift from his father."

Christina glanced at Sonja before saying, "Naturally, we were surprised to find ourselves living next door to the enemy. Shocked, really. But they seem nice, all things considered. For rebels, I mean."

"What do they do over there?" he wanted to know.

Christina said, "Sonja, you can answer that better than I."

Sonja avoided eye contact with Spruill as she said, "The grandmother stays inside mostly. She reads a lot. She knits, and she fixes their food."

"And the boy?"

"He does everything else. He chops wood, hunts, fishes, tends the garden."

"I see," said Spruill. "And spends time here with you?"

Christina answered. "Not much. He taught her to swim, which was a great relief to me given that we are surrounded by water."

"And he defends the rebel cause, no doubt."

Sonja hesitated. "Not that I remember. He worries about his brother, fighting in Virginia."

"But surely he has made derogatory and insulting comments about President Lincoln."

"No."

"Really? I'm surprised. What can you tell me about his field glasses?"

Sonja looked puzzled. "Nothing. I've never seen field glasses there."

Christina spoke. "Has Carter done something wrong? Is he in some kind of trouble?"

"That's what I want to find out. This brother of his," said Spruill, again looking at Sonja, "what does Carter say about his brother's opinion of how the war is going?"

"I doubt he knows his brother's opinion. They are cut off here. They have no way of getting news, or if they do I don't hear of it."

"Has he ever mentioned joining the rebel army?"

"He's too young."

"That was not my question."

Christina injected, "With all due respect, Lieutenant, my daughter is not the enemy."

Spruill flashed a hesitant smile. "I meant no disrespect. I'm merely investigating something that struck me as suspicious. I apologize if I came on a bit strong."

"No," said Sonja evenly, "he's never said he intends to join the rebel army."

"You like this boy."

"As my mother says, they have been nice, and he's the only person here close to my age."

"Which is what?"

Sonja glanced at Christina before saying, "Fifteen."

"As I said, I have my suspicions about what he may be up to, so I did some checking. It may interest both of you to know that his cousin is Barnwell Rhett. Does that name mean anything to you?"

"His grandmother mentioned that name," Christina said.

Spruill steepled his fingers for added authority. "Barnwell Rhett is considered by many to be the instigator of the entire secessionist movement, the patron saint of rebels. That's the family your fisherman comes from. The entire clan should be hung for treason."

"Are there more questions?" Christina asked.

"A request. Would one or both of you conduct me to the property? I'd like to see where the rebels live."

Christina said, "Of course. We want to do all we can to help."

They led Spruill toward the Lodge, passing through the break, then alongside the garden, and arrived at the porch.

Spruill mounted the steps. When he knocked on the door, Soot barked madly from inside.

"Who is it?" demanded Missma.

"Lt. Newton Spruill, United States Navy."

Missma cracked open the door, shushing Soot. When she saw Sonja and Christina standing in the yard, she opened the door wider.

"Good afternoon, madam," Spruill said in a formal tone. "I would like to see your grandson."

"He's fishing. I don't expect him back for hours."

"But until a few minutes ago he was at Three Pines. Are you certain?"

"I'm certain he's not here. This is a one room cabin. I would know if he was here."

"I meant are you certain he's fishing. This seems like an odd time of day for it."

"Oh, do you fish?"

"Not really."

"Well, he does, and he feeds us by doing it, so if he's fishing now it makes sense to do so."

Spruill glanced back at Christina, who suppressed a grin. He said to Missma, "What can you tell me about the field glasses the boy owns."

"Nothing beyond the fact that he has them."

"Do you know where he got them?"

"No, do you?"

"I know only what he told me."

"And what was that?"

"I don't wish to reveal that at this time."

Missma said, "Whatever he told you is true because he's an honest Southern boy, but I have no idea."

Spruill looked around, taking in the whole Lodge with his scan. "I suppose your home used to be in town."

"Our home is still in town."

"Then on behalf of the Union let me thank you for making it so large and comfortable for our soldiers and sailors."

"When you get the bill, I hope you pay it. Is there anything else?"

Spruill turned without further comment and walked slowly down the steps toward Christina. Over his shoulder, he said to Missma, "That's all for now. Tell your grandson that I am watching him, and that I may be back."

"Watch him closely. You may learn to fish." She closed the door.

On their return to Three Pines, Spruill said, "A disagreeable woman."

"But you can hardly blame her, Lieutenant. To be in the twilight of her life and lose everything can't be easy."

"She should have thought of that before bringing all those Africans here. I will be leaving now," said Spruill. "Please keep your eyes and ears open. And I would appreciate it if you would report any activity that could aid the rebel cause."

Christina said, "We are devoted to the Union, Lieutenant."

Spruill mounted his horse, then said, "There is one other matter. From time to time we officers are urged to attend social functions. I am hopeful you, Miss Sunblad, would be willing to accompany me should the occasion arise."

Sonja, unprepared for this overture, looked downward, but Christina seemed to have anticipated it. "That is very kind, Lieutenant, but Sonja is too young. I wish her to be a bit older before accepting such invitations."

Spruill nodded. "I understand. Perhaps another time?"

"Perhaps," said Christina.

As Spruill rode off, Sonja asked, "Do you think Carter is in trouble?"

"I think Lt. Spruill is interested in more than a rebel boy fishing. Did you not notice how he looks at you? How he seemed to be watching your reactions when we went to the Lodge?"

"But he's a grown man."

"And you, my dear, are becoming a grown woman."

• • •

That night, Spruill wrote his sister.
January 21, 1863
Beaufort, S.C.

154

My Dear Hazel:

The plot here thickens and the traitorous pot begins to boil. You will recall my telling you of the rebel I apprehended on the river late last year. He claimed to be fishing. A likely story. I vowed to expose him, and today I made some clear strides in doing so. I traveled to an outpost called Three Pines. Really, I do not see how anyone inhabits this bog. The roads are mere paths that recent rains have turned to mud. Those infernal gnats were out in legions, making my trip there and back an ordeal. I muttered oaths too indelicate to be repeated here.

At Three Pines I met the missionaries assigned there to teach. A mother and daughter from, I believe they said, New Jersey, or somewhere up north. A nice enough pair, doing the Lord's work by bringing education to the savages. I made quite an impression on them in my uniform. The mother is a few years my senior, an attractive woman who, by every word and motion, sought my attentions. So blatant did her flirting become that I became embarrassed for her. And the daughter? She is a fetching woman-child that seemed to be competing with her mother for my favor. I suppose I should not fault them, as they have lived in virtual isolation for many months now, and the sight of a uniformed Union officer at their doorstep must have sent their poor, deprived hearts aflutter. Being a professional, I refused be drawn into their feline competition, and remained above the fray, although seeing the lengths to which they were willing to go to impress me did no damage to my ego.

I went to Three Pines because it borders the cabin where the rebels are holed up. This presented an opportunity for me to question the missionaries, who have lived next to them for nearly a year. They confirmed what I expected. The rebel boy and his grandmother are typical southerners, by and large loathsome people who cannot be trusted in even the smallest matters. Both women are convinced, as I am, that they are spies, and have promised me full cooperation in proving it. The boy rebel was not available for me to confront, but I did meet with the grandmother. Pardon my graphic metaphor, but one wonders how many serpents have suckled at those poisonous breasts. She put up a brave enough front at first, but after a question or two succumbed to the fact that she was no match for a superior intellect. Her answers were lies, and she knew I saw through them. It was pitiful, really.

This investigation has my full attention. The moment I acquire solid proof of felonious treason, I will be promoted (and it has been

155

hinted, jumped a rank or two). I believe my superiors are waking up to the fact that my talents have been sorely underutilized. Had my books, my "pearls" as Kemp called them, not been stolen from me, I would already have advanced. Your news about the aborted auction of the Beaufort library gave me a measure of satisfaction. I wish such wisdom had been on display here before it was shipped north. If it had been, the Spruill Indexing System would have by now guided countless readers to the proper resource. What has happened to the library since?

Only you can fully appreciate what I am about to write. Talking with the rebel grandmother, I saw her clearly formulating lies as she stood there, and in her eyes and on her face I saw the very same patterns I recognized from the face and eyes of "she who shall not be named." I do not know what further proof could be needed that these people are evil. They have all, individually and collectively, grown out of some primordial cesspool. Thank heaven for our New England sensibility, education and refinement.

Your loving brother, Newt.

CHAPTER 30

On February 5, 1863, Carter turned fourteen. He had grown three inches in six months. His voice had deepened into a baritone. Missma regretted having no gift. "It comes too soon after Christmas," she said. He told her he was giving himself a present: Sonja had promised to go gigging with him at Bay Point. She would try out the gig he gave her at Christmas. They would be gone all day and, if he had his way, all night, but he did not mention that last detail of the plan to either Missma or Sonja. Two realities he could not change argued against their going. First, the moon was full so less than ideal for gigging, and second, sailing in the dead of a Lowcountry winter risked chilly discomfort. But the day dawned unseasonably mild, and the moon? At least they would have plenty of light by which to navigate.

When Sonja appeared at the break in early afternoon, her mother came too. Christina insisted on details of this excursion, unlike any Carter and Sonja had taken before. Christina's consent would have been out of the question had the girl not developed into such a powerful swimmer, as Christina observed when Sonja taught her to swim. Christina's stroke would permit survival. Sonja's was competitive.

"You will return tonight?" Christina asked Carter.

"We will try," he said. "But I have sailed where we are going since I was ten, and sometimes the wind or weather make it impossible."

"And if that happens?"

"We will camp on the beach until morning. She'll be fine. I packed a tarp. Don't worry about her. About us." He could see doubt cloud Christina's face.

She said, "I cannot approve, and Carter it has nothing to do with you. I have every confidence with you in a boat on the water. But staying out all night is not appropriate. I'm sorry."

Sonja spoke. "He didn't say we would be gone all night. Only that it was possible. You wouldn't want us risking a return in bad weather, would you?"

"Of course not, which is why you shouldn't make this trip."

Sonja's tone hardened, with a hint of exasperation. It was one Carter had never heard her use with her mother. He wondered if she was like this when she arrived in South Carolina or whether her time here had changed her as he felt his experience at the Lodge changed him. "There is always a risk of weather on the water. That's one thing I've learned since coming here. If we worried about that risk, we would never go anywhere. Carter's very cautious. We'll be fine."

Christina placed her hands firmly on her hips as she addressed Sonja. "I will leave the decision up to you, but I am against it."

"I want to go. I'm going."

Christina, resigned, could not hide her lingering skepticism, but nodded soberly and kissed Sonja's cheek. "I know you will be sensible," she told her. "You are all I have. And you brought what you need? Extra clothes?"

"Yes, Mother. And my gig."

She turned to Carter for yet another assurance. "I'm afraid of that ocean, but you aren't going there, correct?"

"It's possible we will need to run along the shore, but we will never be out of the sight of land. That I can promise."

"Well, you are both braver than I would be, so there is nothing left for me to do but wish you good fishing and a safe return."

Carter and Sonja headed toward the boat. "So we're ready?" she asked.

"Missma likes having Soot with her, but today he is going with us."

He whistled for the dog, who ran ahead of them toward the boat. When the three arrived at the water's edge, she could see he had prepared. The tarp, cross-tied in the bottom of the skiff, bulged. His gig rested beside it.

"What's in there?" she asked, pointing to the tarp.

"Clothes, some food, matches, and dried wood. Kindling, in case we need to start a fire and everything on the beach is wet."

She smiled. "Oh, happy birthday."

"Thanks."

"Want to know what I'm giving you?"

"Do you want to tell me?"

"A big, fat flounder on the tip of my very own gig."

"I'll believe it when I see it," he said, grinning.

"Doubter. I'll show you. And I want to learn how to sail."

"No. You're a girl. Girls can't sail." He knew her well enough to tease her now.

She made a fist and hit him gently in the bicep, noticing that his muscles had grown with his height. "Will you teach me?"

"Take a seat in the bow. Soot, let's go."

The dog and the girl settled into the boat as he unfastened the line, shoved them off, and hopped aboard. She watched him, both because she wished to learn and because she admired the fluid ease with which he worked. So practiced was he at raising the sail, battening the boom, steering the tiller, and catching the wind that it seemed to her that he had trained the boat, and if he could train the boat, he could surely teach her.

Underway, she faced forward, the wind catching her hair. She tilted her face toward the sun. He studied her back, the outline of her set against the blue of the water. The day was as mild as dawn promised. They sailed south, toward

Bay Point. As they neared Hilton Head, they could see the Union pier, moored barges, soldiers and sailors walking along the waterfront. The boat hugged the opposite shore as the sun began to set to their right. "Time to anchor," he said.

He lowered the sail. From behind the tarp he pulled a clawed piece of metal tied to a rope. He dropped it overboard and the boat slowed, then stopped. Tiny waves purled against the side.

"So peaceful here," she said. "But I feel Nature's call."

Carter realized he had never addressed this particular issue. "There are three options," he said. "I can sail us to shore, toward those woods over there. Or you can hop into the water, but it's cold and then you'll be wet. Or you can use the front of the boat as you would use the outhouse. I won't look."

"Promise?"

"Did I let you sink last summer?"

"I trust you. Turn your head and plug your ears."

Later, they watched the sunset. As it disappeared below the horizon, purples and golds reflected off clouds gathered in the west. Soot slept in the bottom of the skiff, his muzzle on one paw.

"I can't believe I've been here for almost a year," she said. "The farm and Philadelphia seem so far away."

"Are you still miserable?"

"I suppose it's okay. I miss my friends."

"Did you have a sweetheart?"

"I was only fourteen."

"Is that too young to like a boy?"

"I suppose not, but no, I didn't have a sweetheart. I've never had one. Did you have one?"

She could see him grin in the waning twilight. "I'm only fourteen, and a few hours ago I was thirteen."

"I guess that's too young," she said, and he regretted his joke. "South Carolina is so different. If we hadn't come, I doubt I would believe a place like this exists."

"I've never been anywhere else," he said. "What is Philadelphia like?"

"A huge city. Big buildings. Horses and carriages everywhere and people in a rush."

"Are there Negroes?"

"Some, but not like here. And they have regular schools to go to."

"Are you sorry you came?"

She hesitated, but said no, she was not sorry. "I see real progress with my students. Some are learning as fast as I can teach them. That pleases me, it pleases Mother, and it must please God, too. And I learned to swim, and soon I will learn to sail. That never would have happened on the farm."

"Do you think He is on the side of the Yankees? God, I mean."

"I do. The scripture condemns slavery. What do you think?"

"I don't know. In my church they preach that God approves of slavery. But if God is with the Yankees, Preston could be in trouble."

"Maybe God protects the good people even when they're on the wrong side."

"I hope you're right. It's time to start gigging."

He raised the anchor and maneuvered the skiff to a hummock just off shore. The moon had not yet risen, so now was their best chance for flounder. He had a castnet, but he wanted what she wanted: to gig her first flounder with her new weapon. He had fished this hummock many times. He knew fish lay below. He impaled a pine knot on a metal pole wedged into the gunwale and lit it. She studied him. Soot wagged his tail in anticipation.

He reached for her arm and guided her to the spot where he stared into the water. "There," he whispered. "See the eye?"

She raised the gig high and thrust downward with a powerful extension of her right arm. She tried to raise the gig but could not.

"You got him!" he said. "Use both arms."

She placed her left hand farther down the shaft and lifted. From the water came a shimmering flounder, speared dead center to the body. She dropped it into the boat and removed the gig.

"You did great," he said. "This is so big it will feed us both. No point in catching fish we can't eat. Are you hungry?"

"Starving."

They landed on Bay Point. Far down the beach, they could see the remnants of Fort Beauregard and a Union signal tower projecting from it. They unloaded the boat. Using only their hands, they dug a hole in the beach. He told her to gather some palmetto fronds while he looked for wood.

"Why not use the kindling you brought?"

"Because we may need it if it rains."

She glanced skyward. The moon was just coming up, big and round and golden, like a heated coin perched on the edge of the world. "Looks like a beautiful night."

"But that can change quickly. You never know here."

When the fire blazed, he unfolded the tarp, extracting from a burlap sack a smaller sack. "Cornmeal," he explained. He returned to the boat, lifted the flounder from it, and kneeled to gut the fish. Next, he fileted it, washing each side in the water. He returned to the fire, bigger than needed to cook because with the sun down the temperature had dropped ten degrees. "We need to let it burn down some. Then, we eat."

Using two long sticks from the tarp, he pierced the filets and sprinkled the cornmeal.

"Won't the sticks catch fire?" she asked.

"Green wood. They will last just long enough."

Together they spread the tarp beside the fire. When the flame died down, they angled the fish over the coals. Sonja reclined, resting her head on her hand, her elbow on the tarp. "Look at that moon," she said.

"After we eat, I have something special planned," he said.

"Tell me."

"I'll have to show you. That way, if it doesn't work, I won't look stupid. We will need to get back in the boat. Is that okay?"

When the fish was done they placed the filets scale sides down in the sand and used their fingers to break off charred pieces of meal-encrusted flesh. When finished, she asked if they should give the hollowed out remains to Soot.

"He won't eat fish," Carter said. "I brought him something. Ready for the big adventure?"

"Yes."

"To the boat, then. Let's pack up."

He piloted into Port Royal Sound, then tacked northeast. It was the reverse of his course on the day he saw the Federal fleet come over the horizon. Now he was running toward Harbor Island. She was watching him, a small glimmer of anticipation evident on her face. He pretended not to notice, concentrating on his steering.

"We're in the ocean!" she exclaimed.

"We are." The full moon was higher, and a white carpet of light ran to it on top of the water.

"Now we will see," he said. He slacked the sail and the skiff slowed. He reached over the gunwale and pounded the side of the boat with his fist.

"What are you doing?"

"If it works, you'll see soon enough. Give it some time." He kept up the knocking in a rhythmic pattern.

She turned back toward the moon, her back to him. Suddenly, her arm shot out, pointing. "Look! Dolphin. Three of them."

He smiled, his teeth gleaming in the moonlight. He raised the sail, and the skiff caught the breeze.

"They're following," she said.

He steered the boat parallel to the shoreline. The dolphins ran a mere ten yards from the boat, as if racing them toward the moon. They dove and arced, leaving a sparkling wake. When they surfaced, the moonlight glistened from their backs and fins. She turned, wide-eyed, to say that she had never seen anything so beautiful. And he was thinking from his seat at the tiller that he too had never seen anything so beautiful, but he was not thinking of the dolphin, and he wanted to sail all night and he wanted that moment to never end.

But it did. The wind picked up, and he instinctively looked over his shoulder.

He tacked toward the beach as the dolphin ran on ahead.

"Why are we turning?" she called out.

He pointed to the horizon behind them. "Storm coming."

And coming fast. They were one hundred yards from shore. Lightning illuminated the thunderhead advancing toward them. For the moment, the moon was still shining brightly, but as the skiff reached the beach, the storm's lashing rains began. They dragged the boat onto the beach, soaked by the rain. He shouldered the bulky tarp and ran toward the tree line. By the light of the moon just before it was obscured by the storm, he bent and anchored a sapling which, when covered by the tarp, formed a rough tent closer to a lean-to. They ducked beneath it just as the pelting, nearly horizontal rain arrived. He was so focused on trying to keep the kindling from getting soaked that it took him a moment to realize she was laughing.

"What an adventure," she said, water beading on her face and flowing in tiny rivulets from her hair. "I'm soaked."

As the storm broke with full force upon the beach, Carter, Sonja and Soot peered out from beneath the tarp, shoulder to shoulder and drenched.

"Cold," she said.

He put his arm around her and moved closer. "Body heat," he said casually.

She scrunched toward him, turning her face to him. When the lightning flashed, it was as if her eyes had a blue current running through them.

She elbowed him. "Did you plan this storm?"

"No. I planned the dolphins."

"Oh. I thought you might have planned the storm so you could get me under this tarp."

"Why would I do that?"

"So you could kiss me."

After a pause, he said, "I want to kiss you, but I didn't plan the storm."

She turned over on her back, looking up at him. "Kiss me then."

"You don't mind?"

"Do I have to kiss you?" she sighed playfully.

As he leaned his head to kiss her, she raised hers to meet him. He had dreamed of this on countless nights. He opened his eyes in hopes of seeing her blue ones so close, but her eyes were closed. She put her arms around his head, moved her lips to his ear, and whispered, "Happy birthday."

"I've never kissed a girl," he said.

"And I have never kissed a rebel."

"But you have kissed?"

"Yes." Then she giggled. "My father. On the cheek. A long time ago. Kiss me again."

The storm passed as quickly as it came upon them. They walked to the beach, shivering as they dug a pit for the fire. The sand was wet only on the surface and an inch or two below. The dry sand beneath still retained some warmth from the day. He placed the kindling, lit a sliver, and blew until the sparks ignited. Wood, damp but usable, lay beneath the better sheltered trees. They crowded the fire, flames now chest high.

"You brought extra clothes," he said. "If they're dry, put them on and bring the wet things to me."

She walked to the tarp, changed behind it, and returned holding the clothes she was wearing minutes before. Spreading them out by the fire, she asked, "Are we here for the night?"

He looked at the sky. "Too dark to navigate. Unless it clears for the moon, we have no choice."

"Then I suppose we make the best of it. Mother will worry, but she must have heard the storm and will understand. We will need more wood."

"And we should move the tarp closer to the fire. It will be cold on this beach before sunup."

Over the next hour they repositioned the tarp, gathered wood, built up the fire. The clothes he wore were nearly dry. The front of the tarp opened toward the fire, while the back slanted down into the sand toward the tree line where they first took shelter. When this was done, they sat on the beach, huddled against each other.

With a twig she drew patterns in the sand. "I can't believe I am here," she said. "A year ago I was riding my horse across farms and now . . ."

"At least you are with your mother."

"What is your grandmother like when I am not there?"

"Missma doesn't change. She has her opinions." He paused before adding, "Like you."

"What's that supposed to mean?"

"You reminded me of her today. Just a little. When you told your mother you were coming on this trip."

With a pout he found charming, she said, "I'll be sixteen in a few months. That's old enough to make decisions like this. Besides, she practically kidnapped me to get me down here. I deserve the right to spend my time as I see fit."

"Funny you should say that. I must have been kidnapped, too, though I never thought of it until you said it."

"You see? We are both living with villains."

"If Missma's a villain, she's a nice one. Most of the time."

"Does she have an opinion of me?"

"She likes you, if that's what you mean. And she doesn't like everyone."

"Oh? Who does she dislike?

"Just be glad you are Swedish and not English."

"Why is that?"

"She has never forgiven them for what they did to her father, my great-grandfather, during the Revolution."

"Valley Forge isn't too far from Chadds Ford. We studied the Revolution in school."

"We lived it here." He related the story Missma had told them as they gathered pecans. "According to Missma, he never got over the loss of those men who laid down their rifles because he told them to."

"Lucky for you that those cousins lived nearby."

He had been staring at the sand as he related the story, but now turned his face to her. "Another cousin, from a different branch of the family, was the traitor who informed the British."

She was silent for a time before saying, "You know so much about who you are and I know so little about my history. My parents hadn't been in the country too long when I was born. Mother doesn't like to talk about Sweden because it reminds her of my father."

"I can't remember a time when I wasn't being taught about the family and about Beaufort. Some of it was boring, but they made sure I learned it."

Sonja nodded. Her pattern in the sand was a series of concentric circles. "Mother likes you, and that is saying something because you are a rebel."

"Does that matter to you?"

She sighed, "It did at first. I didn't know you. But I thought about it. You and your grandmother are victims of the war, just trying to survive. It's not like you are helping the rebels in some way."

"My brother is helping them."

"Should I hold that against you? That wouldn't be fair. I would not kiss your brother, you may be certain of that."

"You would like him."

"There must be lots of nice Southerners, because there are millions of them. But they can't enslave people and they can't break up the United States. No matter how nice they are, they are wrong and they are evil to do these things. You agree, don't you?"

"I don't know. I have never known anyone except Southerners until you moved to Three Pines. If all your friends and your family do and say certain things, and that's all you know, it's hard to call them all evil."

"Still, right is right. You see that. I know you do. You have a good heart."

"Is that why you kissed me?"

"That's one reason."

"What are the others?"

"Let me see. You taught me to swim, for one. You have helped us at the plantation by bringing us fish and game. You gave me a special Christmas present.

You brought me here." She threw him a sly grin. "And you are not bad looking. Oh, and you gave me another reason tonight. You are a good kisser."

He blushed faintly but the sun had now set and his face had become a silhouette.

"Am I a good kisser?" she asked.

"Like I said, my first time. I liked it a lot. I want to do it again."

"Oh, I forgot to tell you. There is a limit of two kisses per day."

"Whose rule is that?"

"Mine. And you have had your two."

As he tackled her gently and lowered her to the beach, she laughed as though he was tickling her. "That's a dumb rule," he said, "and we rebels don't obey dumb rules." He kissed her on the nose, and then on the mouth. She parted her lips slightly and returned the kiss. Soot watched them briefly before turning his stare back to the surf. She was on her back. He hovered over her, propped on his elbow, looking down.

"Mother has mentioned leaving," she said.

"What?"

"Nothing definite. Sometimes she talks about it."

"Why would she do that? I thought she liked teaching the Negroes."

"Yes, but she's been lonely. Think about it. Thanks to you, I have more of a life outside Three Pines than she does."

"That would be terrible. You can't leave."

"Don't panic. I see signs her social life may change."

"What signs?" His lips were an inch from hers.

"Promise not to tell?"

"I promise."

"Mr. Roan? The superintendent? I think she may be sweet on him. She denies it, but I see little signs. I think it would be good for her. Father isn't coming back, and she seems to be the only one who does not see that."

"You don't want to leave, do you?"

"No. Not now. Maybe she and Mr. Roan will start kissing."

"Maybe they already have."

"I doubt that. I would know."

"So will she know you and I have kissed?"

Sonja laughed. "Ha. Not at all. I can be very secretive when I want to be."

"So maybe you can think of something that will help bring them together."

"Play Cupid, you mean?"

"I guess."

"I will think about it. I hope this tax sale doesn't change everything."

"What tax sale?"

"Mother and I went to a big celebration last month. I told you about it."

"When they read that proclamation?"

"The Emancipation Proclamation. Yes, that's the one. Everyone there was talking about a tax sale of rebel property. I suppose since they all left no one has paid their taxes."

"When is it?"

"March. Sometime in March."

"What does that have to do with you?"

"Three Pines will be put up for auction just like the rest of the farms. The new owner could decide to close it, or to live in it, meaning we would have to move. There is even talk of places like it being bought by the freedmen."

"So our house in town might be auctioned?"

"It's possible."

"And the Lodge?"

"That, too."

"I don't want anything to change."

"Out of our hands, and up to God." She breathed deeply and he felt her chest swell beneath him. "I told you a secret about my mother being sweet on Mr. Roan. Now you tell me one. Something you have never told anyone."

His mind flashed to watching her bathe and the trips to Signal Oak. After hesitating, he said, "I'm not sure I should tell you this."

"Why? Is it about me?"

"Do you promise not to tell anyone?"

"Of course."

"It's about Preston. He killed a man. A Yankee soldier in Virginia."

She was silent for a moment, then asked, "How did you find out?"

He was glad he anticipated this question, and replied, "It happened when we were still getting mail."

"War is so horrible. But so is slavery. I feel sure your brother must be very proud of himself."

"No. He learned the man's name, but I've forgotten it. It was early in the war."

"How do you feel about it?"

"He told me before he left that he would do what was asked of him. I guess we all do, and that soldier, whatever his name, could just as easily shot Preston."

"I don't believe you could kill a man. Even a soldier in a war."

He felt the puff of her breath against his lips. "Why do you say that?"

"Like I said, you have a good heart. Do you think you could kill a man?"

"I . . . don't know."

She rolled onto her side. He put his arm around her and pulled her close. She soon fell asleep, while he stared at her profile, inhaling her scent, unwilling to let go of the magic this day brought. He pushed from his thoughts his shameful spying while she bathed, his service to the rebel cause for which she had so little tolerance, because to dwell on them would bring on his inexplicable desire to confess, and to confess risked the joy he felt wrapped around her. Later, he told himself. Another day.

CHAPTER 31

Newton Spruill rode down the main road leading to Three Pines. The Lowcountry bloomed in early April splendor. He passed long tendrils of lavender wisteria twining along fences, the aroma seductive even at this distance. Dogwoods and wild azaleas populated the woods, their delicate whites and pinks set off against the verdant evergreens hosting them. He passed an uncultivated field radiating a blue tinge, loaned for a few weeks by wild toadflax. He cursed this abundance, not because it lacked appeal to the eyes and olfactory, but because with this profusion came pollen, which aggravated his allergies. At one point he began sneezing so violently his horse shied.

He tried to ignore his irritation in favor of his purpose in making this trip. If all went well, he would impress Christina and Sonja, especially the daughter, who he had decided was a flower perfect for picking. That metaphor occurred to him because he spotted in a ditch two matched white Easter lilies. He halted his horse, climbed down, stepped into the ditch and picked them, careful not to disturb the gold-tipped stamens. Women love flowers, he reminded himself, and they love those who give them. He climbed back into the saddle. With one hand he held the lilies and with the other the handkerchief used to blot his running nose and watering eyes.

He urged his horse off the main road onto the dusty lane leading to Three Pines. To his right stretched acres of prepared land, run out and ridged the month before in prelude to planting. Inside the stakes marking the boundaries of a task, teams of workers drilled holes, deposited seeds and covered them with soil. In the far distance he saw the cotton agent, the only person not bent at a ninety-degree angle. He cantered purposely down the lane toward the house.

The front door was open to catch what breeze there was. He knocked. Sonja peeked from an interior doorway, then came forward.

Spruill smiled, extending the flowers. "For the ladies of the house," he said.

"How lovely. Thank you. Mother is teaching. Do you need to see her?"

"Actually, I was hoping to speak with you. Our time together was cut short on my last visit. Pardon me." He turned from her and sneezed into his handkerchief.

Sonja looked doubtful. "With me? What about?"

"If I may come inside."

"It is cooler here on the porch," she said.

"Very well. The porch."

He sat, careful to straighten his uniform tunic. "As I mentioned on my last visit, I have reason to believe the rebel boy next door may be engaged in acts disloyal to the Union." He paused to gauge her reaction.

"Go on," she said.

"As you know, there was a tax sale last month."

"We heard only that Three Pines was purchased by the government. We don't know what they may have planned for the place. We have been anxious about that."

"I wouldn't worry too much. It could be years before anyone focuses on a place as small as this one."

"Is that what you came to tell us? What does that have to do with the rebel?"

Spruill leaned forward conspiratorially. Sonja backed away, thinking his sneezing may be contagious. "The land belonging to the rebels who fled, which were all of them except for the two next door, was sold to others. Only a few rebels found out about the sale. That is because it was hardly publicized. We get a tiny rag called the Port Royal *New South*. Mostly military news and stories. I doubt anyone outside of Beaufort reads it because so few inside Beaufort read it. The other advertisement ran in the *Free South*. Even fewer people read that one. But as I say, a few rebels managed to learn that their property was going to be auctioned, and they hired some locals to pay their taxes."

"I am not clear on the significance . . ."

"The significance is this. Among the few parcels redeemed by payment of the taxes, and therefore spared auction, was the small parcel next door. That odious cabin where the rebels live."

Sonja took this in before replying. "We were told they were a family of means before the war. They also own one of the grand houses in town. Perhaps they had the money to pay the taxes and learned of the sale. You said yourself some did find out in time."

Spruill nodded authoritatively. "I considered that possibility, but here is what I find so odd. Only the parcel next door was redeemed. The house in town which, as you say, is quite grand—I pass by it often—that house in town went to auction. Why would the family save one property and not the other?"

"I don't know, of course, but is that so odd? I have no idea who is living in the Beaufort house, but it cannot be any member of the family. On the other hand, two members of the family live here. If they were going to save a property, that one is the logical choice, particularly if they were short of money. The taxes on the Lodge—that is the name for it—cannot be very high."

"Quite true. The taxes are small. But how did they find out in time to save it?"

"I may be able to help you there," she said. "At the ceremony for the Emancipation Proclamation, everyone talked about the sale. Later, I mentioned it to Carter. That may be how they found out."

"I see," said Spruill. "Yes, that might well explain it."

She probed, wondering where this was headed. "You clearly have notions you are keeping to yourself."

"Forgive my mysteriousness. I fancy myself an amateur detective. A hobby of mine. My thought is that while, as you suggest, there may well be an innocent explanation for how these taxes came to be paid, it is also possible that the boy was being compensated for service to the Confederacy."

"What service can he have performed?"

"That I cannot answer. Not today, at any rate. But I intend to find the answer if there is one. In the meantime, I advise you to be cautious in your dealings with them. Both the boy and the grandmother. If they are guilty of traitorous acts, you could find yourself in a very difficult position if you consort with them. You are much too pretty to be labeled a rebel sympathizer, or worse."

"I appreciate your concern, Lieutenant, but I doubt very much they are doing anything but trying to stay alive. The grandmother is rather stubborn, and because of that they find themselves stranded."

"Keep my advice in mind."

As Spruill retreated toward the main road, Sonja walked to the Lodge. Since their night on the beach, she and Carter had been together at least once a day. In the break, carefully concealed, they kissed and pressed against each other with gathering urgency. They had discovered French kissing, though neither would recognize it by that name, and there was no one to ask. She thought back to a few days before, when he hurt her feelings for the very first time. He mentioned that he planned to go sailing later that day, and she offered to go with him if he could wait until her teaching duties were over. She felt his muscles stiffen and sensed his hesitation. The proposal appeared to take him by surprise. He had stumbled on his words in explaining that no, she could not come today because . . . because he had to catch the tide and therefore could not wait. She found that odd, given the lengths he would go to be with her. It was as if he was avoiding her, and she wondered why.

In fact, he had sailed to Signal Oak that day. He did not know the ramifications of the tax sale he learned about on the beach, but instinctively he perceived it important enough to alert Gabriel. He chided himself for not being prepared for her suggestion, for mumbling an excuse that he knew had been greeted skeptically, and for wounding her, however slightly. And he thought again about what she would do if she discovered his complicity with the Confederacy, his secret ways to help his brother and to gratify his own voyeuristic desire. Was it normal, he asked himself for the hundredth time, for a boy of thirteen (as he was last fall, the last time he followed her to bathe in the creek) to want to see her naked? Was this what thirteen-year-olds do? Did his compulsion to admire her body portend a mental illness? A deviant personality? A character worthy of hell? If their roles were reversed, would a thirteen-year-old Sonja climb a tree

170

with field glasses to see him undress? Was it a normal act if done by a boy and an abnormal one if done by a girl? Abnormal if done by either? There was no one to ask except Gabriel, and it was unlikely he would see him again for months.

She found him driving stakes for tomatoes in the garden. She signaled for him to follow her to the break. Her serious look told him this summons was not about romance.

"That Navy lieutenant is back," she said. "Spruill. He gives me indigestion."

"Like oysters?"

"This is not funny. He is convinced you are a spy."

"What convinces him?"

"Remember I told you about the tax sale? We were on the beach that night."

"I remember. And later you said Three Pines was auctioned."

"Yes, but he told me today that someone paid the taxes on the Lodge. It was not auctioned."

"That's good."

"Good, but the taxes on the Barnwell home in Beaufort were not paid. That house is now owned by someone else, he didn't say who. His theory is that whoever paid the taxes on the Lodge did it in payment for work you are doing for the rebels."

"What is this work I am supposed to be doing?"

"He admits he doesn't know, but he vows to find out."

Carter shook his head. "I don't know what to say. Perhaps Mother found out about the sale."

"He said a few of the families that fled did find out, and they were able to pay the taxes in time. But if your mother learned of it, wouldn't she have also paid the taxes on the Beaufort house?"

"She may not have any money left. She and Uncle Daniel lost a lot in the fire. That is what the Negroes told me. Maybe she only had enough to pay for this place. Maybe she had to borrow even that. I just do not know."

"Spruill said something else. He warned me against being your friend. If you did something unpatriotic, I could get a reputation as a sympathizer."

"Did he say anything else?"

She hesitated. "He wants to call on me."

"Call?"

"Romance."

"Oh. What did you say?"

"I said nothing because Mother told him I wasn't old enough. He bothers me. Everything about him." She paused, then looked at him intently. "Carter, you are not helping the rebels, are you?"

"No."

"And you would tell me if you were, wouldn't you?"

171

"Yes."

"Good, because I tell you everything, and if we are going to do what we do, I don't want secrets between us."

"I want to do what we do. Kiss me."

"Not now. You are sweaty. I have to go back. I will meet you tomorrow."

He returned to the garden. He just lied to her twice, and he slumped under the weight of it. "I tell you everything, and if we are going to do what we do, I don't want secrets between us." What was he doing? He should run after her now, confess before this got any worse, tell her he is compelled to help his brother in any way he can, tell her that he has only known one people in his life, the Southern people, and he loves them and he is not sure if they are right or wrong in this war but he loves them anyway, and he loves her, and he is afraid that truth will cost him what he loves, that which he cannot do without, and that is too much to ask of him. It is too much to ask that he lose his mother and his brother and his home and his blue-eyed love. Too much.

And what about this officer that wants to call on her? The same man who questioned him in the boat that night. He can't bear the thought of sharing her. That cannot happen, but will it?

That evening, Missma said, "You have not said a word all afternoon and you look as if your boat sank."

He looked up absently. "I forgot to tell you. Someone paid the taxes on the Lodge. It wasn't sold in the tax auction."

"Thank God for that blessing. I don't know what we would have done. I suppose Gabriel found some way. What about the house in town?"

He lowered his head and did not answer.

"So that is gone along with everything else."

He did not look up.

"Is that why you are so glum? The loss of the house?"

"I suppose."

Missma stood, crossed the hearth and put her hand on the back of his neck. "There is more to this than the house. Your information comes from Sonja, I take it?"

He nodded.

She patted him gently on the shoulders. "Son, you are dealing with things no fourteen-year-old should have to handle. And for what it's worth, you are doing a mighty fine job of it. Did she hurt your feelings?"

"In a way."

"Would you care to talk about it?"

"I think I need to think it through on my own."

"That is exactly what your father would have said when he was your age, only he didn't face near the hardships you are dealing with. He had his family, his friends, his home. Just remember that girls Sonja's age can be difficult. I was once both."

The fire popped and hissed. He tried to picture Missma as a girl as young as Sonja. The image wouldn't form, and even if it had it wouldn't provide relief from the pit in his stomach, the gloom that settled over him that afternoon. He wondered if sharing with Sonja his need to do what he does for the cause, his cause, Missma's cause, would be understood and accepted for what it is. He doubted it, and if it was, would he be putting her in jeopardy as the lieutenant said? Renouncing his role as a spy seemed the best way to keep Sonja, but with Preston in Virginia fighting, maybe on this very afternoon lying wounded or dead on some battlefield, how could he fail in his meager mission here? Yet he cannot lose her.

He looked up. "I have some decisions to make."

She pinched his scarred earlobe, now completely healed. "And you will make the right ones."

CHAPTER 32

By late spring, life on Cane Island settled into a routine. The war seemed but a distant rumor. Sonja taught in the morning and met with her tutor in the afternoon. That tutor, a Miss Hansfield, had recently arrived from Boston. Unlike her predecessor, whose classes tended to be sporadic, Miss Hansfield was prompt and persistent, arriving on horseback in early afternoon and for two hours demanding Sonja's undivided attention. She was humorless but knowledgeable in mathematics, Latin and history. Her Socratic method assured Sonja's active participation in learning.

Supper at Three Pines was served early, allowing the freedmen who prepared it time to return to their cabins in daylight. Sonja used that time to visit the Lodge, her three quick knocks announcing her arrival. While Missma knitted and Carter read, she studied her lessons, sharing the table and lantern light with him as the day waned. If Sonja had heard news of the war, she shared it, but on most evenings the crackle of the fire and the turning of pages was the dominant sound. A curious peace settled over the Lodge. By unspoken agreement, Carter and Sonja stayed focused on their respective preoccupations. After several such evenings, he realized that this hour, when she was within arm's reach, was the one hour he could fully immerse himself in what he was reading, her mere presence contenting him. For her part, she ignored him completely, with the lone exception of giving him a list of history questions to test her knowledge of wars and dates Miss Hansfield would expect her to know. When Missma, knitting in her rocker, mumbled the answers, Sonja cut her eyes and Carter grinned. When Sonja left, Carter accompanied her to the break, where they embraced. Those ten or fifteen minutes were becoming more heated. Recently, as they kissed, he lowered his hand to her breast. She let it linger there before telling him she needed to go.

• • •

In Charleston, Anna, Abigail and Daniel prepared to leave for Columbia. They had now spent nineteen months with the Singletons, who took them in after the great fire. After a month Daniel had insisted on paying rent, which the Singletons admitted had eased some wartime deprivations. But their daughter, son-in-law and grandson, forced to abandon Vicksburg, Mississippi, were returning to Charleston and needed a place to live. The alternative, their daughter said in a letter, was to "dig a cave in Vicksburg." The house could not accommodate three more people. The Singletons would regret the loss of rental income and the company the homeless trio had provided. Anna, Abigail and Daniel would miss the evenings around the Singleton piano, where Olivia Singleton's lovely alto carried them through old songs reminiscent of antebellum memories.

Anna returned from posting a letter to Uncle Luke notifying him of their decision to accept his offer of shelter. She had just removed her bonnet when through an open window she saw Gabriel Heyward tie his horse in front of the house. She watched him approach, her heart sinking. She had known him all his life. He was, for her and others, a force of nature, a blithe presence in a darkening sky, a lifeline to all the gaiety and charm and exuberance this world held before an abominable war crashed upon them. Gabriel personified what they loved best about what they had lost, and if his shoulders slumped, as Anna saw them do now, if those eyes which were always upturned to new possibilities were cast down, if his radiant smile was shuttered by the taut line of his lips, then the news must be very bad indeed. She knew Preston was in Gettysburg. She met Gabriel midway down the walk and sobbed into his outstretched arms. Neither uttered a word.

Days later, a letter arrived:

> July 24, 1863
> Culpeper, Virginia
>
> Dear Mrs. Barnwell:
> It is with heavy heart that I confirm the death of your son, Sgt. Preston Barnwell. Sgt. Barnwell died of wounds received in the Battle of Gettysburg. He died as he served, heroically. His unit was ordered to attack a defended Union position in a peach orchard. Defying hostile fire, he led a squad of men that fought as bravely as I have ever witnessed in the course of this long war. Your loss is felt by his country and by all who served with this gallant young man, whose memory we will always hold dear.
> I enclose his personal effects, including a letter found on his person in an unaddressed envelope.
>
> With deepest regrets, Joseph B. Kershaw,
> Brigade Commander

Anna opened the letter. At the sight of Preston's pinched script, she broke down.

To the Parents of Edward Lacey:

I do not know if I am doing the right thing in sending you this letter. I am a Confederate soldier of the Palmetto Guard, 2nd South Carolina Infantry. You lost a son to this war and I am responsible. It happened off Nine Mile Road near Fair Oaks, in Virginia. I guess you could say that he and I were in the wrong place at the wrong time. I am so very sorry for your loss, and very sorry to have been the cause of it. He must have been a fine boy. He was brave and did not suffer. I have suffered since, not that I expect or deserve sympathy. This war is an awful thing, and if I am lucky enough to see its end, I will never fight again, no matter the cause.

I come from a small town in South Carolina called Beaufort. It is surrounded by water where we fish and woods where we hunt.

Writing this letter is the hardest thing I have ever done. I ask for your Christian forgiveness but if that is not possible I will understand.

Very truly yours, Preston Barnwell

• • •

In Beaufort, Sonja watched from the porch as Jacob Roan cantered down the lane. By now she was used to his reserved manner, his quiet competence in matters related to the plantation and the freedmen, so to see him waving over his head a paper portended great news. She called to her mother, who joined her on the porch as Roan pulled up.

"Wonderful news," he said, extending the paper. "A glorious victory at Gettysburg. Lee's invasion of Pennsylvania is doomed and the rebels are in retreat. In town they are calling this a turning point sure to hasten the end of the war."

Christina took the paper and scanned the headlines. "Thank the Lord," she said.

"May I see it?" asked Sonja.

"Of course, dear."

Sonja saw Christina linger as Roan dismounted. Of late Christina seemed more focused on him than the war, with telling smiles and admiring nods in his presence. She left them on the porch and retreated to her room with the paper, seized by an odd premonition she would recall later. Seated on her bed, with the paper angled toward the light, she turned past the list of Union casualties to the list, equally long, of Confederate losses. Moments later she rolled the list into a scroll and put it into her pocket, then left the house for the Lodge. Before

176

reaching the break, she heard the echo of Carter's axe. She knew he was laying by wood for the winter and she knew that winter had just become a very long one. Her pace slowed, her legs heavy. When he saw her, he lowered the axe.

As she walked toward him, he sensed her hesitation. Her eyes misted, the blue refracted through moisture as if she had just emerged from swimming in the creek. But her expression lacked the satisfaction he saw then. She stopped close to him, lowered her head, and handed him the scrolled paper. As he studied it, she saw his shoulders sag as the axe fell to the ground. She wrapped her arms around him and pulled him to her. "I am so sorry," she whispered.

At that moment, Missma emerged from the Lodge. Carter saw her over Sonja's shoulder. In an instant she wore the same expression Sonja arrived with, some telepathic intuition of what the paper had confirmed. He managed to say, "The Yankees got Preston, Missma." She lowered herself to a sitting position on the top step, closed her eyes, bowed her head, folded her hands and began to pray.

"I'll come back later," the girl said. As she left, Carter, the paper scrolled in his hand, walked to the steps and sat. He was willing himself not to cry, but he did as Soot licked his face.

Missma opened her eyes and stared down at him. "Such a fine boy. Such a waste. Your mother will be devastated, and because of me we cannot comfort her, nor she comfort us. What a horrible thing this war is, and what a fool I have been for insisting we stay."

"Preston would still be gone," Carter said in a voice barely audible.

Carter ordered Soot to the boat. They were gone overnight. When they returned, he gave no explanation of where they went or what they did. His eyes were red. A stubble of beard was beginning to show. He hugged Missma and said, "I cannot believe he is dead."

In the long days that followed, Carter and Missma mourned someone they loved without his body or any trace of him. None who knew him came to call. No one except Christina and Sonja brought food and commiseration. There was no one to recall, with a rueful smile, the time he learned to recognize poison ivy by climbing a tree full of it to jump from twenty feet into the river. The people who remembered Preston as an industrious boy who would help a neighbor, or to be among the first to volunteer for war, were scattered across South Carolina. Not one man he served with, who knew firsthand what a reliable, positive and brave comrade he was, came to sing praises. They were marching home from Pennsylvania or buried in shallow graves at Gettysburg. No choir gathered to lift voices in lament. No priestly benediction was intoned before the Savior's cross. Preston Barnwell's name appeared on a list, and that was all they had.

A week later, an afternoon shower found them sitting on the porch.

"Carter, I think it is time we considered going to Charleston. Your mother needs you, and you need her. It is not the time to be separated." Then she added,

"If it ever was."

He stared at the planking of the porch. "I've thought about that. I'm not leaving."

"Why?"

The rain fell harder.

"You don't want to go."

"If you know that, you are growing up faster than I realized. When you get to be my age, you will understand why what you say is true. Getting old is difficult. You tell yourself it is part of life, but decline is irreversible. Every day when you wake up you realize that your poor eyesight will be a little poorer tomorrow; that your hearing will be a bit more troublesome; that your memory will slip a notch. I felt that decline—perhaps decay is more descriptive—before the war started and it terrified me. I pictured myself in that room on Bay Street, reading my books, feeling my age, waiting to die. Coming here with you was like a reprieve from all that. I could be useful and to some extent independent. It struck me as a grand adventure, the last of my life before I meet my Maker. Does that make sense?"

He nodded but said nothing.

"I would not take anything for these two years. I have loved them, hardships and all. Here at the Lodge, I told myself I had gotten the best of that decay I feared so much, but of course that is fantasy, as I'm reminded each day. Yesterday, it took me until noon to recall the middle name of my husband, your grand-father. I know it like my own, but I could not summon it try as I might. So at best I have delayed the inevitable. Among my greatest joys has been watching you grow into the man you are becoming. But all good things must come to an end, and I have been selfish long enough. The Yankees won't miss us. We can be in Charleston by tomorrow if this rain lets up."

"I don't want to leave Sonja. And I have work to do here."

"I understand about the girl, but in Charleston that work would be done for you. Others can worry about food and firewood."

"I'm not talking about that kind of work."

It took her a moment. "You mean Signal Oak?"

"Yes."

"Son, you must think that through very carefully. The older you get, the harsher the consequences if you are caught."

"I can do things here I can't do in Charleston. I want to hurt the people that killed Preston."

"Revenge is a natural instinct," she said gently. "Particularly so soon after a tragedy like this. Let some time pass before you take that on."

"My mind is made up."

"What do you plan to do?"

"Be a much better spy than I have been. Up to now I have waited for information to come to me. Now I will seek it out. With the field glasses I can see a lot from the boat. If I can learn about what is where, I will have a better chance of spotting things that could help Gabe. I spent some time at Bay Point after we got the news about Preston. An empty barge was moored at the pier on Hilton Head. The next day they loaded it with some artillery. Why are they doing that, and where is that barge headed? I wouldn't learn just sitting here on the porch."

"Does Sonja know of your plans?"

"No, and you must not tell her."

The next day, he and Sonja met at the break. She kissed him passionately, both because she had missed him and because she meant to again convey her sorrow at his loss. She reminded him the summer was slipping away and he had yet to fulfill his promise to take her to swim in the ocean. The next day, they left early. The weather was hot and clear. On a beach not far from where they camped the night of the storm, they swam. He taught her to ride the waves and to time leaving her feet with their cresting for maximum distance. They ate lunch, kissed deeply on the beach and swam again. In mid-afternoon they returned to the Lodge. For a few hours his sadness was put aside.

In the weeks that followed, he balanced his chores with frequent sails. At times he invited her along, but more often he scheduled his absence when he knew she was teaching. He began doing what he told Missma he would do, visually surveying Beaufort and its surroundings. In the Beaufort River, he pretended to fish while he studied the town. From close in, he didn't need the field glasses, and his fishing aroused no suspicion he was aware of. Over weeks, he noted gradual patterns of coming and going. Shops along Bay Street did brisk business. Supplies were unloaded at the docks. Gunboats tied up for a day or two before heading upriver or down. At times the streets seemed filled with soldiers, and at other times with sailors. The buildings used for hospitals were always busy. He did not know precisely what he was looking for, but he was convinced that by learning what was usual he would spot the unusual when it happened. The sun deepened his tan. At times he actually fished, but more often his hook was bare and his cast net dry so that he need not concentrate on two things at once.

Timing his trips to coincide with Sonja's teaching brought on the guilt that was by now so heavy and so palpable that it felt like a passenger in his boat. He told himself that he would one day soon share with her what he did and why it was so essential that he do it, and that she would understand. She would embrace him as she did when she learned of Preston's death and whisper soothing words of empathy. Such assurances allowed him to focus on the intelligence he was gathering. Yet returning from a morning on the water, steering the boat to shore and resolved to tell her that very afternoon so as to rid himself of that unwanted passenger, his courage failed him. He put it off for another day.

179

On sailing days when he was not fishing near town, he anchored off Bay Point, where he could not see too much without the aid of his field glasses. It was largely boring work, but he stayed with it, convinced he would get a chance to strike a blow with all the intelligence he was gathering. When troops boarded transports at Hilton Head, he counted them, making notes of the numbers and the ships. Often the loaded ships sailed across the bar and headed south toward Savannah, and on occasion they sailed upriver to Beaufort. He sailed the shoreline along the Broad River, sometimes veering into the Whale Branch to pass Signal Oak and at other times meandering into the many creeks diverging from the Broad.

In late August, there were just enough early breezes to cross the Beaufort River for Reggie and bring him back. After Reggie's lesson, they fished but gave it up in favor of swimming from a sandbar in the middle of the river. The water was seasonably warm, relieved occasionally by submerged pockets of cooler current sweeping across their bodies. Reggie expressed his sorrow about Preston to both Carter and Missma, and as they treaded water, hoping for another swirl of the cooler current, he told Carter that Missma had changed. "She not right," he said. Carter responded by submerging.

The following day, wilting in the heat, he waited at the break for Sonja. He saw at once that she was troubled. He moved to kiss her but she recoiled.

"What is it?" he asked.

"That man. Spruill. He came back yesterday."

"So?"

"He's been watching you. He finds it very strange how much time you spend fishing off Beaufort and Bay Point. He actually showed me a chart he is keeping, noting the times you come and go. He . . . bothers me."

"I don't see how he can make trouble for me when I'm fishing."

"You don't know this man. When you anchor off Beaufort, he watches you through field glasses. He says you don't bait your hooks. That you can't really be fishing."

"What does he know? I use lures and flies."

"He knows you're up to something, and he keeps telling me that I will be in trouble if it turns out you aren't fishing."

She took his hands in hers and pulled him close. "I know you're hurting because of Preston. You haven't been the same since the news came. I want to be here for you, especially now when everything is so depressing. And I feel helpless. About all I can do is hug and kiss you and help take your mind off things. But to do that, you have to be honest with me. Something has changed in you that has nothing to do with Preston. You have grown harder, more distant. You never used to be distant. Not from me, anyway."

He sighed heavily. "If I tell you, can I trust you to say nothing to anyone?"

"That's what I have been trying to tell *you*. You can trust me to keep a con-

180

fidence, just the way I trust you."

He began with Gabriel's suggestion on the day he accidentally shot his ear. Gabriel had said there was a way Carter could help. With Preston off fighting, Carter had agreed as a way to do his part. Gabriel had promised news from Anna and had delivered. Gabriel said that all across the South there were home guards, those left behind to defend the town, and that Carter could be that for Beaufort."

"So your cousin talked you into this?"

"It was my decision. I can't blame Gabe. Missma warned me, but I had to be doing something to help Preston. I've wanted to tell you so many times but I just couldn't. I'm sorry I waited so long."

He felt her tense, then pull away. Over her eyes came a dull sheen, as if she was sleepwalking.

"So Spruill is right," she said.

Eyes downcast, he nodded.

"And you lied to me."

"I had to. I worried that you wouldn't understand."

She released his hands. "I'm not sure I do. You're working for a cause I do not believe in. You're helping a side I think is evil. Your brother was not evil—we talked about that. But in this war, one side is God's side and it is not the one you are on."

"It's the only one I know. I did what I had to do."

She looked toward Three Pines. "And I must do what I have to do, even though it will hurt. I have to break this off. You and me. I'm so sorry. You may trust me to keep this secret. I told you I would. But I can't see you again." She leaned forward, kissed his cheek and disappeared through the break.

CHAPTER 33

At the Lodge, the river's celadon hue matched Carter's mood. He told Missma that Preston's death had given him an insight into Madame Defarge, the Parisian woman in *A Tale of Two Cities.*

"And why would that be?" Missma asked. "Such a wicked woman. And heartless. Mr. Dickens makes us believe she a sister of Lady Macbeth."

"When she is knitting the names of all the people the revolution will kill, she is acting out her revenge. I feel that way when I spy on the Yankees. It's not much, but it's better than simply thinking about revenge."

Missma pondered this for a moment, considering her reply. "Don't forget what happened to Madame Defarge. In the end her hatred destroyed her. You can't allow that to do the same to you."

He did his chores mechanically, his mind as blank as he could make it. At least with Preston's loss, stepping up his surveillance spread a tiny ointment on his wound. But Sonja? There was no solace for her loss. For that, the pit he felt in his stomach gaped every time he looked toward Three Pines. Nights were the worst, when thoughts of her filled the Lodge. He did not know it was possible to feel so sad.

Missma saw this but knew that nothing she could say or do would hasten him through this double dose of grief. On a day when he seemed particularly melancholy, she asked him if he planned to sail to Signal Oak, as perhaps there was a letter from Anna.

He stared at her before answering. "You asked me that this morning, Missma. Remember?"

"Did I?"

"You did."

"And what did you say?"

"I said I plan to go tomorrow."

"Yes. Yes you did. I remember now."

Such exchanges were becoming more common.

Christina and Sonja sat on the porch at Three Pines. Tea together in the late afternoon had become a ritual. Trees in the distance were utterly unmoving, still enough in the languid humidity to be painted onto the horizon. They craved iced tea, but there was no ice to be had. As Sonja added lemon, stirred with a pewter spoon, Christina asked the cause of her obvious unhappiness in recent days.

"Everything," Sonja said. "Ruby disrupts my classes. I'm tired of playing nursemaid to her and the others. I'm tired of South Carolina. Don't you think it's time we went back to Pennsylvania? Other missionaries have left. It's not like we haven't done what we came to do. And this heat!"

"I understand how you feel. This is in many ways no life for a girl your age. You've been a good soldier in God's army here. But you didn't complain about the heat last summer."

"So we can go?"

"I would rather not leave at present. Perhaps soon . . ."

"Mother, would this have anything to do with Mr. Roan?"

"And would your wish to leave have anything to do with Carter?"

Sonja sighed. "A little."

"Well, then I will say that my wish to remain does have something to do with Jacob—Mr. Roan. We find we have a lot in common." Then, seemingly happy to change the subject, she asked how Carter was doing.

"He's so sad. He cries when I'm not around. His eyes are red. He says he's better but he spends all his time in the boat alone."

"It must be a horrible blow to both of them. But you haven't been around, have you?"

"Not lately. We had a fight," she said with finality.

"If that's a subject you wish to avoid, we can speak of Jacob. Do you like him?"

"I suppose. I haven't spent too much time around him."

"I have a feeling that will change in the near future. And I've been thinking about your father, who will never leave his life in Sweden." She said this as if expecting her daughter's surprised reaction.

"No, he will not. I think it's time we *both* accepted that."

"I have an idea," Christina said, bringing her teacup down as if punctuating her thought. "Why not go visit Laura for a few days? Things are so much busier there, with people coming and going. And some young soldiers stop in. Perhaps you will meet some boys closer to your age. Lt. Spruill always seems to find a reason to visit us, and his interest is quite obvious. He has said as much. I've heard he also spends time at the Oaks. And Laura would take you with her when she makes her calls on the sick, which would give you a break from your classes."

Sonja's eyes strayed toward the Lodge. "Let me think about it. Maybe."

When Jacob Roan joined them on the porch, he encouraged Sonja to take up her mother's suggestion for time at the Oaks. Of course he would agree, the girl thought. He seemed to agree with everything Christina said or did. He probably just wanted to spend time alone with her. Perhaps her mother's suggestion was for the same reason. Still, the idea had appeal. She wondered if she made the right decision in breaking off with Carter so suddenly. She missed him and worried that she would soften with time and nearness. She decided she would go but wait to tell them.

"I need a favor," said Roan to Sonja. "Can you carry a letter to the boy next door on your next visit?"

Sonja and Christina exchanged glances. Christina cleared her throat and mentioned that because Roan had been away, he was unaware of a change. Sonja no longer went to the Lodge.

"I see," said Roan.

"What is the favor, Jacob? Perhaps I can help," said Christina.

"I have a letter to be delivered to them."

"Oh?"

"I was summoned to meet with a Major Wainwright. They captured a rebel soldier on Lady's Island a couple of weeks ago. He's a cousin of Carter's and was carrying a letter for them. The major said it is a condolence from his mother. The boy was lost at Gettysburg."

"Yes, so sad. Sonja said they are taking it very hard, as I know I would."

"It was kind of you both to pay respects. Not everyone would be so generous with the enemy."

"We did it for the boy. None of this is his fault."

"War inflicts indiscriminate pain. His ancestors have left him a bitter heritage. Even if it ended tomorrow, he and those like him will require generations to recover."

Christina said, "I think about Peter. It's almost impossible to look on the bright side of losing a child so early in his life, but at least he was spared having to fight. He could have been maimed for life, or worse. It is all so terrible. They are saying that at Chickamauga we lost five thousand men killed and ten thousand wounded. In just two days. I can't comprehend carnage on that scale."

"Don't forget the eight thousand prisoners the rebels took. What a debacle, and just when it seemed the momentum was swinging our way. This war has a ways to run yet."

"I wonder if it will last long enough for Carter to enlist. That mother could lose both her sons."

"How old is he?"

"Fourteen, I believe." For confirmation she looked to Sonja, who nodded.

"It's possible. At any rate, here's the letter. Wainwright asked me to get it delivered unless you know of a reason it shouldn't be."

"I feel sure a letter of condolence will be welcome and certainly I have no objections. Leave it on the table. I will take it at the first opportunity."

"Very well. I'm off for a meeting with Philbrick." He looked expectantly at Christina. "You don't trust him, do you?"

She inhaled, her eyes roaming the porch as if in search of the answer. "I can't decide. He seems astute, which is to the benefit of his investors. Still . . ."

"You're wondering if he is serving the freedmen or serving himself."

"Precisely."

"Believe me, you are not alone in your qualms. Others have voiced similar misgivings."

"Perhaps I don't understand what it is he intends to do. I know he bought half of St. Helena at the auction."

Roan shook his head faintly. "Not half, but it's true that his company now controls almost one third of the island. As to what he intends to do, I will learn more at this meeting. I haven't committed to him yet. If he's in it for the wrong reasons, I want no part of it. On the other hand, it could be a good business opportunity and serve the freedmen as well. A win-win proposition, as they say."

"I agree with Laura that the freedmen should own the land they work."

"In fact, some now do. At the tax auction a group of the freedmen pooled their money and bought the land they worked as slaves. About two thousand acres to my understanding."

Christina considered this, her head tilted to one side. "I had not heard. I wonder if Grace and Polk know this. They would be ideal landowners. Perhaps they have some money saved. Do you think there will be another chance for them to buy?"

"I would think so. At the auction the government bid on sixty thousand acres. That purchase included Three Pines, by the way. Everyone assumes the government will want to keep only a portion of that and will sell off the rest at another auction."

Sonja spoke. "So if they have money, Grace and Polk could purchase."

"In principle, yes, but as usual the devil is in the details. The highest bidders prevail, and if those bidders are speculators, the price could be out of reach for people like Grace and Polk, not to mention the fact that the entire character of these islands could change in short order. This plantation, too. Philbrick's advantage is that he put together the consortium with the money to buy, which he insists is an insurance against speculative interests."

Christina said, "As long as he himself is not a speculative interest."

"Time will tell. His company will employ a thousand people. With prompt payment and fair working rules, the freedmen will be better off. As will I, as Philbrick proposes to pay me half the net profits from the crops on my plantations."

"You negotiated that?"

"That's the standing offer to all the superintendents he recruited."

She smiled at him demurely. "And he recruited only the best."

"Thank you. I'll let you know what I learn at the meeting."

CHAPTER 34

S onja visited Laura Towne at the Oaks. Towne taught school, ministered to the sick and distributed clothing sent by the Port Royal Relief Committee in Philadelphia. Her days were long, and her patience seemingly inexhaustible except where the righteousness of abolition was concerned, and there she had no patience at all. Because she constantly interacted with other leaders of the Port Royal Experiment and with the top military brass overseeing Beaufort's occupation, the Oaks was a vortex of activity; a perfect place for Sonja to break the slow routine of life at Three Pines.

But she knew her primary motivation in coming was to distance herself from Carter and the Lodge. She made her decision to break with him viscerally on learning of his deception, and it had felt right since. And because it felt right, she asked herself why it didn't feel good, why she sobbed silently into her pillow at night and avoided looking toward the Lodge in daylight. By her lights he was a traitor and a liar, two loathsome characteristics that should have turned her affections to disgust. Yet she missed him, wondering if she reacted too quickly.

She thought often of their night on the beach and its intimacy. Her mind seemed to be telling her one thing and her heart another. His spying began before she came to South Carolina, so the dilemma had been with him since she arrived. The decision to confide in her must have cost him some sleepless nights, as his absence was costing her now. To break his heart when the death of his brother had already fractured it seemed cruel. She was not a cruel person, she told herself, yet she had acted cruelly. Carter was not a traitor or a liar, yet he had been guilty of both. How could each act so counter to their natures? It was this war, she concluded. War must do things to people that peace cannot. She can't stop the war, but neither could he. They were in it, it surrounded them, and they had as much control of its outcome as a floating leaf had to determine the course of a river.

As soon as Sonja arrived, Towne introduced her to Ellen Murray, who also lived at the Oaks. Murray and Towne were old friends from Philadelphia. Both questioned Sonja extensively on the progress of her students, the teaching techniques found to be best suited for a unique student population, as well as humorous anecdotes that all the teachers were collecting. Within a day Sonja felt at home.

Laura Towne was determined that the girl would see much of what life at Three Pines denied her. On the second full day of Sonja's stay, Towne insisted she accompany her into Beaufort. "I'm taking you to a place we call Hospital 10, where we treat wounded colored soldiers. There are some people there I want you to meet."

Hospital 10 was housed in an antebellum mansion surrounded by ancient oaks that predated the Revolution. "These patients," Towne explained, "are mostly from the 54th Massachusetts Infantry. They led the assault on Fort Wagner near Charleston. Sadly for them, promised reinforcements didn't arrive in time to spare them heavy casualties. More than five hundred were brought here for treatment."

The women were met by Dr. Esther Hawkes, a tall New Hampshire native, the fifth of eight children and a graduate of the New England Female Medical College. She conducted them on a tour of the wards, introducing them to patients in bed after bed.

"So many have left I feel we are abandoned," Hawkes said. "We want to see them go, of course. That is our mission. But now there are fewer than seventy where once there were hundreds."

The soldiers chatted easily with the women. Sonja, whose exposure to blacks up to now had been the Gullah population at Three Pines, was struck by the articulation of these men, and said as much to Hawkes.

"These men have such different backgrounds from the locals who enlisted here in Beaufort with the 1st South Carolina Infantry," Hawkes explained. "While some of them have been slaves, to be sure, most grew up as freedmen in the North and volunteered when the war broke out. We have three college graduates among them. From the accounts I've had of the battle at Fort Wagner, these men performed heroically. They are excellent soldiers, and it's my job to get them ready for duty or to get them well enough to travel home."

They turned a corner. Under a large open window three men rested in separate cots. A black nurse bandaged the right hand of the only man awake. Hawkes said with a grin as they approached, "Here are three of my favorites, all brothers, and all troublemakers."

The patient smiled as he said, "Who you calling a troublemaker?"

"And this," said Hawkes, turning to the nurse, "is Harriet Tubman. Perhaps you've heard of her. She recently helped rescue some freedmen from a rice plantation on the Combahee River." Tubman glanced briefly at the touring women before turning her attention back to her patient.

Towne reached down and took the soldier's other hand. "Thank you for your service to our cause."

"Our cause, too" he replied. "When the war broke out we all volunteered, but nobody would have us. Then Governor Andrew formed the 54th Massachusetts and we came running."

As Towne and Hawkes asked him how he and his brothers were feeling,

Sonja reflected on the fact that these were the first casualties of the war she had been exposed to. The war dictated her life, but the essence of war, the fighting and the wounding and the dying, had been as remote to her as frozen lakes or volcanic ash.

As they left the soldier's bedside, Hawkes said softly, "A fourth brother didn't make it back from Fort Wagner." She led them to another floor. "I have to show you this." She opened a closed door to a room with shelves piled high with watermelons, pumpkins and assorted other fruits. "The colored folks bring these by the oxcart load. They have a lot of pride in their soldiers."

Towne and Sonja thanked Hawkes for their tour. Back outside, Sonja said she had never met a woman doctor. "They are rare," confirmed Towne. "I never completed my training, but I got enough to help the people here. Without me they would have an even more difficult time, poor things."

They met the last ferry of the day and arrived back at the Oaks in early evening. After supper, the head cook, Susannah, told Laura Towne she needed to leave early.

"In a hurry?" Towne asked.

"A shout tonight, Miz Laura."

"Oh my," said Towne to Sonja. "I am so tired after today, but my guess is that you have never been to a shout. You must go, and I must go with you. We'll ask Ellen to come along. I promise you will be highly entertained."

When Ellen agreed, the three women walked by the light of a pitch knot through former slave quarters that still housed those who worked at the Oaks. They paused in front of a small whitewashed building typical of those they had passed. It was dark and quiet.

"This is the house of Auntie Tenah. No one is sure how old she is. Some say one hundred, but I think less. Maybe ninety. This is what they call the Praise House. We come here to read to them and pray with them. I've been here when as many as fifty people were inside, if you can believe it."

"It's tiny," Sonja agreed.

"They are a very spiritual people. I doubt they could have survived the hardships they have faced without that strong faith. They like to listen to the good book, as they call it, and of course they love their hymns, some of which go back to their ancestors' days in Africa. So when they sing, it can get pretty loud in there."

"So that is why it is called a shout?" asked Sonja.

Towne and Murray exchanged a mirthful glance. "Oh, no," said Towne, "a shout is something entirely different, as you will see. I found it shocking when I first arrived. Now I am less put off, but no less amazed."

They continued walking. At the end of the line of cabins they saw one similar to Auntie Tenah's, but more run down. Ellen Murray said, "This is where

Rianna lives. She served at dinner tonight."

Rianna's place was ringed with blacks who, when they saw the women approach, parted like an Old Testament sea to admit them. Inside, a fire blazed in the fireplace and there was no room to sit. The women stood against a wall. Someone began to clap and the others picked it up. A man moved from the crowd into a space at the center of the room. As his eyes rolled up in his head, his arms extended.

"That's the one they call Dutch," whispered Towne. "He leads the shout."

Dutch began to sing in a rich bass, "Sista Rianna sailin' on the Jordan Riva', Roll, Jordan, Roll." Three men close to Dutch began slowly circling him, shuffling their feet and bending at the waist while the crowd kept time. The circling men sang the verse led by Dutch. After several rotations, they turned and reversed direction, still slow and deliberate, shuffling and bending. Dutch reached the end of the verse and began another. "Brudda Ike sailin' on the Jordan Riva', Roll, Jordan, Roll." The clapping intensified. The circling men began stomping their feet between shuffles, and the white women against the wall felt the rhythm in the soles of their feet. Faces of the men and women in the crowd radiated intensity that seemed to heighten with every new verse. Dutch was sweating now, as were the circling men, who had been joined by others although it was becoming difficult to move around Dutch, who remained rooted to his spot. Dutch was also picking up the tempo, which accelerated the clapping. The circling men stomped more emphatically, as if something beneath them must be stamped out, like a fire or a snake. Now the walls vibrated, and with every chorus of "Roll, Jordan, Roll," the crowd sang louder. The escalating mania was a mix of celebration and exorcism, part lifting up and part casting out. It spread to those outside as well, so that the pressure building inside was matched in a frenetic equilibrium. The fire cast hauntingly animated shadows on the walls and ceiling, as if an entire congregation of unloosed spirits had joined. Just when Sonja was convinced that every participant had exhausted his and her reserves of energy, Dutch raised his voice and a renewed fever swept the room. The shouting became a roar. The tempo was now so rapid that those singing along had to be content with short, staccato bursts. The circling reached frenzy as men stomped and bent and writhed at a compulsive pace, several falling to the floor in a possessed heap. Dutch reached a crescendo and finally dropped his head as if seized by death in mid-verse.

Back outside, the women exhaled. Towne said to Sonja, "They will rest for twenty minutes and begin again. It goes on for hours."

"What does it mean?" she asked.

"I'm not sure what it means. It just is."

"At first I found it uplifting, but then it became terrifying."

"My reaction exactly," Murray said and Towne nodded. "Since arriving we have heard so many stories about the plantation owners' fear of slave rebellions. If your experience at Three Pines has been like ours here, you know the Negroes to be, by and large, docile, easy going folk, passive even when it might be in their best interests to be otherwise. There is sweetness about them. But if the shout means anything, I think it means that sweetness conceals an edge, and who could blame them?"

Sonja's stay at the Oaks entered its second week when Towne hosted a small reception for Gen. Saxton and a few of his junior officers. She also invited three Gideonite women, none as young as Sonja for there were none among the missionaries. Seven junior officers turned out in their dress uniforms. Gen. Saxton and Laura Towne made the introductions, then sat off to one side as nature and circumstance combined. Sherry was served, but several of the men had flasks filled with Daddy August's best, although they were careful to keep those out of Gen. Saxton's view. Sonja had never imbibed, but a glass of sherry lightened her mood. The conversation was of the war, of distant homes, of missed families, of the boredoms of camp and the tedium of teaching. Among those surrounding Sonja was Lieutenant Randall Florance, a seemingly shy twenty-two-year-old who lingered at the fringe, listening but saying little. Florance, of Vermont, had a chiseled chin and neatly trimmed moustache. Shy or not, it was he who asked if she would accompany him on a ride through the countryside the following day. Provided Laura Towne was available to chaperone, she told him, she accepted.

She had expected to find Lt. Spruill here, as he seemed to have become a constant in life at Three Pines, but to her relief the invited guests did not include him. His suspicions of Carter, which she now knew to have been well founded, nevertheless rankled her, and there was in Spruill's tone of late an implied threat to her based on a relationship that now appeared part of her past. Just prior to leaving Three Pines for the Oaks, she mentioned Spruill's suspicions to Christina.

"He's imagining things if he believes Carter is a rebel spy," she said, conscious of her deception but determined to honor her pledge to him. "And he tells me I'm placing myself in danger by being Carter's friend."

Christina smiled. "I don't much like his tactics," she said, "but I feel certain he is only pursuing his suit and you have nothing to worry about on that score. He's trying to impress you."

"His suit?"

"His feelings for you. Clearly the lieutenant is smitten."

"He makes me nervous."

"As a woman, you have the ultimate say in such matters. Simply decline his advances."

A foursome left from the Oaks at noon: Laura Towne at the reins, Ellen Murray beside her in front, and Sonja and Lt. Florance seated behind. It was a spectacular fall day, with blue sky, low humidity and a faint breeze of clean air from the east. From the edge of the woods beyond the lane, a white-tailed buck stared at them before darting into the thicket. Beyond the woods, Towne halted the carriage to admire a field of wildflowers. It was the largest such field on the island, she told them, because of cotton's domination. A profusion of gold, yellow and purple spread before them. Sunflowers taller than the rig tilted at them as butterflies flitted among goldenrod and camphorweed.

"Such a splendid sight," said Towne. "Lieutenant, give us some good news about the war. Chickamauga was so distressing."

"A setback, but there will be those in any war. The South has fought better than most in my state predicted. Still, I don't see how the final outcome can be in doubt. The Southerners' only real hope from the outset was that England or France would join as allies, and that hasn't happened. The blockade is denying them what they need, and the lack of manufacturing is beginning to tell. In short, they are facing strangulation. It won't be a pretty death, but death is inevitable. At least that's the way I see it. When it's all said and done, I think their failure at Gettysburg marked the turning point." The mention of Gettysburg reminded Sonja of her last conversation with Carter.

Two days later, Towne asked Sonja to accompany her to a nearby plantation where two children had displayed chills and fever commonly associated with malaria. In the darkened one-room hut, Towne administered quinine and reassured the mother she would come again to check on her patients, a boy six and a girl four. Sonja, observing over Towne's shoulder, thought about her students of the same age. There was satisfaction in teaching them, but to cure them! That would be something. She remembered her visit to the hospital in Beaufort, and the work done by Dr. Hawkes. Two women using their brains and skills to help the sick. For the first time she thought of herself in that role and sensed satisfaction.

During their return to the Oaks, Towne observed that Sonja and Lt. Florance appeared to have gotten along quite well.

"He's very nice," Sonja said.

"Handsome, too."

Sonja had noticed. She was pleased to have shared the company of an attractive, engaging conversationalist. Best of all, she didn't think about Carter once until the mention of Gettysburg.

"He plans to come again tomorrow if his duty schedule permits." She saw concern on Towne's face. "What is it?"

"Those clouds," said Towne. "We are in for a storm."

The storm came upon them as quickly as did the one on the night of the full moon. Black thunderheads replaced sky that had been blue moments before. The wind picked up, gusting in their faces and forcing them to secure their bonnets.

"We are going to get very wet," Sonja said.

"That's not what worries me." Towne was yelling to be heard over the wind. "Bessie, the horse. She's deathly afraid of lightning. She will rear when it strikes."

Moments later, a zigzag bolt of lightning struck nearby. "That was close," Towne yelled, fighting to keep control of the reins as Bessie tried to bolt. "We have to cross the causeway. If she spooks there, we may get tossed into the creek. Can you swim?"

Sonja, holding her bonnet to her head, shouted, "Yes."

"Then let's make a dash for it." The bridge was wide enough to support the carriage but had no rails on either side. Just as the rear wheels rolled onto the planking, an ear-shattering peal of thunder and, simultaneously, a fully charged streak of lightning descended. Bessie reared to her hind legs and skittered sideways, pulling the carriage after her over the edge. Towne and Sonja pitched forward as horse and carriage plunged into the water. They came up sputtering as Towne swam toward the shore they just left; Sonja to the other side. Bessie and the carriage washed twenty yards downstream before the horse gathered her legs and pulled the carriage onto the shore down from where Sonja kneeled and panted heavily. Towne ran across the bridge and joined her there. The women sat to catch their breath, their arms folded on their shaking knees. They exchanged looks. Soon they were both on their backs, convulsed in laughter as the rain fell into their faces, hair and eyes.

CHAPTER 35

A nna, Uncle Daniel and Aunt Abigail sat in the same coach of the South Carolina Railroad as it lumbered from Charleston towards Columbia, but mentally they rode worlds apart on this journey.

Anna thought of Preston, as she had day and night for weeks. She prayed he did not suffer, yet she knew that was unlikely. Certainly she was suffering, unable to eat and managing only the most restless and foreshortened sleep. Because she had been unable to learn details of his death beyond Kershaw's brief note, her mind was left to imagine them. In her daily pilgrimages to St. Philip's, she submerged herself in prayer, giving over to a higher power her worldly grief for Preston and worries about Carter and Missma. On some days she found the renewed strength she sought. On others, she sensed profound stillness, the church a world entirely unto itself where war, conflict and deprivation waited respectfully outside, and on those days she frequently nodded off in mid-prayer, a few moments of the sleep she had sought so desperately the night before. And there were a few days, very few, when she could imagine herself back in the Barnwell pew at St. Helena's, with nothing more pressing than supervising Sunday dinner. What did St. Helena's look like now, she wondered? Was it being used as a church, a hospital, a barracks? As she stared out the window, the flatness of the Lowcountry gradually giving way to the gentle undulations of the interior, she hoped Columbia treated her kindlier than the city she just left.

Daniel stared into the light emitted by the window. "Luke and I haven't lived together since we were boys," he said. "He wasn't easy to live with. Maybe I wasn't either. I hope he's mellowed some, though from his letters I doubt it. Once an idea took hold you couldn't budge him. We had a friend growing up. Jimmy Boland. Luke had killed a rattlesnake and cut off its rattles. He was so proud of those things he hung them on the wall of his room. One day he couldn't find them and accused Jimmy of stealing them because Jimmy had been to see him that day. 'Course, Jimmy denied the whole thing. Luke wouldn't listen. Said he knew Jimmy was jealous of those rattles and had taken 'em when Luke wasn't looking." Daniel shook his head as if recalling his boyhood frustration. "I knew Jimmy pretty well, and I felt sure he wouldn't have done such a thing. So a day or two later, with Luke and Jimmy still arguing and Luke threatening to beat him up if he didn't return those prized rattles, I went into Luke's room and felt behind an old chest. There they were. I brought 'em to Luke but he said it didn't matter, that Jimmy had returned them to keep from being beaten up. Luke never would admit that he had jumped to conclusions in accusing Jimmy. No, Luke has never been one to admit he's wrong. And I fear he's wrong about this war."

"He can be quite argumentative," Abigail injected.

"He can indeed," Daniel agreed, "but he always took up for me if they teased me about being blind. Some will do so, you know. Kids who don't know any better."

Looking at Anna, Abigail said, "He's being loyal because Luke's his brother and that's his nature. Personally, I find Luke very difficult and now we will be living under the same roof." She turned toward Daniel. "And don't tell me he isn't green with jealousy over your success in the cotton business. I hope I can hold my tongue when he climbs on his high horse."

"He has offered help when we're in a fix," Daniel said. "Between the fire and the war it will be years before Charleston can be rebuilt."

"I didn't say I wasn't grateful," Abigail said.

As the train approached the outskirts of Columbia, the contrast with Charleston became stark. The city they left was tired, worn and dispirited. Two and a half years of war, of intermittent shelling, and of Union frigates and gunboats that had become as much a part of the eastern horizon as the morning sun, had Charlestonians drinking the bitter brew concocted first in Columbia, where the Articles of Secession were drawn up. Columbia, on the other hand, appeared as an oasis of prosperity in the moonscape of fallow fields and untended farms the train passed through. Its wide, well-kept streets lined with magnolia and mimosa trees seemed to project a confidence its citizens felt in somehow being insulated from the traumas the rest of the South endured.

Their train lurched to a stop in the South Carolina Railroad Depot half an hour behind schedule. Luke was there to meet them, helping with luggage and settling them into the carriage. He took an indirect route home to show off the improvements since their last visit. First among these was the new Statehouse, an imposing granite structure in the Greek Revival style that was nearly finished when the war broke out. They swung by the college, a mainstay of the town since it opened in 1805. But with all its students off at war, the campus currently served as a hospital complex, where visitors came and went and ambulatory patients sat in gardens for air and sunshine. From the college, Luke turned north toward the business and residential center of the city.

As he had done since they were boys, Luke described to Daniel what surrounded them. "This here's Cotton Town," Luke told them. He pointed to a warehouse. "I've got a lot of money tied up in that building. Been sitting there for months." When Anna asked if there was no demand for it, Luke scoffed. "Oh, the demand is there, but we can't ship it because of the blockade. You got three railroads bringing cotton here from all over the state and no way to ship it to the folks that want it." Luke described for Daniel the sword factory operated by Kraft, Goldsmith, Kraft and Co., where sabers and swords were forged from metal contributed from across the South. They passed the sock factory of John Judge and Co., where a hundred workers labored to produce tubular socks for the Army. Once knitted, the tubes were cut to length, then distributed to five hundred women in Columbia who finish them with knitting needles also manufactured by Judge. Further down Richardson Street, Luke described a factory that made oilcloth and tarpaulins under a contract with the Confederate government, operating out of a complex of offices they also passed. The sidewalks teemed with civilians and soldiers, but the pace was leisurely. He read to Daniel signs advertising sales and placards boasting inventories of coveted items made scarce by the war. In all of his descriptions Luke's voice carried a hint of pride in what Columbia had become; of the contribution it was making to what he consistently referred to as "our sacred cause."

Luke lived alone in a two-story frame house on the corner of Sumter and Blanding streets. His wife died just before the war and his two sons lived out West. The older son, Eli, succumbed to the lure of the California gold rush and never returned. The younger, Alex, worked for a railroad in Kansas City.

Anna wasted no time in making herself useful. She needed the diversion offered by long hours and exhausting labor. She joined the Wayside Home, which greeted transient soldiers and provided them meals. She volunteered at the hospital, sometimes sleeping there when the demand was greatest. Abigail also served at the hospital, although her duties at home demanded a far more limited schedule than Anna's.

Unlike Daniel, Luke had invested in purely Southern enterprises; banks and railroads and shipping lines that were proving riskier bets with each passing month. Should the South suffer defeat, Luke would experience hardship that Daniel and Abigail would be spared. The failings of his business and his fortunes contributed to the somber mood he seemed mired in.

For the first month of their residence in Columbia, the three visitors pointedly avoided the subjects they knew to be flashpoints for Luke's strongly held views. They were grateful for his hospitality, conscious of his glowering depressions and busy acclimating to their new surroundings. As the weeks passed, the new arrivals felt the need to address with Luke their future living plans. They raised the subject after breakfast.

Abigail said, "We are just so grateful to you for opening your home. It has been such a lifesaver for us."

"We won't forget it," echoed Daniel. "We cannot stay here indefinitely, but until the war ends it seems every option we have is fraught with uncertainty."

Luke, seated closest to the fire in the parlor where they were gathered, said, "Stay here as long as you like. You should consider building in Columbia."

"We have discussed that as one alternative," said Abigail. "Of course Charleston will always be home to us, with so many years and friends there."

"Besides," said Daniel with a wry grin, "living here would place the state's two premiere cotton brokers in competition. Do you think the town is big enough for both of us?"

"When this war ends," said Luke, "this town will be big enough for twenty more like us. Everything is going to expand, the likes of which we never expected to see in our lifetimes. Columbia will be the center of the new South. I expect the capital of the Confederate States of America to be moved here. Richmond is too close to the varmints that caused all this. Any man or woman who puts down a stake here is going to be richly rewarded."

"But there are signs," said Daniel with a catch of hesitation, "that the war may not end well."

"Northern propaganda, brother. Don't you be taken in. We have the generals and they don't. Generals win wars. Sure, we suffered a setback at Gettysburg. I would have given anything to see old Abe's face when the Army of Northern Virginia marched up Pennsylvania Avenue with Lee at its head. But that day is coming, and when it does I suspect we will find that cur hiding in the basement, shaking like a sick dog. Look what we did to them at Chickamauga. A few more like that and they will be begging for mercy. They have no stomach for this war, I tell you. Why should they? All we want is to live in peace on our own land under our own government. Do you think they want to fight and die on foreign ground for a bunch of niggers?"

"I wish we shared your confidence," said Abigail gently.

"Do you doubt the sacred cause?"

"As you know, we thought this war ill-advised from the outset," said Daniel. "Even to contemplate it without a European ally was folly."

Luke, eyes cast to the floor, shook his head from side to side and said, "It is a sad day when our sacred cause requires the help of some damn Europeans. Brother, I sometimes wonder where you were raised. You seem to have forgotten the oppression we were subjected to by the Yankee money interests. How they rigged the game in Washington to charge us those high tariffs on things we could only get from them or from Europe. They treated us like we were nothing but their farmers, their hired help to grow what they needed at a pittance of what our products were worth. Then they had the unmitigated gall to gouge us. Nullification was a mistake. I said so at the time. We should have broken with them then and there. Served notice we were not to be trifled, and we were damn sure not going to be told how to treat our slaves, who are our personal property in case anyone has forgotten."

Abigail saw nothing to be gained by contesting Luke's view of slavery. Instead, she said, "How we got here seems less important than where we are. Believe me when I tell you that the people of Charleston are much less optimistic about how this war will end."

"And that is understandable," added Daniel. "The war has been on Charleston's front doorstep since the first shot was fired. We all know how much the Union would love to capture it. The city owes a debt to Gen. Beauregard that it remains free. Brother, do you worry that Columbia will see fighting?"

"Let them try," said Luke. "I pray for it. We will teach them a thing or two about Southern resolve. But I doubt they will come. The odds are too great with us."

"Oh?" said Daniel. "I fully expect them to come sooner or later. Consider the prize. You have kindly taken me to much of the impressive industry here. The railroads come through Columbia. The gunpowder factory is here. Palmetto Iron Works makes ammunition of all varieties. Where would we be without that? The other day you took me to an arms factory, and the Saluda Factory turns out most of the cloth our troops require for uniforms. The paper last week reported that they soon expect to produce a hundred cotton cards a day on the Statehouse grounds. All the notes and bonds that finance this war are printed here. By any objective measure, Columbia would be a far more valuable target than Charleston."

A smile bordering on smugness spread to Luke's lips. "You have made my point. We are too strong for them. All of the resources you named, plus a few you did not, argue against any fighting in Columbia. We are armed and prepared."

"Then why," asked Abigail, "were other cities in the South not equally prepared? Will the manufacturing that is so frowned upon in this state save Columbia's bacon?"

Luke's answer was more of a grumble. "Some folks could have been better ready," he admitted.

Anna asked, "Where would you go if Columbia had to be evacuated?"

"I have not given that the first thought. If Columbia is threatened I expect our whole Army to come to its defense, and for that reason the Yankees will give us a wide berth."

Into the silence that followed, Daniel said, almost as an afterthought, "Mark my words, Brother. Before this is over, the war will come to Columbia."

CHAPTER 36

Sonja returned from the Oaks with the sense of renewal Christina had hoped for. She brought new energy to her classes and had just spent a satisfying morning with her students when her mother informed her of yet another visit from Newton Spruill while she was away.

"He's quite persistent," observed Christina.

"And becoming something of a pest."

"He learned of your stay with Laura Towne and a certain young lieutenant. Florance, I believe?"

"We went riding, chaperoned of course. Randall Florance is good company and I like him. I can't see what that has to do with Lt. Spruill."

"But recall my telling him you needed more time before I thought it appropriate for you to keep company with men. His point has some merit. If you are now mature enough for Lt. Florance . . ."

"That doesn't mean I have to accept Spruill."

"Of course not. You are free to decline, but I can hardly decline for you on the basis of your age. If you don't wish to see Spruill, just tell him so. Tactfully, of course."

"What can I say?"

Christina crooked her arm to draw her daughter in. "That's an issue you will have to address for years to come. It's not always easy, but you might as well start now. And as to Lt. Spruill, I would give some thought to your explanation right away, because he is sure to find out you are back and my guess is that he will waste no time in coming again."

Two days later, Sonja sighed when she saw Spruill approaching because, despite her mother's advice, she had given no thought to the excuse she would offer. And now it was too late.

"Good afternoon, Lieutenant." Her tone was cool but civil.

He removed his cap. "Good afternoon."

"Would you like tea?"

"Thank you, no. I stopped in on a short but to me important matter."

"How can I help you?" she asked, knowing very well the answer.

"You recall my request to be allowed to call upon you."

"Of course, and you no doubt recall my mother's reply."

"Certainly. But I'm renewing my request."

"You learned of my stay at the Oaks and that Lt. Florance accompanied me on a number of outings."

"Precisely," Spruill smiled. "Surely what is good for the goose is good for the gander, so to speak. I ask for no advantage, only an equal chance." His tone was friendly, almost playful.

"I'm very flattered, of course, but I just returned from the Oaks and have hardly had time to settle back in with my students. I wonder if you could be so kind as to give me a day or two to think it over. I asked for the same consideration from Lt. Florance before agreeing to his request." This was untrue, but she sought to soften her response.

"Suppose I come back on Saturday. Would that allow sufficient time?"

"I'm very grateful."

At that moment, Christina joined them, a letter in hand. "Lieutenant, could I prevail upon you for a favor?"

"Of course. Anything."

"You have met our rebel neighbors here, Carter and his grandmother?"

"Yes." Spruill stiffened visibly.

"Carter's brother was killed at Gettysburg."

"I wasn't aware of that."

"Preston was his name. Their mother has written a letter of condolence. I'm told it was found on a captured rebel. I promised Jacob Roan I would deliver it. Would you mind taking it down there? Gettysburg was weeks ago, but nerves are still quite raw."

"You may rely on me."

She handed it to him. "Thank you, Lieutenant. We will see you on your next visit."

Spruill mounted his horse and turned it in the direction of the Lodge. He arrived with the letter in hand. Missma answered his knock.

"Good afternoon, madam. Lt. Spruill. I was here once before."

"I remember."

"I've just come from Three Pines, where I learned about the loss of your grandson. My heartfelt sympathies."

"You are very kind, Lieutenant."

"I was given this letter to give to you. Mrs. Sunblad asked me to deliver it."

Missma eyed the letter, one eyebrow raised. "How did she come by it?"

"Something about a captured rebel. I don't know the particulars."

Missma accepted the letter. "Very well. Thank you for bringing it."

"And your grandson, the other one, where is he?"

"Fishing. He fishes often."

"Yes, he does. Well, I will be on my way. Good day."

CHAPTER 37

On the Saturday Newton Spruill returned to Three Pines, Christina met him on the porch. "Good afternoon, Lieutenant," she said pleasantly. "I can guess why you have come."

He tipped his hat. "She told me I could call on her today."

"Let me see if she is available. Please be seated. The weather is so fine it would be a sin to be inside."

Spruill seated himself as Christina disappeared inside. Long minutes later, Sonja emerged. He rose to greet her.

"Hello, Lieutenant."

"Please, call me Newton."

"Very well, Newton. I was expecting you."

"I hoped you would join me for a drive. It's such a beautiful day."

"Alright. Let me tell Mother."

Sonja and Christina resolved the driving issue several days before, not in anticipation of Spruill's return but in response to a similar request by Lt. Florance, with whom Sonja spent part of the afternoon two days earlier. It had rained that day, so his plan for a buggy ride was spoiled, but they spent pleasant time together on the porch. Both women knew that an unchaperoned girl Sonja's age defied traditional social conventions, whether in North or South. But, they concluded, there was simply no alternative under the unique circumstances presented by life at Three Pines. The only chaperone available was Christina, and her duties prevented it. Sonja was a strong, Christian girl, and Christina trusted her to act accordingly. If the rare neighbor or friend saw her riding with a man and wanted to assume the worst, it couldn't be helped. They agreed that such trips would be taken only in daylight hours. If the destination was an evening party or one of the social events thrown in connection with the upcoming holiday season, she would either spend the night at the home of her hostess, as was typical, or not attend at all.

When she returned from informing Christina, she wore a coat, gloves and a bonnet. He helped her up to the seat of the buckboard.

They left Three Pines, a tendril of dust following. At the main road, Spruill turned east, toward the barrier islands and the sea. He asked about her time at the Oaks, but her impression was that he was waiting for her to finish to take charge of the conversation.

He told her about the family printing business he left in Boston; about an older brother, Winston, who ran it into the ground before Newton stepped in to save it. Spruill was sure Winston had been embezzling from the company, cooking the books in a way he felt certain Newton would never discover, but not only did Newton discover it "by some shrewd analysis," he had his brother prosecuted to boot. He took her on a verbal tour of the plant, desk by desk, job by job. He spoke at length of the press, a Heidelberg, and the challenges presented by certain inks. He detailed patents his company secured on three separate display typefaces. He confided that among men his age in Boston he was "clearly among the elite in income and potential." After an hour, during which she had said virtually nothing, she suggested it was time for them to turn around. On the return trip he told her of the Beaufort library fiasco, which she found more interesting.

"Col. Reynolds claimed he was only carrying out instructions to raise all the money possible by whatever means necessary. So just as the library—are you familiar with the library the rebels had here?"

She shook her head.

"Quite extraordinary for a place like Beaufort. Thousands of some of the best titles. On par with libraries in New England, if that gives you some idea. Fine bindings from some of Europe's best printers."

At the mention of printers, she feared he would again revisit a topic she considered quite exhausted, but he stayed with the library.

"A day or two after the battle at Port Royal Sound, the freedmen ransacked it the way they did all the old homes in town. At the request of my captain, I spent some time organizing it shortly after we arrived. I spent hours there, picking books off the floor, cleaning them, re-shelving them in some logical order. We were on the verge of reopening it to the soldiers and sailors when Col. Reynolds ordered every volume boxed up for shipment north. He planned to auction it off there."

"Was it sold?"

"A few days before the hammer was to fall, Secretary of War Stanton got wind of it. He said the Union does not make war on libraries and put a stop to the auction."

"What happened to the books?"

"The last I heard everything was stored in the attic of one of the Smithsonian buildings. I hope they make the rebels pay to get it back after the war. Would that not be rich?" He threw his head back and laughed skyward. "Making them pay to get their own library back."

Back at Three Pines, he said he would like to call on her again.

"How was it?" Christina asked after she had seen him off.

"Boring," she said. "I learned more about the printing business than I ever wanted to know."

201

"He is a decent looking man."

"I suppose. But he thinks the world of himself, and I have a feeling he looks down on women."

"Did he say that?"

"No. Just a feeling I got as he talked on and on. Oh, well, the day was pretty, and it felt good to get out."

"You get out less now that your friendship with Carter seems to have cooled."

"At least he wasn't boring, and we always did things."

"Have you seen him?"

"Not in several weeks. Since before I went to stay with Miss Towne." She glanced in the direction of the Lodge, but only for a moment.

Days later a package arrived addressed to Sonja. Spruill had gone to obvious expense for the matching bracelets enclosed. Each was highlighted by a turquoise clasp.

"Is that gold?" Sonja asked, pointing to a filigree inlay.

"Gold or not, you cannot accept these," Christina said with a pout. "If he will not take them back, we will donate them to the Relief Committee for the benefit of the freedmen."

"They are very pretty," Sonja said.

Lt. Florance returned. Sonja was happy to see him, and this time the weather permitted an excursion, their first without a chaperone. She liked his ease of manner and his wry sense of humor, so unlike Spruill's self-absorbed formality. At twenty-two, Florance was closer to her age. He told her he was studying at Yale when the war broke out, intending to enter the ministry, but his first year there created doubts he couldn't resolve. "If God created everything, who created God?—things like that. I decided," he said, "that before becoming a soldier in the Lord's army I should become a soldier in another army and make certain it was what I wanted."

"And has your time in South Carolina resolved your doubts?" she wondered.

He grinned. "I hear a voice calling me home but can't decide if it's the Lord's or Vermont's." He took her hand as he halted the buggy. Before turning down the lane on the trip back to Three Pines, he kissed her for the first time. She returned the kiss. She bid him goodbye from the porch and watched as he guided the rig into the well-worn tracings. Christina greeted her when she entered the house.

"You had a visitor, and you will be happy to learn it was not Lt. Spruill. Carter came by and left this." She handed her a folded piece of paper on which her name was written. She opened it in her room.

Dear Sonja.

I told Missma I planned to write to you and she asked me to tell you hello for her. We are doing our best over here at the Lodge. We got a letter from my mother about Preston. Missma said that Navy man Spruill brought it but we cannot figure out how he got the letter. If that is something you know please tell us. Mother said she was sending sugar and tea and other things we need but we did not get them. Only her letter. Thanksgiving is coming and it seems we have less to be thankful for this year. Preston is killed and Mother has moved to Columbia so she is farther away.

Missma has trouble remembering things. Even when I tell her in the morning she sometimes forgets by afternoon. She says it is because she is old, but she never used to forget even when I wished she would.

I miss you. I wish you would come back to see us and to meet me at the break like we used to do. I did not tell you about the things I was doing because I was afraid you would refuse to be my friend. I do not think you should punish me for being honest, as you said you wanted me to be. If I had lied to you, you would still meet me for flounder gigging and kissing so doing the right thing has brought me big trouble. I hate the Yankees for what they have done to Beaufort and for driving Mother away and for killing Preston. I am too young to join the regiment but I could not do nothing. I am not sorry for what I have done. I do not know about all the causes of this war. Missma has explained it and I understand better than I did when it started. I do not think one person should own another. I am glad I do not own anyone and that no one owns me. We were always good to our Negroes and never whipped them or refused to give them food and clothes. Life in Beaufort before this war was the only life I knew and the people that have left are the only people I have ever known. What kind of man would I be if I refused to help my people and did nothing while Preston was off fighting and dying? I would not be much of a man. I hope you will come to see us. Missma misses you like I do.

Your friend, Carter.

CHAPTER 38

J acob Roan brought word of an important meeting to be held at the Brick Baptist Church on St. Helena Island. The subject was land. Grace and Polk, accompanied by Sonja and Christina, were among a hundred freedmen, soldiers and missionaries gathered to hear about the upcoming tax sale. On the way, they talked about the day Sonja and Christina came to their cabin to urge them to consider purchasing land when and if the chance arose. That was the day Christina told them of the purchase by freedmen of two thousand acres at the last auction.

"My people?" said Polk, incredulous. "Two thousand acres?" He turned to Grace, "How much we save?"

At a corner of the cabin, Grace lifted a loose board and removed a clay jar. She brought it to the table and began to count the bills and coins. "Thirty-six dollars and eighty-four cents," she reported. Most of that came from wages eventually received from the cotton agents.

"Don't sound like it buy much land," Polk had said.

"Perhaps enough," Christina had said. "Our president has ordered land to be set aside for heads of families of the African race at the price of just $1.25 per acre. You could buy 20 acres and have money left over."

At the St. Helena meeting, Chaplin French delivered a fine sermon about Moses leading his people to the Promised Land, the crowd's responsive "amen" louder and more robust with each exhortation.

Gen. Saxton followed, outlining the details of the president's plan and the importance of land ownership to their futures. He reminded them that with the privileges of ownership came obligations to participate in the decisions that would affect their communities. "Many of you have seen our surveyors at your plantations, measuring and marking off the twenty acre lots to be auctioned," he said. "You should decide among yourselves and with your neighbors who will get what if there is more than one family interested in the same lot. If you have lived on that lot or farmed it, it is my view that you should have first claim to it, but that rule of thumb will not resolve every conflict. Be generous in your dealings with one another, always remembering the Golden Rule. The sale is set for next February," Saxton continued. "Sometime next month I will publish the procedures to be followed. You should look for them, and if you miss them I feel certain our missionary friends gathered here today will inform you."

Sonja nudged Christina, nodding toward Polk and Grace holding hands.

"Just think," whispered her mother. "Two years ago they were slaves destined for the life of parents who lived and died in the cotton fields. Now, they are learning to read, their daughters are being educated, with decent clothes and shoes that have never been worn by another. And now land!"

When Saxton solicited questions, Polk's hand was the first in the air. How could he be sure he can buy the land he has been tending for years at Three Pines, he wanted to know.

Saxton said, "I am glad you asked because it is important to understand that only on certain plantations will the right to purchase twenty acres at the fixed price of $1.25 per acre be guaranteed. If you do not live on one of those plantations, you can still submit a bid at the auction, but your bid must be the high one to secure your land."

Saxton read the disappointment on Polk's face. "Before you get discouraged," he added, "please know that many of us involved in this process, myself included, believe that far more of the government's land should be made available at this special price, and we are working very hard to make some changes in the current plan."

When the other questions had been answered, the crowd was invited to tour a model cabin, 16 by 20 feet, available for purchase at $25 and capable of being constructed rapidly. Sonja studied Grace and Polk for their reactions, but they seemed to have lost interest, their enthusiasm evaporated. She mentioned this.

"Too good fuh true," Polk said. "No surveyors at Three Pines."

Grace expressed more optimism. She spoke of possible changes to the plan, as Saxton mentioned. Perhaps Three Pines would yet be added to the list of preferred plantations. After all, she reminded him, it was bid in by the government at last spring's auction, so there should be no impediment should the government decide to make additional land available.

Polk agreed she had a point and began to feel better. Then he mentioned another possibility. They could find twenty acres on one of the preferred plantations. It would mean leaving Three Pines, but the chance to own land was too valuable to pass up. They decided Polk would begin the search at once.

While the meeting took place, Newton Spruill returned to Three Pines. The horse and buggy he drove had proven difficult to arrange, but the possibility of a drive in the country with Sonja was reward enough for his trouble. Her maturing breasts and hips occupied more of his daydreams during long, boring hours patrolling waters empty of rebels for a radius of twenty miles. He snapped his whip over the animal in anticipation.

At the porch door he straightened his tunic and knocked. He knocked again. He looked in the nearest window and saw only the main room's bare furnishings. No sound issued from the house. He opened the door, called out, then entered. It would have been odd for someone to be sleeping at that hour, and the doors off the hall stood open. When he confirmed that the house was empty, he walked into a room where Sonja's shirt hung from a hook. He stood for a moment at the foot of the bed, his daydreams resurrected, before approaching her chest of drawers. In the top drawer he rummaged through some socks and scarfs until his hand fingered a drawstring tunneled through a hem at the top of white linen bloomers. He looked behind him, then lifted the underwear to his nose, inhaling. From the folds of the linen a paper fell into the open drawer. On the side facing up was written the word "Sonja." He opened it, scanned the page and tucked the letter into his tunic. Minutes later he mounted the buckboard, the bloomers stashed beneath the seat.

By early November, Polk had traveled to four preferred plantations, with the same results at all. The twenty-acre plots were spoken for, he reported. He was losing hope of becoming a landowner when Gen. Saxton's procedures were published in *Free South*, the local newspaper. As part of her literary instruction, Christina required her pupils to read articles in the paper, so both Polk and Grace became aware of these procedures as soon as they were published. But their reading skills were still rudimentary, and the procedures difficult understand. They sought Christina's help.

"It appears to me," she said, tapping the article with her fingernail, "that all you need to do is file your claim with Saxton's office."

"But for what land?" Grace asked.

"The land right here at Three Pines. Where your garden is."

"But Three Pines ain' on de list," Polk reminded her.

"Yes, but I read this to include more than just the plantations on the list. Listen to what General Saxton said. 'The theory of selection proposed is, to divide up as nearly as possible every alternate quarter section among the freedmen, leaving such other alternate quarter section to such other persons as may wish to buy.' He also uses the term 'preemption right.'"

"What do dat mean?"

"I can't be sure, but to me it means that any freedman who can show he has lived on or farmed the land can claim it. He has rights to it."

"I work dat land fuh ten year."

"Then I think you should follow General Saxton's instructions. Deposit your money at his office along with a description of the land you have been farming. If I were you I would draw a map."

Polk's eyebrows lifted. "Then we get de land?"

"He doesn't promise you get the land."

"We get de money back?"

"Yes, I feel certain your deposit would be returned."

"Then dats what we do."

With the holidays nearing, Jacob Roan returned from a meeting with Edward

Philbrick. He found Sonja and Christina shawled and huddled near the fire.

"Six-thousand-eight-hundred-fifty-dollars?" gasped Christina. "Jacob, we are paid fifty dollars per month here, to teach and to mentor the freedmen. How is such a sum possible?"

"I was as surprised as you are. As excessive as it seems, it must be accurate. Philbrick promised each supervisor half of the profits from the cotton raised on our respective farms."

"But what must he have reaped from that?"

"By contract twenty-five percent. About twenty thousand dollars, and that's after payment of interest to his Boston investors."

"It's shocking."

"Agreed, and it will certainly reinforce the opinions of some that Philbrick is a profiteer in the disguise of a humanitarian."

"Is that your opinion?"

He hesitated. "The man is very astute. He anticipates criticism once these numbers are known so he took some pains to explain to us why these profits are justified. I can see his point because I dealt with the challenges on my plantations. All the supervisors did. We got a late start on the planting. Recall that Philbrick's group didn't acquire the properties until the auction last March. Planting should really have been done in February; March at the latest. Plus, so many of the prime workers have been recruited for the Army. Polk is an exception. So we were short-handed. And while I don't fault the freedmen for not wanting to haul marsh mud to the fields—it is nasty work—that mud is essential as manure, and I had a devil of a time getting my people to do it."

"I suppose," Christina said reluctantly. "But with so much profit perhaps he could have paid the freedmen more."

"No doubt, but Philbrick is against paying wages that will make them complacent. He feels strongly about that."

"I'm happy for you," she said. "And just in time for Christmas."

Grace asked Sonja if she would approach Roan for the use of his carriage. When he agreed, Sonja, Grace, Polk, Sparrow and Lark traveled to the ferry that would take them into Beaufort. They dressed as for church, with the women in their best outfits and Polk in a derby hat. As the buckboard pitched and bounced on the rutted road, they sang "Down in the Lonesome Valley"; "Happy Morning"; "Lord, Remember Me" and "Tell My Jesus, 'Morning'", spirituals that Sonja had learned from them and come to love. Grace clutched a handkerchief in which their land deposit was wrapped, twenty-five dollars to the penny. She counted it three times.

They were greeted efficiently at Gen. Saxton's headquarters. Grace tendered the deposit, which was counted and receipted. Polk handed over his crudely drawn map, which showed his garden in relation to the main house, a large X marking the area they intended to purchase.

On the return trip, Grace clutched the receipt and talked about the cabin they would locate on their land when their savings, now reduced to $11.84, became sufficient to buy one of those cabins they saw at the Brick Baptist Church. Polk smiled broadly at her plan, forecasting record harvests next spring. Behind them, Sparrow peeled an orange, doling out succulent sections like a high priestess administering a sacrament. She and Lark chatted with Sonja about school friends and clothes they planned to make with some broadcloth they had recently received from the Philadelphia Relief Committee. For the four freedmen returning to Three Pines in the late afternoon, savoring the oranges with their faces turned to the setting winter sun, 1864 promised to be a very good year. For Sonja, the outlook was less certain.

1864

CHAPTER 39

Carter now kept a calendar on a pine board he marked with the point of a knife. He regretted his failure to do this when they first came to the Lodge, but it seemed then such a temporary arrangement. Now he wondered if the board will be wide enough to hold the months and years ahead. By that calendar, it was January 3.

With Christmas approaching, he had made a trip to Signal Oak, where this letter awaited him.

December 2, 1863 Columbia, S.C.

Dearest Carter and Missma:
I can only pray you received my letter and the supplies Gabriel brought to you several months ago. I fear you did not. Gabriel has not been seen nor heard from since he agreed to carry them. The Dragoons cannot account for this long absence. They assume he was captured. Given the alternative, I hope they are right. Either way, it is but one more piece of dreadful news from this dreadful war.

To say that I hope this letter finds you well and happy seems grossly inappropriate, as I do not see how you could be either. We all feel Preston's loss, and there are days when I am certain I cannot get out of bed to face another day. We all must have days like that. I have thrown myself into work here, as to stay busy is the only defense I can find to the sadness and depression that overcome me when I am idle. But enough of that, as each of you must be dealing with similar emotions and to dwell on them is to inflict more hurt.

Life here in Columbia is strange. At times you would not know there was a war on. I have spoken to many who seem curiously detached from it, as if the war was going on in Europe. They host their parties and entertain their friends as before. Were it not for the fact that the college is shut down, I suspect social life here would very much be what it was before the war.

But of course the college is shut down, the students off fighting and its buildings being in such demand for hospital rooms. I spend a great deal of time there, doing whatever needs to be done. When I am not there, I am at the Wayside Home, bringing what cheer I can muster to soldiers far from home. I doubt I have ever been more challenged, but as noted above, "enough of that."

Uncle Daniel and Aunt Abigail send their love. And Luke as well, although he is a difficult man to understand. He still insists on the merits of the war despite what Daniel, Abigail and I see as mounting evidence that our suffering is increasing and our prospects for victory less certain. Luke remains entirely confident we will prevail, and while I admire his optimism and wish at times I had more of it, events tell a different story. The other day Uncle Daniel accused him of whistling past the graveyard. He had forgotten I was in the room and immediately regretted his metaphor because of Preston, but I assured him that I knew he meant no harm and that I agreed with the sentiment he expressed. Luke *is* whistling past the graveyard, as are many here, insisting that every setback does nothing more than strengthen Southern resolve, which they seem to believe is in inexhaustible supply. Luke has total faith in Generals Lee, Longstreet, Stewart and Hampton. He insists they are the decisive advantage that will bring victory. His opinion of Gen. Beauregard is less enthused, although his reasoning on that gentleman is unclear to me. Certainly the people we left in Charleston would not trade him for all the generals in the Confederacy, Gen. Lee included.

With the cotton brokerage business all but non-existent, Uncle Daniel has ample time to devote to his precious newspapers. Aunt Abigail reads to him daily, and often he will ask that something he considers particularly important be re-read. I would not want to repay Luke's hospitality, which we all appreciate, by disparaging him, but I am convinced that Uncle Daniel knows more about what is going on here than does his brother, who has lived here all of his adult life. And Uncle Daniel is most concerned that Columbia is not prepared for what may come. "Sleepwalking through the war" is how he puts it.

To state the obvious, I am ready to put 1863 behind me. My ardent prayers are with you both in this holiday season, with the most heartfelt hope that this is the very last Christmas we spend apart. The tragedy of losing Preston is yet another reminder of the need for family, and I will not rest until I am back with mine.

All my love, Anna

Carter read the letter again. Although it was now over a month old, the letter was as close as he had come to his mother in months and seeing her handwriting brought her closer. So Gabriel was missing. Anna's letter was confirmation he was the courier that must have been intercepted with the letter of condolence. Unless he was dead, the Yankees were keeping him somewhere. Beaufort?

A chill, bone deep, swept off the river. He left the relative warmth of the Lodge to chop firewood. Their winter supply was ample, but he felt the need to swing the axe and to strike a blow, even if his target was an inanimate stump. He worked up a sweat in half an hour. It was during his first pause to rest that he heard Missma cry out.

He rushed to the porch, where she lay sprawled.

"I tripped," she said, her eyes watering and her teeth clenched. "My hip."

"Can you walk?"

"No. Carry me inside."

When he placed his arms beneath her, she cried out in pain. "Sorry," he said.

He carried her in and set her gently on her mat. In their time at the Lodge, he had never been behind her partition. He had also never seen her weep and contort as she was doing now. "What should I do?" he asked.

She said, gasping. "I may have broken my hip." She began to moan. "Ohh-hhhhh. Get the laudanum. It's in the cupboard."

He returned with it. She opened it, her hand shaking as she swigged. She grimaced. "Horrid stuff," she said. "Worse than castor oil, but I need it. Now get me my gallon jug. I need to wash this bitter taste from my mouth."

He found and lifted the jug, noting that it was nearly empty.

"Pour some for me. This pain."

He poured some into a cup. Her hand shook as she sipped.

"It's getting low," he said. "Is there anything else that would help?"

"Morphine, but we have none."

"I can go to Three Pines? Ask if they have any."

"I will not be dependent on them."

He added wood to the fire before leaving. At the break, frosted branches snapped as he pushed through. The fields beyond lay frozen and lifeless. Smoke rose from the chimney at Three Pines. His teeth chattered as he covered the distance. He hadn't been there since dropping off the letter to Sonja months ago.

A cook answered his knock. Neither Sonja nor Christina was there. "Be back directly," she said.

He asked her to tell them that his grandmother had hurt herself in a fall and needed help.

Back at the Lodge, he heard Missma's moaning when he reached the porch. "Someone will come soon," he reported.

"This changes everything," she said. "I'm a fool for thinking something like this could not happen."

"Is there anything I can do?"

"Get me a blanket and keep the fire up."

He returned with a blanket and spread it over her. She pulled it to her chin. "Sit here on the bed," she instructed. "This is my punishment for putting you through this. I should never have been so rash. I don't know what I was thinking. But now we are in what my mother would have called a fine fix. I will need to stay in bed until this pain lessens. That could be days, possibly weeks." She paused, her eyes squeezed shut and her teeth clinched. "I will not be able to cook or clean so you will have to take over. I can probably manage to bathe myself for a time, but I will need help with my chamber pot. That's not something a boy, a young man, should have to deal with but it can't be helped. I'm afraid Reggie's lessons are out of the question, so you will need to let him know what has happened. Do you think you can do these things?"

"Yes, ma'am."

"It's terrible to burden you like this."

Soot barked and he heard footsteps on the porch. He opened the door to find Christina and Sonja, bundled in coats, hats and gloves, vapor escaping their noses and mouths. He and Sonja exchanged nervous glances as they walked in. Christina asked what happened.

"She tripped on the porch. She says her hip may be broken."

"In here," Missma called.

They stood over her bed. "I've walked across that threshold a thousand times," Missma said, wincing. "I struck my foot and lost my balance. It was stupid, as many things have been." She winced again and emitted a low "ohhhhhh."

Christina removed a glove and placed her hand on Missma's forehead. Turning to Carter, she said, "Perhaps you can step outside for a few minutes."

He put on his coat and walked onto the porch. Sonja looked so pretty, he thought. Her cheeks were flushed with the chill and her eyes even bluer than he remembered.

Minutes passed. The air outside the Lodge was eerily quiet.

"It could be worse," Christina said as they came out of the Lodge. "The skin is not broken. If it is her hip, as she says it is, at least she is coping with a closed wound. Infection would be the issue otherwise. She's in great pain. The laudanum will help. We have some at Three Pines if she needs more. How will you manage by yourself?"

"I don't know," he said.

Sonja had not spoken, but now said, "I can help."

He stared at her. "That's very kind."

An edgy silence followed. Christina said, "Sonja can look in on her. We will both do what we can, especially in these next few weeks when she is likely to be bedridden. She will need to keep up her strength."

He nodded. "Thank you both for coming."

Christina said simply, "We are neighbors."

When they were gone, he sat in the Lodge, a pencil in hand and a sheet of paper in front. He wrote to his mother. From behind Missma's partition came soft moans mingled with occasional snorts of intermittent sleep. As badly as he felt for her, his spirits rose for the first time in months. Sonja was coming. He would get to see her and speak with her. It was far from what he had, but it was enough for now. He wrote the following letter:

January 1864 The Lodge

Dear Mother:

Thank you for your letter of December 2. Cousin Gabe must have been captured, because we received the letter you sent after the news of Preston, but none of the supplies you sent came with the letter. I do not know how the letter reached us. I hope my cousin is not hurt or killed.

Today there was an accident. Missma tripped on the porch. She says she broke her hip. I carried her to her bed and brought some medicine for the pain. The missionaries at Three Pines came to see her. They say they will help her and me. I will do what I can. I do not know when I will be able to take this letter to Signal Oak.

Please tell Uncle Daniel and Aunt Abigail the news. I miss you very much.

Your son, Carter

In early afternoon, Sonja appeared, businesslike and direct. She seemed to him to be indifferent to the months of absence. Perhaps she had not thought much about him at all, while he had been able to think of little else but her. She went behind Missma's partition and remained there several minutes. He heard them speaking but could not overhear what was said.

When she emerged, she said, "Your grandmother has soiled herself. It will happen often. I need to clean her. I asked her if you can watch what I do. You will need to know when I'm not here. She agreed." She handed him a cloth.

"Soak this in hot water and bring it to me."

He took the heated cloth behind the partition. Missma lay prone, her head elevated slightly on a pillow. Her eyes were closed, but she did not appear to be sleeping. The area around the bed smelled of urine. Sonja untied the drawstring on Missma's bloomers, sliding them down from her hips. He saw a yellowish stain in the crotch of the bloomers. Missma's pubis was shriveled almost to invisibility. Random strands of silver pubic hair protruded. Sonja slid the pants past the knees and off. Missma's legs were thin and varicose, pale white with purple lines and erratic blotches. He saw an oval brown birthmark on her upper left thigh, just below the groin. Sonja placed the warm cloth on Missma's lower abdomen. In a soft voice she asked, "Are you able to clean yourself?"

Without opening her eyes, Missma nodded faintly.

Sonja held the underpants and motioned him from the bed. "I'll have these washed," she said. "And when I come back I'll bring more cloth. She will need a diaper that can be removed easily and washed often. We will need to change the sheets, but not today. It will take both of us to do that."

"Thank you. I would be lost."

"The worst is yet to come. You may have trouble doing what is needed. Perhaps you have never seen a woman's body."

"Yes, I have," he said.

CHAPTER 40

Carter lay on his mat. From beyond Missma's partition came suppressed whimpers. When he looked in on her for the last time, she said through clamped teeth she was trying to use the laudanum sparingly, but that every time she moved so much as a muscle she felt as though a knife pierced her hip. He wondered if she could die during the night.

He got up and went to her. "Missma, would you like me to read to you?"

"Yes," she said instantly. "Anything to take my mind off this. What do we have?"

"*Vanity Fair.*"

The lantern idled on the table, an ornament for months for lack of fuel. He pulled back her partition, propping it against a chair, so he could see her from his seat by the fire. He opened the book, angled it to catch the flickering light, and began to read. She fell asleep by page three.

Sonja came the next morning. She brought a canvas pad she found at Three Pines. She slid it beneath Missma to protect her pallet. She had also cut up a sheet into small squares suitable as diapers. He watched her ministrations with a mixture of gratitude and longing. She remained businesslike and efficient. When Missma napped, they moved to the porch.

"What happens now?" he wanted to know.

"I must ask Laura Towne. She's a doctor. Well, almost. But she will know."

"She can't stay in bed forever. But how long will it take that hip to heal?"

He stared at her. "You got my letter?"

She lowered her eyes to hands folded in her lap. "Yes. I started to reply but wasn't sure what to say. I have missed you."

"For true?"

"Yes, for true."

"What has happened since you . . . left?"

She told him about her stay at Laura Towne's, omitting the young officers that buzzed around her. She was most animated when she spoke of the thunderstorm and their plunge into the creek, smiling as she recalled it. "I was glad I could swim. I owe you for that.

"I spent a day with Laura on her visits to the children who were sick. She was so good with them. She told me about her medical training before she came here. She wanted to become a doctor like the one we met in Beaufort who was taking care of the wounded soldiers. I had never met a woman doctor and I didn't know women could become doctors. I want to be one someday."

"Is that why you are helping me with Missma?"

"That's part of it. And what about you? I know you must miss your brother."

"I miss what I remember. It feels like he left years ago. I still have trouble thinking he won't come back. It seems impossible."

"Are you still doing your . . . work?"

"If you mean scouting out things in Beaufort, I am. I keep track of the river, ships and soldiers going up and down. But now with Missma, who knows? This is a small place, but now I will have to do it all, plus care for her. I need to learn to cook or we will both starve. In a few weeks it will be time to plant. I cut extra wood to keep the Lodge warmer. She likes that."

The next morning, Sonja brought vegetable soup. "She needs to eat," she said. "The cook at Three Pines won't miss this. How was last night?"

"Better. She didn't cry out as much."

When they took the soup behind the partition, a fetid odor hung in the air above the bed. Missma slept. Sonja turned to him. "Let me handle this. You can help me change the sheet. Bring a warm rag." From the fireplace he heard Missma stir. She and Sonja conferred in low tones. When he brought the rag, Sonja handed him the diaper. "Take this outside," she said. "Come back in ten minutes."

When he returned, Missma avoided eye contact. The soup remained covered. Sonja said to her. "We need to move you, Mrs. Barnwell."

"Call me Missma, please."

"As you wish, Missma. Can Carter lift while I slide the clean sheet under you? It will only take a moment."

"You must have a brought a sheet with you. Let's get it over with," she said.

Carter leaned over her. She bent her legs at the knees, wincing as she did so. He positioned one arm under her knees, the other beneath her neck. She weighed less than an armload of firewood, or so it seemed. With her back inches from the bed, Sonja deftly gathered the soiled sheet and positioned the fresh one. He set her down. Missma gripped his hand, transferring her pain.

"You need to eat," Sonja told her.

Sonja uncovered the soup while patiently reminding Carter she would need a spoon. When he brought it, Sonja lifted a spoonful to Missma's mouth, feeding her with the same motions she might have fed a child.

"Very good," Missma said after the first taste. "Carter made this?" It was the first sign of humor since her fall.

As Sonja ladled out the soup, Carter studied her, happy to have the chance to stare while her attention was on Missma. In the three feet separating him from her, he felt the tenderness he used to feel at the break; connected to her though they were not touching. It came to him that this was what he had missed

216

most—Sonja near and relaxed, speaking softly with intimacy the way she did for the first time on the beach that night. Yes, he had longed for the kisses, her tongue seeking his, the heat of her embrace and the press of her body against his. Thrilling, but through their absence he had found a way to endure. But what he witnessed now threatened to overwhelm him. It was touching something he experienced only briefly and thought was lost forever; something to do with his mother, and with Preston, and it had everything to do with Sonja, and the way she gently encouraged Missma to eat a little more, and the way she wiped the corners of her mouth with the spoon.

Sonja looked up at him. "Carter, are you crying?"

He blinked and turned from her. Minutes later she joined him on the porch. She put her arms around him, her head on his chest. They stood for a long time, neither speaking.

CHAPTER 41

In late January, Sonja walked to the cabin occupied by Polk and Grace. She had news she could not wait to share, received the night before from Jacob Roan. Chaplain French had been to Washington and persuaded someone important, perhaps the president himself, to make more land available to the freedmen in the upcoming auction. Now, according to Roan, all land owned by the government not reserved for military or educational purposes could be purchased at the $1.25 per acre rate. The purchaser must have been a resident for six months preceding the sale, be at least twenty-one years of age, and be loyal to the Union. Those conditions met, they could purchase lots of 20 or 40 acres if they took steps to "preempt" the land by living or farming on it. And had not Polk made his deposit and tendered his map? Had he not preempted this land by working it for years? Was he not loyal, long past twenty-one, and living on these islands his entire life?

"Mother and Mr. Roan both believe you qualify," she told them once inside the cabin, where the aroma of fried fatback permeated.

Grace raised both hands toward the roof. "Praise the Lawd!"

Polk grinned at Sonja. "Den I guess I know what I gwine do. Mud my land, das what." He finished the hominy on his tin plate, grabbed a fistful of cornbread where it warmed near the fire, and told them he had work to do.

Grace turned to Sonja. "You see a man mud land? Pickin' cotton ain' nothin' after muddin' land."

"Will Polk mind if I watch?"

"Stay out de way, das all."

Sonja walked to a corner of Polk's plot, where he hitched a mule to the pole sled he used to bring the mud to the fields. If he was conscious of her presence, he didn't show it, focused on the task at hand. He laid the tarp over the runners and tied it at the corners. He led the mule to the creek bank closest to the garden, a distance of a quarter mile. She followed. She watched as he descended the bank, his shovel in one hand and a bushel basket in the other, sinking up to mid-femur. The day was mild for January, and the frigidity of the water seeping into his boots didn't appear to faze him. He began to shovel mud. He lifted the shovel, straining visibly as he shifted his grip to mid-shaft for leverage and positioned it over the basket. The mud plopped to the bottom with a soggy thud. His feet and toes had to be numb. He repeated this for the ten shovelfuls needed to fill the basket. He spiked the shovel at the water's edge, lifted the basket, and shouldered the one-hundred-pound load. He staggered up the bank to the sled, dumping the contents with a satisfied "whew." He began to sweat so removed his coat. He repeated the process until the sled sagged along the ground, at which point he led the mule back to the plot, where furrows from last year's planting ran along like a miniature mountain range.

When Grace joined her, Sonja said Polk needed to rest. Grace shook her head as Polk began using a mattock to break up the first row. Grace explained that the garden soil must be mixed with creek mud before the mud dried, and only when all the mud from the sled had been blended could he afford to rest. When the sled was empty, he cast a glance toward the water, where Beaufort's endless mud awaited.

"I see what you mean," said Sonja as she and Grace walked back toward the cabin.

"That be mens work sho' nuff," Grace said.

At mid-morning, Grace and the girls brought Polk bread, slices of ham and fresh water from the well. While he sat on the ground, Lark told him about a story she wrote that Sonja called "excellent." Sparrow said it was about a lost dog. Grace smiled approvingly. Polk made three more trips before quitting in mid-afternoon. He could barely lift his arms and said that his back felt as if it had been walked on by that elephant he saw in one of the books Christina handed out. The next morning he was there again, hauling another ton of mud from the creek. It took him a week of this routine to fertilize his field.

On the day after he finished the heavy lifting, he stood at the edge of the garden. Grace and the girls were there as Polk explained his decision for a different allocation of the land. He would plant an additional two rows of corn this year, more sweet potatoes and fewer beans. As he walked the perimeter of the plot, pointing, he looked up. Three riders approached. As they drew closer, their Union Army uniforms came into focus.

"Howdy," said Polk when they stopped.

"How do?" said the sergeant, ignoring the women.

Polk did not flinch. "How kin a hep you?" he asked.

"Thinking 'bout buying me some land at the auction," the sergeant said, looking not at Polk but over his head, at the river beyond. "This place ain't reserved for the niggers so I thought I'd take a look-see. Mighty pretty stretch of water yonder."

"'Bout a two hundred acres on Three Pines," Polk said.

"I'm liking this plot right here," the sergeant said. "That garden looks ready to plant."

"Spoken fuh," said Polk.

"Yeah? By who?"

"Me."

"You?" The sergeant laughed as one of the privates chuckled. "You got the kind of money to buy this?"

"Only needs a dollar twenty-five an acre. I gots dat."

"Don't know who told you that but they got it wrong. That price don't get you nothin' if the plantation ain't on that list. And this one ain't. Why I come."

"Dey change dat."

"Well, 'dey change dat' back. Read it yesterday. Get somebody to read *Free South* to you. Yes sir, I just may bid on this one." With another glance at the river beyond, he wheeled, followed by the privates.

Grace felt a sudden heaviness in her limbs, as if it had been she hauling tons of mud instead of Polk, who stared morosely at the ground. Polk, whose first reaction to good news was always to predict that it was "too good fuh true." Maybe he's right, she thought. Sonja, Christina and Jacob Roan seemed well intended, but they were, after all, white people, like the arrogant white sergeant who just left.

Polk turned to her. "I be muddin' nother man's land."

She told the girls to go back to the cabin, and when they were out of earshot said to him, "Maybe, maybe not. We find out."

Polk spit into the soil he had been tending. "Dey ain' never gon let we own no land. Never. I be born at night, but it won't last night. Never."

Grace took his hand and led him toward the main house. "We find out."

When they saw Sonja they repeated what the sergeant said. She said, "I feel sure he is mistaken. Mother or Mister Roan will know."

Roan was away from the plantation, but Christina's head bowed when she emerged from her room.

Sonja repeated the sergeant's statement.

"Oh, Polk, I read that in *Free South* last night. I haven't had a chance to tell you, or you, Sonja. It breaks my heart, but I'm afraid the sergeant is right. The change was changed back. There is so much demand for so little land."

"So what it mean?"

"It means the freedmen have an absolute right to purchase only the plantations on that list. Everything else goes to the high bidder."

"So the sergeant buy my land?"

"The news is even worse where soldiers are concerned. They only have to put up a deposit of twenty-five percent. They get three years to pay the rest."

Polk and Grace turned and walked toward their cabin. Inside, Polk lay on his mat with a groan, as though the labor of the last week had suddenly caught up with him. Grace looked at paper wedged into cracks in the walls, the ill-hinged door that emitted dust, wind and rain, the dirt floor, the roof through which a star or two was visible on clear nights. This shack had never looked so shabby. For the first time since her fullness, she felt again a slave. Her overseer Smits was gone, and old man Boykin, her owner, had never been a presence at the plantation, but she wondered if somehow they were still in her life, part of that great white force which had changed the rules but not the outcome. She was born a slave, and unless the rebels won the war she would die a non-slave, but looking around today it was hard to see a difference. And she wondered what to tell the girls. They had sensed her optimism that with freedom they would see better times, more opportunity, the chance to avoid lives of farming and despair. Thanks to the missionaries, they were learning. Their budding education was no rumor, no dishonored white promise because she saw them come home from school relating stories read in books and with numbers to add and subtract. Perhaps she owed it to them to warn that a change in the rules won't change the outcome, that even as educated non-slaves Lark and Sparrow will still be Negroes, subject to all the hurt and injustice that she and Polk long ago accepted as their lot and God's will.

CHAPTER 42

Around midnight, Carter awoke to a foul odor permeating the Lodge. He knew without asking that Missma had lost control of her bowels. He went to her bedside. She whimpered, whether from pain or embarrassment he could not tell.

"Don't worry, Missma. Sonja showed me what to do." She mumbled, but the only word he understood was "humiliating."

He wet a rag in water kept heated in the fireplace and returned to her. He lifted the hem of her nightgown to expose the diaper. It was soiled through with diarrhea. He pulled the diaper free, then slid his hand beneath her bottom, as Sonja had done. Missma cried out in pain, but it could not be helped. With one hand at the base of her spine, he used the other to spread her legs enough to gain access to the areas that needed to be cleaned. That done, he slipped a fresh diaper under her, tying the corners to keep it in place.

She said, "When I brought us here I thought I could further your education. I did not intend to take it this far."

Before returning to his sleeping mat he placed the soiled diaper into a pot of lye soap. When Sonja arrived the following morning, she complimented him. She brought a stack of fresh diapers. Essential, since Missma's diarrhea had not abated.

"Mother spoke to Laura Towne," she said. "At Missma's age it will take at least a month before she can put pressure on the hip. But she needs to get up and walk when she can stand the pain." She saw the fatigue in his eyes. "I can stay with her this morning. You had a difficult night."

Sonja returned to Three Pines in early afternoon. Christina informed her that "very persistent" Newton Spruill just left.

"Good," Sonja said. "I don't want to see him. I hope he'll stop coming here."

"Then find a tactful way to tell him so. How are things at Carter's?"

Sonja described her morning at the Lodge. Missma dozed off and on, but when awake was able to talk. "I like her spirit," said Sonja. "She doesn't pity herself as some would do in her situation. She pities Carter for what she's putting him through and expresses great guilt for her decision to stay instead of going to Charleston with Carter's mother."

"Does she talk about Carter's mother?"

"Sometimes. I think I would like her if she is as Missma—I call her Missma now because she asked me to—describes. Carter, too. Both sing her praises. A warm woman. They worry about her losing her son."

"That's so very hard. And how is your favorite rebel holding up?"

"I admire Carter for how he takes care of her. He's patient and gentle. When he isn't chopping wood or milking the cow or fixing food or doing the other things he has to do he reads to her. He says her memory is failing. I see that too. She tells me things we talked about just the day before."

"Another reason to dread old age."

"How long do people who break their hips live?"

Christina said, "Laura Towne didn't know. It shortens the life. Of that she was certain. Why do you ask?"

"If she died, I suppose Carter would leave. To join his mother, who he says is now in Columbia. That was in the letter she sent. Which reminds me, he asked me how that letter came to be delivered by Newton Spruill. I couldn't tell him."

"I asked Lt. Spruill to take it there. Jacob gave it to me. He told me how he got it but it was months ago and I've forgotten his explanation. Sometimes I think my memory is getting as bad as Mrs. Barnwell's."

That evening, Sonja put the same question to Jacob Roan, who at first appeared puzzled. "I remember now," he said. "Some major whose name escapes me asked me to deliver it. As I recall they found it on a rebel they captured."

"Carter said the letter mentioned supplies they never received."

"The major did talk about those. They were confiscated. They are rebels, after all. The letter was allowed to go through after being analyzed for any codes or secret messages. A humanitarian gesture. I thought it was the right thing to do."

At the Lodge the following day, Missma's diarrhea was much improved, along with her spirits. Sonja related to Carter the information on Anna's condolence letter. "Who would have brought it?" she asked.

"You're sure he said the rebel was captured?"

"Captured. Yes, he said captured."

"Good. Better than killed. It must have been my cousin Gabe. He came here a couple of times right after the war started. He brought us the cow and Sunset. I wonder what they did with him."

"Mr. Roan didn't say."

From behind her partition Missma called to them. Together they stood at her bedside.

"I heard what you said about that letter," she said. "I hope the Yankees are treating Gabriel well. Now I have a suggestion. You two have been on duty looking after me for too long. It looks like a nice day from what I can see. Why don't you take a sail? I will be fine while you are gone."

Carter looked at Sonja, who said, "A wonderful idea. I haven't been in months. Let me tell Mother where I'm going. She was expecting me."

Thirty minutes later she returned, dressed for sailing. Soot seemed as eager to get on the water as they were. A swift breeze out of the northeast propelled them toward Hilton Head.

"So what is this captured cousin like?" Sonja asked.

At the tiller, Carter smiled. "Cousin Gabe is one of a kind. Missma calls him the ultimate lady's man."

"Perhaps I'll meet him someday."

"Not if I can help it."

"Why would you say that?"

"Cousin Gabe is a charmer. All the girls fall in love with him."

"And you think I would fall in love with him?"

"Well, he's one of us. A rebel, I mean. I know how you feel about those."

"Carter Barnwell, you know no such thing. I ended our . . . friendship not because you are a rebel but because you weren't honest with me. Everything I did with you before that was done with full knowledge you were the enemy." She winked at him. "So, you think I might fall for this cousin? Is he handsome?"

"That's what the ladies say."

"Then I want to meet him."

"You must have met lots of handsome men in the past few months." He was thinking how lovely she looked with the wind in her hair.

"I've met some very nice gentlemen."

"Did you kiss them?"

"That's not a fair question and I won't answer it."

"I guess you're right. It's none of my business."

"But since you asked, and since I promised to always be honest with you, I did kiss one of them several times."

"I wish you weren't so honest."

She laughed. "You didn't ask, but you are a much better kisser than he is."

They stared at each other, quiet for a time. To break the silence, she said, "Missma went out of her way to get us together today. Did you notice?"

"She appreciates all you've done for her. She tells me all the time."

"You didn't ask her to suggest we sail, did you?"

"No. It was her idea. A good idea, but hers."

"It was thoughtful. Still, it surprises me that a proper Southern lady would encourage her grandson to keep company with an abolitionist."

"Missma is certainly a proper Southern lady, but your help to us is more important than your views on slavery."

"Maybe not so proper after all."

His eyes held hers. "What does that mean?"

She draped her hand over the side, letting the river flow through her splayed fingers. She turned her gaze toward the tiny ripples formed. "Oh, just some talk we had one day when you were fishing. If you were fishing."

"Talk about me?"

"About her. A love she had when she was a young woman."

"A man named Marc?"

Sonja nodded.

"I've heard her mention him but that's about all."

"So she never told you what went on in the Lodge?"

He shook his head. "Are you going to tell me?"

She laughed. "Maybe. If you promise to be on your best rebel behavior and stop spying."

"Isn't that what they call blackmail? I'll get Missma to tell me."

"I doubt that. She said it was just between us girls."

They returned with the sun at their backs, daylight beginning to give way to dusk.

She hugged him as she left. It was not the kind of hug he wanted, but it lingered just long enough to remind him of what he had been missing.

At Three Pines, Christina asked about her sail. Then she said, "And you are not going to believe it, but Lt. Spruill was here again. He is truly becoming a pest."

"What did you tell him?"

"The truth. That you were sailing with Carter. He wasn't pleased. Plainly it upset him, although I don't know why he should think he has some claim on your time. You have hardly misled him."

"He's a strange man. Perhaps he will take the hint and quit making the trip."

CHAPTER 43

With her heels in Sunset's flanks, Sonja galloped along a wooded trail near Three Pines. Though it lacked the speed and power of d'Artagnan, the horse had won her heart with its gentle competence over low hurdles of brush and bramble. Now sixteen, the girl relished the freedom she felt when mounted. She had been in South Carolina for two years, longer than most of the missionaries had been willing to stay, and still no girls her age had come to teach. Both horse and rider panted as Sonja pulled up under the arms of a giant water oak.

Her mother was in love, Sonja now knew, despite Christina's denials, going only so far as to admit that she was "very fond of Jacob." But the girl had seen the light in her mother's eyes when Roan returned from his duties at neighboring plantations, noted the devotion she showed in any matter related to his health or comfort, and sensed the loss the moment he left Three Pines. That must be what love is, she reasoned. An absorption in another. An incompletion without that person near. An eagerness to share the most mundane details of a day filled with them, if only to prompt a familiar smile, a tender look of comprehension, of shared experience. Yes, her mother was definitely in love.

She reached down to pat Sunset on the withers. She thought about Randall Florance, his engaging smile, his droll sense of humor, his easy conversation. And too the subtle urge her body was beginning to feel when he kissed her. He held her in a way that suggested he wanted more, and while he had never attempted to move his hands beyond her arms and shoulders, she sometimes wondered what that might feel like. She liked the cut of his uniform, his posture in it, and the sense of security she felt in his presence, a sense she lacked entirely where Newton Spruill was concerned. Spruill was somewhat older than Florance, and something in his manner implied a threat. Florance had soft brown eyes, but the brown of Spruill's eyes was hard and cold. She wasn't sure why she should feel as she did. She should be touched, flattered by Spruill's interest, and by warning her of possible repercussions from an association with a rebel, he had shown he was as protective of her as Florance. Yet she didn't feel protected. Spruill looked at her in a way Florance did not. His eyes took her all in, as if she were a lavish meal about to be devoured. Maybe hunger explained it. Spruill's hunger was palpable, while Florance's was playful and benign.

And what about Carter? She thought back to the day of Missma's fall, her first glimpse of him in months. He looked so different, so much more solid than she remembered. The shirt he wore was too small, his arms strong when he swung the axe. And after their awkward greeting, it took no time to fall back into their old pattern of conversation. If she was as honest with herself as she had been demanding of him, she was glad to see him. Excited even. What could that mean? Did Carter excite her in the same way she was beginning to feel about Florance? If they renewed their kissing at the break, would she wonder what it would be like for Carter's hands to move over her body, or for him to press against her in a way that suggested more? She remembered the warmth of his hand when it lingered briefly on her breast. It surprised and pleased her. But he was a rebel, and a kid. She tightened the reins, turned Sunset toward Three Pines, and cantered home.

She arrived in the middle of an intense conversation between her mother and Grace, who told Christina she did what she could to keep Polk's spirits up, but she lacked a tonic for his profound dejection at learning he would not get his land after all. Like other slaves on Three Pines, Polk had chafed under the despised overseer Smits, for whom nothing was ever done fast or well enough, and who left on the day When Gun Shoot. Polk was known as the best worker on the plantation, but he did not escape the lash for the most trivial of excuses. Smits made daily life harder than it needed to be, but Polk endured, cursing. His anger somehow rendered the hardships tolerable. But Grace told Christina that losing land he never owned had affected him even as his worst days under Smits did not. She had never seen him like this.

According to Grace, he rode to Beaufort by himself to retrieve their deposit. At Gen. Saxton's office, he met freedmen on the same business, and they were as angry as Polk. None understood why so many ready to buy and work the land had been deprived of the right afforded to so few on the preferred plantations. Many had gone to trouble and expense to establish what Gen. Saxton had called preemptive rights in the land, just as the general urged them to do. Had it been a trick from the beginning? The Union right hand didn't appear to know what its left hand was up to. When he learned that the average price paid for an acre in the February auction was $11, he felt both disgusted and foolish. Polk stuffed the refund into his pocket and stormed out of the office. One of the freedmen he spoke with, Linwood, was headed to Daddy August's for some liquid consolation. Polk decided to join him. When he crashed into the cabin late that night, he was thoroughly drunk.

But Grace had bigger concerns than Polk's single night of dissipation. She even managed a smile when she told Christina that the price he paid the next morning inflicted more pain than anything she could have said or done. What worried her, she said, was the fact that he had yet to return to the garden. Spring was coming, and he had not planted so much as a seed of the vegetables they would depend upon for the summer and fall. She confronted him, but he yelled at her, something he rarely did. "Ain' my land. Plantin' on 'nother man's land ain' right."

"He down," said Grace. "He long down."

"And I feel partially responsible," Christina said. "I encouraged you to put in your claim and the deposit. I got your hopes up and feel just awful for doing so. I didn't know the true situation. It seems no one did. You must believe that."

As they talked, Jacob Roan arrived after an absence of several days. He entered the parlor and sensed at once the tension.

"Who died?" he asked.

Christina said, "Polk and Grace lost the land."

Roan nodded. "The auction angered a lot of people."

"Jacob, until the *Free South* is published, we won't know who bought what. Perhaps someone bid for Three Pines. I hope it wasn't that awful sergeant. Do you know what happened?"

"I do. I think we need to speak with Polk."

"He at the house," Grace said.

"Go get him. What I have to say is something you both should hear."

Sonja glanced at her mother, who was staring at Roan with a look of curiosity, but Roan wore his poker face that yielded no clues as to what he had in mind.

At the cabin, Grace went inside to get Polk. Sparrow and Lark read at the table, and though it was only mid-afternoon, Polk slept on his mat. She shook his shoulder. He opened his eyes briefly before closing them again.

"Honey, get up," Grace said. "Massa Jacob here."

Polk turned over, his face toward the wall a few inches away. "What he want?"

"Dunno. Say he need to see we."

Polk sat up and yawned.

Outside, Jacob Roan motioned them all toward the garden. As they walked, Christina took Sonja's hand and whispered, "I think I understand." Sonja looked at Roan to see if anything in his face or motion gave away what Christina had just intuited. They did not. He looked every inch a man on his way to eat breakfast or take a noon-day nap. Polk, by contrast, looked like a man on the way to the gallows. Grace appeared as a woman whose man was being led to the gallows. They arrived at the edge of the garden. It lay exactly as Polk last left it. The combined soil and manure had crusted into a bland settlement.

Roan stooped down and picked up a small stick. He turned to Polk. "Polk, in the days before courthouses and deeds, people transferred property by what was known as livery of season. It's a fancy legal term that is rarely heard today. But when one man handed to another man something from the land like this stick, it passed legal title to that property. As the new owner of Three Pines, I pass this stick to you as proof of your ownership of the 20 acres you filed a claim for."

Christina brought her hands to her face.

Grace looked first to Roan, then to Polk. "Fuh true?" she said.

Said Roan, "I made a lot of money on last year's crop. I decided to invest some of it in a property I know well. Three Pines."

Everyone looked at Polk. He looked down, kicked a clod of dirt by his foot. "I thank you, sir. What I owe yuh?"

"Twenty-five dollars. Pay that and it's all yours."

"I get it," said Grace.

She returned from her cabin in minutes. She counted out twenty-five dollars. Roan pocketed it and turned to Christina and Sonja. "I haven't eaten since this morning." He took an arm of each woman and guided them toward the main house.

Through eyes misting as she walked, Christina whispered, "Thank you, Jacob. I love you for that."

He smiled at her, the poker face gone. "Then it was worth it." They paused, turning back toward the garden, where Polk picked Grace up, swinging her around and around.

CHAPTER 44

Carter's letter to his mother informing her of Missma's fall did not reach Anna until spring. By then, Anna had been in Columbia for months, devoting hundreds of hours to the Wayside Home, bringing to bedraggled soldiers a cheer she usually did not feel herself. She spent almost as much time at the hospital, where she did whatever was needed. She bandaged wounds, emptied bedpans, wrote letters for the wounded, held the hands of the dying, fed the helpless and mopped floors. She rejected proposals of marriage by four patients, but always gently. Her best days came when she was able to close the door of her room at Luke's, fall into bed exhausted, and sleep for a full seven hours.

As soon as she read of Missma's fall, she knew she had to get to Cane Island. Carter could not possibly care for his grandmother. If leaving Beaufort had ever been an option they considered, Anna assumed it would no longer be possible. She must go to them.

She waited for Luke to go to bed early before approaching Abigail and Daniel. "I need to go to Beaufort," she said. "It has been nearly three years since I have seen Carter and Missma and now she is an invalid. I have to reach them somehow."

"We understand," said Abigail. "Can we help?"

"There must be someone who would be willing to take me by boat."

Daniel said, "There is a longshoreman on the Cooper River docks named Munson Russell. Everyone calls him Grip, I cannot remember why. If there is anyone for hire for a job like that, Grip will know. It could be dangerous, and you will need money. Perhaps a lot of money. Abigail and I could lend you what you need. Pay us back when you can."

Anna inhaled. "That would be wonderful. You have been so kind already."

"It is the least we can do," said Abigail. "We think of you as the daughter we never had."

One week later, Daniel and Abigail saw Anna off at the station. She lingered in hugs to both. She found Charleston much as she left it, a dispirited malaise palpable on the streets. She took a hotel room at the Mills House. Early the next morning she hired a carriage to take her to the docks, first asking the driver if he would be willing to seek out a man named Grip and bring him to her. She would pay him extra, she promised. "Tell him Daniel Gregorie sent me."

At the port, the driver left her in the carriage. "The name is Grip you say?"

"That is who I was told to ask for."

The day was grey and overcast, and out to sea lingered dark clouds and Union ships. Her route to Beaufort, if there was to be one, cannot begin here.

Thirty minutes later, she saw the driver in the distance. Beside him walked a shorter man with a limp, a barrel chest and hairy forearms. When they reached the carriage, he said, "Munson Russell at your service. You can call me Grip."

Anna asked the driver to give them some privacy for fifteen minutes. When he hesitated, she assured him of a generous tip. Grip climbed into the carriage and took a seat beside Anna. "Any friend of Daniel's will find a friend in me," he said.

Anna told him of her flight from Beaufort in 1861, of Missma's refusal to leave, of Preston's death and Carter's dilemma. Mostly, she pled with him to help her get to Beaufort.

"First things first, ma'am. I thank you for the life of your patriot son, who gave everything for our cause."

"I thank you for that, Grip."

"As to your need, I would take you myself, but your only chance means navigating the barrier islands, and I ain't done that since '46. I'd land us on a sandbar sure as Christmas."

"Who, then?"

Grip rubbed his chin in contemplation. "Capt'n Gerald's laid up with the typhoid. Capt'n Pete sprung a leak and had to put the *Peacock* in drydock. That shaves the list down to just one, but he ain't the kind of man I'd put a lady like yourself in the care of."

"Forgive me, Grip. I don't want care. I want transportation, and I am prepared to pay."

"Oh, you'll pay, especially if you hire Porter Moss."

"Not Captain Moss?"

"Capt'n is a name we hold for the true salts, the men that respect the water and themselves. Porter is Mr. Moss to me."

"I see. And Mr. Moss. What are his failings?"

Grip rubbed the chin again. "He has a love for the bottle."

"A common affliction."

"And he chases women. All kinds of women."

"Also not rare."

"I will say this about the man. He can sail when he is sober, and he knows those islands like I know the Lord's Prayer."

"Then I suppose I will have to take my chances with his failings. Where can I find him?"

"Sails out of Gilroy Landing on John's Island. His boat is *Cabin Fever*. Not much to look at, but a shallow draft that helps where you are going."

"Gilroy Landing. I will remember that."

"And, ma'am, a word of advice. Don't let him price you up too high. He needs the money, owing to his failings."

"You have been a great help, Grip. I appreciate it, and Uncle Daniel will appreciate it."

"Finer man never drew breath," said Grip, climbing down from the carriage. "Safe travels, ma'am. I hope you get to see your loved ones."

Gilroy Landing proved a generous name for the single dilapidated pier at the end of the lane Anna was directed down. Tied to the sagging planks was a sloop, the name *Cabin Fever* on the stern faintly visible in faded blue paint. Anna called out from the shore.

Her first glimpse of Porter Moss brought to mind all of Grip's forebodings. Something about the way he rose from the low-slung cabin, stretched and stared at her, like a horse he might consider purchasing, conveyed trouble, risk, danger. He disappeared into the cabin, and when he reemerged he was smoking a pipe. A dark stubble mixed with grey covered his cheeks. From his shirt, buttoned at his midsection, dark chest hair protruded. A ponderous belly slumped over his belt. He looked to Anna to be about fifty. "Help you?" he said.

"You are Mister Porter Moss?"

"That I am."

"I am here at the recommendation of Grip."

Moss grinned at her. "I can just imagine what that recommendation sounded like. Grip ain't one of my admirers. I have damn few, truth be told."

"I need your services."

He waved her forward. "Come on board and we will talk about it."

"I am more comfortable here," she said.

Moss sighed. "You sure have been talking to Grip. Have it your way." He stepped onto the planking and walked to her.

"My name is Anna Barnwell. I need to get to Beaufort as soon as possible. I'm prepared to pay as long as the charge is reasonable. Can you help me?"

Moss emitted a low whistle. "Beaufort. Run the blockade."

"I'm afraid so."

"How much can you pay?"

"Tell me your charge."

"Well, it ain't like we post the price like a menu in a boarding house. Lots of things factor in. For a job like this, three thousand should cover it. U.S."

Anna blinked twice. "Three thousand dollars? I don't wish to buy your boat, only to rent it for a day."

Moss lowered his head and cut his eyes upward to hers. "That's just the thing," he said. "We get caught and my boat will belong to the Yankees, same as if you bought it."

"I was told you are a skillful navigator. You should be able to avoid the

Yankees."

"So old Grip said that about me, eh? Mighty nice coming from him. Where in Beaufort do you need to get to?"

"Cane Island. You know it?"

"Sure do. Double trouble. The Union Navy and the Army pickets to worry about. Sounds like a suicide mission."

"I wouldn't ask anyone to commit suicide, and I am certainly not interested in killing myself." There was an edge of exasperation in her tone. "Perhaps you are not the man after all."

"Now hold on. I didn't say I wouldn't do it. Just pointing out the perils is all."

"There is a war on, and we will be sailing into enemy territory. I fully appreciate the perils and assessed them before deciding to go."

"Two Thousand. I'm cheating myself if agree to a dollar less."

Anna squared her shoulders. "I am prepared to pay fifteen hundred, not a dollar more, and there are conditions on my willingness to pay even that."

Moss puffed his pipe and exhaled skyward. "Conditions?"

"I don't mean to offend, but I must be frank in a matter of this importance. There must be no intoxicating spirits on board."

"So old Grip fingered me as a rummy. Anything else?"

"I will require whatever privacy your boat affords."

"Anything else?"

"Yes. One half now and the other half on arrival in Beaufort."

Moss took a long pull on his pipe, his eyes locked on hers. "Conditions one and two I can live with. Can't go along with number three, that half and half."

"It seems fair. We have never dealt with each other before."

"It may be fair, but it ain't smart. It means you have to carry the seven fifty on the trip, and I have to carry it back. I could lose the boat and the cash. When did you want to leave?"

"As soon as possible. Tomorrow morning."

"In that case I will require the fifteen hundred now, so I can stash it in a safe place before we shove off."

"What if you are not here in the morning?"

"Little lady, nobody in these parts wants to see me become the mayor, but I've lived here all my life. I'll be here."

Anna opened her purse and withdrew fifteen hundred dollars in U.S. currency. She had saved herself a thousand dollars, the sum left in the purse, all on loan from Uncle Daniel.

"I see you came prepared."

"As I said, the need is great." She handed him the money.

He counted it. "If you come at seven, we can catch the morning tide. Bring something to eat. We may reach their lines by afternoon, but we will need to

233

anchor until night. We've got some moon, so that will help."

On impulse she extended her hand. "Thank you. I will be here at seven."

He held her hand a moment too long. "Seven it is."

As she returned to her sulky, he said, "I forgot to ask. You coming back with me?"

She turned. "No. Once I get there I will be staying. Forever."

Back at the Mills House, she ordered an ample meal to be packaged and delivered to her before nine p.m. What little sleep she got was restless and intermittent. Fully awake at four a.m., she dressed, taking the remaining one thousand dollars from her purse and concealing it in her corset. By seven she had Gilroy Landing in sight. *Cabin Fever* rocked gently where it did the day before.

As Anna paid the carriage driver, Moss popped his head up from the cabin and beckoned her aboard. In one hand she carried a carpet bag stuffed with clothes and personal items, and in the other the food she ordered the night before. *Cabin Fever* was twenty-five feet long, painted a dingy grey. Its best feature, Anna noted, was the deck, hardwood in need of varnish. The cabin, set just astern of the mast, was a jumbled clutter of Moss's life on board: a grimy sleeping pallet without sheets, a littering of cans and boxes, segments of rope, a pair of binoculars, a straight-back wooden chair. Portholes to port and starboard would admit more light if cleaned. She hoped the musty smell would dissipate once they were under way.

"Before we cast off," Moss said, "I need to tell you the rules. Your main job is to stay out of my way. This boom here will knock you overboard if you ain't looking, so keep your head down. Some folks get seasick if they ride in the cabin. Suit yourself on that. If nature calls, let me know so I can pull to shore. We won't be far from land the way we're going unless we have to make a run for it with Yankees on our tail. I made some extra coffee, so grab a cup if you are inclined. Looks like we drew some fair weather. Let's hope it holds. That is pretty much it. Ready?"

Anna, wary of seasickness and the cabin, sat on the deck beside the mast. From this position she would not only catch the breeze but could lean back against the cabin. She cinched her coat around her in the morning chill, and yes, she was ready. The prospect of seeing Carter and Missma that night had her in an advanced state of anticipation. She nodded to Moss and told him to let her know if she could help.

Moss untied the lines, shoved the pier for separation, and hoisted the mainsail and jib. Both snapped when caught by the wind.

"What river is this?" she asked over her shoulder. Moss was astern, at the tiller.

"Stono. If the wind holds we will be on it for an hour before we get to Wadmalaw Sound."

"When do we have to start worrying about the Yankees?"

"Long about Edisto. I'll tell you when to worry."

The breeze that launched them did not hold. Twenty minutes into the trip the sails went slack. "One thing I can't control," said Moss. "And why we leave early to give ourselves plenty of time." The current carried them leisurely toward Wadmalaw Sound.

In spite of her impatience, Anna began to relax. Grip's warnings about Moss explained her lack of sleep the night before, but this morning he seemed in control as they drifted down the river. Along the banks she saw trees felled by past storms, their roots pried from the ground and bare branches extending from shore. On one high branch she saw a stately peregrine falcon, eyeing them coldly as though they were encroaching on an area he considered his. Minutes later, when a formation of ducks flew overhead, Moss pointed to them. "The wind will pick up soon. Small front coming through."

As predicted, the pale blue sky they began under turned a mottled grey as the sails again filled. By late morning they reached Wadmalaw Sound. The motion of the boat rocked Anna to sleep, and by the time she woke they were half way across the Sound.

At the south end of the Sound they entered a creek that would take them to the Edisto River. Moss guided *Cabin Fever* to shore. "Decent place to take a break and eat," he said.

When Anna returned from the woods bordering the creek, she passed close to Moss as she re-boarded. She distinctly smelled alcohol. He returned her stare with a glassy-eyed grin. Her hands were on her hips as she confronted him.

"Mr. Moss, you have been drinking."

He pushed the air as if to swat her away. "Since about nine a.m., yes ma'am."

"But my condition . . ."

"You said no whisky on board." He stepped unsteadily to the stern, pulled on a rope tied there and brought up a bottle half full of clear liquid. He held it up to her. "See. Not on board. You didn't say nothing about overboard."

She let out a rasp of disgust and turned her back.

"Don't you worry none, little lady. I can sail these creeks drunk as a lord with my eyes shut. If you'll take a seat I'll get us underway." He slurred "underway" to something closer to "unnaway."

She returned to her place, fuming, her back to Moss, her jaw set and her eyes ablaze. "What next?" she demanded over her shoulder.

"Sail this creek to just before the Edisto. Then we wait for dark. If you're a praying woman you need to pray these clouds clear, 'cause we will need a little moon. Not too much. Just a little."

I need to pray for more than that, she thought but did not say. The boat eased back into the channel. The woods were behind them, and ahead broad savannahs of spartina grass stretched to the horizon, the golden hue grass swaying in the wind that powered their sails. Anna recognized the peculiar aroma of marsh, tide and mud; the smell of home. She focused on her reunion, pushing away the vulnerability she felt at the mercy of a drunken pilot. Carter would be almost a man, a head taller than herself, she predicted. And who could have foreseen that Missma would still be vibrant three years later? She must be frail by now, but perhaps her rugged living conditions had strengthened her. In letters, Carter and Missma seemed to be getting along personally; Anna was anxious to observe the relationship that had evolved. How good it would feel to embrace them both again. She could not summon even a remnant of the anger she once felt at Missma. What mattered now was only that they all be together, and remain together. She tingled in anticipation.

She was brought from her daydream by a crunching sound and a sudden lurching of the boat, its forward progress arrested. She looked back at Moss.

"Oyster bank," he said. "With tide this low, hard to avoid them. Don't worry."

He trimmed a sail and the stern of the boat swung downstream. Moments later they backed off the bank. He tacked to recover the proper direction. She breathed easier.

The sun, masked for most of the afternoon by a veil of thin grey overcast, was setting. Moss lowered the sails, glided *Cabin Fever* to shore, and announced they would remain here until dark. "Edisto just around that bend," he said, pointing toward the darkening horizon.

Anna debated a confrontation. By his halting movements and the slurring of words, she knew his level of drunkenness had spiked. She risked making the situation worse, but decided it was worth a try. She rose and made her way to the stern, where Moss sat at the tiller.

"Mr. Moss, I demand you honor our agreement. You must stop drinking now."

Moss raised his eyes as if surprised to find her there. "And if I don't?"

Frustration overcame her. Close to tears, she said, "I haven't seen my son and his grandmother in three years. I'll die if I don't reach them. I paid you well to bring me here, and we will have a chance if you are sober. I am begging you."

Moss stood, towering over her and bringing his face down to within inches of hers, his bloodshot eyes leering at her and his breath reeking of whisky. He said, "I love it when a woman begs." He lowered his eyes to her breasts. She recoiled, and he grabbed her by the shoulders, pulling her to him. "I'm thinkin' you brought some money with you. Maybe tucked away inside your clothes. Should I take me a little look-see? Maybe feel around until I find what I'm lookin' for. Go ahead, scream," he said. "There ain't one person in twenty miles of here. I could beat you, have my way with you and throw you overboard for the crabs and no one would ever know. And I just might do it. Been a spell since I had a woman, and a long spell since I had one as fine as you."

His grip was so forceful she winced in pain, openly weeping now. "Don't hurt me," she pleaded.

"Then sit down and shut your mouth about my drinkin'. One more word and I've told you what is going to happen." He released her shoulder. She returned to her place by the mast, shaking uncontrollably. Minutes passed. Her shoulder throbbed. As she stared into the gathering darkness, she heard him snoring. She turned. He slumped across the gunwale, one hand on the tiller even though the boat was grounded. His head lolled back, mouth open.

Moss awakened with a snort. He reached for the bottle at his feet, took a long pull, and stoppered it again. He stood, turned toward the creek, unbuttoned his fly, and peed over the side. Anna, facing forward, heard his urine empty into the current. She shuddered, folding her arms against the chill settling over the marsh.

Moss said, "Better take care of business here. There'll be no stops till we get where we're goin'."

"Let's get started," she said.

Moss climbed out, shoved off and tumbled back in, cursing as he hit his head against the tiller. When he raised the sails, the boat glided cleanly into the channel taking them to the Edisto.

"I can smell 'em now. Yankees," he said.

Anna scanned the ribbon of dark water unrolling in front. She saw no lights. The sky had cleared enough for a quarter moon to peak through. That, at least, was one positive. An hour later they reached the mouth of the river, where Moss tacked south across St. Helena's Sound. On this leg they would sail over open water for five miles.

Whitecaps lapped against the sides. Moss yelled to be heard over the sound of the wind, which picked up when they entered the Sound. "Over there." He pointed.

Off the starboard bow Anna saw the lights of a ship or gunboat. It was far away and did not appear to be closing. She could see nothing of the far shore and wondered how Moss could possibly navigate to the straight they would need to enter; the narrow passage separating Harbor Island from St. Helena's Island. That was his problem, she told herself, knowing that it was equally her problem. To have her fate in this man's hands galled; the fact that she was warned cold comfort. She kept a wary eye on the lights to starboard, which gradually receded to invisibility.

After what seemed hours, she made out the faint features of land ahead. She could not be certain, but she thought she saw the straight. Perhaps Moss had brought them in after all. Afraid of the answer, she called back, "What is that?"

"Harbor Island," he said.

The tingle of nearing home returned. She was back. A few miles separated her from all she had been holding onto. *Cabin Fever* glided silently through the straight.

They entered Harbor River, protected from the sea by barrier islands. The winds slackened and whitecaps turned to feeble ripples of tide. They cleared Harbor Island on the port side, then sailed past Hunting Island. A few more miles, Anna told herself. She looked back. Moss took another swig from the bottle. They entered Station Creek, which would connect them to the Beaufort River. They had sailed about a mile when Anna felt the dreaded sensation of wood ploughing into an unseen bottom. The boat stopped. They had run aground. Moss lowered the sails to keep them from keeling over.

"What happened?" Anna asked.

"Sandbar. Musta strayed from the channel. Or it could be a new one."

"Can you get us off?"

"Not likely."

"You freed us from the oyster bed."

"This is a sandbar. Not the same. We're stuck until the tide floats us off."

Anna wanted to scream. "When will that be?"

"I figure about daylight. Nothing to do but wait it out." He went below, and soon the sound of his snoring filled the cabin.

Anna wondered if things could get worse when the wind slacked, then died altogether. With the stillness came mosquitoes, buzzing about her in relentless torment. She relieved herself over the side, then stretched out on the deck, pulled her coat over her head, and tried to sleep on what would be the longest night of her life.

Cabin Fever rocked as a flood tide lifted it from its immurement. The sun was not yet up. Anna wakened to the sound of Moss urinating off the stern. His bottle was empty, so unless he had another he would be forced into sobriety. Every bone in Anna's body ached; her back spasmed. An oozing between her legs signaled the beginning of her period. She fought the urge to scratch the scar from her surgery, which seemed to itch at the most inconvenient times. She was miserable. Get me there, she thought over and over.

In a series of narrow passages along Station Creek, Moss proved his worth as a sailor when sober. He exhibited skills in tacking and coming about that were possessed by only the most seasoned. But the sun was up as they entered the Beaufort River. To their left lay Hilton Head, its sprawling wharfs and tethered ships clearly visible. To their right, eight miles away, lay Cane Island. To reach it, they must sail in open water in clear daylight.

They had just made the turn into the river when she heard Moss say, "Trouble." He pointed toward Hilton Head. From out of Skull Creek came a boat trailing steam.

"Could be routine patrol," Moss said.

The boat steaming toward them was the gunship *Danforth* that, from its path, appeared to have been lying in wait. It crossed Port Royal Sound, closing fast, and overtook them easily. From *Danforth* came the order to halt or else. They could see the mounted guns trained on them. Moss had no choice. He lowered his sails as the gunship came alongside. Anna and Moss were briefly questioned by a lieutenant while a chief searched *Cabin Fever*. The lieutenant ordered Moss and Anna to board *Danforth*. The chief stayed aboard *Cabin Fever* to pilot it to a Union marina on Skull Creek. Anna was standing at the rail when *Danforth* motored past Cane Island. She saw the Lodge, a tendril of smoke rising from its chimney. Carter and Missma were in there. She knew it. She could feel it. The Lodge was as welcoming as she imagined, and as unattainable as a moated castle on a distant mountain. She stared at it just a moment longer, then turned away.

In Beaufort, Moss was incarcerated in the same cell holding Gabriel Heyward. Anna was put on the first Union ship headed north. By evening she was back in Charleston, exhausted, broken and utterly unsure of what she should do next.

CHAPTER 45

Sonja left the Lodge, pleased with Missma's recent progress. Her pain had subsided to a tolerable level, her dependence on laudanum reduced, and her mood less mercurial. As Sonja bathed her this morning, she mentioned walking "in a day or so." She entered the break. Dogwoods and honeysuckle bloomed. From within their delicate white and pink petals came fragrant echoes of spring as mockingbirds and brown thrashers joyfully called to mates.

She paused to talk with Polk, planting his garden with renewed urgency. On some days the family worked among the neatly defined furrows, but Polk and Grace discouraged the girls from too much knowledge of the fields. They did not want to raise farmers, and the knowledge they wanted their daughters to acquire was not to be found there.

At the main house, with no one home, she made herself tea and had just opened a book when there was a knock at the door. Newton Spruill stood on the porch. She did her best to hide her irritation.

"Good afternoon," he said cheerfully. "Beautiful day for a drive, don't you think?"

"Hello, Lieutenant."

"Please, Newton."

"Newton, it's so thoughtful of you to come all this way, but I really don't believe I can go with you today. I have a headache that is killing me."

"It's quite a long way out here. Are you sure you are not up to it?"

"Very sure."

"That's unfortunate, because there is something important I wish to discuss. It concerns your rebel friend."

"Oh?"

"As you know, I have long suspected he has been passing information to the traitors. Now I have proof, and with it I am confident he will be arrested and charged. That's what I wished to discuss. Are you certain you can't go with me? We don't have to make a day of it. All I ask is an hour or two."

"Very well. I suppose my headache can tolerate an hour or two."

He held out his hand to help her into the buckboard but she ignored it, seating herself at maximum distance from him. At the end of the lane he turned on the main road toward the barrier islands.

"I read where Jacob Roan bought Three Pines," he said. "That must provide some reassurance for you and your mother."

"It's a comfort. It also allowed some special freedmen on the property to buy twenty acres. That made us all very happy." She did not wish to appear too anxious regarding whatever proof Spruill thought he had, hoping he would broach the subject, which he did.

"I hope you realize that my true interest where the rebel is concerned is your welfare. I'm fond of you, as I hope my suit has made plain. Your continued association with a spy will do your reputation great damage, and it could lead to severe consequences. That's why I have made it my business to protect you as best I can. Before it's too late."

"You mentioned proof."

"A letter has come into my possession. In it he very clearly admits to treasonous activity."

"A letter? Addressed to whom?"

"To you."

"Me? How would you come by a letter addressed to me?"

He halted the carriage and turned to her. "Let me acquaint you with some facts of life, young lady. You are in a war zone. Good Union men are dying for our cause. I happen to be an officer in the Union Navy, and as such I owe it to my country to do all I can to protect those in harm's way. That duty gives me broad powers to seek out and find evidence wherever it lies. Never mind how I obtained the letter, but rest assured I have the authority to possess it."

She had received only one letter from Carter, the one she put in her top drawer. It was months ago. In that letter, did he say he was spying?

"'I am not sorry for anything I have done,'" Spruill said. "Do those words ring a bell?"

Her eyes flashed. "You have been in my room?"

"Very briefly, for a completely legitimate reason, I assure you. As I said, this is war."

"I cannot believe you would go through my things!"

"I appreciate the danger you are putting yourself in, even if you are too young and naive to fully perceive it."

"What is it you want, Lieutenant?"

"Your company. I want companionship. I want to protect you, and in the process I believe you will come to think of me as I think of you. We can go for rides, as we are doing now. I'm in a position to take you to parties and dances. We could picnic. There are many activities open to someone with my resources. But they are not things I wish to do alone."

"And if I should agree?"

"For as long as you agree, I don't see how I can share the letter with authorities. The rebel clearly implicates you in his treason. I would not be much of a protector if I threw you into such peril."

She stared at him. "It's been an hour. I would like to return now. My head hurts, and I need time to think about this."

"Of course. Suppose we agree that I will return in one week for your answer. That should be enough time, don't you think?"

They returned to Three Pines in silence. At the house, she climbed down without bidding him goodbye. In her room, she searched her dresser. Not only was the letter gone, but she now knew the fate of her bloomers in which the letter was wrapped. What kind of man would be so lewd? And what exactly did that letter say?

She put that question to Carter. Missma slept, and they stood together on the porch. She related Spruill's visit.

Carter looked dazed. "It was so long ago. I don't remember exactly what I said."

"Did you mention Signal Oak?"

"I could have."

"Did you say you were spying?"

"It's possible."

"He quoted one line. 'I am not sorry for what I have done.'"

"Yes, I did say that."

"I remember that line, too. I wish I remembered more. I suppose I should have destroyed the letter."

"What should we do?"

"You can't be arrested. What would happen to Missma? I can't do what you do here, even if I were to move to the Lodge."

"He came into your room. He had no right. You should report him."

"I thought of that. But if the letter is as damaging as he says, are the authorities going to care how he came by it? And how much trouble would it cause me if you can be convicted of spying? These are things I don't know."

Into the silence she said, "I should go with him. There are worse fates. A buggy ride now and then won't kill me."

"I hate to see him get his way. He isn't the man you kissed, is he?"

"Please. I have better taste than that."

"You would do this for me?"

"For both of us. And for Missma."

"Still. Thank you."

"You are welcome. And rebel, one day you may have to do something for me."

A week later, Missma took her first steps in over two months. Standing by her bedside, Carter and Sonja helped her to her feet. She leaned on the back of a chair. By moving the chair forward she could maintain her balance. Her face was a study in concentration as she shuffled forward. Between pushing the chair and moving her feet, she tired easily, but the next day she repeated the process. Her pain now was as much from bed sores as from the hip. To the relief of all, she was able to manage her chamber pot. Sonja acknowledged the progress when she said, "That is one tough old lady."

Spruill returned for Sonja's answer which, when she gave it, prompted from him lavish praise for her maturity. "You won't regret it," he said, even as she thought she may very well. She accompanied him on a two-hour buggy ride. The day was mild, and not even Spruill's company could dull the scent of honeysuckle or the raw beauty of unfolding magnolia blossoms. She decided to survive this indenture by focusing on her surroundings. A party or dance would allow her to meet other people; broaden her horizons. She resolved to take something positive from her Spruill experience.

By late spring, Missma had progressed sufficiently to discard the laudanum. She did not trust her balance, so discarding the chair to aid her walking was not an option. Carter became used to the sound of the chair being pushed across the plank flooring. But Missma was still in, if not pain, significant discomfort. She sighed as she hobbled, often emitting a "whew" or groan when she rose or sat. Her movements were slow, deliberate. It took her half an hour to dress.

While Carter was pleased she had regained at least partial independence, he worried that Sonja's visits would become less frequent as a result. But they continued. On days when he was hunting, fishing or sailing, he did not see her, but Missma told him how long she stayed and what they discussed. That was, she reported the subject of their discussions when she could remember, but with increasing frequency she could not. On those occasions she fell back on vague generalities like "we talked about the news at Three Pines," without saying what that news was, or "we talked about her teaching," without repeating details of their exchange. He knew she was covering her dementia as best she could, and she had days when complete lucidity replaced it.

With Carter there, Sonja was cordial, friendly, engaging, yet reticent. She held back, cautious where he was concerned. He remembered his times with her at the break, when they kissed and pressed against each other, and she seemed open and unguarded. He wanted that back. She felt something for him, but it was not what she felt before. Maybe, he thought, she had outgrown him, that she had matured in ways that, for him to appreciate, would require equal maturity on his part. She could be waiting for him to grow up. Perhaps the man she kissed was now the recipient of her unguarded openness. The longing he felt from the first came back every time they were together. He knew it was wrong for him to be thankful Missma broke her hip, but he was.

Newton Spruill continued to demand access to Sonja as his price for not having Carter arrested. He came to Three Pines as often as his duty schedule allowed, pressing his perceived advantage by ever-longer buggy rides when weather permitted and extended stays on the porch when it did not. Sonja's tolerance for him mystified Christina, who resisted the urge to pry. Sonja returned from buggy rides in a notably foul mood, deepening the mystery as to why she went at all. She brightened when Christina joined them on the porch and on several occasions had made excuses to Spruill that Christina knew not to be true. After one such session, when Sonja pleaded an excess of work for her tutor, expected the next day, Christina confronted her.

"Your tutor hasn't been here for weeks. Why don't you simply tell the lieutenant you don't wish to see him?"

"I can't. Not now."

"And where is that nice Lieutenant Florance?"

"They transferred him."

On a buggy ride in late summer, Spruill said he had just received orders for a one-month assignment, but would return. He reached for her hand. Sonja let him hold it, grateful for the reprieve his absence would bring.

When Spruill's assignment ended, he predictably presented himself at Three Pines. On that day, Sonja went eagerly. Perfect temperature, low humidity and cloudless skies made a ride into the country pleasant even with Spruill. Orange daylilies grew in profusion along the road, and Sonja was sorry when Spruill turned off that road onto a lane they had not previously been down. Trees lined either side as far as she could see. Spruill's mood was typically talkative. He reached for her hand to resume the intimacy he assumed had been established.

When they had driven several hundred yards down this deserted lane, Spruill stopped the buggy, turning to her.

"We have seen each other often this year," he said. "I've grown very fond of you, and I have every reason to think you feel the same." He paused, then said, "May I kiss you?"

She shrugged. "If you like."

He slid over and kissed her, a chaste kiss she did not return.

"Heaven," he said. "How about another?" With this kiss he put his arms around her and pulled her to him. She pulled back.

"That's more than a kiss," she said, "and not appropriate."

"Why not?" he said. "I've been a patient man. I think I'm entitled to a little affection from you."

"I agreed to accompany you, and I have done so. I did not agree to do more."

"But doing more is part of human nature."

"Not mine," she said with growing awareness of her isolation on this lane.

"Oh? I am willing to wager you have done more with that rebel you are so fond of."

"With all due respect, Newton, what I do with Carter is my business."

"It is mine as well. Have you forgotten the letter?"

"Not for a moment."

He reached into his coat and withdrew a tangle of cotton she recognized as her missing bloomers. As she snatched them, he seized her wrists. He brought his face to within inches of hers. "I have been in this God-forsaken place for over two years serving my country. It's very lonely for a man without female companionship. The least you can do is provide some in ways that matter most."

"Lieutenant, you are hurting me."

He tightened his grip, moving his face even closer. "I will not let go. I have waited long enough."

"What are you going to do?"

"I would rather show you." He released one wrist and moved his hand to cup her breast. With her now free hand she tried to remove his but he squeezed the breast until her eyes filled with tears. She screamed. He slapped her and again seized her wrist, lowering her hand to his fly. "There," he said. "Doesn't that feel good?"

"Let go of me."

"Get in the back," he said, jerking her arm.

She balled her fist and brought it down hard on his groin. When he yelped and doubled over, she raised one leg and with it shoved him off the seat. He fell head-first to the ground. She dropped the bloomers at her feet, took tight hold of the reins and with a snapping motion began to drive. Immediately from under the buggy she heard a cry of pain. She had run over Spruill's ankle. She drove for a minute before turning the buggy around. The lane was narrow and she must pass Spruill, who lay in the roadway holding his ankle. The buggy gathered speed as she steered it toward him. He rolled into the ditch as she passed.

Where the lane joined the main road she halted the rig, looking over her shoulder. Spruill was nowhere in sight. She panted heavily, shaking so that holding the reins steady was impossible. With frequent glances back, she waited for her breathing to slow. She saw the bloomers at her feet, reminding her that Spruill still had the letter. And she had a Union buckboard that would require explanations at Three Pines. She turned the rig around and started slowly back down the lane. She could hear him moaning as she approached. She stopped, looking down at him sprawled in the ditch.

"I need help," he said. "My ankle may be broken."

"I hope it is. I will leave the buckboard near the entrance to Three Pines. How you get there is your problem. If you make trouble for Carter or me with that letter, I will tell your superiors how your ankle came to be hurt. Do you understand?"

Spruill nodded, his face grimacing.

She picked up the bloomers and waved them at him. "Now that I know your hands have been on these, I could never wear them again. But they will burn, as I hope you do."

CHAPTER 46

Late August heat settled over the Lowcountry. Nothing moved but the tides. At Three Pines, they watched the barometer for readings that portended a hurricane, and there were days when they would welcome one as relief from the heat.

But weather was not the main concern. The week before, Grace came to the house hysterical, saying Polk had been taken by four men in a buckboard as he tended his garden. Between sobs, she told Sonja, Roan and Christina of having witnessed the shabbily dressed white men chase Polk down, subdue him and throw him into the back of the wagon. Roan told her of the $100 bounty the Union now paid recruiters who persuaded freedmen to join the Army.

"They're having trouble meeting their quotas with volunteers," Roan had said. "The bounty was approved as an incentive to recruiters to find those willing to join."

Grace screamed, "Polk ain' joinin' no Army. Not now!"

Roan tried to calm her. "I've heard of these men. They sign the recruitment papers for the men they kidnap. Let me look into it."

Two days later, Roan reported to Sonja and Christina that Polk's enlistment form showed his signature, undoubtedly forged. It was Polk's word against that of the four henchmen, who all swore Polk came willingly despite the sizable knot on his head. "I spoke to Polk," Roan said, "and while he could leave any time, Three Pines is the only place he wants to go. The Army would bring him back and charge him with desertion. They want some corroboration of Polk's claim that it's a forgery."

In his absence, Grace and the girls devoted extra time to the garden, leaving fewer hours to study and learn.

Missma hobbled around the Lodge. Another slip and fall would be fatal. She grew weaker, the effort required to move her chair taxing her strength to a degree it did not just several months before. Prior to her fall, leaving Beaufort was always an option, but now she was immured at the Lodge. Anna or other family members would have to come to her when and if the war ended.

And it appeared the war was ending. Sonja read to Missma news of it from *Free South*. From that weekly newspaper, Carter and Missma formed their opinion that the Confederacy could not withstand the Union's mounting strength. They had learned there was now a general named Sherman with an Army of 60,000 men moving through Georgia toward Atlanta. Missma forgot things, but she remembered the name Sherman.

In September, the heat broke. Carter wrote to Anna. "I'm going to take Sonja with me," he told Missma.

"Is that wise?"

"I have already told her how I use Signal Oak to communicate."

"But you have not told her where it is located. Once she knows, the Union knows."

"She won't reveal it. I'm sure of that."

"Has she said that?"

"She will."

"Do what you think best."

When Sonja arrived that morning, she carried cornbread still warm and six eggs. Carter asked if she would like to go sailing.

"To Signal Oak," he said.

"You trust me with knowing where it is?"

"Yes."

"Then I think my answer is perhaps. If you are going there on personal business, I will go. If the trip involves work for the rebels, then I will stay here with Missma."

"I'm taking a letter to my mother. I never know until I get there whether something is waiting for me."

"When do we leave?"

"I'm ready now."

With Soot in the bow, they took the long way, around the tip of Parris Island and up the Broad River. The boat was beginning to show its lack of maintenance for what would soon be the third anniversary of life at the Lodge. The sail frayed. He lacked the heavy thread and canvas necessary for repairs, even if he knew how to make them. Barnacles on the sides and bottom required constant scraping in a losing effort to reduce drag in the water. The loss of the boat would bring new and severe hardships.

The temperature was mild and the winds fair. In the west, grey clouds scudded along the horizon. A formation of ducks flew over, a reminder of seasons in transition. Sonja, sitting forward, turned now and then to smile at him, enjoying the day and the chance to again be on water. And they both felt unspoken relief to be away from the Lodge, where an atmosphere of decay permeated the enclosed space.

He piloted them into the Whale Branch. When Signal Oak came into view, he pointed. To her it seemed just another water oak bedecked in Spanish moss. The boat glided into reach of the lowest limb, and he tied them to it.

Together they stepped to the second limb. He led her along it to the trunk. "In there," he said, pointing to the hollow. He reached in. "Nothing for me here." He removed his letter from his pocket and deposited it. "Confederate post office," he said. "No stamp needed." He reached up, grabbed a large ligament of Spanish moss, and draped it across mid-limb.

"What is that about?" she wanted to know.

"To let them know I have left something."

"Clever," she said. "Unless a big wind comes along."

"A hurricane, maybe. Otherwise, that stuff clings more than you think." They returned to the boat.

"Is someone watching us now?" she asked.

"I never know. They must check the limb to look for moss, but I don't know when. Maybe days after I leave. Maybe they are looking now."

"This all seems very strange to me," she said. "Here I am with you at a secret rebel location. Does it seem strange to you?"

He sat down beside her. "Things have seemed strange to me for three years. I don't know if I'll ever understand it."

"It, or me?"

"Both."

"Listen, rebel boy, the war is complicated but I really am not. I came here to teach ignorant people. I admit I didn't want to come at first, but Mother thought it would be a good experience for me and it has been. So I owe it to her that I'm here. But I knew inside that slavery was wrong, and the Bible says it is wrong, so my duty was clear. I wish you felt the way I do, because then we could be what we were. I miss what we had. I would love to have it again. I don't know if it's possible."

He looked at her hard. "Did you and your family ever own slaves?"

"Of course not."

"Did any of the neighbors of your farm in Pennsylvania own slaves?"

"Not that I know of. I feel certain not."

"So you have a strongly held belief in something you had no personal experience with until you came here, is that right?"

"Well . . . I suppose that's true. Does that matter?"

He shifted his gaze across the creek, where the Confederates, if they were watching, had them in view. "I think it might. I was twelve when this war started. I was born here and have never been farther from Beaufort than Charleston in my life. The system here, the one you believe is so terrible, is the only one I've ever known. The people who owned others and the people they owned are the only people I've ever known. Suppose a whole bunch of people from South Carolina had come to your farm in Pennsylvania one day to preach against owning cows and pigs and horses and goats."

"But people are not animals."

"I'm not saying they are. Of course they are different. But would you have turned on your parents and your neighbors if you came to think owning animals was wrong?"

"If I studied the matter and concluded it was wrong, I think I would have done what I could to change the situation."

"When you were twelve?"

She started to respond, then remained silent, thinking.

"What you forget," he continued, "is that what you found when you got here was my whole world. I hunted and I fished with Preston. We sailed like you and I are doing today. We pulled shrimp from the creeks and oysters from the banks. We were happy in the house in Beaufort with Mother and Missma. I had cousins and friends all over town. I knew them and they knew me. That was what we had here. And overnight it disappeared. When I was twelve. I don't see how you can hold it against me that I helped my brother and the only things I have ever known."

She said, "I do understand that you were very young to have to make the kind of decisions you had to make."

He nodded, looking at the bottom of the boat.

"But what about now?" she asked. "You will be sixteen in February. How do you feel about these things now that you are older?"

"About slavery? I can see that it was wrong. Mother didn't like it and always treated our people well and fairly. They seemed happy enough to me."

"Then they were more fortunate than most. If you could hear some of the stories we hear at Three Pines, you would be shocked. The overseer there, a man named Smits, was subhuman. The cruelty. Did you ever hear about something they call the Smits treatment?"

"No."

"This man had a punishment for slaves he considered out of line. Maybe they ran away or stole a chicken or something. Anyway, he put human waste—the slave's own waste—into the slave's mouth and made sure it stayed there by tying his jaw shut so he couldn't swallow. He was forced to hold it for hours."

Carter's face registered disbelief. "Nothing like that ever happened to our Negroes."

"You didn't live on a plantation, where most of them stay. We've heard of other things just as bad. Beatings and shootings and starvations."

"I can't defend that if it happened."

"It happened. It would still be happening if the war had not come along. And you are helping the people that did it. Those same people that are over there now, watching us. Maybe your family was innocent of such things, but Southerners as a people were not innocent."

"I had to help Preston."

"That's different. I understand your loyalty to him. I truly do. But he's gone."

"Over a year now. I still can't believe he's not coming home. That I will never see him again."

"You could honor his memory by refusing to help them anymore. Then you and I could go back to the way things used to be."

"No. No we could not."

She stared at him. "No?"

"No, because if we are to have what we had I need to be honest with you. And I haven't been."

"You admitted you spied and lied to me about it."

"I did other spying I have not admitted."

"Are you going to tell me?"

He took a deep breath. "You came to the creek to bathe. Early in the morning. I followed you. I climbed a tree and watched. I knew it was wrong, and I told myself I would never do it again, but then I did. With field glasses. I was ashamed. I still am."

She reached for his hand. "So how did I look?"

"The most beautiful thing I've ever seen."

"Kiss me," she said. "Like we used to."

For the next few minutes they were a tumble of arms, legs, tongues, and lips. Catching her breath, she whispered into his ear, "I hope those rebels are watching."

"I guess we should start back," he said. Soot, bored by the romance, resumed his spot in the bow. As they re-entered the Broad River, she said that in light of the new honesty between them, she must tell him about Spruill.

"I was terrified," she said. "He went crazy. I swear I never did a single thing to cause him to think he could take liberties with me. We were on that lonely road with no one for miles. I know what he had in mind, and I suppose he could have killed me after that. My breast turned black and blue. It was awful."

"Did you report him?"

"No. I still could, but I was afraid of what he would do with that letter. I asked him to show it to me but of course he wouldn't. I'm sure he broke something when the carriage wheel ran over his leg. He was holding his ankle. I wonder how he got back without being able to walk, not that I care. We were miles from anywhere."

"I would like to break his other leg," said Carter.

"One and only one good thing came of it," she said. "He's been holding that letter over my head, and now I have violence to hold over his head. I think whatever advantage he thought he had is gone. I don't intend to see him ever again."

Back at the Lodge, he saw her to the break, where they pressed together in an extended embrace. He reveled in the feel of her, in her openness to him that he once again sensed as a tangible thing. When they parted, she started toward

Three Pines, then turned to say, "Next spring, when the water warms up, why don't you bathe with me?"

CHAPTER 47

As Thanksgiving approached, Carter stood on the roof of the Lodge, trying to repair a small leak that had developed near the base of the chimney. Better to deal with it now than during a winter nor'easter. He looked up to see a rider in the distance, visible to him only because he was eighteen feet off the ground. The rider wore bright scarlet pants and a blue tunic, the distinctive uniform of the 1st South Carolina Infantry. When Carter recognized the rider as Reggie, it was all he could do to maintain his balance. He waved his arms and Reggie waved back. The two old friends embraced as Reggie dismounted.

"What is this?" Carter demanded, pointing to the uniform. "You, a soldier? Wait until Missma sees you."

Inside the Lodge, Missma napped, but stirred when she heard them. They heard the clump, clump shuffle of her chair as she emerged from behind her partition. She stared at Reggie, grinning broadly, as if she was seeing a phantom. He stood still as she moved closer, looking him up and down with bewilderment.

"As I live and breathe," she said.

"Howdy, Miz Martha," he said. "I in de Army now."

"Reggie, you look like a natural leader in that uniform. We have missed you. Sit down and tell us how this happened."

Reggie sat erect as he related the story. He told them of a man named Hunter who approached him when Portia was away, of her dismay at learning what he had done, of a promised hundred dollar bonus, which the Army said it paid to Hunter but of which Reggie received only twenty dollars. "An' Massa Hunter, he gone." But once in, Reggie found he liked the military. The order of things bore enough similarity to the order he imposed upon his plants and shrubs. The praise he received from his superiors, white and black, filled a void left by an absent father. Camaraderie with older soldiers coincided with an evolving maturity. His ability to read and write with some proficiency had already led to a promotion, with more promised. Regular pay had partially salved the wound left by Hunter's cheating. Some of that pay was going to Portia, and the rest set aside to one day open a nursery.

"Any fighting yet?" Carter asked.

Reggie shook his head. "But soon," he said. He told them that his unit had been ordered to join other units, including the now-famous 54th Massachusetts, in an assault on the railroad at the end of the month. They would sail up the Broad River for an attack on the junction at Gopher Hill. "General Sherman, he comin'. Done burned Atlanta and mo' fuh de same fuh Savannah."

"I hope he has no plans to burn Beaufort," said Missma.

"Dunno, but he comin'."

Reggie, absent from the Lodge for months, wanted all the news of Anna. He expressed concern for Missma's hip, but she made light of it, saying only that her fall had proved "a pain for everyone." Carter suggested he change out of his uniform so they could fish, but Reggie was due back at camp by sundown. He left them with a half-wave, half-salute and a promise to return.

The next day, Carter met Sonja at the break. They had resumed the pattern of intimacy both had missed. Then, while she tended Missma, he sailed to Hilton Head, where he saw an assembly of the transports the Union would need for the assault Reggie revealed. Artillery was being loaded onto barges. He sailed to Beaufort, where bustle on the wharf sent a similar signal.

Back at the Lodge, Sonja was gone. He related what he saw. Missma said, "I told Sonja nothing about Reggie's information. I thought the less said, the better."

He did not reply, conscious he had now reached a crossroads he had known was inevitable. Miles to the east, Confederate soldiers, his people, Preston's people, Gabe's people, were relying on him as their eyes and ears. Thanks to Reggie, and confirmed by his own observations, he possessed vital information which, if delivered timely, was likely to save Confederate lives, maybe even Gabe's life if he had somehow escaped capture and rejoined his unit. And it could save the railroad, still in Confederate hands despite Union efforts to interdict it. His duty had never been clearer. Preston did his duty and he died doing it. The least Carter could do was make a trip up the river with a message.

Yet he had Sonja back. Did he promise her at Signal Oak that day he would never spy again? No. He did not make that promise. He confessed to watching her bathe, but he never said he would not serve his country, and the Confederate States of America was still his country. Preston's country. Anna's and Missma's and Cousin Gabe's country. If he could make the trip to Signal Oak without Sonja finding out . . . but there it was again, the gnawing at his insides he had felt by keeping things from her, and that he had not missed since ridding himself of it in the boat at Signal Oak. Can he go back to that? With the openness they now enjoyed, she would know he was hiding something. He could not go back to again deceiving her. He could not stand the gnawing and he could not risk disappointing her that way. That much was clearly understood in the boat, and it had been reinforced and reaffirmed by every long embrace since, with every eager probe of her tongue to his, with every press of her breasts against him, with each riveting look from those blue eyes she had said without saying, "I trust you." He cannot forfeit that trust.

So whatever he decided must be shared with her. She would have to understand. But would she? Did he? If warning Gabe's men allowed them to prepare, wouldn't Reggie be in greater danger with the loss of surprise? Could he choose between Gabe and Reggie? Perhaps, he thought, he was asking the wrong questions. The world he came into when he was twelve was made for him. But soon he would be sixteen, almost a man. If the war was about slavery and slavery was wrong, the war must be wrong. And if his age and immaturity when it started relieved him of the responsibility for difficult judgments, didn't his aspirations for manhood now demand that he make them? The swelling in his groin when Sonja pressed against him was a man's swelling. To meet her eyes on her level required a man's resolve. The time had come, he thought, to become that man.

He met her at the break the next morning. It was chilly, and she was bundled in her winter coat, but opened it to feel what she needed as much as he did. As she leaned her head on his shoulder, he told her of Reggie's disclosure and his reconnoiter of the buildups at Hilton Head and Beaufort. She drew back to look at him.

"No," he said. "I will not go to Signal Oak."

She pulled him to her and whispered, "I love you, rebel."

1865

CHAPTER 48

Following her return to Columbia from her aborted effort to reach Cane Island, Anna experienced persistent depression. Abigail and Daniel did what they could to cheer her up and assured her on several occasions that the loss of their money to Moss meant nothing. "You tried," Abigail repeated. But in fact they too had cause to be dejected for reasons unrelated to money and that could be summed up in one word: Sherman.

Anna found her blues most severe when she was idle. Throughout the fall, Thanksgiving and Christmas, she worked like a woman possessed, as she wondered at times if she was.

Her frenzy of activity did not prevent her from noticing signs that Columbia was at last waking to its vulnerability. The city's method of coping mirrored hers; keep busy and hope for the best. January 17 marked the official opening of the Great Bazaar, conceived and organized by the ladies of Columbia to raise funds for the troops. The House and Senate chambers of the old state house had been designated to host the event, scheduled to last for several days. Each state would provide donated items from that state to be auctioned, raffled or sold. Anna had been assigned to Virginia's exhibit area. When she arrived, the air in the chambers was electric. Everyone talked at once, with animated gestures and contorted faces, and the subject was not the Bazaar, nor the troops, nor the status of the Confederacy. The subject was Sherman. Just after New Year's, portions of Sherman's army crossed into South Carolina from Savannah, which had surrendered to him after his "march to the sea." With a force of 60,000 men, Sherman was a military juggernaut, but where is he headed? Speculation divided equally among Augusta, Charleston and Columbia. As she made her way to her assigned station, she overheard snippets of the only conversation being held: "burn everything in his path," "suffer like Atlanta," "ruthless criminals disguised as soldiers."

Anna took her place behind the Virginia donations. There were peach preserves, maple sugared pecans, a handmade quilt with the great seal of the Confederacy emblazoned in the center, a case of French wine that made it through the blockade, Smithfield hams, orange marmalades, bolts of broadcloth, crocheted sweaters, deep dish apple pies and more. She had worn her best dress and smiled at each potential customer as she greeted them. It was what she could do for her state; there was nothing she could do about Sherman. Working with Anna at the Virginia exhibit was Mrs. Malinda Pringle, who assured that "we in Columbia have nothing to fear, but I tremble for poor Charleston when Sherman arrives."

• • •

Since arriving at Luke's, Abigail had resisted numerous temptations to make changes in the house. Her early suggestion that a small rug be relocated from the foyer to a place in the living room had been met with frosty skepticism. The rug tended to gather when trafficked, and on several occasions Daniel had almost tripped. But Luke liked things the way they were, and the mere suggestion that improvements could be made seemed to be taken as implied criticism. The rug remained in the foyer. One change during her stay had been suggested by Luke when she brought out the door knocker she had salvaged from their Charleston home. Though slightly misshapen from the heat, it remained functional, prompting Luke to suggest they install it on his front door, which lacked one. "You can take it back when you leave," he said.

In mid-February, a neighbor summoned Abigail with that same door knocker. He was leaving, he told her, and asked her to keep an eye on his home next door. In the distance the sound of cannon jarred them both. "Sherman," Daniel said. "Our last defense is at the Congaree. If they get across, we are doomed."

"Can we hold them?" Anna asked.

"Yes," said Luke. When he added, "We *must* hold them at the Congaree," Anna could only think back to declarations four years earlier: "The forts on Hilton Head and Bay Point must hold."

"No," said Daniel. "They are far too strong. I fear they will be in the city in a day or two. Governor McGrath declared martial law. It is the beginning of the end."

Anna looked at Abigail. "Is it that bad?"

Luke stamped his foot. "No, I tell you. Our boys will rally yet. Why, Wade Hampton is here. No better general lives unless it be Robert E. Lee himself. He will protect the capital to the last man."

Abigail dropped her eyes as Daniel shook his head. "Brother, how I pray you are right, but I fear you are living on hope, and hope has run out. Sherman's target has been Columbia all along. His feints at Charleston and Augusta were designed to throw us off. To keep us guessing. Sadly, they worked. Now he is here. We must prepare for dark days."

"Should we leave?" Abigail asked Daniel.

"I will not leave my home," said Luke. "I have more faith in our forces than you do. They will find a way to stop the Yankees. Besides, Sherman gave Savannah honorable terms, much to my surprise. Why shouldn't he do the same for Columbia? Everyone was predicting he would put Savannah to the torch, but it did not happen."

Daniel admitted that this was possible. "But my frustration, one that I know we all share, is getting accurate information. We cannot, it seems to me, make a decision about leaving based on all the rumors flying about this city. The newspapers say one thing, the people another, the politicians yet another. We should go out tomorrow and see for ourselves."

That night, Anna fell into bed exhausted. Not even the bombardment of Union positions on the Congaree by Confederate batteries kept her from sleeping soundly.

The morning of the 16th dawned clear and bright. After a delayed breakfast, they decided to follow Daniel's suggestion by seeing firsthand what was happening. Luke drove the carriage, with Anna sitting beside. From the seat behind, Abigail gave Daniel a running account of all she saw, as she had done for years.

They proceeded down Richardson Street, jammed with carts and carriages. A trip that usually required fifteen minutes consumed an hour and a half. It seemed every pedestrian carried something—a lamp, a suitcase, a box of papers. At the government offices, workers carried out armloads of papers, and they piled them randomly in the nearest carts. Luke stopped one of them long enough to ask what was happening.

"The government has been told to evacuate," the man said. "The governor is leaving and so are we."

Their next stop was Cotton Town. They crossed Upper Boundary on Richardson Street, where Luke brought the carriage to a stop. He turned toward Daniel.

"Brother," said Luke, "you cannot believe it. All that cotton that was in the warehouses is now in the street. I know all the people here. Let me ask some questions." He handed the reins to Anna and dismounted, returning fifteen minutes later.

"They tell me General Beauregard ordered this. Seems he plans to ship it north so the Yankees won't get it, but no one seems to know how the cotton is to get from here to the rail station. Total confusion in there," he said, pointing to the nearest warehouse.

It was late afternoon when their buckboard came within view of the Broad River Bridge, a covered two-lane wooden span. As Anna, Abigail, Daniel and Luke passed near, they spotted the first Confederate soldiers they had seen in their day-long tour around the capital.

"What do you see?" demanded Daniel.

"Our soldiers are running on the bridge," Abigail said.

"Toward us or away?"

"Toward," she said. "And now the bridge is on fire. Oh, those poor men."

"That can only mean Sherman has crossed the Saluda. He is on our doorstep, and as soon as he can bridge the Broad, he'll take Columbia."

The four in the carriage had seen enough. The flames from the bridge brought back to Anna, Abigail and Daniel the painful night in Charleston when so much was lost. They cannot escape fire, or so it seemed. Back at Luke's, they discussed leaving.

"Never," said Luke. "I would not give the Yankee dogs the satisfaction. I do not need to be part of this discussion. You three do what you think best. For my part, I am going to bury my plate and other valuables in the backyard." He left them to do precisely that.

"I doubt we can get out," Daniel said. "The train stations will be overrun."

"Surely Sherman does not plan to burn the entire city down," Abigail said, more in hope than conviction.

"I cannot imagine fleeing," said Anna. "I am so tired. And to where?"

"Not Charleston," said Daniel. "There is talk of it being evacuated as well."

"We are trapped," said Abigail.

The following morning, the 17th, a tremendous explosion jarred them and the rest of Columbia awake. Luke, in his nightshirt, raced to the roof, returning out of breath. "Smoke is coming from the railroad depot. I must go out. Lock the door and let no one in."

He returned hours later. "I would not have believed it," he said, his eyes wide, "had I not seen it myself. The Yankees built a pontoon bridge over the Broad last night. I saw hundreds crossing it. Maybe thousands. And they are already getting liquored up in Cotton Town."

Daniel asked if he had seen smoke.

"The depot is still smoking and I saw some in Cotton Town, too."

Daniel let out a gasp. "Liquor and soldiers are a bad combination. I hope our people aren't so rash as to fire the cotton."

Luke, standing near the fireplace, said, "Better to fire it than let the Yankees have it."

Daniel brought his cane down with such force it snapped in two, the lower half rolling to within inches of Luke's feet. "Fool!" he shouted. "You would not say that if you had been through what we saw in Charleston. A breeze could set the whole city on fire and there is no one to put it out. Our government has abandoned us. Do you truly expect a bunch of drunken Yankees to lift a finger to help? It is madness."

Luke reached for a shotgun leaning in a corner. "I can't control the Yankees or a fire, but I'll be damned if they'll take what I've worked hard to get."

The four spent the afternoon in the parlor, huddled near the fireplace but cold nonetheless. All conversation seemed futile. Having decided to stay, with leaving no longer an option, they waited for events outside to decide their fates. At mid-afternoon, Luke spied a neighbor walking briskly by. He hailed him. The neighbor said he had been to Richardson Street, that all was panic, confusion and chaos; shops being looted by both townspeople and soldiers, liquor flowing freely. "Are they fighting?" Luke asked, but the neighbor hurried on before he could answer.

In early evening, Luke returned to his roof. An orange glow loomed against the sky in the vicinity of Cotton Town. Returning to the parlor, he reported what he'd seen. He had just reassured them that he thought them at no risk of fire when there were three sharp strikes of Abigail's door knocker.

Luke walked to the door carrying the shotgun. "Who is it?" he demanded.

"Private Fortnoy, United States Army."

Luke stiffened. "What do you want?"

"Hoping you could spare a little grub." Fornoy's slurred speech made it difficult to understand him through the door.

"He sounds drunk," Abigail said, approaching the door.

Luke shouted, "We got nothing here for Yankees 'cept some buckshot, so you best move along." He mounted the stairs. Anna, alarmed at what he might do, followed. On the second floor, Luke opened a window above the front stoop. He leaned out brandishing the weapon. "If you don't leave my property now I'll shoot you, and don't think I won't."

Anna grabbed Luke's arm. "Is it wise to antagonize him, Uncle Luke? He may have a gun. We don't know what he will do. Maybe if we give him some food he'll be on his way."

Fornoy looked up. He turned and walked away, unsteady on his feet. In the street, he turned back. "Case you ain't heard, reb, General Sherman and about ten thousand of his friends just showed up."

Luke patted the shotgun. "You tell Sherman and the rest of the Yankee scum I'm waitin' for 'em." He slammed the window down and wheeled on Anna. "You see? Do you see what Yankees do when you show them some gumption? If our boys had stood up to them like I did, we wouldn't be in the mess we got now." He screamed at her. "But no, our so-called leaders fiddled and fiddled and let Sherman march in here without a real fight. No Yankee is setting foot in my house unless it is over my dead body. Now get out of my way."

Anna recoiled, caught off guard by Luke's menacing glare directed at her. It was as though the soldier's pounding on the door snapped something inside Luke. She turned from him and sought the shelter of her room across the hall.

She closed the door and fell onto the bed, her breath coming in gulps. She heard Luke trudge down the stairs. From the floor below his voice boomed, raving to Abigail and Daniel about "the gall of the man" and "Sherman devils."

Anna was unsure how much time passed. Gradually, Luke's downstairs ranting became less audible. She thought sleep would be impossible, with Sherman's next move unknowable and Columbia seemingly on the edge of surrender. It occurred to her that this could be the deciding night of the entire war, yet she sensed drowsiness overtaking her. Her nightmare with Moss and her return to a city under invasion . . .

Daniel was the first to yell "Fire!" Anna bolted awake. She ran to the door, opened it, and saw smoke coming up the stairs. She started down, hearing Abigail's plea for help and Luke's panicked screams. When she reached the penultimate step, she could not see or breathe. Nor could she stand the heat radiating from below. The lower hem of her dress caught fire. She sprinted back up the stairs, into her room. She smothered the hem with a blanket, then raised the only window. Outside, a magnolia tree hugged the house. She had admired it often, and never more than now, as with a short leap it offered the potential for escape. She took a final look at the room, flames now visible in the hall outside her door. She remembered that the money she brought back from Charleston was still in her dresser drawer. She got it, stuffed it into her bodice, and returned to the window. She climbed onto the sill, focused on the closest limb and leaped. She caught the limb beneath her elbows, her breath knocked from her but she held on. With her feet she probed for the branch below. Sensing it, she walked along it until she reached the trunk. She descended, carefully at first but then the heat from the house drove her. She fell from the lowest limb, turning her ankle when she landed. She crawled from the base on her hands and knees. A flash illuminated her shadow on the ground in front of her as the magnolia tree erupted in flames.

CHAPTER 49

Christmas of 1864 came and went at the Lodge virtually unnoticed, the pall of winter, war and Missma's infirmity saturating the Lodge like a suffocating vapor; the miasma of defeat and resignation.

In late January, on an afternoon after her teaching duties were over, Sonja brought oatmeal sprinkled with cinnamon. Missma took it in half-spoon portions, her appetite all but gone. She ate to forestall starvation, but not even the cinnamon, a spice long since unavailable at the Lodge, could interest her in more than a few bites. Carter joined Sonja at her bedside.

"Give us the news," Missma said. "It can't be good, so don't worry about sad tidings. What is Sherman up to now that he has captured Savannah? I suppose he will burn Beaufort next."

"The Union captured the railroad," Sonja said. "A few days ago. General Sherman's army is marching north, but no one is quite sure where he is headed. He has no cause to burn Beaufort."

"Carter read to me the newspaper you brought. He had no cause to burn half of Georgia, but he did."

So they finally got the railroad, Carter thought. After all this time. He wondered if he could have prevented it with some timely information. Probably not, he told himself. "I want to sail," he said. "There may be a letter from Mother. Can you go?"

"I promised Sparrow and Lark I would read with them this afternoon."

At Signal Oak, he reached into the hollow and withdrew a thin envelope, his mother's distinct handwriting a welcome sight. He had not heard from her in weeks.

> January 18, 1865
> Columbia, S.C.
>
> Dearest Carter and Missma:
> I hope and pray this letter finds you safe. I will keep this short as the mail will soon post and no one can be sure how much longer it will deliver. Columbia grows more anxious by the day, with fierce arguments over where Sherman is headed next. Those arguments rage even in my own house, where Luke insists Columbia is immune and Daniel believes it to be Sherman's ultimate objective.

At the Great Bazaar just concluded, I learned information that is my reason for writing. A lady with whom I served is being courted by a major who is currently on leave from his unit in Charleston (and expects that leave to be canceled at any moment due to Sherman). He visited her briefly at our booth yesterday, and when I heard him mention the Charleston Light Dragoons I asked if there was news of Gabriel. He has escaped!! Or at least that is the rumor among his comrades. Supposedly a Negro from Beaufort who crossed the picket lines worked at the jail where they were holding him. If true, this is the only good news I can remember in months.

If there is a silver lining in any of these clouds, it is that this war may soon be over. While not a popular view, I believe the South is on its last leg. All the estimates of the Union's superior resources seem to be coming to pass. If we are to lose, let it be quickly so we can be reunited.

You are in my heart and prayers daily. Stay strong, as I am doing my best to do. The thought that Preston may have died in vain is too painful to dwell upon, yet I do.

All my love,
Mother

Back at the Lodge, he read the letter to Missma. She asked him to read it again. Her eyes were closed, her face expressionless, but at the news of Gabriel's escape the faintest smile formed. "All devil," she whispered. "That boy is all devil."

CHAPTER 50

Through the sunshine of a February afternoon, Sonja looked out the window of the Lodge.

"Carter. Soldiers."

Moments later they heard boots on the steps, then two sharp knocks at the door. "Open up, rebels."

Carter opened the door to find Newton Spruill standing in front of two uniformed men.

Over his shoulder, Spruill said, "Look around the place. Under it, too." He walked in. Sonja and Carter both noted his limp. At the sight of Sonja, standing at the window, he said, "I should have known I would find you here."

Carter said, "My grandmother is sick. She has been helping me take care of her."

"Yes, she seems to have a soft spot when it comes to the rebellion. Where is Gabriel Heyward?"

"I don't know," Carter said.

"You admit you know him?"

"He's my cousin."

"When did you last see him?"

"I don't remember. Two years ago?"

"He was captured trying to come here."

Carter stared at Spruill but said nothing.

"How old are you, boy?"

"Sixteen, sir."

"The rebels are drafting sixteens now. Why aren't you in the Army?"

"I guess they don't know I'm here."

Spruill glanced quickly toward Sonja. "We can remedy that."

From behind Missma's partition came the scrape of her chair against the floor. "I remember you," she said, emerging.

"And I remember you," Spruill said. "Not pleasantly."

"Good. I have no cause to be pleasant to invaders."

Spruill looked around. "If I find one speck of evidence that Heyward has been here I will have you all shot."

Missma wheezed audibly. "If Gabriel Heyward was anywhere near here, someone would have already been shot, and it would not be us."

"I would be careful with talk like that, old woman. I could still charge your grandson with treason."

Sonja spoke, still at the window. "That would be a very bad idea, Lieutenant. I feel sure you know why."

Inspection took only minutes. As they were leaving, Spruill said, "He has been here. Or he will be here. I will be watching." Capturing Sonja in his gaze, he assured, "I am always watching." Sonja and Carter waited for them to pass into the break before turning from the window.

Missma said, "If those are the only soldiers chasing Gabriel, we have nothing to worry about. I need to lie down."

After helping Missma onto her pallet, Carter and Sonja sat near the fire. He said, "Do you think Spruill was bluffing about fixing that? We must be getting desperate if they would send someone here to get me."

"He's so much wind," Sonja said. She smiled. "A shame he has that limp." Then, turning serious, she said, "Would you fight?"

"I fought my war here."

There was silence broken only by Missma's wheezing from behind the partition. Sonja reached for his hand. She lowered her voice to a whisper, glancing over her shoulder. "I have to tell you something. I've been putting it off and I was hoping you wouldn't hear it from Spruill. General Sherman burned Columbia. The reports are very preliminary and I have seen no list of casualties but the damage was great. Hundreds of houses destroyed."

Carter stared at her. "Mother."

"Shhh," she whispered. "I don't think this is news that should be shared with your grandmother. She's too frail."

At that instant Missma coughed violently. They rose together and went to her side.

"You don't sound good, Missma," Carter said. "Your cough is getting worse."

"That's because I have consumption," she said, her voice a whisper.

"Consumption is very serious," Sonja said.

"No, child, it's fatal. It will kill me soon, perhaps today. My mother died of it and I nursed her until the end. I recognize . . ." Another coughing spell interrupted.

Carter leaned close. "What can we do?"

"Build up the fire. Then come sit with me."

When they were at her bedside, Missma reached for Carter's hand. "A few weeks ago, on a morning you were shrimping, Sonja and I had a talk. She will tell you about it sometime. It was the story of an old beau of mine named Marc. We were very much in love but matters neither of us could control came between us. If I could leave you with any advice, I'd say don't let that happen to you. You are both still so young with so much ahead of you. But you have lived more since we came to the Lodge than most people your age. Mature beyond your years, as they say. I don't know what your future holds. My crystal ball becomes less reliable by the minute. When the war ends, and I pray it does, you will be faced with decisions. My one regret in going now is that I will not know how this turns out. Maybe, if there is a heaven, I will get to watch from a privileged perch, to spy on you from above. I hope so. But I want to tell you this. You two share something special. It's rare and it's valuable. Carter, it may be the only thing of value you have left when this war ends. You will both decide what you will decide, and I cannot decide for you and would not if I could. But I hope I am right in the prediction I am taking with me. Speaking of which, I want to be buried here, at the Lodge, under that magnolia nearest the garden. Other than making very sure I am dead first, that is all I ask. Now, I am tired of talking."

Carter squeezed her hand. "I wish Mother was here."

"It is better this way, my boy" Missma said. "I fear she still has not forgiven me."

He smiled. "I believe she has, or will. Thank you for bringing me here, Missma. What a time we have had."

"Will you read to me?"

"*A Tale of Two Cities?*"

"Good. Begin at the beginning. I never tire of hearing Mr. Dickens."

He got the book and brought it to her bedside while Sonja looked on. By the time Jerry Cruncher stopped the mail coach on the road to Dover, Missma labored to breathe as the rattle in her chest became more pronounced. Her fingers kneaded the top fringe of her blanket, pulled to her chin. He stopped reading, looking to Sonja in helpless resignation. He felt there must be something he could do besides read, but he was at a loss to know what, so he began again. Her eyes remained closed as the heaving of her chest slowed and her fingers stilled. By the time Jarvis Lorry met Lucie Manette at the Inn, Missma was gone.

Sonja watched over her for any signs of life, taking her pulse every few minutes. Meanwhile, Carter began digging the grave. The roots of the magnolia made this difficult, as seemed appropriate on a difficult day. After a time, Sonja covered Missma's head with the sheet and returned to Three Pines, bringing Christina back with her. Christina lowered the sheet, raised the eyelids, checked the pulse, listened to the chest, and confirmed what they all knew. She knelt beside the bed and said a prayer.

She repeated the prayer late in the afternoon after they had put Missma in the grave, wrapped in a sheet. Sonja, Christina and Soot stood at the foot as Carter shoveled dirt over her. By sunset, all had been done. The women embraced Carter without words before returning to Three Pines. Carter, exhausted by the digging, entered the Lodge to spend his first night alone.

CHAPTER 51

The following day Carter, Sonja and Soot went sailing. Before leaving they opened the door and windows to allow fresh air to replace the scent of decay. Decisions, postponed in view of Missma's declining health, were now essential.

"So what are you going to do, rebel?"

"What are we going to do," he corrected.

"There is talk of us leaving now that the war seems to be ending."

"Whatever we do I hope we will do it together."

"I want that also," she said. "Missma wanted it, too."

"You must have won her over if she talked with you about that Marc fellow. She mentioned him a couple of times."

"Did she tell you he was a Tory?"

"She didn't tell me anything about him. Do you want to steer?"

"Sure." He slid toward the bow as she took the tiller and continued. "She fell in love with a Tory from Charleston, but after what the British did to her father she couldn't bring herself to marry into that family. Marc's family was even close with the man who betrayed her father's trust."

"I should be grateful she didn't marry him. I wouldn't be here."

"She said she made the right decision, but it took her years to get over Marc. It was obvious to me why she wanted to tell me. You can love someone even though you disagree with them on something as big as loyalty to your country."

"Or secession?"

"I suppose. She shared another detail she said she was too embarrassed to tell her grandson." She eyed him playfully. "She's gone now so she won't mind me telling you, but I think I'll wait until you're older."

"What? I'm sixteen. Old enough to hear anything she told you."

"Not really. We eighteen-year-olds know so much more than you children."

"Yeah, well you treated me like a kid for a long time."

"You were a kid."

"I want to know what she told you."

"I don't know if I should say. It might give you ideas. Ideas that could get us into trouble."

"I won't let you steer unless you tell me."

"That Lodge holds memories for her. When she decided she couldn't marry Marc, she brought him there to tell him. She said the Lodge had just been built,

266

so everything was new. She asked him if he had ever been with a woman . . . in the Biblical way. Do you know what I mean by that?"

He nodded. "I think so."

"I'm sure you do. When the Bible speaks of some man knowing some woman, it's pretty obvious what's going on. Anyway, Missma had never known a man in the Biblical way and she gave herself to Marc. That night. In the Lodge. In the same bed she died in yesterday."

"No wonder she wanted to come back."

"I find that very romantic, don't you?"

He crawled to the stern and took her hand with a sly grin. "Very romantic. And it gives me ideas."

She jerked her hand away. "Well, you can just put that idea away until you're grown. That bath with me in the spring is the closest you're going to get." She tousled his hair as she did the first time he took her gigging.

"I need to find my mother if she's still alive. I could take my chances with the blockade and sail to Charleston. Now that Missma is gone, you are the only thing keeping me here." He stared at her. "Will you go with me?"

"I've thought about that. But where would we go? How would we live?"

"I have no answers. All I know for certain is that for more than three years I've survived here. I have no idea what the world will look like after this war. You told me Sherman burned Columbia, and what else did he burn? Maybe they will burn Charleston before it's over. Living there may be harder than living here has been. But I can't leave you."

"I'll have to think about it. Mother will object, of course. But I will talk with her. It's a big decision."

Back at the Lodge, they closed the windows and built up the fire. Carter was employing his improved cooking skills when there was a loud rap on the door. "Gabe!" he exclaimed. Moments later Gabriel Heyward entered.

"Damn, boy, you've grown," said Gabriel. "I left a boy and here you are a man. And this must be the girl I heard about. Howdy, darlin', Gabriel Heyward at your service." Sonja smiled as Gabriel put his arm lightly around her shoulder. "You and I need to spend a lifetime getting to know one another. How's about we get married tomorrow?"

She laughed. "I've been warned about you."

"Me? I'm as harmless as a scorpion in an old lady's bloomers."

"So I've heard."

"Cousin Gabe, the Yankees are looking for you."

"It's worse than that. One of their people spotted me on the road. He was in a wagon so it will take him some time to sound an alarm, but they will know I'm here. I'm some kind of hungry. If you give me some food I'll be on my way."

"You can't leave."

"I can't stay here. I figure they'll be here within the hour."

"Then let's go all to Charleston."

"What about granny? Where is she, anyway?"

Carter and Sonja exchanged looks. "Out back," he said. "Under the magnolia tree."

"One great old lady. Did she suffer?"

"She broke her hip last year. A lot of pain. I think she was ready to go. And for all I know, Mother is gone, too. Sherman burned Columbia."

"I heard about that. A couple of the Negroes over at our plantation told me. But we can talk about that later. No time now."

Carter turned to Sonja. "Will you go with us?"

"You know I will."

"Pack light, because with you, Gabe, Soot and me, the boat will be crowded. There will be some danger. We could get stopped. They will arrest Gabriel and me. I'm not sure what would happen to you and Soot."

"Then we better not get caught."

Sonja ran to Three Pines. She was out of breath, stuffing clothes into a carpetbag when Christina walked by her door. Sonja motioned her in and closed the door behind her. "Carter and I are leaving," she said. "I don't know when I will be back."

Christina's face tensed. "I was afraid of this. I forbid it."

"Mother, I'm eighteen. It's what I have to do."

"Where will you go?"

"His cousin Gabriel is at the Lodge. There is talk of Charleston. Carter needs to find out what happened to his mother."

"Your students . . ."

"That's a problem. Can you help? Sparrow and Lark are ready for your advanced class anyway. Tell them I will see them again."

"You're leaving now?"

"They are waiting for me."

Christina looked toward the floor and shook her head slowly, as if puzzled. "I brought you here, us here, three years ago not knowing what we were getting into. It has been an adventure, has it not?"

"The greatest one I could have imagined."

"You are quite serious about Carter. That surprises me."

"It surprised me more. It happened so gradually. He was such a kid when we got here. But he grew up. We both did."

"I worry that the attraction is one of necessity. You both had each other with no one else around your age."

"If that's the attraction, we will find out. But I believe it's more than that."

"You go by boat?"

"Yes. And for once I hope our side is asleep. For this one night I will have to be a Confederate. Carter says he and Gabriel will be arrested if we are caught."

Christina embraced her. "My daughter the rebel. Wait, please." She started out of the room.

"Mother, I have to go."

Christina disappeared. Moments later she returned, clutching a handful of Greenbacks. "I know you have some, but you'll need more. Don't let them get wet." Sonja thrust them into her bag. In her haste several fell to the floor. She stooped to pick them up.

While Sonja was bidding her mother goodbye and Gabriel ate, Carter carried water and a change of clothes to the boat. Returning to the Lodge, he took a final look around. He picked up *A Tale of Two Cities*. He knew with indwelling certainty that the boy he was and the man he would become had both been shaped and molded in this room. Part of him would stay here always. He went outside. By the magnolia tree he knelt, placed his hand on the earth, and thanked Missma for all she did. It was, he told her, the best of times and the worst of times, and he smiled, knowing she would understand.

Sonja returned, panting heavily from her sprint. "Ready," she said. "And Carter, there's a rider galloping up the lane. From a distance it looks like Spruill. I don't think he saw me, but we better leave now."

Gabriel emerged from the Lodge carrying the cast iron pot. With Soot in the lead, all ran for the boat. Sonja jumped aboard as Carter and Gabriel shoved off. They were twenty-five yards offshore when Newton Spruill appeared on the bank. He drew his revolver and leveled it at the boat. A second later a bullet ripped through the sail just above Sonja's shoulder. Carter, at the tiller and closest to Spruill, shoved her down. "Hand me the rifle," he yelled to Gabe, who reached for it just as the gunwale beside him exploded, sending wood splinters in all directions.

Carter grabbed the rifle, lowered his profile, and steadied the barrel on the gunwale. Spruill was squarely in his sights. Spruill fired again, and this time water roiled behind them. Carter drew a bead on Spruill's chest. He was about to squeeze the trigger when Sonja's words came back to him. "You could not kill a man." He lowered his aim and fired. Spruill grabbed his knee and fell to the shore, his revolver flying from his hand into the water.

Gabriel said, "At least he won't be telegraphing Hilton Head."

Carter stared at Spruill, writhing in pain, before turning his back to the shore and seizing the tiller. "Hilton Head is not what worries me," he said.

"Patrols?" asked Sonja.

He nodded. "We stand no chance against their gunboats in open water. For all we know they heard the shots. Sound carries a long way on a day like today. Station Creek is our best hope."

"Is it far?" she asked.

"Seven or eight miles. We passed it the night of the dolphins. Unless they stop us we should make it by late afternoon.

Gabriel said. "You just shot a Union officer. There will be hell to pay if we are caught, not that I'm sorry you did it. He was shooting to kill."

Sonja reached for Carter's free hand. "You did the right thing. I knew you would. Whatever happens, I'm proud of you." Across Port Royal Sound, she saw the pier at Hilton Head and the now completed reception center, where she and the others first set foot in South Carolina. What was then a chaotic outpost appeared, even from this distance, to be a thriving town.

They had Station Creek in sight when Gabriel, looking to starboard, said, "Trouble."

Carter followed his gaze to see a gunboat speeding out of Skull Creek. "Here they come." He gauged the wind, hoping it held for what he knew would be a race to the mouth of the creek. "It will be close," he said.

"Is there anything I can do?" Sonja asked.

"Pray," he said.

"*Danforth,*" said Gabriel, training field glasses at the gunship closing the gap.

Carter's head whipped around. "*Danforth?* That's the boat that carried Mother to Beaufort."

"What are you talking about?" Gabriel asked.

"No time for that now," he said. Then a smile formed on his lips. He grinned at Sonja.

"What?" she asked.

"*Danforth* is about to learn something about this river."

"It better learn fast because they are gaining on us," said Gabriel, his usually unflappable demeanor at risk. "If this wind dies, so do we."

"They think they will head us off," Carter said. "See that hummock guarding the creek? What they may not know is that there is another one, further out, just below the water. They are headed right for it."

Moments later, the gunboat confirmed his prediction by a seizure so immediate that those on deck pitched forward and the sailor at the bow went head first overboard. It was as if the ship had hit an invisible wall. Sailors, regaining their feet, rushed to the railings as the ejected man stood, his feet planted on the submarined island that evidently did not appear on Union charts. On the deck, there was much pointing but little action with the sole exception of a sailor amidships, who raised a rifle and fired toward the skiff, but it was out of range and the bullet plunked short of its target, a tiny plume of water marking the entry point into the river. Gabriel stood and doffed his hat at the *Danforth*.

"My prayer was answered," Sonja said, and despite the tension laughed at Gabriel's taunting and at the sight of the drenched Union sailor walking toward the marooned gunboat. She reached back to place a hand on Carter's arm, taut as he gripped the tiller. "I like Gabriel," she said.

The sun was setting as they entered the creek, a meandering stream that would carry them into Harbor River. "If the breeze holds we should make St. Helena Sound in a few hours."

"Then what?" Sonja asked.

"Edisto," Carter said.

"But the Union will be waiting, will they not?"

Carter smiled at her in the waning daylight. "Whose side are you on?"

"Don't tease me," she said.

"*Danforth* could be stranded until the tide changes. Even if it manages to get off that reef, by the time it returns to Hilton Head it will be late. The Union doesn't have a ship or boat that can reach us unless the wind dies and we are delayed for a day or two. None of their boats navigate these creeks, so they will send a steamer around Bay Point. By then we'll be near Charleston."

"I have people on the Wadmalaw if we can make it past Edisto." Gabriel said. "Good people."

"Is Edisto far?" she wanted to know.

Carter said, "You can see it across the sound, but there will be five miles of rough open water we will need to cross. Tomorrow morning if the wind is right."

"Enough stew in this pot to last us a couple of days," Gabriel said.

Carter asked, "What was it like to be a Yankee prisoner, Cousin Gabe?"

"Best time of my life," he said. "Old Gabe knows some poker, and those Yankee guards lined up to give me their specie. Two of them tried to settle their debts with Confederate money. I told them that dog wouldn't hunt, and unless they paid up, I would haunt them after the war, coming to their homes in Connecticut and Massachusetts and teaching their children to sing Dixie. On the night I escaped, I left them each a written tally of what they owed me."

Progress through the creek was slowed by an ebbing tide and slackening winds. At one point Carter and Gabriel climbed out, forced to pull the boat through chilly, shallow water. Near dawn, Gabriel snored evenly, curled up with Soot in the bow. At the stern, Carter and Sonja looked toward Edisto.

She took his hand. "What is going to happen to us, rebel?"

He pulled her close with one arm and with the other pointed north. "If we make it across that sound, we will be safe."

"Then our war is over," she said, as a new day broke cold and clear.

The End

ACKNOWLEDGMENTS

My deeply felt thanks to those who helped me on the long road which writing historical fiction becomes. Some early readers proved particularly helpful: Brian Robinson of Dallas, Texas, whom I met in San Miguel de Allende, Mexico, and who has shown himself to be a fine judge of the printed word; my great and historically savvy friend Jim Russell of Westlawn, Virginia; Beaufort's premier historian, Lawrence Rowland, whose encyclopedic recall of Lowcountry history is unsurpassed; and best-selling author John Jakes, whose comments on the manuscript prompted significant revisions.

Thanks also to my editor, John Burbage, for his insights and encouragement, and to Gill Guerry, who once again worked his cover magic. And to the Pat Conroy Literary Center, which continues to inspire us to keep Pat's literary legacy alive.

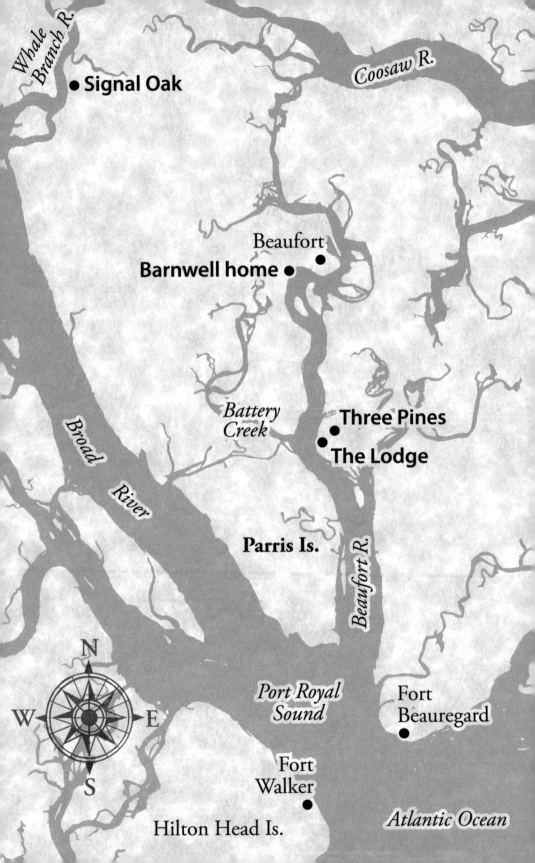